GHOSTLY FEARS

A Harper Harlow Mystery Book 13

LILY HARPER HART

HarperHart Publications

ONE

"**A**nd then Harper thought I was dead ... and cried. Jared was excited for a little bit because he thought that meant he would never have to share her again. Alas, I was only sleeping and all is right with the world."

Zander Pritchett, his eyes sparkling, told the story for what must have been the eighth time since returning from a mutual vacation with his best friend and her fiancé. The unfortunate target of his story, his boyfriend Shawn Donovan, merely shook his head and laughed at Jared Monroe's stony expression.

"That is not what happened," Jared snapped. He was growing increasingly annoyed with the story. The first time Zander filled in his boyfriend, he expected a few dramatic embellishments. It was Zander, after all. That's what he did. Every time the gregarious man told the story, however, it grew in size. "Also, I'm fine sharing Harper with you. She's too much woman for one man."

For her part, Harper Harlow merely arched an eyebrow as she picked through the takeout Jared had brought for dinner. He went with their favorite diner — so it was burgers and fries all around — and she couldn't help feeling a bit disappointed after the luxurious food they ate on the cruise ship for the better part of a week. It wasn't that the burgers were bad as much as they weren't decadent. She happened to love a decadent meal.

"That was a compliment," Jared offered when Harper didn't immediately give him grief.

"I'm sure it was." Her expression was hard to read, which made Jared wonder if he was in trouble.

"Actually, you're just enough woman for one man ... as long as I'm that man."

Slowly, Harper's lips curved. "I'm not angry. I was just thinking."

"About what?"

"How much I miss seafood."

"Not me," Zander countered. He seemed fine with his burger, which was out of place because he was the fussiest eater of their little group. "I'm happy for a little piece of home." He turned a set of adoring eyes on Shawn. "I'm also happy for a big piece of home."

Jared mimed gagging, a response Zander often reserved for when he had to play witness to his best friend and her cuddly paramour, and grinned when Zander skewered him with a harsh look. "Oh, it's not so funny when you're the one on the receiving end, huh?"

Zander rolled his eyes. "I have no idea what you're talking about."

"Really? You used to do your 'I'm going to throw up' dance whenever I said something mushy to Harper when we were first dating. I remember it well. You said you based it on the New Kids on the Block."

"Oh, right." Zander laughed at the memory, not embarrassed in the least. "I forgot about that. I'm awesome at that dance."

"You are," Harper agreed, opting to sample her food. She was starving and there was no way Jared could procure blackened sea scallops at the snap of his fingers, especially in Michigan when winter was trying to cling to the area with ragged fingernails. "I remember when you spent weeks watching all the old boy band videos on MTV so you could learn the dances. You were convinced you were destined to be a backup dancer."

Zander's expression was withering. "Um ... I've never been convinced that I should be a backup anything," he countered. "I'm a headliner, my friend. I always have been. I thought I would be the face of the group, the one who gets all the attention while the others are left being bitter and jealous."

"Yeah, Heart," Jared teased, amused despite himself. "How could you not realize that Zander is built to be the face of a group?"

Zander ignored the sarcasm and barreled forward. "I'm being serious. I would be the Jordan Knight of New Kids on the Block."

Harper wrinkled her forehead as she doused her fries with ketchup. "Isn't Donnie Wahlberg considered the most successful member of that group?"

"Donnie is famous for being an actor. Jordan was the true musician ... and best dancer. Donnie didn't stay in his lane. Everyone knows boy band members should always stay in their lane."

To Harper, the statement didn't make a lot of sense. She bit into her burger and methodically chewed as she mulled Zander's theory. "I like Donnie Wahlberg," she said upon swallowing. "In fact, I much prefer him to his brother as an actor. I can't say as I've ever really listened to New Kids on the Block's music, but I'm betting he would be my favorite member. I prefer real music, though."

"How is 'Step by Step' not real music? They're going to get to you, girl."

Harper recognized the lyric, but only vaguely. "You need to stop quoting boy band lyrics to me. It's getting weird."

"Totally weird," Jared teased. "Let's talk about something everyone can enjoy. I know, let's talk about how Zander passed out on the deck and drooled in front of half the ship." Jared knew he was playing with fire before Zander's expression turned to molten lava, but he was willing to risk it since they were no longer sharing a roof. He and Harper had their own house. Sure, it was only across the street — so that meant there wasn't much of a buffer zone — but they had strong locks and it was cold out. Zander had been complaining about the frigid temperatures since they returned. He was unlikely to risk the cold for petty payback.

At least Jared hoped that was true.

"Did I mention that I'm sick of you?" Zander intoned. "I mean ... seriously sick of you. I'm so sick of you they need to think of another word for it. You are the Debbie Downer of our group. No, truly. You always have to suck the fun out of everything."

Sensing trouble, Shawn interjected himself into the conversation to direct Zander and Jared to a topic that wouldn't cause fur to fly. "Tell me about the entertainment. I've heard they have great shows on cruise ships."

"We didn't go to a lot of the shows," Jared replied, his gaze never moving from Zander. Something unsavory looked to be silently passing between them and it made Harper and Shawn unbelievably nervous. "We had other things going on, like looking for Zander."

"I was never missing," Zander shot back. "I knew where I was the entire time."

Harper cleared her throat to get everybody's attention. "I don't want to infringe on the completely unnecessary fight, but I'm going to. We don't need this." She was serious. "We're all friends, right? We're all in love with each other."

"I'm only in love with Shawn and you," Zander countered. "I could take or leave him." He made a dismissive hand motion in Jared's direction. "I find him ridiculously annoying."

Jared wasn't bothered by Zander's opinion. "I'm only in love with you,

Heart. I like Shawn a great deal, don't get me wrong, but I could take or leave your best friend right now ... especially after he horned in on our romantic vacation."

Harper's heart dropped. She knew this argument was far from over. They'd gotten into it a few times in recent weeks. Jared wanted a romantic trip that consisted of just the two of them. Harper was all for it, until she remembered she and Zander had booked a work cruise years in advance. Luckily they'd thought ahead and purchased extra tickets in case they were in relationships when the cruise finally rolled around. That worked out well for Harper and Jared, but not so much for Shawn, who owned his own business and couldn't get away.

"Do you want to know what I think?" Shawn interjected, his tone forceful. He was used to the occasional territorial meltdown between the two men. They'd been going at each other since he became involved with Zander. At first, he found the group dynamics daunting. Now he was used to them. He wasn't particularly worried about things getting physical between the two men, but it wasn't unheard of for one (or both of them, quite frankly) to pout for a day or two. That put a strain on Harper's mental health and Shawn's patience quotient.

"I always want to hear what you have to say," Zander replied, a serene smile on his face. "You always take my side so it's good for my ego."

Shawn sighed. He loved Zander, but he was a handful. "Well, I'm not on your side today." He didn't shrink when Zander's eyes turned dark. "Don't look at me that way. I think you're both being idiots. From Jared's perspective, though, it has to be difficult for him to listen to you tell the same story for what's probably the fiftieth time."

"I haven't told it more than two times," Zander countered as Harper and Jared snorted in unison. "I haven't."

"You've told it at least eight times since you've been back," Shawn countered calmly. "I'm betting you told it a few times on the ship."

"Try twenty times," Jared muttered.

"I did not." Zander was shrill. "I was very poised in the face of my almost death."

Harper focused on her burger so she wouldn't have to take sides. Just like Shawn, she was sick of the arguments. She wasn't sick enough to paint herself as a target for both men if they got angry enough, however.

Shawn, apparently, was willing to be the designated bad guy of the evening. "I happen to believe that Jared was just as worried as Harper when they heard there was a body on deck and they couldn't find you. You two may drive each other crazy, but you've bonded over one thing ... and she's sitting on the floor stuffing her face."

Harper looked up guiltily, causing Jared to laugh as Zander smirked. "I'm just sitting here minding my own business," she offered.

"You are," Shawn agreed. "I think it's because you're sick of the fighting. Next time there's a group vacation, it's probably best if we all go so we don't have to deal with ... whatever this is ... again. I imagine you've had enough of it."

"I really have." Harper was relieved to have someone in the room who understood her feelings. "I love them both ... but, boy, they are a lot to deal with."

Shawn chuckled appreciatively as Jared moved his hand to Harper's back. Regret, bitter and strong, coursed through him. The last thing he wanted to do was make his fiancée uncomfortable. They were supposed to be resting, living it up before they all returned to their regular jobs. This was not the best way to get her to relax.

"I'm sorry," he offered, meaning it. "I didn't mean to let this happen ... again."

"You never mean to let it happen. Sometimes you simply can't stop yourself. I don't want to fight, though. I just want to relax. Traveling always takes it out of me. This time is no different. Can't we just have a moratorium on arguments for at least — I don't know — seventy-two hours or something?"

Jared nodded without hesitation. "I think that's a fantastic idea."

"I don't know if I can last that long," Zander admitted. "I'll do my best, though."

"That's all I ask," Harper encouraged. "I ... ." She trailed off when there was a knock at the door. "Is someone expecting visitors?"

"Not particularly," Zander replied, getting to his feet. "I haven't seen anyone since I got back, though. I guess it could be my mother ... although I promised to stop in and see her tomorrow. She wants to hear all about my trip. I bet my near-death experience will really get her going."

Jared made a face. "Your poor mother."

"You haven't met her," Harper countered. "There's nothing poor about her. Trust me. She's a ... well, let's just say there's a reason Zander turned out the way he did."

"There really is," Shawn agreed. "I thought she was going to be one of those sweet and doting women when I first met her. It turns out ... she's something else entirely. I'm betting she was a helicopter mother before they were cool."

Jared had no idea what a helicopter mother was, but it didn't sound good.

He watched with a general sense of curiosity as Zander trudged to the door and opened it. The look of surprise on Zander's face told Jared he wasn't expecting whoever was on the other side of the threshold.

"Can I help you?" Zander asked. "I ... are you lost?"

The voice that answered was rich, deep and nuanced. "I don't believe I'm lost." He rattled off the address of the house. "I'm in the right location, correct?"

"You are." Zander took a step back and motioned for the gentleman to enter. He seemed confused ... even more so than usual. "You look familiar. I feel like I should know you."

"My name is Byron Jessup. I'm sure you've heard of me."

The name meant nothing to Jared, but it obviously meant something to Harper and Zander because the atmosphere in the room almost immediately changed.

"Holy crap." Harper scampered to her feet, her dinner forgotten, and joined Zander in front of the door. "You really are Byron Jessup, aren't you? I can't believe you're here."

"Yes, well ... um ... I have a matter to discuss with you. You're Harper Harlow, correct? I've seen you on television a few times, and you have quite the reputation in paranormal circles."

Jared had no idea what was going on, but the man's sudden appearance made him nervous. He sensed something profound was about to go down. "I'm sorry. I don't mean to be rude, but I'm not familiar with you." He wiped his hands on a napkin before jutting one out in greeting. "Jared Monroe. I'm a detective with the Whisper Cove Police Department."

Byron accepted the proffered hand. "I know who you are. I had an aide research Ms. Harlow extensively and your name came up multiple times in conjunction with her."

"You had an aide research Harper?" Jared was becoming more and more uncomfortable with the conversation. "May I ask why?"

"I find I am in need of her expertise."

Harper shifted from one foot to the other, uncomfortable. "Is this about Jennifer?"

Jared felt as if he was wading through quicksand as he tried to keep up with the conversation. "Who is Jennifer?"

Harper merely shook her head and remained focused on Byron. "I knew her because we went to school together. You probably know that, though."

"I do," Byron confirmed stiffly. "And, as a matter of fact, this *is* about Jennifer. I was hoping you might be able to help me find her. You are a ghost hunter, correct? I want you to find my daughter's ghost."

Jared openly gaped. "Your daughter is dead? Did something happen to her recently?"

"My daughter is missing," Byron corrected. "She has been for a long time. I happen to believe that she's most likely dead. I want Ms. Harlow to prove – or even disprove, quite frankly – that assumption."

"You want me to prove it how?" Harper hedged.

"I'm hosting a special event at my home." Byron was all business. There was no inflection in his voice, no emotion. He appeared to be nothing more than a businessman about to cut a deal. "I have invited some of the most renowned psychics in the country — and others like yourself — and the goal is to prove Jennifer is dead, hopefully somehow figure out what happened, and put her to rest. She deserves peace."

Harper remained rooted to her spot, flummoxed.

"I'm still behind," Jared noted. "Does someone want to fill me in?"

"Not right now," Zander replied, brushing off Jared's question with impatience. "We'll fill you in later. We're talking to Mr. Jessup now." His smile was so broad when he turned to the smartly-dressed visitor, it threatened to swallow his entire face. "We would be happy to participate in your event."

Harper opened her mouth to argue with her best friend but no sound came out and no one looked in her direction.

Byron didn't smile, simply nodding instead. "Wonderful." He dug in his pocket and came back with two envelopes. "These are invitations to the event. Please contact my butler with your confirmation and he will handle room arrangements. Thank you so much for your time."

He turned to leave, but Harper stopped him.

"Wait." She appeared confused. "Just so I'm understanding, you want us to join forces with psychics and other ghost hunters to find Jennifer. That's what you're saying, right?"

"It is."

"But ... why now?"

"Don't you think it's time?"

Honestly, Harper understood what he was trying to do. She wasn't particularly fond of his attitude, though, and she didn't like his description of the setup. "We don't usually work this way," she explained. "I've never worked with the sort of people you're referring to and I'm not sure it's a good idea."

"It's a great idea," Zander argued. "This way you won't have to do all of the heavy lifting."

"Zander, just ... stay out of this for a second," Harper argued. "I need to talk to Mr. Jessup. I don't want to agree to something that I don't think is a good idea."

"Your partner already agreed," Byron pointed out. "The deal is done."

"No, it's really not." Harper shook her head. "I'm not trying to be difficult, but I don't like the way this sounds. You haven't given us any specifics."

"And what specifics are you in need of?"

"Well, for starters, how is this going to work? Do you have reason to believe your daughter died in the home?"

"No. What does that matter?"

"Her ghost might not be hanging around the house if she died elsewhere. I've found that it's impossible to predict exactly how a displaced soul reacts. I mean ... it's possible Jennifer returned to your home because that's what she was familiar with, but it's also possible she's somewhere else entirely."

"Why do you think I'm hiring you? I can't be bothered with logistics I don't understand. That's your job."

Harper made a protesting sound. "See, that's another thing. You didn't mention hiring us. You just said you wanted us to come out and hang around other people and look for your daughter."

"I'm aware that your time is valuable. I don't expect you to do it for free."

Oddly enough, since Harper knew the girl in question, she probably would've volunteered her services for free. She'd always wondered what happened to Jennifer Jessup. It was one of those stories that never seemed to die because there was no closure. Byron's attitude bothered her on so many different levels, though, she wasn't sure where to start.

"I don't think it's a good idea," Harper supplied, making up her mind on the spot. "I can't commit to something like this without more details."

"There are details in your invitations," Byron replied, his tone clipped. "Payment information and expected duties are also outlined. I'm assuming you'll want to talk with your business partner. Please call my butler either way when you've made your decision. Thank you very much for your time."

He started toward the door, causing another bout of irritation to flow through Harper.

"We've already made up our minds," she called out.

"Speak for yourself," Zander grumbled.

"I just don't think it's our thing," she added.

"I expect you to reconsider when you've read the invitations. Have a nice evening."

With those words, he was gone ... and Harper was left with nothing but questions and an angry partner. She skirted around Zander and returned to her dinner, sliding to the floor as he glared at her.

"Well, that was stupid," Zander announced. "Do you want to tell me what you were thinking? Oh, wait, you weren't thinking. That much is obvious."

"Zander." Harper's voice was low and full of warning. "Just let it go. I'm focusing on dinner. After that, we'll leave and get out of your hair."

"Whatever." Zander's attitude was on full display. "I think we've actually managed to spend too much time with each other for once. I never thought it would happen, but there it is."

Harper couldn't help but agree.

TWO

J ared wisely kept his mouth shut until they returned home. The usually
warm and comforting relationship Harper and Zander shared was
chilly and dark for the rest of the evening. Jared couldn't wait to
escape. If Harper's reaction when they hit the street – and she could
finally breathe again – was any indication, she wholeheartedly agreed.

"Well, that was an interesting evening," Jared quipped as they climbed the
steps to their front porch.

"I think we need a break."

He stilled. "You and me?" His heart shuddered at the thought.

"What?" Her sea-blue eyes clouded as she looked at him. "Oh, you thought
... no. I wasn't talking about you and me." She shook her head and let out a
nervous laugh. "I definitely wasn't talking about us. I meant you and I should
take a break from Zander. A few days of distance might be a good thing."

They were words Jared wanted to hear for a long time. He liked Zander —
no, really — and he knew Harper adored the man. They had a bond that
couldn't be shaken, to the point where they were tragically co-dependent and
finished each other's sentences most of the time.

When Jared first met Harper, he found her relationship with Zander to be
troublesome. He couldn't imagine not enjoying her presence, to the point
where he sometimes wondered if love at first sight was really a thing because
he seemed to be infatuated from the start. Zander's refusal to give them room
to grow, oxygen so the roots of their relationship could form a solid anchor,
was a constant sore spot.

Somewhere along the way, though, things had shifted. Harper's happiness became the most important thing to Jared. She needed Zander. That meant Jared had to find a way to put up with the man because he needed Harper. Once Shawn entered the picture, things honestly got better. Zander no longer insisted on spending all his time with Harper and Jared. He had his own romance to focus on, and it was a welcome change.

That didn't mean Harper and Zander embraced the notion of distance. They were still all up in each other's business. They were far too involved with each other, as far as Jared was concerned. Things were getting better, though. The new house helped. They were embracing independence while still maintaining their close friendship.

However, the past few days had been a test and it appeared no one was in line to receive a passing grade.

"I think you're just crabby and need a good night's sleep," Jared countered, holding open the door so she could step inside. He wanted to help, but he knew better than saying anything negative about Zander. It wouldn't go over well and simply result in another kind of fight ... and it was one Jared refused to engage in. He'd learned his lesson over the time they'd been together. Harper might find herself irritated and at the end of her rope, but she was always going to be on Zander's side when it came to a fight. Jared was careful never to make her choose, and not simply because he was afraid she would occasionally pick Zander over him. It was also because he worried she would tire of having to choose between them.

Quite frankly, he and Zander had come to a meeting of the minds. They agreed to get along better for Harper's sake. Somehow that agreement fell by the wayside this week and Jared still wasn't certain how it happened.

"How about I make you some hot chocolate and we get comfortable in front of the fireplace?" he suggested. "You're agitated and need to calm down. The best way to do that is hot chocolate."

She cast him a sidelong look. "How do you know hot chocolate will fix this?"

"Because I know you." He helped her out of her coat. "This isn't as big of a deal as you seem to think it is," he promised. "Seriously. You both had an off night — I didn't exactly make things better — and now everyone is angry. I don't think it helps that Byron Jessup stopped by and roiled up an already unsettled atmosphere. What's his deal, by the way?"

Harper sighed and rubbed her forehead. "Can we get comfortable before I tell that story? I'm still not exactly sure what happened there. I also want to see that invitation. Did you bring it with you?"

He nodded and dug in his pocket, coming back with one of the envelopes.

"It's right here. Zander seemed excited at the prospect of being involved in this."

"That's because Zander can't see the bigger picture."

"And you can?"

"I see ... trouble." She took the envelope and stared at it. "I'm going to get into some comfortable clothes. Can you make the hot chocolate and meet me in front of the fire in ten minutes?"

He nodded without hesitation. "Yes. Will you tell me everything that's bothering you?"

"Yeah, although I'm not even sure I understand everything that's bothering me."

"Well, then we'll figure it out together."

She mustered her first real smile in almost two hours. "That sounds like a plan."

HARPER WORE HER FAVORITE FUZZY pajama pants and one of Jared's oversized sweatshirts when she returned to the living room. He had hot chocolate waiting on the table and a blanket settled on the floor in front of the fireplace. The room felt cozy and warm.

"This is nice." Harper beamed at him as he lifted the blanket so she could get comfortable next to him. "Do you know one of the things I like most about you?"

"My rugged good looks?"

"That goes without saying." She giggled as he tucked her in tightly at his side. "I like that you're fine when I would rather dress like this than go all Victoria's Secret crazy."

"Well, as happy as I am when you decide to go Victoria's Secret crazy — and that's a delightful way to refer to it — I like it when you're snuggly and comfortable, too. I happen to think this outfit is the epitome of sexy."

She laughed, warmth filling her face and causing him to want to burrow closer. He loved these shared moments. They were what he lived for.

"Tell me about Byron Jessup," he prodded, causing the smile to slip. He immediately regretted his impatience.

"It's kind of a long story."

"I like long stories."

"Right. Well ... it all started about nine years ago. I guess it was closer to ten now — man, am I getting old — and I remember the timing exactly because it was right around our high school graduation. It will be ten years exactly in May."

"Okay." Jared was familiar enough with Harper's moods that he knew not to push her. Allowing her to tell the story in her own time was best. "Drink your hot chocolate before it gets cold."

Harper did as instructed, making a happy groaning noise as the chocolate-y goodness hit her lips. "Oh, I'm pretty sure this is what Heaven tastes like."

He laughed, watching her profile as she sobered.

"So, the Jessups are rich. I mean ... like Scrooge McDuck rich. They could fill a pool with gold coins and dive into it. That's how rich they are."

"I'm not familiar with the name, but I gathered that from the way he was dressed. I'm pretty sure that was a twenty-thousand-dollar suit."

Harper had trouble wrapping her head around that. "Why would anyone spend that much on a suit?"

"I don't know. You'll have to ask him."

"I think I'll pass. Anyway, they don't technically live in Whisper Cove. They live on their own island in Lake St. Clair. Jennifer went to school with us, though."

"I'm surprised, if they're so rich, that she went to public school. You would think that they would get private tutors or send her to boarding school or something."

"I never really thought about it," Harper admitted. "That's true. Jennifer was always a nice girl, though. She was shy and you never would've known by interacting with her that she lived a life of rampant privilege.

"I mean ... she participated in all the school fundraisers," she continued. "She baked her own stuff for bake sales and sold wrapping paper on the streets. She didn't wear expensive clothes. I'm sure she had name brand stuff, don't get me wrong, but it wasn't the sort of stuff that stood out.

"She worked on the school paper, was nice to everyone, and tried really hard not to stand out. I think she was embarrassed by the money. I don't remember thinking that back then, but looking back now, that's how it seems to me. She really didn't want people treating her differently simply because her father was rich."

"She sounds like a person who ascended beyond her circumstances," Jared noted. "I mean, honestly, she could've gotten away with being a real little jerk to all the other kids. She didn't go that route, though. A lot of kids in her position might have."

"Yeah." Harper took on a far-off expression. "She was always really nice."

Jared's fingers were gentle as he slipped a strand of hair behind her ear. "Were you tight with her?"

"We were friendly. I don't know that I would say we were tight. I was tight with Zander and I remember hanging out with her a few times. It's just ...

Zander sucks all the oxygen out of a room. He doesn't always mean to, but he somehow manages it. I didn't have a lot of time for anybody else, and since we both felt like outsiders it didn't make sense to let too many people into our secret group."

"It sounds like Jennifer would've been a good fit, though."

"It does." Harper bobbed her head. "Anyway, Jennifer participated in a lot of school functions. She was very academically minded. She was on the student council and a member of the National Honor Society. She was in the French club and donated her time at a retirement center. She was a very giving girl."

"And yet she died," Jared noted.

"No, she disappeared," Harper corrected quickly. "We don't know that she died. We simply know that one day she was no longer here and nobody has any idea what happened to her."

Jared's heart gave a little heave. It reminded him of another story he'd heard upon arriving in Whisper Cove. This one involved Harper's former boyfriend, Quinn, who was thought dead in a car accident. Since she could see and talk to ghosts, she spent months — years really — searching the surrounding fields and woods looking for his ghost. She wanted to help him pass over.

It turned out, however, that Quinn wasn't dead at all. In fact, he was very much alive ... and dangerous. He returned from the dead with an unbelievable story — one that had a soap opera twist — and tried to bond with Harper again. The truth eventually came out, but Harper was hurt in the process. Jared didn't want that to happen again. Still, he was curious.

"What are the specifics of her disappearance? I mean ... what happened?"

"I'm not sure I ever heard the real story," she admitted, sipping her hot chocolate. "There were several versions going around. The first is that she ran away. People said that she hated her father because he had a reputation for being cold and distant. People said she hid her allowance for a year and ran away with enough money to live on without ever working a day in her life."

Jared cocked a curious eyebrow. "Did you believe that?"

"Not even a little. Like I said, I wasn't really tight with Jennifer, but I liked her. We talked a few times. Once, for example, there was a talent show at school. Zander and I were doing an act together — even though I was mortified at the prospect because I'm tone deaf — and my parents came to watch the show.

"I was backstage and terrified and I complained nonstop about my parents being there," she continued. "I said I wished they wouldn't come. Jennifer gave me this sad little smile that I didn't understand. She said I was lucky that my parents bothered to come, even if it embarrassed me. She also said her father never once came to a single event at the school and only her grandmother bothered to at least try to be present for certain events."

Jared stirred. "Is that true?"

"I don't know. I don't ever remember seeing Byron Jessup at anything."

"That had to be hard on her."

"I think it was."

"After meeting him tonight, he didn't exactly come across as father of the year. I mean, on one hand, he's obviously concerned about what happened to his daughter. He wasn't exactly what I would call emotional, though."

"He never was. Even in the days right after she disappeared, he would go on television and barely blink while droning on about offering money as a reward for anyone who could find her. Even then I understood there was something off about his reaction. He was willing to invest money in her well-being but not love. It was ... weird."

"You don't know that he didn't love her," Jared argued. "Some people simply have difficulty expressing themselves."

"And I get that. I do. It was still weird."

"Did you believe Jennifer ran away?"

Harper cocked her head, considering. "I guess part of me thought it was a possibility," she replied after a beat. "She never seemed happy. I never saw her laughing simply for the joy of being happy. Her life was about obligation and the things she had to do. There were never things she simply wanted to do and enjoy. I don't think she was allowed."

"That sounds like a very sad existence. Maybe she did run away. I would run away from a life like that. Was she an adult when this went down?"

"Yeah. She'd just turned eighteen. Why does that matter?"

"Because, if she was an adult, she wasn't breaking the law. Even if someone found her, they would have no jurisdiction to drag her back. That could've been a deliberate decision."

"I guess."

"You don't look convinced."

"That's because I'm not. The thing is, Jennifer was always sad, but she was always trying to make her father happy, too. I don't think she would've purposely hurt him by taking off, no notice or anything, and leaving him to always wonder. She was fairly straightforward. I think she would've at least sent a letter after the fact."

"How do you know she didn't do that?"

"Because he's looking for psychics and ghost hunters to prove she's dead."

"Good point." That brought the conversation full circle and Jared had another question. "How come you don't want to help? I mean ... it seems like you really liked her. Even though her father is a cold fish, this is the sort of situation where you could shine. Don't you want to help that girl who was always so sad?"

"Yeah." Harper bobbed her head and answered without hesitation. "I've always wanted to help her. I even went out to the area near the island a few times when I was a kid hoping to see a ghost. I thought I could at least point the police in the right direction. I never found her ... but I don't think I tried very hard either."

"You said that she might not have died out there," Jared reminded her. "She could've died somewhere else."

"Yup. Which means finding where would be practically impossible."

"So ... you're not going because it would be a waste of time?"

The question caught Harper off guard. "Do you think I should go?"

"I think it's unlike you not to even consider it." He chose his words carefully. "This young woman was your friend. Sure, not to the same level as Zander, but she was most definitely your friend. The fact that you don't want to look at all is ... confusing. You're usually gung-ho to help."

"I know. It's just ... ." Harper trailed off. She wasn't sure how to explain herself. "First off, the prospect of the other psychics and ghost hunters is daunting. I don't know that I want to be pitted against someone else. It makes me nervous just thinking about it."

"Then don't look at it as a competition. Look at it as an opportunity. This is a young woman you knew. Her father, whether you like him or not, obviously cares enough to pull out all the stops in a last-ditch effort to find her. You have the opportunity to give him some peace. Why not take it?"

"Because ... because ... ." Harper didn't have an acceptable answer. She realized that now. "Probably because Zander agreed without asking me and I didn't like Jessup's attitude," she admitted, rueful. "That's definitely not fair to Jennifer, though."

"It's not," Jared agreed. "This isn't about being fair, though. Life isn't fair. Still, I think you're going to regret it if you don't at least give it a shot. As far as I can see, the only thing you're going to lose in the attempt is time. Jessup is paying for your time, so not even that is true."

"Yeah." Harper stared at the envelope on the table. "Maybe I spoke too soon. It couldn't hurt to at least read the invitation."

"There you go." He pressed a kiss to her cheek. "Just think about it. I happen to believe you're going to change your mind once you sleep on it."

"Maybe."

"I guess we'll find out tomorrow." Sensing she was ready to relax, he tickled her ribs and made her squirm. "When Zander climbs into our bed before dawn to make up tomorrow, make sure you guys don't wake me. I plan to tire myself out with you before bed tonight."

Harper's mouth dropped open. "That's not going to happen, the making up thing, I mean."

"Oh, it's totally going to happen."

"It is not. I'm really mad at him."

They both knew that wouldn't last.

"Would you care to place a wager on that?" Jared challenged.

"Absolutely. What are the stakes?"

His grin turned devilish. "What if I show you instead of tell you?"

Harper's eyes flashed with impish delight. "Show me what you've got."

"Finally, something I really want to do."

That went for both of them.

THREE

J ared wasn't surprised when he woke up to whispering the next morning. When he shifted to look at the other side of the bed — sure enough — Zander was there and he and Harper were looking over the invitations.

"I take it you two have made up," he murmured, rolling to his back. He was shirtless, and he couldn't remember if he'd tugged on boxer shorts before falling asleep. A quick check told him he had, which was probably because he knew he would wake up to this exact situation.

"Yes, we're in love again," Zander drawled. His hair was a mess and he looked to be in his pajamas. Jared deduced he slept poorly the night before and let himself into their house as soon as he could reasonably explain his presence.

A quick look at the clock told Jared it was barely seven. "Couldn't you have waited to fall back in love until after breakfast?"

Zander solemnly shook his head. "I'm in love with you again, too. Just FYI."

Jared groaned. Even though Zander worked his last nerve – and often – the man had charm oozing out of every pore. It wasn't hard to figure out what kept Harper and Zander attached. They loved each other like siblings ... which meant there would always be breakups and make-ups in their future.

"I don't want to be the one to ruin this lovely moment, but ... I thought we had an agreement about when you could sneak into the house and climb in bed with us." Jared never thought he would utter a sentence like that in his life. He'd said it more than once by now, which was ludicrous. "I thought it was supposed to be a weekend thing. Isn't that what we agreed on?"

"Not if Harper and I are making up. I get a pass if we're making up."

Jared thought about arguing, but the look on Harper's face had him stowing his opinion. "Fine. That can be an addendum to the main rule. However, there will be a limit of how many fights are allowed a month." He was well aware of how Zander's mind worked. If Zander thought he'd found a loophole, he would exploit it at every turn. "No more than one fight a month."

Zander's mouth dropped open in mock outrage. "I can't control my emotions. You know darned well we'll fight more than once a month."

"Then you'll have to wait until we're awake to make up. That has to be a rule." Jared's gaze was firm when it landed on Harper.

"He's right, Zander," she noted, sighing when Zander glared at her. "It's only fair. He deserves privacy in his own bedroom."

"Whatever." Zander's distaste for the conversational turn was obvious. "We're still in the middle of making up, so you can't boot me."

"There would be no point in booting you now. I'm fine with it." Jared dragged a hand through his hair and fixed his eyes on a happy Harper. He couldn't help returning her smile. He would put up with a morning visit from Zander every single day for the rest of their lives if she could always be that happy.

Of course, he had no intention of telling Zander that.

"How did you sleep?" Harper asked, leaning over so she could give him a kiss.

"Good. How about you?"

She merely shrugged, telling Jared that her slumber hadn't been nearly as restful as his. "You should've woken me up," he chided.

"I didn't want to interrupt your snoring."

He tweaked her nose. "Funny girl. What about the invitations? Is there anything interesting there?"

"You tell me." Harper retrieved the invitation from Zander and handed it to her fiancé.

Jared rubbed his eyes and propped himself up on a pillow before focusing on the rectangular card. "They expect you to stay at the house overnight."

"Several nights," Harper corrected. "It's part of the package. If we want to get paid, we have to stay even though we're local. They expect results from this, and they believe we'll have better luck contacting Jennifer's spirit if we're there at night."

"What do you think?"

"I think I've seen more ghosts during the day than I have at night, but it doesn't really matter. I mean ... staying there isn't going to kill us. Besides, I've always kind of wanted to see that house."

"You mean castle," Zander corrected. "It's not just a house. It's a castle."

Jared looked to Harper for an explanation.

"It is kind of a castle," she admitted. "It has turrets and everything. The only houses I've seen that are similar are the ones down in Grosse Pointe. You know, the really old ones in the ritzy neighborhoods that survived the blight crackdown."

Jared was familiar with the houses in question. "So ... basically you're saying it's a mansion."

"Castle," Zander muttered.

Jared shot him a look. "I get it. You said it was on an island. How does that work?"

"It's in Lake St. Clair," Harper explained. "It's not a big island and it technically doesn't seem like an island because it's only like a quarter of a mile from land, but you need a boat to get out there unless you're really motivated for a swim in warm weather."

"How big is the island?"

"About twenty acres," Zander replied. "It's big enough for them to spread out — they have things like a boathouse, their own cemetery, a barn, and all that other neat stuff — but it's not as if someone can get lost on the property."

To Jared, the comment was telling. "So, you're basically saying that you don't believe Jennifer got turned around and died on the property by accident or anything."

"I sincerely doubt it."

"Besides, they had searchers out there," Harper offered. "They had dogs and a lot of volunteers. If she'd fallen and hit her head or something, they would've found her."

"Right." Jared rubbed his stubbled jaw, thoughtful. "How would she have gotten off the island? I mean ... how does anyone get to and from the island?"

"There's a ferry," Harper replied. "It can hold a few vehicles, I think. Like three or four. The Jessup family pays for it. They also control it. It's not as if random people can hop the ferry and ride out to the island."

"So, if Jennifer left, she left on the ferry. That's what you're saying."

"In theory," Harper hedged. "That's not quite the way it was done in practice. I happen to know she had her own little boat — she told me about it — and she used to motor it between the island and mainland herself. There was a special place for her to anchor it and then she had her own car in the lot at the marina."

"You said she disappeared right before graduation. That would mean it was warmer around then, right?"

"May is hit or miss. The days are pretty warm, but the nights are still relatively cool."

"Okay, if she was determined, though, she could've made it off the island herself. Where was her boat found? Was it on the mainland?"

Harper shrugged. "I honestly don't know."

"You never asked?"

"I never thought to ask. I was a kid. Er, well, I was technically almost an adult, but it's not as if I was a grown-up. We were thinking about graduation and all that stuff." Harper's cheeks flushed with shame. "And, before you ask, I'm embarrassed that I didn't bother to look into the details. You're right. I should know these things."

"That's not what I was saying," Jared protested. "I just thought you might've followed up on the details after the fact. I mean, when you came back from college, you guys started a business pretty quickly, right? I would think finding the ghost of a girl you went to high school with would be right up your alley."

"I never really thought about it," Harper admitted, chewing on her bottom lip. "I probably should have. I'm not certain why I never thought about it. You're right. It makes sense ... at least on the surface."

"Maybe you didn't think about it because you're not convinced she's dead."

"Maybe." Harper's expression was hard to read. "I don't know what to think."

Jared flicked his eyes to Zander. "What about you? What do you think?"

"I don't know what to think either," Zander replied, stretching. "Jennifer was a really nice girl. She always took time to talk to me, laughed at my jokes. She was one of the few people who didn't call me names or make fun of me because I was gay. She didn't ask questions about it either. She simply accepted it and that was it."

"I would like to pull some information on this old case before we head out there," Jared supplied. "What time are we supposed to arrive?"

Harper's eyebrows migrated north. "What are you talking about?"

"Are you saying you two aren't going?" Jared was legitimately surprised. "I thought for sure you would change your mind once you slept on it."

"I did change my mind. It's just ... you made it sound as if you're going with us."

"I *am* going with you." He was matter-of-fact. "I'm part of the team, right?"

"Absolutely." Harper bobbed her head. "You're also a part of the team who has a job."

"Which I don't have to return to until Monday at the earliest. It's the weekend. If you guys are still there by the time I'm expected back, I'll make my decision then. As for now, I don't see why you can't consider me part of the team."

"Are you sure?" Harper was pleased but dubious. "You really want to go with us?"

Before Jared could answer, Zander inserted himself into the conversation. "Hold up." He raised his hand. "If your boyfriend is going, then my boyfriend is going. There's no way I'm going to be the third wheel again."

"I think that's a fabulous idea," Jared enthused. "If Shawn is there, you'll be less likely to sleep in our room with us."

"Oh, you wish." Zander rolled his eyes, although he looked intrigued at the prospect. "I wonder if he'd be interested in going."

"I'm guessing he would," Harper offered. "The thing is, we need to take Eric and Molly, too." She was referring to their co-workers and friends at Ghost Hunters, Inc. — or GHI to those in the know — and she was earnest as she delivered the news. "They can't be left behind a second time."

Jared focused his full attention on the invitation again. "It doesn't say you're limited as to the number of people you can bring with you. It just says to call this butler guy with the number of guests and time of your arrival."

"And you honestly think they won't put up a fight for six guests?"

"Zander said it's a castle," Jared pointed out. "I'm betting they have room."

"I'm betting they do, too." Zander wiggled off the bed, happily grinning as he grabbed his coat from the chair in the corner. "I need to get home and pack. I also need to talk to Shawn. He might not even realize I'm gone."

"You didn't tell him before you left?" Jared made a face. "You're an astonishingly good boyfriend."

Zander refused to be dragged into another fight. "Harp, call me when you know the details of our pickup. I'll see you later this afternoon. I love you." He gave her a quick kiss, one that was designed to irritate Jared. Instead, it made the taciturn cop smile. "I'm not real thrilled with you," Zander announced, meeting Jared's gaze.

"You love me, too, and you know it."

"Not right now."

"Oh, now that really hurts."

"Yeah, yeah, yeah." Zander hurried to the door. "This is going to be fun. I can't wait to find Jennifer's ghost. I bet she has fun stories to tell."

Harper kept her smile in place until he disappeared and then she let her real emotions take over.

"Why are you frowning?" Jared asked.

"Because you're right. I don't know that I believe Jennifer is dead. Part of me thinks she really did run away."

"Why is that an issue? If she's not dead, her father should be happy."

"Unless she really doesn't want to be found."

"You don't have to find her if she's still among the living. That invitation says you're required to talk to her if she's dead. That's it."

"I guess you're right." She forced a smile and turned to him. "I'm starving. What do you think about making breakfast and then hashing out a few of the logistics on this? I'm glad to have you along for the ride, by the way."

He chuckled. "Do I have to refer to you as my boss?"

"Yes. I'm going to be really bossy."

"Somehow I think I can live with that."

HARPER AND JARED WERE JUST SITTING down to eggs, hash browns, toast, and bacon when the front door of the house popped open.

Initially, Jared assumed it was Zander returning for whatever packing catastrophe he'd managed to come up with in thirty-five minutes. Instead, though, he found Phil and Gloria Harlow meandering through the house ... and they were holding hands.

"Oh, geez." The comment was out of his mouth before he thought better of it.

When Harper lifted her head and found her parents entering the dining room, she was flabbergasted. "What are you guys doing here ... and together?"

Instead of apologizing — which any normal parent would've done — Gloria went on the offensive. "Can't we visit our only daughter?"

Harper considered her answer for a full beat. "No." She shook her head. "You two have to knock ... and stop doing that." She jabbed a finger toward their linked hands. "That is just too much."

"You've seen people hold hands before," Gloria countered, frowning when Phil moved to separate himself from her. "Don't let her boss you around. She has to learn that not everything is going to be done on her timetable, and to her preferences."

"This is her house," Phil said. "If she's uncomfortable ... ."

"Oh, I'm uncomfortable." Harper shook her head and stared at her plate. She often wondered why she couldn't have normal parents. Sure, there was probably no textbook definition of "normal" when it came to parents, but anything different from how her parents acted would be welcome. "You guys are supposed to be getting divorced."

"Well, that's what we're here to talk to you about," Phil hedged. He looked distinctly uncomfortable, to the point where Jared felt sorry for him.

"Do you want to sit down?" Jared offered, gesturing toward the other end of the table. "There's coffee in the pot. We ate all the food, but I could make more if you're hungry."

"We've already eaten. Thank you, though."

"Wow, everyone is so polite," Harper intoned, wrinkling her nose when Phil pulled out Gloria's chair so she could sit. "So very, very polite."

"Is there something wrong with that?" Gloria challenged, her eyes flashing.

"There's so much wrong with what you two are doing that I don't know where to start."

"Heart." Jared put his hand to Harper's back. He understood what was upsetting her. For as long as he'd known her, Phil and Gloria had been going through the most tempestuous divorce known to man. They'd been arguing about spoons, toilet paper, and even wicker furniture that was so old you couldn't sit on it without falling through and landing on the pavement. He'd assumed, like everyone else, that they hated each other.

He'd been wrong.

Several weeks before, in the middle of a murder investigation revolving around Gloria's current boyfriend, Harper and Jared walked in on them ... spending quality time together ... under their own roof. Come to find out, it was a normal occurrence and they had no intention of stopping. Harper was still traumatized by what she witnessed.

"I'm sorry." Harper held up her hands in capitulation. "I simply don't understand what's going on. Are you guys back together?"

"Well, we've been giving that some thought," Phil hedged. "We've found that we really don't thrive when we're under the same roof."

"Not even a little," Gloria agreed.

"We fight. We call each other names. Occasionally we throw things."

"I throw things," Gloria corrected. "Your father doesn't. He's not a victim of his own toxic masculinity. I read about that affliction online, by the way, and I can't tell you how happy I am that it doesn't pertain to your father."

Harper could do nothing but openly gape.

"So, you're not getting back together?" Jared prodded, confused. If they weren't getting back together, why were they holding hands?

"We didn't say that," Gloria offered hurriedly. "We said we couldn't live together."

"So, what does that leave?" Harper asked, finding her voice.

"We're going to keep separate roofs and go out together several times a week."

"You're dating," Harper surmised. "You're going to date each other."

"Essentially." Gloria bobbed her head. "We're tabling the divorce while we date each other."

"Does that mean you're going to work on getting back together?" Harper queried.

"Perhaps, or we might just try to come up with a sex schedule or something. It's all up in the air."

"Oh, geez." Harper dropped her head into her hands as Jared fought the mad urge to laugh. The situation shouldn't be funny ... and yet all he wanted to do was laugh.

"Basically we're saying that we love each other, but we don't know if we can live together," Phil offered. "We just thought you should know."

"Well, thanks for that," Harper said sarcastically. "I can't tell you how happy I am to hear that."

"You're welcome."

4

FOUR

They took two vehicles, mostly for practical reasons. Eric and Molly rode in one vehicle with all the equipment. Everyone else piled into Jared's truck for the half-hour ride to the ferry dock. Jared, who hadn't spent much time riding on ferries that carried vehicles, was amused at the sight.

"This is huge."

Harper arched an eyebrow as she looked around. It was cold, the wind bitter, but Jared insisted on getting out so he could see things up close and personal.

"Compared to the ferry that crosses Lake Michigan, this is tiny," she countered, burrowing into her coat. "I thought it was supposed to be spring. It doesn't feel like spring."

Jared automatically moved behind her so he could snuggle close. "I think it's cool."

He seemed excited, which made Harper happy, but she was moody thanks to the biting wind. "I know this is a man thing, but I can't take the cold." She shivered before reaching into his pocket to retrieve the keys. "I'm going to sit in the truck and keep warm."

"Okay." Jared wasn't bothered about being abandoned. He gave her a quick kiss. "I'll be back in a few minutes."

"Don't hurry on my account. I know you want to look around. Go ahead and do your thing. It's not as if we're not all going to the same place."

"Good point."

Harper was only in the truck for two minutes, the heat vent pointed directly at her, when Zander hopped in to join her.

"This is the absolute worst," he complained, lowering his face so the warm air blasted directly on it. "Shawn is out there acting like it's some grand adventure. I think he's lost his mind."

Harper laughed, genuinely amused. She was relieved they'd made up, although that was never in doubt. They were lifers when it came to friendship. Nothing could ever tear them apart for more than a few days.

"I think it must be something we don't understand." She shivered a bit even as the truck started to warm. "Jared thinks it's the neatest thing ever, too."

"I'm pretty sure he thinks you're the neatest thing ever." Zander rested his head against the steering wheel. Instead of hopping in the back, he opted to be upfront with his best friend. He would have to move when Jared returned, but for now he was perfectly happy. "So, I've been thinking about Jennifer."

The comment, seemingly from out of nowhere, filled Harper with surprise. "I have, too."

"Really? What have you been feeling?"

"Ridiculous guilt."

"You have?" Zander exhaled heavily, relief palpable. "I'm so glad I'm not the only one. Shawn asked me about her last night after you guys left — and I'd already ranted and raved about how I was never going to forgive you for like an hour — and he asked a few questions that made me feel like a jerk."

Harper was legitimately curious. "Like what?"

"Like ... how come we didn't invite her to hang out with us more if she was so obviously lonely." His smile was rueful. "I don't remember considering it when we were kids but, looking back, it seems like something we should've done."

Harper had come to the same realization. "Yeah. Jared asked me the same stuff. He asked me why I didn't come up here looking for her after she disappeared, other than those two days when I didn't put a lot of effort into it. I already knew what I could do, and it would've been helpful to try and find Jennifer. I never did, though."

"I don't blame you for that. I mean ... you were a kid. You were still careful about putting your powers on display. That was before we had any idea what we were going to do with our lives."

"I wasn't a kid, though. Not really. I was an adult. That's right before we graduated. I should've helped."

"Under most circumstances, you would've readily volunteered. I wonder why you didn't back then."

"I've been wondering that, too, and I haven't come up with anything that doesn't make me feel uncomfortable. You know, Jared mentioned that she was an outsider like us. That she didn't fit in with the other kids and never had friends of her own to confide in. I can't remember her hanging out with anyone, can you?"

Zander pursed his lips. "Not especially," he confirmed after a beat. "I mean ... she was friendly with everybody, but she wasn't exactly tight with anybody in particular."

"No, and that really bothers me." Harper looked around to make sure Jared and Shawn weren't heading back in their direction. She wasn't exactly keen to admit to the next part. "All I can come up with is that we shut her out because of the money. It's like we naturally assumed she couldn't be one of us because her father was rich, and that seems awfully judgmental for a gay guy trying to find himself and a girl who could talk to ghosts."

Instead of commiserating with her, Zander's eyes lit with mirth. "We were the dynamic duo. Ghost girl and gay guy. Remember when we started that club?"

Harper smirked at the memory. "Yeah. It was you and me against the world. I can't help but wonder if Jennifer wouldn't have benefitted from having someone to talk to, like you and me used to talk to one another."

"I'm sure she could have, and I regret that we were so self-absorbed that we couldn't see she was in pain. However, we can't go back in time and change that. All we can do is move forward and try to right some past wrongs while we're out here."

"Yeah." Harper took on a far-off expression as she turned her attention out the window. "What did you think about her father? I've been trying to think back regarding him, too, and I can only ever remember seeing him at school events a few times."

"I think he acts like he's got a really uncomfortable stick wedged up his you-know-what. He's a huge jerk. That doesn't mean he didn't love Jennifer, or that he doesn't feel her loss. He might be one of those guys who can't display his emotions in the correct way."

"Good point." Harper had been thinking the same thing. Of course, she'd also been wondering if this was all for show and he was hoping to take suspicion off himself once and for all. "Do you remember when it first happened? The police questioned him and we were all atwitter. We thought that meant he had to be guilty."

"I remember." Zander turned grim. "That was the talk of the town. I heard my mother and Mel gossiping behind closed doors. Mel was a detective back then, of course, and he liked to gossip even when it was against the rules."

In addition to being Zander's uncle, Mel was also Jared's partner so Harper was well aware of his penchant for talking out of turn. He was like an uncle to her, though, so she forgave him everything. He'd been the source of endless amusement and numerous ridiculous outings back in the day. "What did he say?"

"He said there was some question about why Byron waited as long as he did to report Jennifer missing. Apparently it was more than a day before he filed the report."

Harper's eyes went wide. "Seriously? That doesn't sound like a concerned parent."

"No, but it was more than that. Mel said that Byron didn't even realize she was missing. Apparently one of the maids told him that she hadn't slept in her bed and then he searched the island for her before finally calling for help. By then no one had seen her for like thirty-six hours."

Now that he mentioned it, Harper vaguely remembered reading something like that in the newspaper. "Right. People theorized he kept it to himself because he actually did something to her. After the fact, though, a lot of people came to his defense and said that he wasn't a killer, just neglectful."

"Right. Plus, as far as I remember, almost everyone believed that Jennifer ran away. There was no evidence she was taken and people assumed she had enough money to run and hide."

"But did she have enough money to hide from the investigators her father most likely hired? That's the question. Jennifer was a smart girl, but she didn't seem all that worldly. She also would've been planning this long before she carried it out and nobody found any evidence of that."

"Yeah." Zander stroked his chin, thoughtful. "Do you think Byron will open up about all that?"

Harper had been asking herself the same question. The only answer she could come up with was a resounding no.

TWENTY MINUTES LATER, JARED PULLED into the long and winding driveway that led to Jessup Manor. Harper explained the family gave it that moniker years before, when Jennifer was in high school and after Byron's mother gave the house to him, and she'd acted mortified when word got out.

"Well, I get why you guys refer to it as a castle," Jared noted, parking in the spot indicated by a uniformed attendant. "This place is ... unreal. It reminds me of a hotel more than a house."

"It's ostentatious," Harper agreed. "Still, I've always wanted to see inside. A visit is fine. I much prefer our place to this one, though."

Jared chuckled. "Yeah. You can't tell me you wouldn't want to live in a castle. I'm pretty sure I'll never make enough for that to become a reality."

"I don't want to live in a castle." Harper was matter-of-fact. "A home isn't about size or the number of items you can fit inside of it. Home is about this." She reached over and pressed her hand to the spot above his heart.

"No, home is about this," Jared countered, giving her a soft kiss before collecting his keys. Zander mimed gagging from behind them, but Jared ignored him. "This is going to be an interesting weekend. Let's see if we can find a traumatized ghost, shall we?"

Harper nodded without hesitation. "Yeah. There's Mr. Jessup now. I guess he was expecting us." She inclined her chin toward the front walk, which looked to be made out of river rock paving stones. "I hope I don't trip over my tongue because I'm too nervous to talk."

"It will be fine," Jared reassured her. "We're all here together. It's going to be okay."

Harper could only hope that was true. Still, she was a professional. She was determined to approach this job like she would anything else. That's why she had a friendly but relaxed smile on her face when she greeted Byron. "It's nice to see you again, Mr. Jessup." She extended her hand.

Because it was a social nicety that he couldn't simply ignore, Byron took it. He wasn't exactly gregarious in his greeting, though. "Ms. Harlow. It will probably be easier, less rigid, if you call me Byron."

Harper noted that he didn't say he wanted her to call him Byron because it was less informal. He was simply insisting on it because he didn't want people to talk, whisper about him being unapproachable behind his back. "Sure. Where would you like us to go?"

"Well, there's been some discussion about that." Byron slid his eyes to the gentleman standing next to him, a staid individual with snowy white hair — even though he was probably only in his fifties — and a suit that looked as if it cost more than Harper's car. "Your contingent is by far the largest we have coming in."

Harper balked. "You didn't say there was a limit."

Byron offered up an impatient hand wave. "And there's not. You're also the one closest to this location, so it makes sense that you would be bringing more people with you. You're the only one I've hired who actually knew Jennifer."

"She was a really sweet girl," Harper said automatically.

"She was dependable," Byron agreed. "She was not the type to wander off alone. That's why I know someone took her. She wouldn't willingly leave."

"Hopefully we'll be able to prove that," Harper offered, immediately wishing she'd phrased it a different way. "I don't mean I hope that she's dead. That would be weird. You know what I mean, though."

Byron arched an eyebrow. "I believe I do. As it stands, your group is rather large. This is Bates, my butler. We've been discussing the lodging arrangements and we believe it would be best for your group to take over the guesthouse. There are four bedrooms, a private bathroom and kitchen, and basically anything else you could possibly need."

Harper's initial reaction was disappointment. She wanted to see the main house. Then she realized she would still be visiting. This way, though, she would have space to retreat to that was set back from the rest of the guests. This really was the best of both worlds.

"The guesthouse sounds great," she enthused. "We have a lot of equipment and this will allow us to pick and choose what we need depending on the specific situation."

"Then it worked out well." Byron looked bored, as if he was in distress having to talk to people below his financial station.

His reaction had Harper biting the inside of her cheek. "If you show us which direction to head, I'm sure we can figure the rest out ourselves."

"Bates will handle that," Byron offered. "He runs the house."

"Kind of like Bates on *Downton Abbey*, right?" Zander asked, his eyes sparkling.

The butler's expression never changed. "It's not like that at all."

Zander was taken aback by the cool dismissal. He was used to people falling all over him — rich people, poor people, outgoing people, introverts ... it didn't matter — and he clearly wasn't happy with the current tone of the visit. "I didn't mean it in a bad way. I just ... you know, Bates."

"I'm familiar with the television show," Bates said dryly. "I can assure you that our duties are completely dissimilar."

Amused despite herself, it took everything Harper had to keep from barking out a raucous laugh. "I'm sure the duties are completely different," she reassured him. "I mean ... you probably don't have to help Mr. Jessup get dressed or anything, right?"

"Not more than three times a week."

Harper pressed her lips together and widened her eyes as she glanced at Jared. It was obvious he was as amused with the conversation as she was.

"Well, we thank you for helping us," Jared said finally. "We're looking forward to this weekend. Knowing we don't have to worry about any of the equipment is a great relief."

"I'm sure." Bates' expression was almost a sneer. "And what sort of equipment does a ghost hunter require?"

His disdain was evident and it set Harper's teeth on edge. "You would be surprised. We have EVP recorders, EMF meters, laser grid kits, a spirit box, Mel Meters ... and the rest. Just the normal stuff."

"I'm afraid I've never heard of any of that. It doesn't sound normal to me."

"Well, I'm sure there are things in your world that don't sound normal to us," Harper pointed out. "That doesn't mean they're not real."

"I suppose." Bates opted for silence for the rest of the trip. He didn't speak again until they were positioned in front of what was termed "a small guest-house." It was three times as big as Harper's house. "Will this do?" he asked primly.

Harper hoped she wasn't openly gaping because it would give the ostentatious man a reason to judge her. "It will be fine," she replied crisply. "This is a work trip, not a vacation. We don't need cushy accommodations."

Jared arched a delighted eyebrow as he scooted around her, his arms laden with bags. He was genuinely amused with her attitude. He held it together until they were inside — Bates on his way back to the main house — and then asked the obvious question.

"What was that about?"

"I don't like his attitude," Harper automatically complained. "It was like he was silently judging us."

"I have news for you: There was nothing silent about his judgment. Still, you usually don't react to things like that."

"I know." Harper let loose a long sigh. "I don't know what's wrong with me. I'm on edge or something. I don't know how to explain it."

"Well, now that you're here and the initial meeting is over, maybe you'll calm down some, huh?" He dropped the bags he was carrying and crossed to her so he could give her a hug. "This is going to be a tense weekend — I can already see that — but it's nothing you can't handle."

Harper nodded as she returned his embrace. She recognized she was on edge and needed to calm herself. It was obvious to pretty much everyone, and she wasn't the sort to turn away from introspection.

"Let's get the equipment unpacked and put it on the dining room table," she suggested after a beat. "I don't think we're going to be doing a lot of eating out here. Then, after, we can check out the grounds."

"I don't think we're going to have time for that," Eric offered, his attention on a sheet of paper he found on the counter.

"What is that?" Harper asked, curiosity getting the better of her.

"This is an itinerary. We're expected in the main house in two hours for a cocktail meet-and-greet. After that, dinner will be served. Dress is casual ... but no ripped jeans or visible bra straps."

Harper furrowed her brow. "It doesn't really say that, does it?"

"As a matter of fact, it does."

She scowled. "I'm really starting to dislike these people."

"Just remember that you're here for Jennifer and not her father," Jared noted. "It's only one weekend. I'm sure we can all make it work."

Harper was no longer sure that was true, but she kept her opinion to herself. There was no point in begging for trouble. They would have to head off each problem when it became apparent. There was nothing else they could do.

FIVE

Harper opted for simple black pants and a cashmere sweater, a Christmas gift from Jared that he loved seeing her in because the rich blue set off her eyes.

"You look nice," he noted as he straightened his tie in their bedroom mirror.

"Thank you," she beamed ... and then decided to help, sliding in front of him so she could attack the crooked scrap of fabric. "I don't think you have to wear a tie if you don't want to."

"It's the first night. I figure I should probably make a good impression because I'm basically the only one who doesn't have a legitimate reason for being here."

"Shawn doesn't either," she offered helpfully, grinning when he kissed the tip of her nose. "Also, you do have a legitimate reason for being here. I want you with me."

"Then I guess it's good that I always want to be with you."

"Most definitely." She rolled her neck as she finished, her hands light as she brushed them over his suit jacket. "You clean up really well."

He cocked his head to the side. There was something about her demeanor he couldn't quite put his finger on. She was melancholy, quiet, but he sensed an eruption would eventually come if she didn't vent her emotions better. "Do you want to talk about what's bothering you?"

She was taken aback. "Why do you think something is bothering me?"

"Because I've met you."

"Why else?"

He almost laughed. Almost. He didn't think she was purposely being funny, though. "You might feel better if you tell me," he offered, tugging a reluctant sigh from her lips.

"You're going to think I'm being ridiculous."

"Try me."

"It's the other psychics and hunters. I haven't really thought about them until now — mostly because I was more interested in seeing Jessup Manor — but now that we're finally going to meet them, I can't help being afraid."

Jared didn't know what to make of the statement. "I'm not sure what to say. Do you need me to tell you that you're better than all of them or that it's okay to step back and let them dominate the room? I could go either way with this one."

The indecision on his face caused Harper to giggle. "I guess I'm nervous that they'll be better than me," she admitted, sheepish. "I never thought this would be a genuine concern for me, but this situation is different from anything else I've ever been part of. I can't help but wonder if Byron is setting us up to be in competition with one another."

"I think that's a fair question. He seems to be the sort. It doesn't matter, though. It doesn't matter what these other people think. It doesn't matter what sort of show they intend to put on. All that matters is that you're an authentic person and you're here for a legitimate reason ... to help people. We don't know the motivations of these other people, but I very much doubt they're all pure as the driven snow."

Harper hadn't considered that, but now that she did, she found she over-whelmingly agreed. "We have to be careful. Odds are, not all these people will be trustworthy."

"That's exactly what I was thinking." He cupped her chin and kissed her. "I think it's time we head up, though. We shouldn't be late. I don't think Byron Jessup is the sort of guy who finds tardiness whimsical."

"Yeah. We should definitely head up."

BECAUSE IT SEEMED RUDE NOT TO, Harper knocked on the front door and waited for Bates to answer. If he was surprised to see them, he didn't show it.

"We weren't sure if we should knock," Harper offered lamely.

"Knocking is always appreciated," Bates replied. "The other guests are assembled in the parlor. This way, please."

Harper made a face behind the man's back — one that made Jared choke on his tongue — but she held it together as the stiff butler showed them through the house. She was relieved when they arrived at their destination and found the other guests seemed to take the missive for casual dressing to heart. There wasn't a ripped jean in sight but there were a few pairs of Levi's that boasted frayed seams.

"Harper Harlow and ... guests," Bates announced when they arrived in the room. "There are drinks at the bar — no gratuities are necessary because our host has arranged to cover that — and Mr. Jessup will be joining the party imminently. Please enjoy yourselves ... within reason."

Zander's eyes lit with insult as the butler escaped from the room. "Why did he look at me when he said that 'within reason' part?" he exploded.

"Maybe because it's easy to see that you're the type who will dance on tables," Jared shot back.

"That is a bigoted thing to say," Zander sniffed. "I can't believe you're dating a man who would think that, Harp. I just can't even ... ."

Months past, Jared would've fallen for the act. He knew better now. "Oh, don't even." He made a face. "I didn't say that because you're gay. I said it because you're a loud drunk."

"Oh." Zander brightened considerably. "Well, that's perfectly acceptable." He shuffled toward the bar. "Speaking of that, I'm thinking it's a Grasshopper sort of night. What do you think, Harp?"

"I think I'm sticking to water," Harper automatically replied. "I think you should, too."

"Absolutely not." Zander squared his broad shoulders. "I'm going to see how the other half drinks and there's absolutely nothing you can do about it."

"Then knock yourself out." Harper kept close to Jared as she swiveled to focus on the rest of the room. To her utter surprise, she recognized some of the faces milling about and socializing. "That's Madeline Baxter." She made the announcement a bit more loudly than she intended.

Jared cocked an eyebrow. "Is that name supposed to mean something to me?"

"It should," Zander replied, appearing on the other side of Jared with a glass full of some green concoction gripped in his hand.

"That was fast," Harper muttered. "Are the bartenders magical or something?"

"Let's just say they're not Tom Cruise but they're pretty freaking sly. I'm impressed ... and it's good to boot."

"That's great," Jared drawled sarcastically. "As long as your tastebuds are happy, we're all good."

Zander's eye roll was pronounced. "Who beat you with the crabby stick?"

"I asked you a question," Jared reminded her. "Who is Madeline Baxter?"

"It's the blonde over there in the corner," Harper supplied, keeping her voice low. "See the one in the dress that basically covers nothing?"

Jared's eyes went wide when he finally found the woman Harper was referring to. "I believe I see her."

Harper, not amused in the least, elbowed him in the stomach. "You'd better not like what you see."

"I only like what I see when I'm looking at you. Who is she, though?"

"She's a former cheerleader and the bane of my existence," Zander volunteered. "If evil had a face, it would belong to Madeline Baxter."

Harper shot him a quelling look. "Let's not exaggerate," she suggested. "She might've changed since high school."

"You went to high school with her?" Jared was officially intrigued. "Why is she here?"

"Because she's married to Byron Jessup."

Jared opened his mouth to respond and then snapped it shut, taking a moment to absorb the news and regroup before speaking. "Just so I'm clear — and I'm not casting aspersions on anyone here, I'm seeking clarification for my own edification — that woman went to high school with you and Zander and now she's married to Byron Jessup? She's young enough to be his daughter."

"She's most definitely young enough to be his daughter," Harper agreed. "Ironically enough, Madeline was always jealous of Jennifer in high school and gave her a hard time. She started dating Byron publicly not long after Jennifer disappeared. It was quite the scandal ... although most people let it go because they believed Byron was grieving."

"You don't believe that, huh?"

"I don't think Byron cares about anyone but himself. Appearance is everything with him, so all he cared about was other people coveting what he had ... like a young wife."

"Still, that's kind of gross," Jared pressed. "I wonder what Jennifer would've thought of that."

"Maybe we'll get a chance to ask her," Harper suggested.

"Fair enough." Jared inclined his chin toward the older couple sitting across from Madeline. "Who are they?"

"George and Evangeline Jessup," Harper supplied. "They're Byron Jessup's parents."

"They don't look happy to be here."

"Not even a little," Harper agreed. "I don't know much about them. I know they had money but not the sort of money their son possesses. There was a rumor at one time that George and his son were warring over who was more important to the family legacy – the house went with the status, but it was Evangeline's to pass on when she deemed it necessary – but I think they were legitimately the only two who cared."

"Awesome," Jared intoned. "What about the others?"

"That's Richard." Harper extended her finger toward a handsome man standing next to the couch where George and Evangeline reclined. "He's Jennifer's brother. He's two years older, was in college at the time she disappeared."

"I didn't realize she had a brother." Jared straightened and studied the man, who was dressed for success but appeared to be morose and surly. "He doesn't look happy to be here either."

"I don't want to make excuses for these people, but if you look at it from their point of view, this all probably seems ridiculous," Harper said. "I mean, think about it. Jennifer has been missing for ten years. Suddenly Byron has decided that he's going to amass a bunch of psychics and ghost hunters — people they probably assume are kooks — to discover what happened. It can't be easy to swallow."

"I guess." Jared was thoughtful. "The fact that they're here seems to suggest to me that Byron is in charge of pretty much everything where this family is concerned. If they don't want to be here and yet still attended ... well ... that means he's controlling the purse strings and they all know it."

"You assume this has something to do with money," Harper noted. "That's not necessarily true. Maybe they're upset he's doing this and hanging tight because they want to make sure Jennifer's memory isn't trampled."

"Are you sure that's not wishful thinking?"

"No, but I don't always want to be the jaded person who assumes the negative."

"And you think that's what I'm doing?"

"No. I just ... it's weird, but I don't want to hate all of these people." It was hard for Harper to admit. "I'm here to help Jennifer if I can. At least one of these people has to be worthy of sympathy. Otherwise, it's going to be hard to keep my eyes on the bigger picture without getting bitter."

Jared understood exactly what she was saying. "Fair enough." He slipped his arm around her waist. "What about the others? Do you recognize any of them?"

"That's Bertie Nixon," Zander volunteered, tipping his head toward the far-right corner. "He's a local attorney. I know because he handled my grandfather's will, the probate and stuff. I bet he's here representing the financial needs of the family."

"That makes sense," Jared acknowledged. "Perhaps the other family members are here because they believe Byron has lost his mind and they want the probate lawyer present to strip power from him."

Harper scorched him with a dark look. "And that's not jaded?"

Jared had the grace to be abashed. "That probably came out a little harsher than I intended."

"Just a little bit," she agreed, turning to the other three people in the room. They were dressed more colorfully than the rest, and Harper had a feeling they were the psychics she would be pitted against. "I guess that's the other 'talent.'"

Jared slid her a sidelong look before focusing on the individuals in question. "Does anyone recognize them?"

"I do," Molly offered, her hair a violent shade of purple this week. She wore a pretty black dress that showed off her shoulders and seemed in awe as she stared at the man holding court in the middle of the group. "That's Harris Fontaine."

The name meant nothing to Harper. "Should I know who that is?"

"I'm on it," Jared offered, typing on his phone. "Oh, here he is. Wow. He's considered a psychic to the stars. He has a bunch of celebrities who supposedly use his services religiously."

"I don't think that's anything to get excited about," Harper said petulantly.

"Oh, so cute," Jared teased, squeezing her tighter. "If I was a famous star, you would still be my favorite psychic."

"I'm not a psychic."

Jared stilled. "I guess not. How do you think of yourself?"

"As awesome," Zander answered for her.

"That goes without saying," Jared acknowledged. "How else, though?"

She shrugged, noncommittal. "I'm just ... Harper."

"No, you're special. How do you want us referring to your gift?"

Harper shifted from one foot to the other, clearly uncomfortable. "I don't know. I ... just call me a ghost hunter. That's what I am."

Jared found her reaction peculiar and looked to Zander for help. For once, Harper's best friend looked as stymied as Jared felt. He didn't appear to have any easy answers.

"I'll run Harris Fontaine before dinner and see if I find anything good," Jared said finally, opting to put off pressuring Harper on the issue until later in the evening ... when they were alone and she didn't have to worry about censoring her thoughts. "What about the other two, the women?"

"I'm pretty sure the one in the bright scarf with all the jewelry is Delphine Winston," Molly replied, squinting to get a better look at the woman in the muted light. "She's based out of New Orleans. She's considered a bruja, although I'm not certain if she's the real deal or a fraud. So many of the faces coming out of the Quarter are fakes that I'm leery of all of them now."

Jared didn't want to look like a rube, but he was behind. "What's a bruja?"

"A witch," Eric replied. "Molly endlessly researches all this stuff because she's obsessed with the paranormal."

"You think witches are real?" Jared asked Molly with an arched eyebrow.

Harper slid her boyfriend a sidelong look. "I happen to believe witches are real, too. In case you've forgotten, we met one not too long ago."

Jared was chagrined. "I remember, but I didn't really consider her a witch."

"Oh, she was a witch. She didn't want to view herself that way, but she was still a witch. As for this woman … ." Harper trailed off as she went back to staring. Delphine appeared to be the gregarious sort. She was the life of the party, telling spirited stories and causing Harris to break out in raucous guffaws. She was clearly putting on a show.

"Do you think she's real?" Jared asked after a beat. "I mean … I realize you can't possibly know beyond a shadow of a doubt, but if you're real, there's every possibility one of the others is real, too."

"I don't know," she answered after a moment's contemplation. "It's too soon to tell. I need to get to know her. I agree it's possible one of these people is the real deal."

"What about the last one?" Jared asked, gesturing toward a pretty woman, long red hair hanging to her waist. She had high cheekbones and looked to be enjoying herself, although her expression suggested polite interest in whatever Harris was saying rather than genuine curiosity.

"Her name is Margot Markham," Shawn volunteered, joining the group from behind. "I know because I asked Bates. I was curious about everyone as much as you guys and figured he had answers. He says Byron selected half the psychics and Madeline added a few names of her own to the list."

"I can't believe he willingly shared," Harper noted. "That doesn't seem like his style. He thinks we're beneath him."

"I don't know that he really believes that," Shawn hedged. "He clearly wants people to believe he feels that way. I get a sense everything he does is for show, and he's not particularly happy about it. That's neither here nor there, though."

"What did he tell you about Margot?" Jared asked.

"Just that she's a psychic of some renown and made a name for herself with some murder on the west side of the state. I'm not sure if she actually solved it … or found the victim … or something else. That's all he said."

"I can run the information easily enough," Jared offered. "I think it's smart to get background on all three of these people ... just in case."

Harper couldn't find reason to argue with his assessment. "Yeah. I definitely think that's a good idea." Her eyes traveled back to where the Jessup family was sitting, unhappiness practically oozing from the corner. "You might want to see what you can pull on them, too. I mean ... odds are long that any of them are involved, but it can't possibly hurt to check."

Jared followed her gaze and grimly nodded. "You read my mind. I want to check on all of them, too. I'm especially interested in Madeline. I know you said the relationship between her and Byron didn't start until after Jennifer went missing, but what if that's not true?"

Harper's stomach twisted at what Jared was suggesting. "You think Byron was involved with her before? You know that means he would've been messing around with her when she was still in high school, right? She graduated with us."

"I know. Would she have been an adult at the time?"

Harper shrugged. "I don't know. I have no idea when her birthday is."

"It's something to check out. It could be nothing. Maybe Madeline visited at the time to offer her condolences or help and one thing led to another. I just want to make sure."

"It makes sense to me," Harper supplied. "I find their entire relationship weird."

"Then I'll look. Other than that, I suggest we try to get through dinner and see where that leaves us."

"Sounds like a plan to me."

SIX

D inner was an uncomfortable affair. For some reason, someone — Harper had a strong suspicion it was Bates because he seemed evil — set up a seating chart that isolated her from the other members of her group.

She didn't like it.

To her left was Evangeline, a woman who seemed as uncomfortable as Harper felt. She kept focusing on her plate to the detriment of everything else, including conversation. Harper wasn't particularly excited about the set-up but recognized it would be worse if she made it through dinner without a single comment.

"So ... I believe you're on a committee with my mother," she hedged after a beat, antsy. "The library committee or something. I can't remember the exact name of it."

Evangeline arched an eyebrow and pinned Harper with a look. "Oh, really?" She said it in such a manner Harper couldn't help but wonder if she was judging her by her outfit ... and by extension her mother. Gloria wouldn't like that. "And who is your mother?"

Harper was legitimately afraid to answer the question. "Um ... Gloria Harlow." She didn't see where she had much choice so she simply went for it.

"You're Gloria's daughter?" Evangeline's expression was hard to read. "You don't look much like her."

Since Harper found her mother's devotion to fashion somewhat embarrassing — especially in southeastern Michigan, where a hoodie was considered the height of subtle elegance — she took the comment as a compliment. "Thank you."

Amusement, faint as a whisper, flitted across Evangeline's face. "How do you know I don't like your mother?"

"Because very few people like my mother. There are times I don't like her. Just recently she was a suspect in a murder. I was playing the odds."

This time Evangeline laughed, genuinely amused. "I take it you got your father's sense of humor. I've always been fond of Phil. He's a bit of a card, but he has a good heart."

Harper couldn't argue with that sentiment. Even though she was agitated with her parents — to a level she never thought possible — he was still a good man. He always listened to her, tried to help, and yeah, occasionally he gave the most ridiculous advice ever, but he honestly tried to help when the opportunity arose. That was more than she could say for her mother.

"He does have a good heart," she agreed, her eyes moving farther down the table, to where Jared sat between Delphine and Bertie. He seemed to be listening intently to whatever Bertie was saying, something Harper couldn't fathom because she was bored out of her mind. "Are you on board with this?" she asked on a whim.

Margot, who was seated on Harper's right, swiveled at the question. She looked genuinely interested in the answer, although she didn't insert herself into the conversation.

"Am I on board with what?" Evangeline's expression reflected confusion.

"This." Harper gestured toward the huge table. "Your son has assembled a bunch of psychics and ghost hunters — people I would assume you don't believe in — and wants us to discover what happened to your granddaughter. I can't imagine that's easy for you."

Evangeline worked her jaw, and for a brief moment Harper sensed real anger simmering under the surface. Ultimately, though, she collected herself. "I'm here, aren't I?"

"That's not really an answer."

"What sort of answer do you require?"

"The truth." Harper was determined to get a real answer from the woman. "I knew Jennifer in high school. I'm only telling you because I'm not sure you were aware. She hung around with my friend Zander and me sometimes ... although, in hindsight, we wish we'd gone out of our way to spend more time with her."

"I'm sure that would've made things better," Evangeline said dryly, causing

Harper's lips to twitch. "As for what's going on here, I don't know what to think about it. You're right about me not believing in psychics and the like." Her gaze was pointed when it landed on Harper. "That being said, you have an interesting reputation."

Harper swallowed hard at the insinuation. "What is that supposed to mean?"

"It means you have an interesting reputation. You've been in the newspapers several times. You found that girl in high school, saved her life. I remember listening to Jennifer go on and on about it. She thought it was a marvelous thing. Other people were more suspicious."

Harper felt distinctly uncomfortable being at the center of the conversation. "Well, we don't have to talk about that."

"Why? It's your exploits that got you here in the first place. You've been at the center of quite a few high-profile investigations, including that little girl who went missing before Christmas."

"That was pure luck."

"Really?" Evangeline arched a challenging eyebrow. "My understanding is that you found another girl in a shed. She'd been dead for years. Her mother was arrested for murdering her and kidnapping the other girl."

Harper shifted on her chair, uncomfortable. "Well ... I don't know what you want me to say," she said finally. "On one hand, I get that you don't believe in all this stuff and I figure I should play along for your benefit because I was taught to respect my elders. On the other hand, I did everything you said. I found Zoe and put Chloe to rest. I'm not ashamed of that."

"You shouldn't be. Those were both wonderful accomplishments. I'm hopeful you can help my son the same way."

"But you don't think I can," Harper surmised.

"Let's just say that I think Whisper Cove has seen its fair share of miracles for one year. I don't believe we're due for another. If you'll excuse me." She dabbed at her mouth with her napkin and stood. "I believe I'm done for the evening. It was nice meeting you, Harper. Tell your father I said hello."

With those words, she was gone, and Harper was left with more questions than answers.

"That was interesting," Margot noted, speaking for the first time.

Harper slid her eyes to the young woman. She was quiet, shy, and seemed happiest hanging back and surveying the landscape rather than making waves. Harper liked that about her, although she wasn't sure she trusted her. It could simply be that Margot was smarter than everyone else in the room.

"What did you find interesting about it?" Harper asked.

"She doesn't want to get her hopes up," Margo replied without hesitation. "On one hand, the idea of getting answers excites her. She'd like to at least know what happened to her granddaughter. On the other, if somehow it's proven that Jennifer is dead, she'll lose hope. That's the only thing that's been fueling her for the past ten years."

Harper wasn't sure she agreed with that assessment. She found it insightful, though, and filed it away to think about later. "I think this is a family at odds," she offered finally, her gaze bouncing toward the end of the table, to where Richard sat with Zander. They looked to be the only two individuals enjoying each other's company, and Richard roared with laughter at some story Zander told. "I think some want answers and others would be happy with the memory of Jennifer going away."

"I can't disagree with you there." Margot's gaze fell on Madeline, who was sitting between Shawn and Harris. She participated in polite conversation with both but didn't appear engaged. "Do you think we'll find her?"

Harper shrugged, noncommittal. "We don't even know she's dead. I don't know what to expect."

"If she's not dead, where has she been?"

"Maybe she's been hiding. Maybe she adopted a new identity, a new life. There are a myriad of possibilities."

"Do you really think that's possible?"

"Yes. Do I think it's probable? It's too soon to say." She turned back to her prime rib. "This is really good. I guess we can't complain about that."

"I'm a vegetarian."

Harper's gaze flitted to the woman's plate and she realized not a single thing had been touched. "Oh, well, sucks for you."

Margot laughed. "I'll survive. There's always bread."

"That's the way to look at it. Who doesn't love bread?"

"Nobody I know."

AFTER DINNER, BYRON LEFT the bulk of his family in the parlor and led Harper, Harris, Delphine, and Margot to the second floor. Harper's team trailed behind, seemingly unsure what they should do, but Byron completely ignored them and focused on the willowy blonde.

"This is Jennifer's room," he intoned as he pushed open the door. "I've changed nothing since she went missing."

Harper's discomfort jumped to the point where she turned itchy as she found herself looking at a child's room. Technically, she guessed it belonged to a teenager. It was vastly different from the room she had when eighteen, though.

"Oh, this is weird," Jared muttered, moving in behind her as he surveyed the room. "It's like ... ."

"A little girl's room," Harper finished, her heart giving a tremendous heave as she lifted her eyes to the top of the canopy bed. "I always wanted one of these ... when I was eight."

"It's a little girly," Jared admitted. The room set off a number of red flags in his busy brain. "Is this what your room looked like when you were eighteen?"

Harper shook her head. "No. I had rock posters everywhere ... and I was obsessed with Colin Farrell so I had pictures of him taped to my mirror. I had makeup all over the place ... and Zander kept his hair products at my house because he didn't want his mother to know what he was spending his money on."

Jared smiled. He could picture Zander and Harper sitting on her bed, futzing with each other's hair and makeup while gossiping about everyone in their school. It was a warm vision. Jennifer's room was vastly different. "Yeah, well ... I really want to get a look at the original missing person's report. Mel is pulling it for me."

Harper couldn't contain her surprise. "You've been in contact with Mel?"

"I wanted him to know where we were in case these people turned into murderous cretins."

"Oh, right. Smart." Harper flashed a bright smile and patted his arm before moving toward the nightstand. There was one photo in the room. It was a framed snapshot, and at the center of it were Madeline and Jennifer. It seemed out of place in the room, and for some reason it set Harper's teeth on edge. "Has this always been here?" Harper asked, snagging the photo.

Byron furrowed his brow as he slid his eyes in her direction, frowning when he realized what she was holding up. "No. Where did that come from?" He grabbed the frame and searched the room, his eyes ultimately falling on Madeline, who had trailed after the rest of the group. "Did you put this here?"

The woman's cheeks colored. "So what? We were friends."

"That's not exactly how I remember it." Byron's tone was tart. "Is this even a real photograph?" He stared hard at the image. "Did you pay someone to create this? I'm pretty sure Jennifer never posed with you. She didn't particularly like you ... especially toward the end."

Harper tilted her head to the side, suspicious. She decided to play a hunch. "Is that because she found out the two of you were seeing each other? That had to be hard on her."

Before Byron could open his mouth, Madeline took control of the conversation. Harper was hoping that would be the case.

"She was just jealous," Madeline hissed. "She melted down when she caught us together, accused me of only wanting to hang out with her so I could get close to her father. She was rude and judgmental, and I absolutely hated her for it. She was impossible to be around ... and all because she was jealous that her father liked me more than her. I mean ... really."

Harper pursed her lips as she slid her eyes to Byron. He understood what she'd just admitted. Madeline was still operating in the dark.

"Madeline, if you don't have anything constructive to add to the conversation, perhaps you should go downstairs," Byron suggested. "Isn't one of those Real Housewives and Insipid Women shows you like — the ones you aspire to be worthy to be on — airing a marathon or something? Why don't you take a bottle of wine upstairs and focus on that? I'll handle this."

Madeline showed her true colors, the doting wife disappearing. "You can't just cut me out of this. I'm part of this family, too."

"For now." Byron's expression was cold. "That can be remedied, something I'm giving serious thought to. Now, if you don't mind, I would like to focus on someone of actual importance to me." He shoved the photo frame in Madeline's direction. "You are not allowed in this room. We've been over this a million times. I will have Mrs. Sanders go through the closet and chest of drawers tomorrow. If any of Jennifer's things are missing, I can guarantee you won't like what happens."

Madeline's eyes reflected murderous intent as they landed on Harper. "This is all your fault," she hissed. "Why couldn't you just mind your own business? I mean ... really. You were such a freak in school. When Byron mentioned he was calling you, I told him it was a bad idea. He should've listened to me.

"You're so ... low class," she continued, obviously warming to her subject. "You don't have the same breeding as we do. You don't belong out here. You brought your stupid fairy friend — he was always obnoxious and people laughed behind his back — and neither one of you belong here."

She was haughty enough that Harper's temper snapped. When the blond ghost hunter took a deliberate step in the woman's direction, Jared intercepted her quickly.

"Heart, that's not a good idea," he said on a murmur, carefully snagging her arm. "She's trying to bait you."

"I don't care what she says about me," Harper growled. "She can't go after Zander. I won't allow it."

For a brief instant, Jared got a picture of how Harper must have spent her teenage years. Her devotion to Zander, while sometimes irritating, was a thing of beauty. She didn't care if Madeline disparaged her. She did care about Zander feeling even a moment's discomfort.

"Mr. Jessup, I think we need to have a discussion," Jared noted, motioning toward the hallway with his hand. "Harp, stay here with Zander. Check out the room and ... do your thing. I'll talk to Mr. Jessup and his wife."

Harper glared at the other woman, fire practically coming out of her eyes. "I'll make you cry if you're not careful," she warned, fury practically oozing from every pore. "I mean ... I'll make you cry like a little girl."

Jared had never seen Harper quite so aggressive and he was amused despite himself. "Rein it in, Tiger," he teased, squeezing her hand. "I'll be right back."

Jared made sure to snag Madeline from the corner before exiting the room. He had no intention of leaving her behind to wreak havoc on Harper's already frayed emotions. "You, too." She put up a fight, but Jared refused to let her escape.

"I'm not going to let this viper harass Harper to the point of no return," he announced when it was just the three of them in the hallway. He had on his "no-nonsense" cop face and it was clear he wasn't in the mood to play games. "She agreed to come here even though her initial instinct was to say no. She's in a different position from these other people because she knew Jennifer."

"I would think that would make things easier for her," Madeline shot back. "Unless ... wait ... is she a fraud?" Her eyes lit with mirth at the suggestion. "I bet she is. I always knew it back in high school. People would fall all over her because she supposedly found missing people, but I knew better. She was faking all of it because she liked being the center of attention."

Jared pinned her with a hard look. "I don't like you," he announced, not caring in the least that it could be construed as rude. "Do you know what I just heard with that little speech? You were jealous of Harper in high school because you wanted all the attention and couldn't understand when someone else garnered it. I don't really care about your issues."

Madeline opened her mouth to argue, but Jared held up his hand to silence her. "I'm talking now," he insisted, pinning her with a look before turning to Byron. "I don't want to be difficult. This is Harper's gig and I'm basically along for moral support because she knew Jennifer and feels guilty for not looking for her earlier. However, there are certain things I won't put up with.

"The first is insults to her," he continued. "And before you open your mouth, Madeline, an insult against Zander is an insult against Harper. They're just that close. You don't have to get along with them, but you do have to show them a modicum of respect. That only seems fair."

"Well, I don't care what you think is fair," Madeline shot back.

"I do," Byron interjected, his expression never changing. "I understand what you're saying, Mr. Monroe, and I happen to agree. If my wife cannot be pleasant, then she will not be part of the action."

Jared smiled as Madeline's mouth dropped open. She clearly expected her husband to side with her, to the point where she was furious when it didn't happen. "That's all I ask." He skirted around Madeline. "Now, if you'll excuse me, I want to see the show. Have a lovely rest of your evening."

SEVEN

Jared could hear Madeline complaining to Byron as he returned to Jennifer's room. For his part, Byron didn't appear to have much sympathy for the woman's plight. He told her, in no uncertain terms, that she was to shut up and get out. Then he left her to fume and returned to the group. He seemed keen to watch the action.

"I sense a great deal of strife," Harris intoned, adopting a creepy voice as he closed his eyes and looked to the ceiling. "The spirit who lived here for the entirety of her life was not a happy one."

Harper frowned at the man. She didn't enjoy the theatrics. "You don't know she's a spirit," she countered. "There's no way to tell that from what we have in this room. It's not as if Jennifer's spirit is in here."

"You don't know that," Harris shot back, agitation on full display. "She could be here ... simply hiding."

"But ... she's not." Harper wasn't in the mood for games. "This room doesn't even feel like her. Are you sure this was her room since she was a kid?" She pinned Byron with a probing look. "This doesn't feel like Jennifer to me."

Instead of being offended, Byron appeared genuinely intrigued. "I was not aware that you were that close with my daughter."

Harper refused to let the comment grate. "I don't know that 'close' is the appropriate word. We hung out a little bit. We knew each other well enough to talk from time to time. I know that this isn't the sort of stuff she liked."

"And what sort of stuff did she like?" Harris asked, haughty.

"Books," Harper replied simply. "She loved reading ... and she had this shirt, something about books being new adventures. I can't remember the exact saying."

Byron nodded his head, impressed. "You're right, of course. This was her bedroom, but she only slept here. She wanted to change it when she got older, but my mother decorated it and insisted it had to stay the same. Jennifer spent all her time elsewhere."

"And where was that?" Jared asked.

Instead of answering, Byron motioned for everyone to follow him. The trip through the massive house took a full four minutes. When they arrived at their destination, though, Harper sighed and started nodding as she stepped into the ornate library.

"This feels like her," she intoned, glancing around. Her gaze immediately fell on the comfortable couch and chairs positioned in the center of the room. "She spent all her time in here, including sleeping when she could get away with it, right?"

Byron nodded, his eyes appraising as he looked Harper up and down in a new light. "She did. I never understood it, but she always loved this room."

"What's not to love?" Zander enthused, moving to the couch and looking up. There was a skylight overhead. "I bet she lied here every night and dreamed about what her life was going to be like when she finally got out."

Byron stiffened at the words, and the look Harper shot in his direction was apologetic.

"He didn't mean that the way it sounded," she offered quickly. "It's more that ... every kid stares at the sky and dreams how his or her life is going to turn out. Jennifer was probably no different."

"Except she *is* different," Byron countered, recovering. "My daughter never got a chance to grow up. She never got a chance to even try to make the dreams come true. That's why all of you are here. I want to know what happened to her, and where I can go to find her body. I want to put her to rest."

Harper didn't take the man's gruff tone to heart. She understood he was covering. Part of him wanted to explode all over Zander. The other part recognized there was truth in the words. That was even harder for him to accept, because it was clear he was a man struggling with duty and regret. Even though Harper didn't particularly like the man, she could see he was torn apart by what happened to his family ... whatever that was.

"Tell me about the last time you saw Jennifer," Harper instructed, changing the subject. "How did she seem?"

Byron was taken aback by the question. "What does that have to do with anything?"

"More than you might think," Jared offered. "I know you're convinced your daughter has to be dead, but we have no proof of that. Is it possible she was upset with you, that she wanted to run away and managed to carry it out?"

Byron made a series of protesting sounds with his mouth. "That's the most ludicrous thing I've ever heard," he said finally, his temper coming out to play. "I mean ... how could a child manage to stay hidden for so long? Even if you're right and she did run away, she couldn't have stayed hidden for such a long time. It's simply not possible."

That wasn't a denial, Harper realized. "That's not what I asked." She was firm as she held the older man's gaze. "What was your last interaction like?"

"I don't remember." Byron's demeanor was stiff as he straightened his shoulders. "Now, if you'll excuse me, I have other tasks to attend to around the house. You're free to look around as long as you wish. Breakfast will be served at eight o'clock tomorrow morning. I expect you to be prompt ... and find the answers I'm looking for. Tonight was a simple introduction. Tomorrow will be much more."

He turned on his heel to leave and Harper opened her mouth to call after him, an apology on the tip of her tongue, but Jared offered her a subtle head shake. She snapped her mouth shut and nodded, silently agreeing with him. Begging Byron to stay and share information with the group wasn't the way to proceed. The man needed to participate of his own free will. It was the only way this would work.

"Goodnight," Harris called to his back. "I'll find your daughter tomorrow."

Delphine waited until she was certain Byron was no longer in hearing distance and then dropped a withering look on the psychic to the stars. "You are such a suck-up, Harris. How do you breathe with your head so far up our benefactor's behind?"

Harris's expression was dark. "You're a troll, Delphine. I can't believe you even got tapped for this one. It's as if the man has no taste. I mean ... look at this one." He gestured toward Harper, causing her to balk. "She's a local who has only found a few missing people. She hasn't talked to any dead celebrities or anything."

Delphine snorted. "We can't all be more interested in the performance than the outcome."

Harper's frown was so deep the lines ingrained in her forehead looked etched. "I don't like the way you guys are talking. We're not here to put on a show. We're here to find out what happened to Jennifer."

Delphine and Harris snorted in unison.

"If that's what you need to tell yourself," Harris drawled. "I don't know about the rest of you, but I'm heading back to the parlor to have a few drinks.

I might as well get as much out of this trip as possible, because I have a feeling I'm not going to be able to milk it overly long thanks to you imbeciles."

Harper took offense at the remark. "I don't need to take your crap."

"You don't," Harris agreed. "I think you should pack your hurt feelings and attitude and leave this island. You're harshing my vibe."

Harper looked to Zander to confirm that was an insult. "Should I smack him for that?"

"I'll do it for you," Zander offered, stepping in that direction.

"Nobody is smacking anybody," Shawn warned, sliding in front of Zander. "In fact, I think this conversation has gone on long enough for one night. If the rest of you want drinks in the parlor, that's certainly your prerogative. We have an early morning, though, and I'm betting it's going to be a long day. We're heading back and getting some sleep."

Jared shot the calm man a grateful look. "That's exactly what we're doing," he agreed, keeping Harper secured at his side. "We're all going to bed and getting a good night's sleep. Hopefully we'll be able to approach this fresh tomorrow."

"Speak for yourself." Harris was derisive. "I have plans to make friends with a bottle of Johnny Walker Black tonight. There's nothing you can do to stop me."

Jared wasn't in the mood for a pissing contest. He reminded himself that Harris wasn't his responsibility. "Knock yourself out."

"I intend to."

HARPER SLEPT FITFULLY, DREAMS OF ODD GHOSTS – not Jennifer – tumbling through her head. She woke rested but edgy, although her ragged emotions smoothed at the edges when she opened her eyes and found Jared staring at her.

"Hey." Her voice was a warm murmur.

"Hey." He tightened his arms around her and graced her with a gentle kiss. "How are you feeling?"

She wasn't expecting that particular question. "Am I supposed to be feeling a specific way?"

He shrugged, noncommittal. "I don't know. I figured you might be a little agitated about what happened last night."

"Which part?" She was rueful. "Are you talking about Harris being a world-class jerk? Or how about Madeline admitting she was sleeping with Byron before Jennifer disappeared? She essentially confirmed she was having an affair with an older man when she was underage."

"I heard that." Jared rubbed his stubbled cheek against her soft skin, thoughtful. "I'm not sure what I'm supposed to think about that, but I find it interesting."

"I know what to think about it. It's gross. Can you arrest and lock him up or has the statute of limitations passed?"

Jared wasn't sure how to answer the question. "The age of consent in Michigan is seventeen. There's literally nothing I could do ... even if she was still seventeen and they went at it in front of us. He didn't technically break the law."

Harper was horrified. "He dated his daughter's friend. That's totally gross."

"I happen to agree with you. I'm guessing that Madeline had an inkling what she was doing when that went down, though. I don't get the feeling that she was some innocent girl taken advantage of by a lecherous old man."

Harper immediately started shaking her head. "Um, no. Madeline may have been worldly. She might even have befriended Jennifer with the strict intention of seducing her father. That doesn't mean that Byron's hands in this are clean. Whether it was against the law or not, it was morally corrupt and I find him disgusting."

Jared chuckled, genuinely amused. "Tell me how you really feel."

"That is how I really feel. I think Byron is gross. Besides, you saw Madeline last night. She's acting out because this didn't turn out how she thought it would."

She's obviously a very unhappy woman," Jared supplied. Why do you think she had that photo made up and put in Jennifer's room like that? I mean ... that is weird."

"It is." Harper rolled her neck until it cracked, causing Jared to move his hands to her tense muscles so he could work out some of the kinks congregating there. "I wonder if she did it to alleviate some form of guilt she's carrying around."

"What do you mean?"

"It's obvious Madeline befriended Jennifer in the first place to get close to Byron. She probably had a plan from the start, wanted to seduce him and maybe get some money out of him. She got everything she wanted ... except a real partner. I'm guessing she thought Byron would go weak in the knees because of her age and beauty and give her whatever she wanted. That's not exactly what happened."

"No, Byron most definitely has no love for her," Jared agreed. "I don't know if he ever did. He probably had lust at one time, but I'm still unsure why they got married. Byron treats her like a possession more than a partner. Do you know if that's the way he treated Jennifer's mother? Speaking of that, what happened to her? Where is she?"

"She died when Jennifer was a kid." Harper took on a far-off expression as she tried to remember. "I think she had breast cancer but actually died in a car accident on the way to the treatments or something. I remember that Byron funded a lot of experimental treatments for her because I heard my parents talking. They couldn't believe the specialists he was flying in."

"He had money," Jared pointed out. "If you have money and someone you care about is sick, you're going to pull out all the stops."

"Yeah. I obviously didn't know them back then. I got the impression that Byron loved her and was devastated when she died. She was sick a long time ... and there wasn't a lot of hope for her. The accident, though, stole her before they were ready. I think it was a terrible death."

"I think all death is terrible if you love someone." Jared stroked his hand down the back of Harper's head. "Do you think I wouldn't do whatever I possibly could to keep you with me if I were in that position?"

"I don't like thinking about it at all."

"Me neither." He brushed his lips against her forehead and involuntarily shuddered. He definitely didn't want to think about that. "The mother's death might explain Byron's demeanor. He's a cold man, detached from the world. Perhaps he's that way because the worst has already happened to him. Maybe he simply never got over his wife's death."

"I get that, but he still had two children," Harper pointed out. "Richard and Jennifer were still there ... and young. They needed someone to take care of them, to love them. He owed them that. They didn't ask to be brought into this world and neglected."

"I see you have some strong feelings on the subject." Jared was amused despite himself as he held her gaze. "How do you know they were neglected?"

"Because Jennifer mentioned being raised by the house matron. That's what she called her. Mrs. Steuben, the house matron. It was very weird ... and I had no idea what a house matron was. I'm still not sure I do."

"Ah." Jared's heart gave a little roll. "Still, it had to be hard on Byron. He obviously loved his wife, to the point where I don't think he's gotten over her death to this day. That could be why he treats Madeline the way he does. She's not responsible, but he's bitter about having to live a non-authentic life with someone else and he takes it out on her."

Harper tilted her head to the side. "I never considered that, but it makes sense. Still, I don't understand why Madeline would put up with this. She's still a young woman. Why not divorce him and find someone who will actually love her?"

"I think that answer is obvious. The money."

"Right." Harper made a face. "I bet she signed a pre-nup because she assumed she would be able to soften him up at a later date and get him to throw it out."

"My guess is that's why most people sign pre-nups. Still, if she's truly miserable — and she appears to have an awful life — wouldn't it make sense to abandon the money and move on?"

"Some people think money is more important than love."

"I'm glad we don't feel that way." He snuggled close and gave her another kiss. "I can't imagine not loving you so much that it puts a little ache in me," he admitted. "I wouldn't want to anchor myself to someone for an extended amount of time if I didn't love them. That seems like such a waste."

"I'm right there with you. Not everyone believes like we do, though. There's nothing we can do about it. In fact ... ." She trailed off when there was a knock at the door, lifting her head as Zander threw it open and crossed the threshold.

"That was very good," Jared encouraged. "The knocking was a nice touch. Next time, wait for us to tell you to come in. That will complete the effect."

Zander ignored the dig and focused on Harper. "You guys need to get up. Our presence is requested at the main house."

That sounded ominous. Harper struggled to a sitting position and held Zander's gaze. "Why do I think something bad happened?"

"Because you're a smart woman," Zander replied. "Bates just dropped by. He's informed us that we're required at the main house because Madeline has gone missing."

"What?" Harper was flabbergasted. "How did she go missing? We're on a freaking island."

"Your guess is as good as mine. We've been summoned, though. My guess is there's going to be trouble if we don't head down there."

Jared was already halfway out of bed. "We'll get dressed and meet you at the front door in ten minutes. I'm guessing this is not a good development."

Zander's expression was wry. "What was your first clue?"

8

EIGHT

Harper's hair was still wet when they headed toward the main house. Jared frowned when he realized she'd merely pulled it back, away from her face, rather than drying it.

"You're going to get sick," he chided. "We could've waited ten minutes for you to dry your hair."

"It's fine." She waved the comment off in a haphazard manner. "You don't really get sick from anything other than germs no matter what anyone says."

"Oh, that's not true," Zander countered, walking several paces behind them with Shawn at his side. He'd obviously been listening to the conversation. "Don't you remember that time when we were kids and my feet got wet while we were building that fort outside and I spent the next two weeks in bed with pneumonia because of it?"

Harper slowed her pace and shot him an incredulous look over her shoulder. "Not really. I'm pretty sure that didn't happen."

Zander made a protesting sound that reminded Jared of a squawking bird. "It most definitely did happen. I was in bed for two weeks. I could've died."

Harper slowly shook her head. "No, that's not what happened. I heard my parents talking. Your mother was being overprotective and got angry because your feet were wet and told you that you were sick. You weren't really sick ... and you didn't get pneumonia. You just spent two weeks in bed watching television for no good reason."

Zander's expression turned dark. "No. I think I would remember that."

"And I think I would remember if you got pneumonia and almost died."

"No." Zander's expression was plaintive when he turned to Shawn. "I was sick. I swear it."

Shawn looked caught. "I'm sure you were."

"See." Zander was haughty when he glanced back at Harper. "Shawn knows me second best and he thinks I was really sick."

Harper fought the urge to roll her eyes ... and failed. "Oh, come on. He's just saying that because he loves you and doesn't want to get in a fight when there's a missing woman to worry about. I bet he really agrees with me that your mother convinced you that you were sick and you've turned it into a big thing in your head when it was actually nothing."

Zander worked his jaw, incredulous. "I was at death's door!"

"Shh." Shawn put a finger to his lips and shook his head as they approached the front door. "Now is not the time for this discussion. A woman is missing ... and that's on top of another woman being missing for ten years. I don't think now is time for the great pneumonia debate."

"Fine." Fire filled Zander's eyes. "Just know that I will be putting a reminder in my calendar so we can pick up where we left off once we get home."

"I think we're all looking forward to that." Shawn briefly held Jared's gaze before scowling. "It's not funny."

"It's kind of funny," Jared argued. "I can't tell you how glad I am that you're in our lives now, man. Before, that fight would've turned into a screaming match and I would've had to feed Harper ice cream all day to get her out of her funk. Now you're here to do the heavy lifting. It's awesome."

Shawn rolled his eyes. "Let's just see what the big deal is, huh?"

"Absolutely."

THIS TIME THEY DIDN'T KNOCK, instead pushing open the front door and stepping inside without drawing attention to themselves. Harper wasn't sure if it was planned — if it was, it was an ingenious idea on someone's part — but they ended up slipping into the front foyer and playing witness to an argument without anyone realizing they'd arrived.

"I think we should call the police," Evangeline argued, her hands on her hips. "I don't think this is something we should be messing around with." She seemed agitated, which surprised Harper because the older woman had been so muted the night before.

Standing across from her, George was the picture of bored understatement. "She's probably at the salon or something ... or online shopping. Heck, for all we know, she could be hiding in a closet because someone said they would play Hide and Seek with her and she's too stupid to realize everyone else already quit the game. There's no reason to get worked up."

"She's missing," Evangeline pressed, her jaw tightening in profile. "Don't you find that odd? We're all here to find out what happened to Jennifer, who went missing, and now Madeline is missing."

"We're all here to watch Byron go through a mid-life crisis in slow motion," George countered, his tone dismissive. "I told him months ago that he was going off the deep end when he insisted on hiring that private investigator to search for Jennifer. She's been dead since the start of this and everyone knows it. He simply refuses to see it."

That was interesting, Harper internally mused. George was convinced his granddaughter was dead. Evangeline, however, seemed to have hope. How much hope was the question ... but there was definitely hope.

"It doesn't matter if Byron is going off the deep end," Evangeline snapped. "What matters is that Madeline is missing. I think there's something wrong with that scenario ... like really wrong. Maybe we should call the police."

"And tell them what?" George was exasperated. "Do you think they'll race out here to start looking for her because she's feeling petulant and wants some attention? I'm guessing they'll tell us we can't even file a report for twenty-four hours."

Harper was about to open her mouth and tell them that Jared could answer that question when he took the opportunity out of her hands. Jared cleared his throat, causing both of the elder Jessup family members to jerk their eyes away from each other and toward the door, and offered a strained smile.

"I don't want to interrupt, but I'm with the Whisper Cove Police Department," he explained. "I might be able to help you."

Evangeline looked relieved at the news. "Oh, well, good."

George was another story. "How can you be a police officer *and* a ghost hunter? I thought you needed to pass a mental fitness test to be issued a service revolver. Did you lie or something to get through it?"

Jared's eyebrows drew together. "Not last time I checked," he said dryly. "I'm not a ghost hunter, though."

George's lips twisted into something akin to a sneer. "You're with the ghost-hunting contingent."

"I'm with Harper," he clarified. "She's my fiancée."

"Oh, so basically you're acting as her chaperone." George's disdain was evident. "That's probably wise because this entire weekend is going to turn into a psych experiment before it's all said and done. The fact that you're a cop is beneficial, though. My daughter-in-law is missing. Go ... find her." He extended his fingers and wiggled them, as if giving Jared a menial order.

"How about I get some information first?" Jared countered, his smile never wavering. There was danger in his eyes, though. Harper recognized it. His patience was wearing thin and George would be wise not to push him too far.

George obviously didn't recognize that. "What more information do you need? She's not here this morning. We've looked everywhere. Obviously something has happened to her."

"I'm not sure how you jumped to that conclusion," Jared shot back. "I would like to talk to Byron, though. Where is he?"

"In the parlor," Evangeline replied, effectively cutting off her husband before he could say some other ridiculous thing. "Follow me." She led the small group through the house with ease and precision, nodding to a few staff members as she passed. It struck Harper that Evangeline was essentially the lady of the house even though the title should've belonged to Madeline.

"When was the last time anyone saw Madeline?" Harper asked.

"I'm not sure," Evangeline replied. "My understanding is that it was sometime last night, when everyone was upstairs ... perhaps hanging around Jennifer's room."

Harper exchanged a quick look with Jared. That meant they could've been the last people to see Madeline. Did that mean something?

Byron sat on a small settee, the newspaper open and his primary focus when they invaded the room. Margot, Delphine, Richard, and Bertie were also present ... although they'd wisely scattered across the room and were not crowding Byron.

"I see you finally decided to join us," Byron said dryly, snapping the newspaper before folding it and placing it on the table. "I believe I need your services."

Initially, Harper believed he was talking to her and was confused. Then she realized Jared was standing directly behind her, his hand on the small of her back, and Byron was talking through her. It was as if she didn't even exist.

"You need my help?" Jared queried, unsure. "May I ask why?"

"My wife is missing."

"That seems to be the word spreading through the house," Jared acknowledged. "How do you know she's missing?"

Byron blinked several times in rapid succession and Harper was convinced he had a snarky response on the tip of his tongue. He managed to hold it back, though. "Because no one can find her."

Jared wasn't deterred by the answer. "And where have you looked for her?"

"Everywhere."

"Everywhere?" Jared hiked an eyebrow. "I very much doubt you could've searched everywhere in this house in the space of an hour or so. When did you realize she was missing?"

"About forty-five minutes ago," Byron replied. "The kitchen staff pointed out she didn't appear with a menu this morning — that's part of her regular routine — and when I checked her room she wasn't in there."

Something occurred to Harper and she blurted out a question before she could think better of it. "You guys don't share a room?"

Annoyance, fast and hot, took over Byron's features. "Not that it's any of your business, but I cannot sleep if there's any noise or light in my room. I need complete and total darkness, silence. That means I have to sleep in my own room. It's not a big deal. Many couples have the same arrangement."

"Okay, well ... ." Harper licked her lips and risked a glance at Jared. He was obviously thinking the same thing she was. "I think we should search the house," she said. "We need to get everyone together and go through every inch of the house. We can't leave one room unturned."

"You do that," Byron suggested, reclaiming his newspaper and focusing on it. "If you find her, tell her breakfast is late and I'm not happy."

Harper's mouth dropped open, but Jared pulled her away from the uninterested man before she could put him on blast. "Not now," he murmured, dragging her with him despite the token protests she put up. She really did want to give Byron a piece of her mind. "It's not worth it."

"He doesn't even care."

"I'm starting to think none of these people care about each other. It doesn't matter, though. We need to search for Madeline. She's our primary concern."

"Then we should get to it."

ULTIMATELY THEY BROKE INTO VARIOUS teams. Harper and Jared tagged Richard to go with them because they needed someone familiar with the house. Shawn and Zander teamed with Evangeline. Everyone else — minus Harris, who was apparently nursing a hangover and dragging — paired off with various staff members.

Harper was still fuming about Byron's refusal to join in the effort to find his own wife when they hit the third floor twenty minutes later.

"I know he's your father, but he's a jerk," Harper raged as she followed Richard through the quiet hallway. "I mean ... a real jerk. A total and complete jerk. He's king of the jerks."

Jared pinned her with a quelling look. "You're talking about Richard's father, Harper," he prodded gently.

"No. It's okay." Richard was blasé as they wandered down the hallway. He didn't look especially happy about being dragged along for the search but wasn't particularly sour about it either. He seemed more curious than anything else. "My father isn't the easiest person to deal with."

"That's an understatement," Harper muttered under her breath, determined to be mindful of Richard's feelings. She understood a little too well about having a difficult parent. Even though Harper found her mother intolerable at times, she remained loyal to the woman. She couldn't fault Richard for doing the same.

Instead of being offended, Richard slid her a small smile. "I remember you," he noted as he opened the first door to allow Jared entrance. He explained the bulk of the rooms on the third floor were not currently in use so he had to retrieve a set of keys from Bates before they headed up. "From high school, I mean. I remember you."

"You do?" Harper couldn't hide her surprise. "You were two years ahead of me. I thought for sure I wouldn't be on your radar."

Jared kept one ear on the conversation as he checked beneath the bed and inside the closet. He saw no reason to interrupt, though. Harper was good with people. She knew how to draw out information. He figured it was best to let her do her thing while they searched.

"People told stories about you in whispers," Richard explained. "People said you could see ghosts. I heard a few people talking about it one day when you walked by and someone explained that you found some girl's body after a car accident. People were saying it was a miracle you pulled it off or something."

Harper wet her lips. She was familiar with the girl in question. "Yeah, well, that was a long time ago."

"You don't have to be uncomfortable," Richard offered quickly as he locked the door and led them to the next room. "I thought it was an interesting story. I'm sure you got grief about it from other people, but I was never one of those who thought you were a quack."

"That's reassuring," Harper offered. "Er, well, kind of."

He chuckled at her expression. "You were also famous because of your relationship with Zander. He had a certain reputation, and because you refused to separate from him, you did as well."

"I don't really want to talk about Zander," Harper warned. "If you're going to say something that's going to tick me off ... ." She left the threat hanging.

"Why would I say something about Zander that's going to tick you off?"

Harper held out her hands and shrugged. "You would be surprised at the heinous things people say."

"I'm sure. I happen to like Zander, though. He sat next to me at dinner last night. He's very funny."

"Yes, he should have his own comedy show," Jared intoned as he finished up another room. "Next."

Harper opted to take advantage of the conversational lull to ask Richard about his stepmother, who was technically two years younger than him. "How come your father isn't worried about Madeline? I mean ... I get that they're not close. I saw them interacting last night. It was ... not pleasant. It was so not pleasant I'm thinking about instituting a rule that Jared and I can never sleep apart once we get married because I don't want to risk whatever happened between your father and Madeline happening to him and me."

Jared reached over and snagged her hand, giving it a solid squeeze. "That's never going to happen, but I'm fine with the rule."

"I don't think you two need to worry about that," Richard offered. "No, seriously. I know I don't know you very well, but I've watched you together since your arrival. You're in tune with one another, attracted to one another, and constantly seeking out the other. That's the exact opposite of Dad and Madeline."

"Were they always like that?" Jared asked as Richard showed them into another room.

"Pretty much," Richard confirmed. "I mean, don't get me wrong, I think my father enjoyed having sex with her at some point. How else would they have ever gotten together, right? He never loved her, though. He loved my mother and her death almost broke him. Since he couldn't marry for love again, he decided to marry for stature. Having a young woman on his arm made his business associates talk ... and he liked that. Unfortunately, he didn't like Madeline."

"Yeah, Harper and I were talking about that last night," Jared hedged as he dropped to his knees again to stare under a bed. "I'm assuming your father forced Madeline to sign a pre-nup before they got married. Why would she stick around now given the way he treats her?"

"You'll have to ask her that," Richard replied. "I never understood why she married him in the first place. I always assumed he made some sort of promise to her, that if they made it to a certain point, he would tear up the pre-nup and she would be able to inherit. I'm pretty sure that never happened, though."

"How sure?" Harper queried.

"Well, I heard Madeline screaming at him before you guys all arrived yesterday. Apparently he puts her on an allowance. She's only allowed to spend so much a day ... and then she gets an extra amount per month for big purchases, but if she makes a big purchase she can't make another for three months."

Harper was horrified. "No way. That's … ridiculous."

"That's my father." Richard locked the room and pointed toward the last one in the hallway. "I don't mean to tell you your business, Detective Monroe, But Madeline is known for taking off for several hours — even days sometimes — and then coming back after a trip to the spa or mall. She always denies doing it for the drama, but we all know that's how she rolls."

Jared wasn't surprised by the tidbit. "I figured last night that she has a dramatic side. It also doesn't surprise me that she'll get attention any way she can. She seems starved for it. Given the situation, though, we have to look for her. I mean … it's too weird not to."

Richard held up his hands in capitulation. "I get it. I'm not telling you how to conduct your search. I just don't want you to beat yourself up if we don't find her. Odds are she'll show up when she thinks Dad is more likely to buy her something extravagant."

"Does he reward this sort of behavior?" Jared was legitimately curious.

"No. He will reward her for being quiet for an extended period of time. If she's gone, she's quiet. That's all my father cares about."

Harper felt sick to her stomach. "Let's check the last room and then rendezvous with the others. I think we need to check the grounds, too."

Jared nodded. "I'm right there with you. That's definitely next."

9

NINE

The initial search of the house came up empty. Harper wasn't surprised. That didn't mean she was done looking, though.

"We need to search the grounds." She was adamant as she bundled up in the guesthouse, tugging a knit cap over her ears to protect her from the cold and grabbing the gloves she brought with her. "It got down to the twenties overnight. If she was outside and exposed ... ."

Jared cocked his head as he watched her. He sensed she was determined. In truth, he wasn't opposed to looking for Madeline. That didn't mean he wanted Harper turning this into a thing.

"You heard Richard," he noted as he grabbed his own knit cap. "She's known for taking off when she wants attention. That's probably what happened here."

"Except she never gets the attention she wants when she does this. Oh, and this is different. I can't help but wonder if this has something to do with Jennifer ... and we can't overlook anything if that's the case."

"Harper, how could this possibly have anything to do with Jennifer? She's been gone ten years."

"Yes, but we're all here searching for her. Byron wants answers. Perhaps someone took Madeline to distract us from looking into the past."

Jared ran his tongue over his teeth, conflicted. He had a specific opinion about Madeline, but he wasn't sure his girlfriend was in the mood to hear it. As if reading his mind, Harper stopped flitting about the room and gathering her bulky outdoor things and regarded him with unreadable eyes.

"What?"

"I didn't say anything," Jared replied hurriedly.

"You're thinking something."

"I *am* thinking something," he agreed. "I'm thinking that … I love you very much."

She made a face, but Jared didn't miss the way her lips curved. Essentially she believed he was being ridiculous but always enjoyed hearing him proclaim his love. He understood the reaction because he often felt the same way. "What else are you thinking?"

He opted for honesty. "I don't think you're going to want to hear it."

"Try me."

"Okay." He sucked in a measured breath. "I think Madeline has always been jealous of Jennifer. Whether it's rational or not, she's always been in her shadow. Jennifer disappeared and, to this day, Byron is determined to find her. Things didn't go well for Madeline, probably not even close to what she planned.

"In her head, she was probably picturing extravagant shopping trips and a partner, a besotted lover, who would dote on her because of her youth," he continued. "Instead she got a man who very clearly loved his first wife, never got over her death, and mostly cared about himself. What little time he had on the side was now dedicated to finding his missing daughter, a girl who was set up to be Madeline's nemesis."

Harper blew a raspberry, catching him by surprise. "If Madeline had issues with Jennifer, they were her issues. Trust me. Jennifer never went out of her way to be friendly with Madeline. That means Madeline used Jennifer to get close to her father. I'm not blind."

"And yet you still seem to think she's in potential danger despite everything you know about her personality."

"I don't like the timing," Harper corrected. "The timing is what throws me. Why would she take off and do this ridiculous crap when there's a house full of people to give her the attention she obviously craves? I can see doing it when it's just the family. There are outsiders in the house, though. She'll finally get the attention she believes she deserves."

Jared wanted to argue with the sentiment, but the more he thought about it, the more it made sense. "Okay, I get that," he conceded after a beat. "However, how could this possibly have anything to do with Jennifer?"

"I'm not saying it has anything to do with her in the sense that someone took Jennifer and now, ten years later, someone has returned to take Madeline. Like … it's a serial killer for girls who were of a certain age together."

"That's good, since you're their age."

Harper hadn't thought of that. "Anyway ... ." She shook her head to dislodge the thought and focused her full attention on Jared. "What if someone actually did something to Jennifer? I'm talking someone in the house. Maybe nerves are frayed or on display and causing Madeline to disappear is simply a way to direct attention elsewhere."

Jared stroked his jaw as he considered the suggestion. "I guess that's possible," he supplied after a beat. "I don't know how probable it is, though. It seems as if you're grasping to me."

"Maybe I am," Harper conceded. "That doesn't change the fact that I have a feeling." She gestured toward her stomach. "There's a big ball of anxiety sitting in there — I've felt this way since we first got the news — and I can't shake the feeling that something bad might've happened to Madeline. I don't know how to explain it."

He let loose a sigh. She was too earnest to deny. "Then we'll look for her. I was going to look anyway because I feel it's my duty. I thought maybe you would stay here, stay warm. I guess not, huh?"

"No. We're a team. We do everything together."

"Fair enough." He leaned over and gave her a quick kiss before straightening her cap. "Did I mention how cute I find you when you're all bundled up like this?"

"No."

"Well, you're adorable." His smile was whimsical. "You're like an exotic little snow bunny."

"Winter is almost over. You probably should've brought this up sooner if you want to take advantage of it."

"Oh, I've taken advantage of it. You just didn't realize it at the time. Besides, as much as I like you in the cap, I like you in a hammock better. I'm ready for spring."

Harper managed a smile at his enthusiasm. "So am I. It's still a bit off, though. Right now, our biggest concern is finding Madeline."

"So that's what we'll do." It was as simple as that. Jared gestured toward the door. "Come on. Richard said he would meet us at the stables and facilitate an introduction to the staff down there. We probably shouldn't keep him waiting."

"Good idea."

RICHARD WAS ALREADY WAITING in front of the massive stable when Harper and Jared arrived. He didn't look agitated, as if he was angry because they were late. Still, Jared offered up a sincere apology.

"It took us a few minutes to find our hats and gloves. I want to make sure Harper doesn't catch a chill."

Richard smiled. "Of course. Don't worry about it. I should've told you that the stables are heated, though. She's unlikely to get a chill in here." He pulled open the door and, sure enough, a blast of warm air smacked Harper directly in the face.

"Oh, wow. Neat." Harper was all smiles as she stepped through the door and found herself in another world. "Oh, my ... will you look at this?" She hurried to the closest stall, where a black horse of majestic beauty looked at her from over the door. His stall was three times as big as others she'd seen at area horse barns. "This is amazing."

Jared smiled as he watched her reach a tentative hand up to pet the horse. The animal made a snorting sound but accepted the attention without complaint. "I didn't know you liked horses," he noted. "There's a place over on the east side, close to the lake, that allows horse rides on the beach. We should go this summer."

"Okay." Harper was happy at the prospect. "I do like horses. I've only ridden a few times, but it's been great fun each time."

"Then I'll definitely make it happen." Jared watched her for another moment and then focused on Richard. "Did Madeline spend a lot of time down here?"

"Actually, she did," he confirmed as they walked down the hallway toward the office. "She loved the horses. I think they were the one thing my father willingly gave her because he wasn't much of an animal person."

Harper was understandably confused. "I don't understand. If your father doesn't like horses, why does he have like ... ten of them?"

"Because he likes being important. Having horses is something important people do. I'm sure he read that in a magazine or something at a certain point. That's why he got the horses. It's also why he's on the waiting list for a Tesla, even though he doesn't really want one."

Sadly, Harper understood exactly what he was saying. "Image is very important to your father."

"Image is everything," he corrected. "That's why he married Madeline in the first place. He knew people would talk, but he didn't care. To him, it's better to be the center of attention — even if it's for negative reasons — than to be ignored."

"That makes me feel sorry for him," she admitted. "It's too bad he couldn't get out of his own head long enough to try and find some happiness. I mean ... I know he loved your mother. To tune himself out to the possibility of ever loving another, though, seems like the exact opposite of what she would've wanted."

"I think people tried telling my father that over the years, but he wouldn't listen." Richard was rueful. "He's not always easy to deal with. He's ... set in his ways."

"We can't really focus on him right now," Jared noted. "We need to focus on Madeline. If she's in trouble, we need to find her. If she's simply taken off because she wants attention ... well ... at least we'll know."

"There is that," Richard agreed. "Believe it or not, as much as I don't like Madeline, I don't want anything bad to happen to her. That's more for my father than her, of course, but it's still true. As much as my father dislikes putting up with her, the guilt he would feel if something actually happened ... well ... let's just say I don't think he would get over it."

Harper understood what he was saying. "Yeah. I understand. Madeline is the girl who cried wolf. She's taken off a bunch of times because she's desperate for attention. The problem is, if you always assume that's what she's doing, the one time she might need real help you'll be less likely to go to her aid."

"I don't happen to believe that's on me," Richard argued. "She's the one who keeps doing this."

"I understand." And, because she did, Harper let it go. Still, she pointed toward the door at the end of the hallway. "What's down there?"

"It goes to the attic and doesn't open. I don't even know where the key is. There's no way she's up there ... where it's dusty and mice might live. Trust me."

LEE TRAVERS WAS THE HEAD of the stable. He was a horse man with a lot of history in the area. Due to Byron's dislike of animals — and apparently anything that caused a normal person to smile — Harper couldn't help wondering why Lee would take on a job for a man who had no skin in the riding game. It became apparent why this was the perfect job for Lee within a few minutes of questioning him.

"I have complete autonomy over the horses," Lee explained. "I can enter them into whatever shows I want. If I think there's a real chance of them placing, I call Mr. Jessup so he can attend, but I don't mind him taking the glory."

"That's good," Jared encouraged. "We're actually wondering about Madeline, though. She appears to have gone missing."

Lee exchanged a quick look with Richard, something unsaid passing between them.

"We're well aware that Madeline takes off occasionally because she's looking for attention," Jared added. "We're not idiots. However, it does seem unlikely that Madeline would want to take off now because there are so many people in the house lined up to give her the attention she craves."

"I didn't even consider that," Richard intoned. "That's true, though. Why would she take off now?"

"Maybe she wanted everyone to search for her," Lee suggested. "That seems right up her alley."

"Perhaps," Jared conceded. "I'm a police officer, though. It's my job to make sure she's not in trouble."

"I understand. I don't know what to tell you, though. She hasn't been out here."

"Do you monitor this place throughout the night?" Jared queried. "I mean ... do you keep the doors locked? Is someone always watching the horses?"

"Oh, well ... not always," he conceded. "We don't have anyone in here overnight unless one of the animals is sick. As for locking this place, we don't because someone would have to basically swim over from the mainland and even when the weather is great, that doesn't happen."

Jared understood what he was saying. "So, it's possible she could've visited."

"It's possible," Lee acknowledged. "I think it's unlikely, though. There's nothing down here to benefit her. There's not even any furniture, other than a few chairs. No television."

Jared nodded, contemplative. "If she was going to leave the island, how would she do it? I'm guessing she would have to take a boat, right?"

Richard stirred. "Not necessarily. She has access to the ferry captain. She could've called and demanded he facilitate a ride back to the mainland for her."

"Has she ever done that?"

"Yes."

"In the middle of the night?"

"I'm not sure," Richard hedged. "I guess it's possible."

"Can you get the ferry captain on the line for me?"

"I can, but we have another option that will probably be easier," Richard replied. "The garage is behind the house. All the vehicles are kept there. If one is missing, the garage manager will know it."

"You have a garage manager?" Harper was flabbergasted. "How is that a full-time job?"

Richard chuckled hollowly. "You'll have to ask my father."

. . .

TONY DELUCA WAS IN OVERALLS and working on the engine of a Bentley when the trio entered the garage. He glanced up, a rag in his hand as he wiped off a piece of equipment that Harper didn't recognize. He seemed surprised to find visitors darkening his door.

"Is something wrong?" he asked automatically.

"Maybe," Richard replied. "We're looking for Madeline. Have you seen her?"

The laugh Tony let loose was long and drawn out. "Why would she possibly be hanging out here? This isn't exactly a hot spot of activity."

"No, but we're trying to ascertain if Madeline left the island," Jared interjected. "My understanding is that you maintain the vehicles, as well as keep track of them. Do you happen to know if any of the vehicles are missing?" A quick scan around the massive garage told Jared that some sort of detailed list might have to be utilized to ascertain the answer.

"There's nothing missing," Tony automatically answered.

"Are you sure?"

He nodded as he placed the car part on a workbench and wandered over to a computer resting on a large desk in the corner. "Every vehicle Mr. Jessup owns is listed right here. Besides that, though, I know this garage backwards and forwards. I would know if Madeline left, and her cars are still here."

"She has more than one car?" Jared queried. "Can you point them out to me?"

"Sure." Tony pointed toward a Mercedes and an Aston Martin, both blue in color. "Those two belong to her."

Jared immediately headed in that direction, reaching for the door on the Mercedes so he could search inside. "How often does she take out a vehicle?"

Tony held out his hands and shrugged. "Not very often. If she wants to go out, most of the time she takes the limo so someone else is responsible for driving. She insists on it for her hair and nail appointments."

"She thought others would covet the life she was leading if she was in a limo," Harper surmised.

"I'm guessing that's true, too," Jared confirmed, feeling under the vehicle seat. "There's nothing in here. This car is pristine. You could eat off every surface."

"Please don't do that." Tony's grin was tight. "I'm the one that has to keep all the vehicles cleaned."

"And apparently tune them up, huh?" Jared arched an eyebrow and stared at the part Tony had left behind. "I'm guessing you have this place set up so you know if someone enters the garage."

"That's correct." Tony bobbed his head. "I'm responsible for all the vehicles so I lock the doors every night. Mr. Jessup is usually in by seven or eight unless he has a specific function. If that happens, Carlos knows the code to get into the garage."

"And who is Carlos?"

"The chauffeur," Richard replied. "He's the standard driver for my father and Madeline."

"Is he housed on the island?"

"Actually, he's not. He was for a few years, but then he got married. He lives a few miles from the ferry, with his wife and twin sons."

"Does he come to the island every day?"

"Um ... I don't think so." Richard looked as if he was concentrating. "I think he does in the summer because it's more likely someone will want to leave on a whim. Not in the winter, though. There are days the weather is too rough for the ferry. There are also days when there is absolutely nothing going on."

"That doesn't seem like a full-time job," Jared noted. "How does he make enough to keep working for your father?"

"If my father likes an employee, he makes sure to pay enough that no one ever wants to leave. That's why he has a renowned chef, mechanic, horse trainer, and landscaper on his payroll even though he doesn't have enough work to keep them busy. Basically most of these people are working part time but getting quadruple wages."

"I would like to argue because that makes me sound greedy, but it's true," Tony said. "I'm paid very well, so it's kind of like being semi-retired."

Jared could understand the appeal. "What about Madeline? Did she enter your garage last night?"

"No, and neither did Carlos. He dropped off Mr. Jessup yesterday morning and then split because he knew his services wouldn't be needed for the rest of the weekend. I talked to him. He had no intention of coming back."

"So, basically you're saying odds are good that Madeline didn't leave the property."

"That would be my guess."

Jared rolled his neck and stared at the ceiling, lost in thought. "So ... where is she?"

That was the question plaguing Harper, too. Where could the woman have possibly gone?

TEN

By the time Harper and Jared reunited with the rest of their group, they were no closer to finding Madeline than when they started. The house had been searched from top to bottom –twice – and there was no sign of her. The only people that seemed to care were the ones belonging to Harper's group. Everyone else was either over it or convinced she would show up when she got bored.

"I don't like this," Harper groused as they sat in the parlor shortly before lunch. They were offered cocktails, which everybody turned down because they were there to work, and found themselves ostracized because of their insistence on taking Madeline's disappearance seriously.

"None of them bothered to look," Shawn volunteered from his spot next to Zander on the couch. They were holding hands, looked relaxed, but Harper detected an edge of vitriol in his voice. "By the way, if I ever go missing, I don't want them on my search team."

Harper couldn't blame him. "Did you guys find anything?"

"No." Zander shook his head. "We talked to a few of the maids, though. We thought maybe they came across the clothes Madeline was wearing last evening. We thought it would at least give us a timeframe to work with if they discovered the outfit."

Harper brightened. "That's good thinking. What did they say?"

"That they couldn't find the outfit. I figured I would recognize it easily enough so I went into her closet but ... nada."

Harper frowned. "I guess that means she was still wearing it when ... she did whatever she did."

"That's the problem," Jared noted, sparing a quick glance for the rest of the room to make sure no one was eavesdropping. "We have no idea if she left this house of her own volition or was taken. Given the things we know about her, I would assume it was on her own but ... the timing is troubling."

"Okay, since nobody else is doing it, I'll ask the obvious question," Eric said. "Why would someone take Madeline at the same time people are out here looking for answers on Jennifer?"

"There could be any number of reasons," Jared replied, opting for honesty. "Just off the top of my head, someone could be nervous because we're here investigating Jennifer's disappearance and this individual doesn't want us looking at him or her so Madeline makes a good distraction."

"You think someone in the house killed her?" Eric was officially intrigued. "Who? You think it was a family member, right? That's what you're saying."

Jared immediately started shaking his head. "Not necessarily. A lot of people are employed here. A lot of people cross on and off the island on any given week. It could be someone who works here, or visits frequently. It doesn't necessarily have to be a family member."

"Except it makes more sense for it to be a family member," Harper volunteered, drawing Jared's unreadable eyes to her. "I just mean that murder is rarely carried out by someone who doesn't know the victim. I'm not saying it never happens, but it's certainly not common."

"No, I would agree with that assessment," Jared said slowly, nodding as he considered her words. "We simply don't have enough information. I would like a clearer picture of Jennifer, to be honest. You guys gave me a basic overview but that's not enough for me to truly understand her."

"That's all we know, though." Harper shifted on her chair, frowning when Jared grabbed her hand to calm her. "I feel bad that we don't know more about her but ... that's it."

"I'm not admonishing you," Jared reassured her. "I didn't mean for that to come out as a personal attack. That's not how it was meant."

Harper relaxed, but only marginally. "Okay. I'm sorry. I took that personally and I didn't mean to. What do you think we should be doing? There's a cemetery on the island. We could go check that out ... or maybe wander around the woods."

Jared didn't look thrilled with the prospect. "The snow is going to be deeper in the areas covered by trees," he pointed out. "It takes the sun longer to penetrate through the branches. That means wading through all the snow is going to take a lot of energy, and potentially be dangerous."

Harper refused to let it go. "Or we could stumble across her footprints."

Jared opened his mouth to argue but thought better of it. "That's a fair point. Maybe we can head out after lunch." He didn't appear keen on the idea. "Or maybe you and Zander should stay here, question more of the staff, and try to get a feeling for what's going on. Shawn and I can wander down to the woods."

Harper was instantly suspicious. "Why do you want us to stay here?"

"I didn't say I *wanted* you to stay here. I merely said it might be a good idea if you and Zander stay here because that allows us to split our efforts."

Harper didn't miss the fact that he avoided eye contact when he uttered the words. "You are a terrible liar," she hissed, frustration wafting off her. "You really don't want me with you. I don't understand."

"Hey!" Jared extended a warning finger and finally met her gaze. "I always want you with me. I'm just not certain that taking you down to the woods is a good idea."

Harper refused to back down. "Why?"

"Because ... because ... ."

"Because he's afraid there will be a dead body down there," Zander volunteered out of nowhere, his gaze on his cuticles. He appeared bored. "He thinks, if someone killed Madeline, she's likely down there and he doesn't want you to see it."

Harper made a protesting sound. "I've seen dead bodies before."

"This is a person you went to high school with. Plus ... well ... you kind of called her out about the photo last night. I'm worried that will make you feel guilty."

"I'm not sorry about pointing out the photo. It seemed out of place ... and it was."

"It definitely was," Jared agreed, unruffled. "I still think it might be better if you stayed up here with Zander. That way we won't have to worry about either of you ... or listen to him complain."

Harper's eyes widened when she realized the real reason Jared didn't want her chasing him to the woods, and then she had to bite the inside of her cheek to keep from laughing. For his part, Zander wasn't even paying attention to the conversation.

"We'll stay here and talk to the workers," he said, holding his hands side by side and looking at the fingernails on both. "I really need a good winter moisturizer. The dry air is murder on my hands."

"We'll shop for something as soon as we get back," Shawn promised, amusement flitting across his features. "As for the walk to the woods, I'm all for it. Let's hit lunch first, though."

Jared nodded. "Yeah. We missed breakfast and I'm starving. I hope they have something good."

THE TABLE WAS ARRANGED WITH name tags for everyone ... again. Harper had to roll her eyes when she realized Jared was seated across from her rather than next to her. That was going to make whispering about the others practically impossible. In addition, Byron arranged his place at the head of the table, to Harper's right, and Harris was awarded the spot to her left.

"This is ... delightful," she muttered as she settled into her chair and unfolded her napkin.

For his part, Harris had only just joined the rest of the group and he seemed out of it and sluggish. "It smells great," he enthused, his eyes bloodshot and red-rimmed. "Is that crab salad? I happen to love crab salad." He reached for a platter of sandwiches as a woman carried it to the table. She smoothly sidestepped him and slid it to the center of the table while Harris made a series of groaning noises.

"You could've just handed it to me," he complained.

Instead of immediately responding, the woman whipped out a pair of tongs and scooped up a sandwich, depositing it on his plate before doing the same for Harper, Byron, and Jared. "Do you need anything else, sir?" she asked her boss.

Byron shook his head as he placed his napkin in his lap. "No. Thank you, Delia. It looks wonderful."

"Certainly, sir." She curtsied — something Harper didn't know was still in practice — and then headed out, disappearing from view. Harper waited until she was gone to add potato salad and what looked to be handmade potato chips to her plate.

"This looks great," she enthused, trying to gear herself up for another uncomfortable meal. At least she had Jared this time, she told herself. Sure, he was all the way across the table, but she could at least exchange amused glances with him when no one was looking.

"Crab salad is a favorite of mine," Byron announced, catching Harper off guard when he added chips to his plate. "Jennifer liked this meal, too. She used to ask for it all the time."

Harper's forehead wrinkled. "This particular meal?"

Byron nodded. "She loved crab salad, but the chips were a favorite. She wasn't allowed to have a lot of unhealthy food — something she didn't like — so the chips were an extravagance that she looked forward to each week."

"Why wasn't she allowed to have unhealthy food?" Jared asked, his plate already laden with items. He clearly wasn't kidding when he said he was hungry, his enthusiasm for lunch making Harper smile. There wasn't a single open spot on his plate. "I would think that junk food is a rite of passage for a teenager."

Byron cast a sidelong look at Jared's plate and merely shook his head. "She was on a special diet. We had a dietitian called in when Jennifer was fourteen because she put on ten pounds in four months during the eighth grade."

Harper stilled, dumbfounded. She had to have heard that wrong. There was no other explanation. "Excuse me?"

"She put on ten pounds," Byron repeated, obviously missing the potential mayhem loitering in Harper's eyes. "I was worried she would develop bad eating habits so her junk food allowance was limited."

Harper was officially annoyed. "Was Richard's junk food allowance limited?"

"What? Of course not. He was never fat."

"I knew Jennifer. She was never fat either."

"I told you. She put on ten pounds. We didn't want it to become twenty so we limited her calories. It wasn't a big deal."

It felt like a big deal to Harper. All she could think about were the sleepovers she and Zander used to share, the nights when they would go through an entire box of Little Debbie snack cakes, a huge bag of chips, and that was on top of the endless candy they used to inhale. Zander was a big fan of licorice ropes and was convinced he could eat ten in one night. He'd actually managed to prove it once.

"God forbid she put on ten pounds." Harper's eyes filled with fire at the same moment Jared kicked her under the table to get her attention. Because she knew he would make her feel ridiculous about her reaction, she refused to meet his gaze. "I mean ... ten pounds makes her a real oinker, right?"

Byron's expression was hard to read as he turned his full attention to Harper. "I can't help but feel as if I've offended you. That wasn't my intention. You're clearly not overweight. You can eat as many chips as you like."

"That's really not the point," Harper shot back. "Why would you possibly make your only daughter feel as if she was less than normal because she put on a few pounds? That is not the end of the world. Trust me."

"I didn't want her being unhealthy."

"It seems to me that you wanted to give the illusion of the perfect family," Harper countered, opting to go for broke. She was tired of tiptoeing around this man and his bad attitude. He was surrounded by people who never told him no and she was fed up with biting her tongue. "That's what you're most interested in, right? Looking perfect. You don't care if it's true as long as those watching from outside believe the false image you're painting."

"Oh, geez." Jared slapped his hand to his forehead and continued shoveling in food. Harper was convinced he thought it would be taken away from him at any second and he had to inhale it while he still had the opportunity.

"I honestly didn't mean to offend you," Byron repeated. "That was not my intention. It was also not my intention to upset my daughter. Do you think she sat around and plotted my death with the same look on her face that you boast now?"

Harper found the question odd. "I don't know a lot of kids who sit around and plot their parents' deaths. Sure, occasionally you wish for an errant train to hit your mother or father and put them in a coma for a bit, but you don't wish for death. I guarantee that's not what Jennifer wanted."

"How can you be sure?" Byron looked legitimately curious. "I mean ... she's been gone a very long time. When I think back to the girl I knew, I often wonder what sort of woman she would've become. Would she have been the sort of woman who hates her father? I can't rule it out."

The question, the naked emotion under it, were the first hints for Harper that Byron was a real person with genuine emotions. "My mother drives me crazy," she announced out of nowhere. "No, true story. Just a few weeks ago she was a suspect in the murder of her boyfriend. Two days later — like, literally two days later — I walked in on her and my father having sex.

"My parents have been acting as if they hate each other since I was a little kid and I thought for sure they were only staying together until I graduated from high school," she continued. "They made it a lot longer than that. When I asked them why they did the bad thing — and in my house, no less — they gave me a lot of answers. The one that stuck with me, though, is probably the one that fits your circumstances, too.

"You can't choose who you love. You can only decide to embrace that love or push it out of your mind. I think Jennifer loved you a great deal. I think she wanted to make you proud. I also think you were so lost in grief due to losing your wife you didn't give Jennifer the attention she needed."

Byron arched an eyebrow. "Apparently you're not afraid to give your opinion."

"I'm really not," Harper agreed. "Besides, I think you want to hear the truth. Maybe not always, but in this particular case, you need to know exactly what you did wrong. You weren't a very good father to Jennifer. All she wanted was your time and you were too busy to give it to her. You can't go back and fix that. You can move forward, though.

"I think you called us here because that's what you truly want," she continued. "You've been letting Jennifer's disappearance hang over your family for a long time. You need answers more than anything because you feel frozen in place. You can't do anything until you know ... and that's the simple truth of it."

Byron looked impressed. "You're good at reading people."

"You're not hard to read."

"Does that mean you'll be able to find Jennifer's ghost, put her to rest?"

Harper stalled on the question, unsure how to answer. Finally, she shook her head. "I can't answer that. I've seen nothing to indicate that Jennifer's spirit is still hanging around this house. It's difficult because we don't know where she was killed.

"Well, actually, we don't know *if* she was killed at all," she continued. "I know you don't want to hear it, but are you absolutely sure that Jennifer didn't run off to start a life someplace else?"

"I'm absolutely positive."

He sounded sure of himself, but Jared was still interested in drilling down on this particular topic. "Ignore your opinion on the subject. From a practical standpoint, could she have gotten access to enough money to run off with?"

"She didn't."

"I'm not asking if she did or didn't." Jared was firm. "I'm asking if she *could* have run."

Byron worked his jaw, his mind busy. Finally, he nodded. "She could've run. She had money in her account, enough to get out of the state with. She couldn't have lived on it for long, but if she was really determined, she had enough money to run."

"How much is enough?" Harper asked.

"Twenty grand."

Harper's mouth dropped open. "That's more than enough to flee the state on. She could've lived for two years on that money if she found the right place and opted to be frugal."

"Certainly not." Byron immediately started shaking his head. "There's no way she could've lived on so little money."

Harper didn't believe that for a second. "Well ... she obviously could've run if she wanted. You're certain she didn't make it off the island, though, right?"

"Absolutely certain," Byron confirmed, bobbing his head. "There's no way she got off this island without someone noticing. It's impossible. That's why I think something happened to her here. I need you to find what that something is."

She felt caught. "I'll do my best."

"Oh, you're going to be the one to come up with all the answers," Byron supplied, a knowing look on his face. "I have no doubt about that. Some of the others may be flashier, but I think you have the most substance. I've always thought that."

"Not everything you read in the paper is true," Harper cautioned.

"I've been following your work for a very long time, my dear. I'm confident you're exactly the one I've been looking for. You'll find the answers I need."

Harper could only hope his faith wasn't misplaced.

ELEVEN

Part of Harper was put out that Jared wanted to leave her at the main house to check the woods. The other part was glad because she had a hunt of her own she wanted to participate in ... and she felt it was better to conduct it away from his watchful gaze.

Unfortunately for her, Zander wasn't the type to entertain himself and he followed her out of the parlor when she tried to slip out unnoticed.

"Where do you think you're going?" he questioned her back, causing her to cringe.

"I didn't think you were watching," she grumbled.

"I'm always watching. I'm the Great Zander ... or Zandini. What do you think sounds better?"

Harper wasn't expecting the question. "I have no idea. Whichever one floats your boat is fine with me."

"I'm going with Zandini. I think it's more festive. Anyway, I'm the Great Zandini and I know all and see all. You can't put one over on me no matter how hard you try. I knew you were going to sneak out before Shawn and Jared left. By the way, you're not fooling anyone with that 'stiff upper lip' thing you're trying to pull off. You're going to give Jared grief about treating you like a girl before the night is out."

Harper thought she should argue – she was a feminist at heart, after all – but she didn't have the energy. "I'm heading upstairs."

"Why?"

"Because ... I just am."

"Yeah, that's not going to work on me. I need more of an explanation than that."

Harper let loose a sigh, the sound long and drawn out. "Fine." She held up her hands. "If you must know, I want to look around the house ... and I want to do it at a time when no one is looking over my shoulder."

Zander was fine breaking the rules. He'd been that way since he was three and his mother told him his face would freeze that way if he wasn't careful. He risked it all the same because he figured it was worth it. He had no problem searching the Jessup house without invitation. He simply wanted to know why first.

"Harp, I think it would be better for both of us if you just told me what you were looking for. You're not good at the subterfuge. You never have been. Can't you just tell me? We're wasting time."

He was right. Harper hated to admit it, but she had no choice. "I have a feeling," she started, searching for the right words. "I've had it since we arrived. I feel like someone is watching me."

Zander didn't as much as blink. "I'm sure half the people here are watching you. Some think you're a kook because you can see ghosts and others think you're awesome because you can see ghosts. It's pretty much a mixed crowd."

"Not a human someone."

"Oh." Realization dawned on him. "You think a ghost is here. Have you seen it? Is it Jennifer?"

"I haven't seen it. I've just felt eyes a few times. The first was when we arrived, but I brushed it off because I figured there were people watching outside. The second was at dinner last night. It was really foggy out. Do you remember?"

He nodded. "Yeah. It's because the air is getting warmer and the ground is still cold. It creates nonstop fog. You used to think it was romantic when we were kids."

"Yes, well, now when I'm staying at a huge house on an isolated island I think it's a little creepy. That's neither here nor there, though."

"Okay. Fair enough. Are you saying you saw a ghost in the fog?"

"It's more something I felt. I don't know how to explain it." She heaved out a sigh. "Then I felt it again when we were searching the third floor today. There was that door Richard said didn't open, the old attic door. I swear I could feel someone on the other side. It was as if ... I don't know ... someone was beckoning to me."

All traces of mirth were gone from Zander's face. "Do you think it was Jennifer?"

"I don't know." That was the truth. Harper was honestly at a loss. "I don't know if it's even a thing. I just know that I have to look. You don't have to go with me, though. I'm not making you."

"Don't be ridiculous." Zander let loose an exaggerated eye roll. "The mistress of the house went missing last night. Whether she's really missing or took the day off to drink and garner attention, I can't say. It doesn't matter, though. I'm not letting you out of my sight."

Despite herself, Harper laughed. She didn't want to encourage him, but she couldn't help herself. "Then let's head up and see what we can find, shall we?"

Zander held out his arm so she could take it. "It would be my pleasure."

"YOU SEEM AGITATED."

Shawn waited until he and Jared were far away from the house to start talking. While he didn't know Jared as well as he did Zander and Harper, the two men were quickly forging a bond that no one else could replicate. Because Zander and Harper's relationship was so strong – and, frankly, co-dependent – they needed strong partners. That's where Shawn and Jared came in ... and seemingly excelled more than anyone who came before them. Shawn recognized fairly quickly once it was just the two of them that Jared was struggling.

"I don't like this place," Jared admitted, not missing a beat. "Not even a little. It feels ... off. I don't know how to explain it."

"I get what you're saying." Shawn was the easygoing sort so he fell into step with Jared and let the detective's wave of unease break against him without flinching. "This place should be welcoming and awesome, but it feels overstuffed and uncomfortable. The people who live here – with the possible exception of Richard, who doesn't seem like such a bad guy – aren't good people. It's hard to feel they've earned this utopia."

"I don't know that I exactly feel that," Jared hedged. "It's more that ... this place is what so many people would dream about. I mean it's a castle. That's what Zander called it and he was right. It's a castle and it should be full of princesses ... and jesters ... and magic. Instead we have a family that is rudderless, a girl who went missing and no one did a thing about it for ten years, and a father who seems to have lost all reason for living when his wife died, leaving his children to basically fend for themselves."

Despite the serious conversational topic, Shawn grinned. "That's basically what I said."

Jared barked out a laugh, amused. "I'm being a little dramatic. I get it. It's just ... I'm bothered by the fact that Jennifer Jessup went missing ten years ago and nobody did a thing to find her. And, yes, I'm including my own partner in that when I say it."

Understanding bloomed in the back of Shawn's mind. "Have you considered calling him to ask why?"

"I kind of did ask why and he hemmed and hawed around. He didn't give me a real answer. I think that's because he feels guilty."

"Odds are she's dead, right?"

"I honestly don't know." Jared held out his gloved hands and shrugged. "I think there are arguments to be made on both sides."

"What sort of arguments?"

"It sounds to me like Jennifer was a very unhappy young woman. She was eighteen when she disappeared. That very well could be because she was finally an adult and made a plan for escape. If she did run, I'm not sure we should find her."

"You're bothered by the notion that she didn't run, though," Shawn surmised. "You're afraid she's been dead or in trouble all this time and no one raced to her rescue. You can't blame that on yourself. You weren't here. You were a kid back then and you didn't even live on this side of the state."

"All of that is true. That doesn't change the fact that this situation feels ... wrong. As for trouble, I don't think that's a possibility. She either willingly went missing or was killed back then and no one discovered her body."

"Do you think someone in her family did it?"

"I can't rule them out. I don't know what to think. I'm simply bothered by the whole thing."

"Fair enough. Why did you really want me to head out here with you? Is it because you didn't want to listen to Zander whine about how cold it is, or is it because you're afraid we're going to find something?"

Jared had to give the other man credit. It was an insightful question. "Would you think less of me if it's a little of both?"

Shawn barked out a laugh. "No. I'm right there with you. I'm a little afraid of what we might find, too."

"It's not that I'm afraid what we might find," Jared corrected. "It's more that I'm afraid there might be more going on here than we realize. I don't know what that 'more' is yet, but I'm determined to find out."

"So, let's find out."

Jared mustered a smile. "I just hope Zander and Harper are staying out of trouble at the main house. I'm worried they're going to stumble into mayhem."

"It will hardly be the first time."

"That doesn't make me feel any better."

. . .

FINDING THEIR WAY BACK TO THE third floor was more difficult than Harper and Zander imagined. It took them a full fifteen minutes to plot the correct course thanks to the house's winding hallways and muted decorations. Every corner of the house seemed to look exactly the same as the next corner. Harper found it disconcerting.

"You know, we used to make jokes as kids about living in a castle, but I don't think it sounds nearly as much fun as it used to."

Zander made a face. "Bite your tongue. Our castle would look nothing like this. We would have some color in our world ... some spark ... some pizzazz." He wrinkled his nose and glared at a dull painting of a woman standing in front of a fence. "We would definitely have some decent art."

Harper snickered as she stared at the woman in question. "Is that supposed to be a famous painting or something?"

"Not that I'm aware of."

"It's pretty ugly."

"It definitely is."

They continued staring for a long beat, only shifting their attention when a distinctive sound bubbled at their backs. Harper recognized the noise as coming from a man. Someone – and she had a pretty good idea who – had cleared his throat to get their attention.

"Oh, bugger it," Zander muttered.

"You need to stop watching the BBC," Harper complained. "Americans don't use the word 'bugger' and you know it."

"The cool ones do." Zander lifted his chin and met Bates' serious gaze as he turned. "Good afternoon, kind sir. Is it tea time? I'm always up for a spot of tea."

Instead of yelling, or demanding answers about what they were doing, Bates made a tsking sound and shook his head. "Listen to your friend. You watch too much television. I'm not like the Bates character on *Downton Abbey*."

"You could be like him," Zander argued. "All you have to do is give it a try ... and master a British accent. You would be so much cooler with a British accent."

"I would prefer not walking around the house with a fake accent," Bates countered. "It's a personal choice but one I've become comfortable with."

"See!" Zander jabbed a finger in the finicky butler's direction. "That was a very Bates-like thing to say."

It took everything Harper had to swallow her laughter. Thankfully Bates looked more amused than annoyed.

"Yes, well, we'll have to table that particular conversation for when I'm dead." Bates turned his attention to Harper. "May I ask what you're doing up here? I wasn't aware that any group activities were scheduled in this part of the house this afternoon."

Zander lowered his voice to a conspiratorial whisper. "That's snooty butler for 'how dare you wander throughout my castle,'" he offered helpfully.

Harper couldn't contain her laughter. "I figured out what he was really saying myself."

"I don't care that you're up here," Bates corrected quickly. He seemed much more at ease than he had been the previous day when greeting them, which Harper found interesting. "Mr. Jessup told me to give you free rein in the house. He's convinced you're the one who is going to come up with the answers he needs. It's just ... no one else is wandering around up here."

"Oh, well ... ." Harper felt caught. Ultimately, she wouldn't lower herself to lying. "There's a door up here. It's down at the end of the hall. I saw it when we were searching with Richard. He said there was no key to the lock but ... I feel the need to get in that room."

Bates' expression was hard to read. "May I ask what you expect to find in there?"

"I honestly don't know. I simply feel I need to look."

"In that room there?" He pointed toward the end of the hallway, to the doorway that called to Harper. When she nodded, he let loose a sigh. "Well, the reason Richard didn't allow you to enter that room is because we no longer have a key to it. He's not the only one shut out of that room. I am as well."

"Oh." Harper struggled to swallow her disappointment. "It's just the attic, right? How come you haven't had the door replaced? I would think there's stuff stored up there that you need."

"Not really. It's a big house. We have more than enough storage space without having to climb the old stairs that lead to the attic room."

There was something about his tone that set Harper's teeth on edge. "What's up there?"

"What makes you think anything is up there?"

"Because I know something is. You're being purposely evasive and I felt something from that room earlier. There's something there."

"Oh, geez." Zander made a horrified face. "You don't think Jennifer has been locked up there for ten years, do you? That is like ... too horrific to consider."

"I don't think it's Jennifer," Harper supplied. "I do think there's something up there, though, and I would really like to see what it is."

Bates let loose a long-suffering sigh, as if he was under duress and no one in the entire world had ever suffered as much as him. He was being overly dramatic as far as Harper was concerned, but she had no intention of letting up. "We really don't have a key."

Harper regarded him for a long beat. "You know what's up there, though, don't you?"

"I've seen photos of the room once before. I've never actually been inside. There honestly is nothing of consequence in that room."

"Then tell me what's in there."

"You're making a mountain out of a molehill," Bates insisted. "That is a room that fell into disuse a long time ago. It belonged to the first mistress of the house, Mrs. Coltraine. Her first name was Beatrice."

Harper didn't recognize the name. "I think she was before my time."

"She most certainly was," Bates agreed. "She was long before my time, too. She was Mr. Jessup's grandmother on his mother's side. They're the ones who built this house."

"I vaguely remember hearing that when I was a kid," Harper volunteered. "They were essentially the richest people in the area. They bought the island for very little and then employed a bunch of people to build the house. It was a big deal at the time, right?"

"It was. It was during a down economic time and the people in the area were grateful for the work that was being thrown their way."

"And that was her room?" Harper queried. She was legitimately confused. "Why was she kept in the attic? Was there something wrong with her? Wait ... I don't want to know. She wasn't some horrible monster or anything, was she?"

"Harper watches too many horror movies," Zander volunteered when Bates shot a questioning look in his direction. "Her imagination runs wild at the worst possible times. She can't help it."

"Ah." Bates smiled. "Well, in this particular case, it's unnecessary. Miss Jennifer was never in that room either. It's been locked for at least fifty years."

"But what's up there?" Harper pressed.

"It's a sewing room. Mrs. Coltraine liked to sew and she wanted a place where no one could bug her. She picked that room herself. She was the only one who had a key. Her husband doted on her some and he made sure she had her privacy ... and when she died, no one ever found the key. Her husband was so distraught he ordered everyone to leave the room as it was, a memorial to her, and over the years the key was lost."

Harper thought that was a ridiculous way to waste a room, but it was sort of romantic, too. "You're sure nobody has been up there, right?"

"I guarantee it. I shudder to think how that room looks now. It's probably a big dust ball. No one has set foot up there in at least fifty years. I believe Mr. Jessup was born after his grandmother died and I'm fairly certain he has never seen the inside of that room either. I guarantee Miss Jennifer isn't up there."

It made sense in a weird way and yet Harper couldn't tear her eyes from the door. "I guess it's nothing then." She wasn't convinced, but Bates clearly couldn't help her. Jared, however, was another story. She would hit him up for his lock-picking skills if it became necessary. "It was just a feeling, after all."

12

TWELVE

Harper couldn't get the sewing room out of her mind. It bothered her. Sure, Bates was friendlier than he had been on the day of their arrival, but there was something about the man's demeanor that made her leery.

He was stuffy, of course. She would expect nothing less from a man in his station. He was expected to represent Byron, be the face of the house. That meant jocularity was probably frowned upon.

"You know what?" Harper asked Zander as they made their way back to the guesthouse. "If we ever get that castle we dreamed about when we were kids, we're having a funny butler."

Zander slid her a sidelong look, legitimately amused. "And that declaration came to your mind just now because ... ?"

"Because Bates is zero fun at all. If you're going to have a butler, he should be fun."

"Like the butler in *Clue*?"

Harper laughed. That was one of their favorite movies. "We should have a viewing of that soon. The next snowstorm, we're totally there."

"Do you think we should introduce Shawn and Jared to *Clue* night?"

Harper tilted her head, considering. "We could."

"Yeah."

"Or we could keep that as something just for ourselves."

He broke into a wide grin. "Good idea. We need a few things that are just for us."

"We certainly do," she agreed, stomping her feet to dislodge the muck as they reached the front door. "How long do you think Jared and Shawn are going to be?"

"I don't know. Are you worried?"

That wasn't the word Harper would've chosen ... although it wasn't all that far off. "No. I want to talk to Jared, though."

"You mean you want to fight with him." Zander wasn't an idiot. He knew Harper was agitated about being left behind. Even though it wasn't necessary for her to make the trek to the woods, she'd convinced herself Jared didn't want her along because she was a girl, and that mentality always rubbed her the wrong way. "If it's any consolation, I really do think he was more worried about taking me to the woods than you."

"Did I say I was upset?"

"No, but you're doing that raised voice thing you do when you're about to get surly. I would recommend against that right now since we're all stuck in this guesthouse together and there's nowhere to escape if a big fight breaks out."

Harper had considered that herself. "What if it's just a little fight?"

"One where you pout and he gives in and promises you a really long massage?"

She bobbed her head. "Yeah, something like that."

"I think that is perfectly acceptable under the circumstances."

"Good."

THEY STRIPPED OUT OF THEIR coats and boots once inside. Eric and Molly were in the living room, sitting so close they were practically on top of one another. Harper found the scene cute, especially since they'd built a fire and looked altogether cozy.

"Would you like us to leave so you can continue doing ... whatever it is you're doing?" Harper called out.

Eric's cheeks colored with embarrassment when he realized they were no longer alone, but Molly didn't appear bothered in the least.

"Actually, no. We have some big things to show you." She seemed excited, to the point where Harper was intrigued.

"What did you find?"

"Come and have a seat and we'll show you."

Harper and Zander exchanged a look. Molly was the enthusiastic sort. That was why they hired her as an intern when she applied for an open position even though she had no employment history in the field. There was just something about her that called to both of them. Even though there were other candidates who had better credentials, Harper and Zander had been sold on her from the start. Her energy was appealing ... and it remained so years after the fact.

"Sure." Harper was more than happy to get comfortable in front of the fire. "What have you got?"

"Look at this." Molly turned the laptop she was sharing with Eric so Harper and Zander could see the screen. "What do you see?"

Harper furrowed her brow as she leaned closer. The screen was relatively dark, which was normal given the software they were using, and she had to take a moment to orient herself to the map on the screen.

"There are multiple hotspots," Zander noted. "There are like ... four or five of them."

"Exactly." Molly bobbed her head, excited. "You know what that means, right?"

"There's paranormal activity here," Zander replied. "I don't think that surprises anyone."

"But to have multiple hotspots in one area like this is ... it's a unique find."

Harper reached over so she could snag the laptop and get a better look. "What's over here on the grounds? And how did you get such an expansive scan? We've never gotten a scan like this before."

"That is Eric's doing." Molly cast her boyfriend a proud look. "He's been making some tweaks to the equipment. He took that old radar scanner we got at the estate sale a few months ago and modified it."

"Modified it how?"

"Radar scanners are supposed to measure movement," Eric explained. He wasn't as prone to dramatic fits as Molly, but even he looked excited. "Police use them when setting speed traps."

"I'm well aware," Zander said dryly. "I've been nabbed in a couple of traps."

"I think we all have," Harper added. "What does that have to do with what you've done here?"

"Ghosts are energy," Eric explained. "Energy registers on EMF readers. EMF readers aren't all that different from radar guns. I basically combined the two, so now our radar gun can register moving EMF trails."

Harper wasn't sure she understood, but she was impressed. "Are you serious? That's amazing."

"I've tested it a few times, but I wasn't sure it was really working until I tested it here. There are huge open expanses of space that have nothing that should read on the gun. We're getting readings, though."

"Ghosts?" Zander asked.

Eric's smile faltered. "That's the question. I obviously can't see ghosts to confirm. I was hoping we could take fresh readings and head out with Harper to see if it's really working. She should be able to identify a ghost."

Even though she was warm and comfortable, Harper was eager to test the theory ... and not simply because Eric had obviously put so much work into the project. "Let's do it." She handed back the computer and stood. "Try to find something outside of the house. I would like a break from those people if we can manage and I don't want to answer a bunch of questions about what we're doing. If this thing really works, I think Eric is going to have quite the moneymaker on his hands."

The dark-haired man balked. "What do you mean?"

"This could be a valuable tool," Harper pointed out. "You created it. If it works, you can manufacture and sell them to other people. Do you know how many people would jump at the chance to get their hands on something like this? We're hardly the only ghost hunters out and about in the world."

"Yeah, but ... you mean you think I should sell it?" He looked puzzled.

It was obvious to Harper he hadn't gotten past the initial excitement to realize what this could mean for his future. "If it works, I think you should sell it. I'm not sure it will happen overnight — you're going to have to build a few more and make sure you can replicate the effect — but this could turn into a huge deal."

"You could be rich," Molly enthused.

Eric's cheeks turned a dark shade of red. "I don't know about rich."

"I do." Zander clapped his hand to Eric's shoulder. "We'll be able to say we knew you when. That's still a bit off. Let's see if it really works first."

Eric dumbly nodded as he got to his feet. "Yeah. Let's see if it works."

THE MOST OBVIOUS PLACE TO CHECK was the cemetery. Harper knew there was a burial ground on the island, but one of the hotspots seemed to point directly toward it ... which made sense.

It took the foursome almost ten minutes to find the cemetery, but once they did, the screen on Eric's phone lit up. He'd created an app to transfer the information to a mobile device so they didn't have to carry around a laptop. It was ingenious really.

"Okay. If this is working, we should see it light up even more now that we're directly on top of the location," he said, handing the radar gun to Molly and pointing it at the cemetery. "Here we go."

Harper watched, anticipation coursing through her, and studied the tiny cemetery. If she had to guess, there were less than twenty graves. In the center of the parcel rested an ornate mausoleum, which looked to be a replica of the house. The windows were stained glass, and small turrets jutted into the sky.

"That's really cute, huh?" Molly noted, following Harper's gaze. "It's like a little dollhouse."

"I don't know that I would want to play with that dollhouse," she said dryly. "It's neat looking, though. Maybe a little over-the-top."

"Oh, everything about this place is over-the-top," Molly noted. "It's still cool. I mean ... who wouldn't want to live in a castle?"

Harper and Zander exchanged a quick look.

"You'd need a better butler, though," Molly added after a beat, thoughtful. "The one they have here is zero fun. You totally need a fun one."

"That sounds awesome," Zander agreed, grinning.

"Okay, the readings should be coming in," Eric announced. He was completely focused. Harper couldn't blame him. This was an exciting moment. It's not every day that you create something that could legitimately change a small portion of the world. She remembered how she felt the first time she constructed one of the dreamcatchers she now used on a regular basis to help troubled souls to pass over. She'd been proud ... and that was nothing compared to what Eric had built.

"What do you see, Molly?" he asked.

"Um ... it's lighting up." Molly almost squealed she was so excited. "Look at that."

Harper glanced at the small screen over her shoulder, her heart giving a little leap when the multicolored blob on the screen actually moved. "There's something here." She jerked her head in the direction of the mausoleum. She wasn't exactly an expert at reading maps, but she was fairly certain the spirit was located close to the building. "Come on."

She led the way to the gate, fumbling with the lock twice before she could open it. She didn't look behind her to make sure the others were following. Instead, she barreled forward and hurried around the side of the mausoleum. She wasn't sure what she would find, but the blur of ghostly light that sped away from her and disappeared around the other side of the building gave her a small jolt.

"Oh, wow."

"What do you see?" Molly asked, breathless as she caught up. "Did you see something?"

"Definitely." Harper slowly nodded her head. "There was something back here. I couldn't make out a form, just the energy trail. Whatever it is — whoever it is — is feeling shy. They zipped around the other side of the mausoleum."

Eric craned his neck so he could check the phone in Molly's hand. "The signal moved on the phone, too."

"It really is working." Harper was beyond excited. "Wow. Eric, this is an amazing invention. This is ... where is she now?"

Eric was as giddy as he was capable of getting as he pressed the radar trigger again. "Just a second."

"She?" Zander asked, cocking an eyebrow. "How do you know it's a she?"

That was a good question. Harper didn't have a good answer. "It's just a feeling," she said after a beat. "I don't know how to explain it. The energy feels female."

"Perhaps we'll be able to tweak the program to ascertain that eventually," Eric supplied. "I mean ... I'm not sure how, but it feels as if things are opening up for us."

Harper grinned. "They're definitely opening up."

"She should be over there." Eric pointed toward the far side of the mausoleum. "Maybe this time just Harper should approach. We might be frightening her wandering around in a big clump like this."

"Good idea," Molly said. "We'll wait here."

Harper happily embraced the suggestion and moved away from the group. This time when she readied herself to cross the last corner, she offered up a few words of greeting. "We don't want to hurt you," she called out. "I swear we're not dangerous. We just want to talk to you."

The ghost didn't answer, so Harper tried one more time. "We're here to help," she added. "We can make things better for you. I swear it."

She took a tentative step around the mausoleum, sucking in a breath when she caught sight of the female ghost for the first time. She didn't recognize the face. It was old and well-lined, and somehow dignified. She wore a dress that felt somewhat dated, a high neck and unforgiving waist on full display. Harper had a feeling she'd been here a long time.

"Hello. I'm Harper Harlow." She hoped she came off as friendly rather than deranged. "What's your name?"

The woman cocked her head to the side, as if surprised to be addressed. She'd probably been ignored for so long she no longer tried to interact with the living, Harper surmised. That notion made her inexplicably sad.

"You can see me?" the woman asked finally, her voice hesitant.

Harper nodded. "Yeah. I can see and hear you."

"But ... how?"

"I have a special ability. It's something I was born with."

"You were born with it?" The ghost cocked her head to the side, obviously confused. "How does that work?"

"Well ... it's a long story."

"Long story." The ghost took on a far-off expression, as if disappearing into her own mind for a short bit, and then recovered quickly. "You shouldn't be here. This is private land."

"It's okay. We were invited. Byron invited us."

"Byron?" She made a face. "That can't be right."

"Do you know Byron?" Harper couldn't be certain, but she was operating under the assumption that the ethereal woman she was staring at was none other than Byron's grandmother, the woman who died and left her sewing room locked for fifty years after the fact. She obviously had no proof of that, but she was comfortable with the assumption.

"I know Byron," the ghost replied. "I don't know how you know him, but I know him."

"He invited us here. We're trying to help him find his daughter. She's ... missing. She's been missing a long time. Do you know what happened to her?"

"I ... ." The question seemed to confuse the woman. "You shouldn't be here," she said finally. "This isn't a place for people like you. You should leave."

"We're only here until we find Jennifer."

"No. You should leave now."

"We won't be here long," Harper repeated. "Maybe you can help us. Do you know if there are others like you here? Other ... ghosts?"

The question was enough to rattle the woman and she immediately started shaking her head. "You shouldn't be here. Leave now."

"We're not here to hurt anyone," Harper reassured her.

"Leave now!" she bellowed, her eyes going wide. Before Harper could press her further, however, she disappeared.

"She's gone," Eric announced from behind Harper, disappointment lacing his tone. "She was there one second and gone the next."

"Why did she leave?" Zander asked, joining Harper. "Did you say something?"

Harper shot him a withering look. "Are you asking if I scared the ghost?"

"I'm just asking what happened." He raised his hands in mock surrender. "I wasn't accusing you of anything."

Harper heaved out a sigh. She knew better than taking out her frustrations on Zander. "She was scattered. She seemed confused. I think it was mentioning ghosts that really got her going. She was following the conversation before then. That seemed to be too much for her, though."

"Oh, well ... maybe we'll get another chance. She lives here, right? She'll probably come back once we're gone."

"Maybe," Harper agreed, dragging a restless hand through her hair. "I don't think she's going to come back as long as we're here, though. We should head back."

The group fell into step with one another, Molly excitedly chattering away as Harper thought through the interaction again. "I think she was Byron's grandmother," she offered after a few minutes.

"The woman who locked her sewing room and no one has opened it since?" Zander queried.

"One and the same."

"Why do you think that?"

"She had on this dated dress. It looked homemade even though the people who lived here obviously had money to purchase haberdashery in a store."

"Good word." Zander grinned. "Do you have any other reason for assuming it's her?"

"No. It's just a feeling."

"Well, a feeling is good enough for me." He slung his arm around her shoulders. "You knew it was a female and you were right. Now we just have to figure out what happened to her ... and get her to trust us long enough to start talking. That shouldn't be so hard to do, right?"

Harper wasn't so sure, but she kept her opinion to herself. She needed to think. There had to be a way to draw the woman back. She was convinced of that.

13

THIRTEEN

Jared, upon returning to the guesthouse, didn't fully understand the implications of Eric's new invention, but Harper was so gung-ho he listened to her explain it – twice – before simply nodding.

"That sounds great."

Harper stared at him for a long beat. "You don't get it."

"No," he agreed. "I don't get it. You obviously do, though, and if you're excited, I'm excited."

"Except you're not excited."

He sighed. "Maybe you guys can go out after dinner and show me. I'm sure I'll understand if I see it in person."

She nodded but knew that wouldn't happen. "Actually, we already have something scheduled for after dinner." She held up the invitation that arrived while they'd been out exploring the grounds. "Our presence is required at a séance."

Jared frowned as he took the invitation. "A séance?" He was clearly dubious. "How does that work?"

Harper held her hands out and shrugged. "I have no idea. I'm not really a séance person."

"Can we get out of it?"

The question caught her off guard. "I don't know. I mean ... Byron is paying us to be here. From the sound of the invitation, this is Harris's idea. I'm sure he wants to put himself on display and act like an idiot. He might actually be able to draw a ghost or two in, though. Who is to say?"

"I'm to say. I don't happen to believe he's the real deal."

Harper couldn't stop herself from smiling. "I think a lot of the people in this business are frauds."

"You're not." He was stalwart and loyal above all else, which was one of the things Harper loved most about him. "You're the real deal. I think you should be calling all the shots."

"That's funny because Zander believes he should be calling all the shots."

"No. It should be you." He managed a smile as he leaned in to kiss her. They'd retired to their bedroom for a bit of alone time before dinner once he returned from his trip to the woods. He pictured some cuddle time, and maybe a little something else. She was agitated, though, even though she did her best to cover. "What's wrong, Heart?" His fingers were gentle as he brushed her hair away from her face.

"What makes you think anything is wrong?"

"You have an expressive face and you're not a very good actress."

She frowned. "Should I take that as an insult?"

"Absolutely not. I like that you're straightforward and there are never any games." He leaned close and pressed his lips to her neck. "Er, well, any games that we both don't want to play."

She laughed as she slid her arms around his neck and leaned close. She needed this, she realized. She needed to be close to him, to be held by him. He anchored her and that's what she needed now.

"What's wrong?" he repeated, growing more concerned.

"Nothing is wrong," she reassured him quickly, pulling back so she could look into his eyes. "I'm fine. I just ... we saw a ghost."

"Jennifer?"

Harper shook her head. "I don't know who she was. I have a feeling she was Byron's grandmother, Beatrice."

"What makes you say that?"

Harper told him about the rest of her day, about trying to get into the upstairs room and her conversation with Bates. As she talked, she allowed Jared to direct her toward the bed so they could get comfortable and wrap themselves around one another. When she was finished, he was thoughtful.

"It sounds like she doesn't understand what's going on," he noted. He understood more about the ghost world than he ever thought possible thanks to his relationship with Harper. "Why do you think she's hanging around?"

Harper shrugged. "I honestly have no idea. I guess something traumatic happened to her back in the day, but I haven't been able to find anything on how she died. It was a long time ago and there's no information on the internet."

Jared pursed his lips as he stared into her eyes. "Well ... maybe she'll grow to trust you."

"We don't have a lot of time left here. I mean ... I'm starting to wonder why Byron even invited us. We've done nothing to track down the truth regarding Jennifer's disappearance."

"Maybe Byron just wants to think he's doing something. I mean ... it has to be hard. That's his daughter. She vanished into thin air one day. He's been plagued with questions for ten years. It can't be easy."

"I get that." Harper was earnest. "I do. That doesn't change the fact that we still have no idea if Jennifer is even dead. I mean ... she could've run. That's a legitimate possibility. Byron doesn't want to see it, but if Jennifer was really as unhappy as she seemed, why would she stay?"

He shrugged. "I don't have an answer for you."

"I don't have an answer for me either." She pressed her head to his chest as he stroked her hair. "Sometimes I wish I didn't see ghosts."

He arched an eyebrow, surprised. "Why do you say that?"

"Because I'm supposed to have this special gift that helps people and what's the point of being odd and different if I can't help people? I'm not helping anyone right now."

"That's not true." He scooched lower on the bed and lifted her chin so he could stare into her eyes. "You're helping me."

"With what?"

"This." He kissed her, grinning when she rolled her eyes. "And this." He kissed her again, nudging loose a sigh.

"You're pretty charming when you want to be," she noted as she stared at his curved smile. "I love you, Jared."

"I love you, too."

"I kind of want to tune out the rest of the world for an hour or so," she admitted, mischief flitting through her eyes. "Do you have any ideas for distracting me?"

His face split with a wide grin. "As a matter of fact, I do."

"Somehow I knew you were going to say that."

TWO HOURS LATER, THEY MADE THEIR way to the main house. Everybody else was already seated and Harper offered up a lame apology when they settled at the table.

"Sorry we're late."

Byron smiled indulgently at her. "That's quite all right. I assume you were preparing for Mr. Fontaine's séance this evening. I have to admit, I'm looking forward to it. He believes we might even be able to have a conversation with Jennifer."

Harper didn't bother hiding her surprise as she shifted her eyes to the psychic in question. Byron had arranged the seating chart to make sure Harris was to his right and Harper to his left this evening. It seemed – at least to Harper – to signify a change in the pecking order. Since Jared was seated next to her for the first time since arriving, though, Harper was fine with it.

"I don't really participate in a lot of séances," she admitted after a beat. "They're not part of my work."

"And how do you communicate with the dead?" Harris asked.

"Usually I just have a conversation with them."

"But ... how do you call them?"

"I don't call them. I usually stumble across them and ask a few questions. Occasionally I get called to a home because of a troublesome haunting and I have to capture a ghost so I can send it to the other side. It's basically a fifty-fifty split."

Harris's expression was hard to read. "I see ... and you actually make money doing this?"

"I do." Harper bobbed her head, doing her best to keep from snapping at the man. He had one of those tones that stabbed to her very marrow. "How do you communicate with ghosts?"

"I force them to come to me." Harris puffed out his chest, obviously feeling very self-important. "It's necessary to set the right tone when dealing with the dead. They can make life difficult for the living if you don't make them aware you're in charge."

Harper kept her face placid, but just barely. "And how do you let them know you're in charge?"

"By calling to them, of course. If you can force them to appear when they don't wish to do so, you become their master. Surely you already know this."

"Not really." Harper forced a flat smile. "That's not how I operate."

"Perhaps that's because you don't know what you're doing."

Jared stirred. "I've seen Harper work her magic more times than I can count. She knows what she's doing."

"You're her fiancé, right? I believe you're required to say that." Harris didn't wait for Jared to respond, instead turning his full attention to Byron. "I believe we should have the séance in the library, the one where your daughter enjoyed spending her time. That's probably where her ghost will feel most comfortable."

Byron nodded without hesitation. "That sounds like a fine idea to me."

Harper narrowed her eyes as she met Harris's gaze. There was an unsaid challenge passing between them, but she refused to call him out in front of an audience. If he wanted to put himself on display with a séance, who was she to judge? Sure, she had her doubts it would work, but it was his show.

Honestly, she was mildly curious to see how it would all turn out.

BY THE TIME THEY FINISHED DINNER and escaped to the library, Harris made a big show of giving Byron a list of things he would need for the séance. That meant the library was dripping in ambiance when they arrived ... and a bevy of small candles.

"This is perfect," Harris announced, rubbing his hands together. "This is everything I need."

Harper glared at him out of the corner of her eye before folding her arms over her chest and leaning against a wall. She was embarrassed for him ... an emotion that he neither seemed capable of recognizing nor admitting to.

"We don't have to stay," Jared whispered as he slid behind her. "I know this isn't your idea of fun."

"Actually, I want to see what he does," she admitted. "I assume he's going to make a jackass of himself. I'm just curious how far he's willing to take it."

What Jared didn't tell her was that he believed Harris was willing to take it all the way. He figured he would simply let her enjoy the show and be surprised.

Harris clearly relished being the center of attention because he made a series of humming noises, as if testing the ambiance, and then held out his hands as he sat cross-legged on the ground. "The spirits are ready," he announced.

Harper rolled her eyes until they landed on Margot, who was having the exact same reaction as her. Delphine, however, appeared intrigued and readily joined Harris on the floor. Apparently she wanted to bask in his attention.

"I'll help call to the spirits," she offered.

Harris pinned her with a serious look. "I don't need help. You'll screw it up if you're not careful."

"Nonsense. I've been doing this for years. I've never failed when it comes to a séance."

"Neither have I."

"So ... this should work out well."

Harper pressed her lips together to keep from laughing and slid her eyes to Jared. He looked as amused as she felt and he slipped his arm around her waist to keep her close.

Harris and Delphine spent the next ten minutes chanting over top of one another, fighting to see which one could draw the most attention. A quick look at the Jessups told Harper they were already bored with the show. Well ... other than Byron. He seemed legitimately taken with Harris's efforts.

And then the man started calling out Jennifer's name. He did it in such a loud voice he caused Harper to jolt.

"What the ... ?"

Jared tugged her tighter against him, frowning. "That's ridiculous," he muttered under his breath.

Byron seemed to feel the exact opposite. "Is it Jennifer? Is she here?"

"She's here," Harris intoned, causing Harper to straighten. When she looked around the room, she came up empty.

"She has a message for you," Delphine added. "She wants you to know that what happened to her wasn't your fault."

Harris openly glared. "She's talking to me, not you."

"She's talking to both of us."

"Oh, geez," Harper muttered, shaking her head. "She's not even here."

Byron shushed her and focused on Harris. "What is she saying? Does she know what happened to her? Where can I find her body? I want to put her to rest?"

"Her voice is very faint," Harris explained. "It's going to take a moment – and absolute silence – for me to make out what she's saying. I'm going to need everybody's cooperation."

"I can't even ... ." Harper pulled away from Jared and circled, her gaze going to the second floor of the library as she shook her head. When her gaze finally focused, her heart skipped a beat as she realized an ethereal face was watching them.

"Jared." She gripped his hand tightly, drawing his attention to the second floor.

Of course, he couldn't see anything. "Is it her?" he whispered, keeping his lips close to Harper's ear as Harris continued acting for the crowd.

"It's not Jennifer." Harper sighed as her gaze locked with that of Beatrice. The ghost looked just as worried as she had earlier in the evening. She wasn't, however, alone. She had two friends with her, both female, and both dressed in outfits that went out of style a good fifty years before. "I don't think Jennifer is here."

Jared moved his hand to her back and lightly rubbed as he stared at the spot that had captivated her attention. There were times he wished he could see what she did simply so she wouldn't always be alone when the terrifying things appeared. There were other times he was glad he couldn't see because he was convinced it was something that would forever change his outlook on life. He didn't know how Harper managed to function – and well – seeing the things she did.

"Tell Byron," Jared suggested. "He should know he's being taken for a ride."

Harper shifted her eyes back to Harris, who was nowhere near done putting on a show. "If I do that, I'll look like I'm jealous or something because I haven't found any answers. It's not exactly as if I've found any proof that she's still alive."

Jared studied her for a long beat. "Well, then I don't know what to tell you."

Harper didn't know what to do either. Because of that, she remained where she was and watched Harris lie through his teeth.

"She says that there was an accident," Harris explained. "She was out walking in the woods and she fell, hurt herself. No one came to save her. She died out there alone, but she doesn't blame you."

Byron exhaled heavily. "Where is she? I want to find her, bring her home."

Harper frowned. This was a ridiculous load of nonsense as far as she was concerned. Apparently she wasn't the only one who believed that.

"There's no ghost here," Margot announced, taking everyone in the room by surprise. She didn't look up, didn't take in the three ghosts watching the show with impassioned faces. Instead, she remained focused on Harris. "Jennifer isn't here. You're making it up."

Harris's eyes filled with fire. "I most certainly am not making it up. I'm an expert. There's a reason my services are in such high demand. Jennifer is here."

Byron glanced between his two "experts" before shifting his eyes to Harper. "What do you think?"

She sucked in a breath. She hated being put on the spot. "I think that she's not here." No matter how she felt about what was going on, Harper couldn't lie. She didn't have it in her. "I think someone else is here, though. Maybe a couple of someones, in fact."

Byron wrinkled his forehead. "Someone else? I don't understand."

"Your grandmother. How did she die?"

"Grandma Beatrice? I ... she died in her sleep."

Harper glanced at the ghost on the second floor. "I don't think that's true. Is that what you were told?"

Byron was officially bewildered. "What does my grandmother have to do with Jennifer's death?"

"Probably nothing. I don't know that Jennifer is dead, though. No matter what Harris tells you, she's not here. He's making it up."

Harris hopped to his feet, fury on full display. "That is a vicious lie. She's here. She doesn't want you agonizing over her death. She's mostly at peace."

"If she is dead, she won't be at peace until she crosses over," Harper countered. "She's not here, though. We don't know what happened to her. That's the truth."

"I know." Harris refused to back down. "It was an accident. She wants her father to find peace."

"I want her father to find peace, too," Harper offered. "This isn't the way, though. I won't participate in a lie."

"Then perhaps you should leave," Harris suggested. "If you don't believe, why are you even here?"

Byron found his voice. "Because I want her here. Harper knew Jennifer. As for all of this ... I need time to think." He looked conflicted ... and shaken. "I'm sure you can entertain yourselves for the rest of the evening. I need to retire."

He was already out of the room before Harris found his voice.

"Well, I hope you're happy." His gaze was dour when it landed on Harper. "You're totally ruining this for everybody. This trip has turned into a whole bunch of suck."

Harper couldn't agree more. The trip sucked ... but that didn't mean it was a total loss. She flicked her eyes back to the second floor and found the ghosts were gone. There were souls on the property who had answers. She simply needed to track them down and make them talk.

That was going to be easier said than done.

FOURTEEN

Harper woke cocooned in warmth, Jared's breath hot on the back of her neck. Once Delphine and Harris started arguing the night before, they excused themselves for bed. Zander and Shawn stayed behind, seemingly amused by the show. Harper expected a full report when they left the relative safety of their bedroom ... but she wasn't in the mood to deal with it yet.

"What are you thinking?" Jared murmured, his voice thick with sleep. "I know what I'm thinking. It's too early to get up."

Harper smiled as she rolled to face him, taking a moment to enjoy his stubbled profile. "You're so pretty."

He snorted. "I was just going to say the same thing about you."

"Oh, yeah?" She snuggled closer. "If we were home, I would suggest we spend the day being pretty together in bed. Like ... the entire day. We could order food delivered and everything."

He arched an eyebrow, amused. "Do you want to go home? I can have us there in an hour. We can be undressed and back in bed before breakfast."

She considered the question. "I want to go home."

Her answer surprised him. "Okay. Then we'll go home."

"I want to go home, but I can't just yet," she clarified. "Something is really wrong here. I mean ... really off. There are three ghosts running around."

He nodded without hesitation. "So ... duty calls, huh?"

She nodded. "Next weekend, though, we're doing the 'stay in bed all day and live on love' thing. I'm going to insist on it."

"I'll be right there insisting on it, too." He gave her a soft kiss and then sobered. "Tell me what you're thinking about the ghosts. I know we talked about it last night, but I never really got a feel for what you think is going on."

"I don't know what's going on." Harper rolled to her back and dragged a hand through her hair as she stared at the ceiling fan. "I need to talk to Beatrice."

"To be fair, you don't know that's who you're dealing with. You have a feeling – and I tend to think all your feelings are golden – but we don't have proof yet. Maybe we should check the house for photographs. That, at least, would be something."

Harper brightened considerably. "I hadn't thought of that. I ... ." She trailed off when there was a knock at the door, propping herself on an elbow as Jared sighed and called for whoever was trying to invade their morning to come in.

To absolutely nobody's surprise, it was Zander.

"Oh, good, you're up." He hurried into the room on bare feet and climbed in on Harper's side of the bed without invitation. "It's freezing this morning. It's so cold it's foggy again."

Jared shifted his eyes to the window and frowned when he realized Zander was correct. "I don't think there's any sun in our forecast today."

"Which sucks," Zander supplied. "If you're going to live on an island, don't you think it should be sunny all the time? I know all those stories we read as kids talked about fog outside of castles, but this is getting ridiculous."

"It's still technically winter in Michigan," Harper pointed out. "I think this is normal if you're going to live here."

"Then maybe we should move."

"I think Jared and Shawn might put up a fight."

"I know I will," Jared agreed. "I happen to like Michigan. Yeah, the winters are brutal sometimes, but the spring, summer, and fall are great. You can live with a little cold."

"Whatever." Zander rolled his eyes to the ceiling. "By the way, you guys missed quite the show last night. Harris and Delphine got absolutely blasted and started calling each other frauds in front of the Jessup family."

Harper didn't always understand Zander's penchant for gossip but this was news she was eager to hear. "Really? What did the Jessups do?"

"Well, George called them both frauds – and added Margot in for good measure – and stormed off not long after you guys left. Evangeline hung around for about an hour and then quietly said her goodnights. Richard hung around for the duration. So did the lawyer."

Harper was officially intrigued. "Does anyone else wonder why the lawyer is hanging around? I mean ... that's weird, right?"

"I would think it's weird," Jared agreed, rubbing his chin as he thoughtfully deconstructed the Jessup family in his mind. "Of course, I don't think they're a normal family. I mean ... does anyone think these people love each other?"

Harper slid her eyes to him. "I think they're a family who struggles ... and often. We don't know what they were like before Jennifer disappeared, or Byron's wife died. It sounds to me as if her death was the catalyst that changed everything."

"Maybe. You said Jennifer was unhappy in high school, though. You said her father was never around."

"We don't know that he wasn't around before her mother died. Maybe he wallowed in grief so far that he simply couldn't climb out of it. I mean ... I like to think that I would be strong if the same thing happened to me, but I'm not sure I could ever get over losing you.

"Think about it: Say we have two kids and ten years from now something happens to me," she continued. "Do you think you would be the same person with our kids if you had to raise them alone?"

Jared wasn't a fan of the game. "I would prefer not talking about this."

"It's a legitimate question." Harper refused to let him off the hook. "If I died, do you honestly think you would be the same person?"

"Just for the record, your answer should be 'no,'" Zander offered helpfully. "You're supposed to say that you would never get over the loss of her."

Jared glared at him. "Thank you for telling me how I should feel, Zander," he drawled. "I don't know how I managed to get through the day before you were a regular part of my life telling me how to feel."

Harper sensed trouble and quickly backtracked. "You know what? You don't have to answer. It was a stupid question."

"No, it wasn't." Jared caught her hand before she could escape and sucked in a breath. "You want to know if I would be like Byron and shut down if something were to happen to you. That's not an easy question to answer.

"The thing is, you're the love of my life," he explained, earnestness on full display. "I mean ... the absolute love of my life. There is no one I will ever love like you. Not ever. Losing you would cripple me and I know I wouldn't be the same man.

"That being said, if we have kids – which I'm looking forward to doing one day – I would understand that I have a responsibility to those children," he continued. "I would hope that I was capable of pulling myself together to take care of our children the way you would want me to. I would always miss you, and long for the day when we're reunited, but I would not neglect my children in the process."

Harper beamed at him. "That was a good answer."

"It was," Zander agreed. "You wouldn't be alone, though. You would have me. I would help you."

Oddly enough, Jared took comfort in the offer. "Thank you. I don't want to play this game any longer, though. You're not going anywhere. In sixty years, it's still going to be you and me together."

"And me," Zander added.

"And Zander." Jared grinned as he pressed a kiss against the corner of her mouth. "We're going to have endless days where we don't have to get out of bed. That's all still in front of us."

"We just have to get through this first," Harper noted, sighing. "I guess that means we should get ready for breakfast, huh? I think this is basically the last day for the investigation. We're supposed to leave tomorrow morning."

"And I'm looking forward to it," Jared said. "I'm a little worried that you're not going to let it go if you don't find answers."

Harper's smile was rueful. "You know me too well. I can't let this go. Not yet."

"Because you feel guilty about not helping Jennifer more when you were in school?"

"Partially. I also feel guilty for not thinking about her enough since she disappeared. She deserved someone to remember her."

Jared let loose a long-suffering sigh. "That doesn't necessarily fall on you."

"No, but I still want to help. I'm not ready to give up yet."

"Then we won't give up." Jared was matter-of-fact. "We'll keep plugging away until we find answers. That will start at breakfast again. I'm going to call Mel and ask him to check with Madeline's family to see if she's shown up back on the mainland. I'm still not convinced her disappearance should be ignored."

"That's a good idea. While you're doing that, I'm going to hop in the shower. I don't want to be late this morning. I would like a chance to talk to Byron alone, before Harris and Delphine show up and start putting on another show."

"I'm sure that can be arranged. I'll handle interference if need be." He leaned closer to her, ignoring the fact that Zander was watching them. "It's going to be you and me forever," he whispered. "You're never getting rid of me ... and I won't let you go."

She smiled. "I think we're going to be happy for a long time. You don't need to worry."

"I *know* we're going to be happy for a long time. There's no doubt in my mind."

TRUE TO HIS WORD, JARED MANAGED to isolate Byron when they reached the main house. He stood in the doorway, standing guard, and allowed Harper to sit down in private with the man without the threat of one of the two idiots – which is how he was mentally referring to them now – interrupting.

"How are you feeling?" Harper asked as she sat down across from him. She couldn't help noticing he seemed paler and more wan than normal.

"I'm fine," Byron replied, forcing a smile for her benefit. "I hope you didn't spend the evening worrying about me."

"Maybe just a little." Harper held her index finger and thumb about an inch apart and offered him a rueful smile. "I wanted to talk to you about a few things. I feel as if I might be talking out of turn here, but I feel it's important that you not get taken for a ride."

Byron's expression didn't change. "And you're worried that Delphine and Harris are doing exactly that."

He was more observant than Harper gave him credit for. "Maybe a little," she conceded. "Last night they were putting on a show. I need you to understand that Jennifer wasn't there. I don't know what that means, but I'm bothered by what I saw."

"Harris tried to track me down after I retired last night. He said you were the one putting on a show."

"I'm sure he did." Harper wasn't surprised by the statement. Jared, however, scowled from his spot in the doorway.

"She's not putting on a show," Jared argued. "I know this is hard for you to believe, but she's the real deal. I've seen her in action more times than I can count. She's not lying to you."

Byron flicked his eyes to Jared, seemingly amused. "You're very loyal to her. It helps that you're a police detective in good standing. Your opinion matters. And, yes, I researched you just as thoroughly as Harper.

"That being said, this whole weekend is something of an experiment," he continued. "I don't know what I expect to happen. I'm not an idiot, though. I knew when I invited all of you here that it was likely there would be a fraud or two in my midst."

His gaze was heavy when it snagged with Harper's sea-blue eyes. "There are stories about you in this area. Some people speak about you reverently. Others think you're a grifter. I've read every story on you I could find."

Jared bristled. "She's not a grifter."

Byron chuckled. "No. I don't believe she is. For her to inspire such loyalty in you is a testament to who she is. I don't know what I believe about Jennifer. I go back and forth, my emotions all over the place. It's hard for me to even admit to myself what I want."

Harper licked her lips, uncertain how far she truly wanted to push things. She'd come this far, though. Turning back now seemed a mistake. "We're worried about Madeline," she admitted, going for broke. "I know you're not, but we are. Jared called his partner this morning and Mel is going to check with Madeline's family to see if she's shown up over there."

"You really don't have to worry about her," Byron countered. "She does this all the time. She's looking for attention. She doesn't care if it's negative or positive. That's who she is. She thinks she can emotionally blackmail me into giving her what she wants."

"And what's that?" Jared asked, legitimately curious.

"She wants me to rip up the pre-nup. She's been after me to do it practically since the moment we married. I told her before she signed it that I would never destroy it. She apparently thought she could convince me otherwise."

"Do you even love her?" Harper asked, the question escaping before she thought better of it. "I'm not judging you or anything," she added hurriedly. "You don't seem to love her, though."

"Not everyone is blessed with true love." His smile was small but genuine. "You and your friend here obviously love each other. It's written all over your faces whenever you look at one another. I had that sort of love with my first wife. You don't get blessed twice."

"You don't know that," Harper argued. "I can guarantee you don't get blessed twice if you don't open yourself up to it. Have you considered divorcing Madeline, letting her go? She might be better off."

"I've been considering that a great deal of late. I don't know what I'm going to do. You don't have to worry about her, though. She'll turn up. She always does."

"And you're sure this is all about money?" Jared queried. "If you've told her over and over you won't tear up the pre-nup, why does she persist?"

"At this point I believe she's under the impression she's wasted ten years of her life," Byron replied. "She's convinced I'll come to my senses and leave her Jennifer's half of my estate. That's not going to happen, though."

Harper couldn't contain her surprise. "Are you going to leave half your estate to Jennifer even now? I thought you believed she was dead."

"I do. It's too much for me to consider the alternative. I believe she's dead

... but there's a chance she's not. As it stands now, my estate will be split in two. Richard will get one half. Jennifer the other. It will be held in trust for twenty years after my death to see if she surfaces. If she doesn't, then the money will be doled out to her favorite charities after the fact."

Harper was impressed. "That's a good thing," she enthused, impulsively reaching forward to grip his hand. "That's a really good thing. That's some-thing Jennifer would've really liked."

"I thought you didn't know her very well."

"I didn't, but I know that about her. She had a giving soul and I think she would've liked knowing that you were helping people because of her after the fact."

"Yes, well ... ." He rolled his neck and collected himself. "Part of me is angry with her. If she really did take off, it was cruel of her to treat me this way. I don't pretend to have been the perfect father, but she didn't even give me the option of correcting my mistakes.

"Whenever I think about that too hard, though, I hate myself," he contin-ued. "I feel she's dead. She wasn't the type to take off that way. Something happened to her ... and that makes me feel guilty for a different reason. I need to know what happened."

His eyes were cool, clear, when they locked with Harper's conflicted orbs. "I meant what I said the other night. I believe you're the one who is going to find her. You don't have to worry about me falling victim to Harris or Delphine. I'm not a moron. Just ... find what happened to Jennifer. I need that from you."

"I'm going to try," Harper promised. "There is one thing I need from you before I can move forward, though."

"What's that?"

"Do you have a photograph of your grandmother?"

The question obviously caught Byron off guard. "I'm sure I do. Why?"

"Because Jennifer's ghost may not be hanging around, but I'm pretty sure your grandmother's ghost is ... and she's not alone. She's skittish and won't talk to me, but I'm going to change that. I simply want to confirm I'm dealing with who I think I'm dealing with before I tackle trying to communicate with her again."

"Fair enough. I don't know why she would be hanging around, though. She really did die in her sleep. It was peaceful."

Harper felt in her heart that wasn't true. For now, she kept her opinion to herself. "Let's take it one step at a time and see what we can come up with, huh?"

"That sounds like a fine idea."

FIFTEEN

Harper's conversation with Byron left her with more questions than answers ... and the big ones revolved around money.

"Can I ask you something?" she asked Jared as he poured juice from the small drink cart in the parlor.

"Generally I would say yes without even thinking about it, but you have your serious face on."

Harper merely stared at him and blinked, eliciting a sigh.

"What's your question?" he prodded.

"Can you ever imagine marrying strictly for money? I mean ... can you imagine a life of being with someone that doesn't revolve around love?"

"Not even a little." He answered without hesitation. "Not all people are alike, though. Money doesn't mean as much to you and me. We want enough to be comfortable and not constantly struggle, don't get me wrong, but we don't need what they have here."

"And what do they have here?"

"Comfort but not happiness. I would much rather have the happiness."

Harper couldn't disagree with that assessment. "I've been thinking back to high school a lot."

Jared had already figured that out himself. "Are you thinking about Jennifer again? Heart, I don't think obsessing about what you didn't do back then is smart."

"I'm actually not thinking about Jennifer. I'm thinking about Madeline."

"Oh. That makes sense." Jared handed her a glass of juice. "Are you wondering if she was always the sort of person who was willing to throw happiness out the window for money?"

"Kind of," Harper hedged. "She was never a nice girl, though. That's probably not a surprise to you, but she was never the sort of person you simply wanted to hang around and have a good time with."

"I'm guessing there was static between her and you over Zander." It was a statement more than a question.

"Probably not like you're thinking," Harper countered hurriedly. "She didn't give him a hard time because he was gay. She gave him a hard time because, much like her, he always wanted to be the center of attention."

Jared was thoughtful as he led her to one of the small settees. "Basically you're saying she was always starved for attention. Tell me about her home life. When I asked Mel to check in with her parents, he made an odd groaning sound."

Harper chuckled. "Yes, well, her mother is very much like my mother. She owns the hair salon in town."

Jared frowned. "I can't imagine your mother cutting hair. That doesn't seem like much of a power position."

"Oh, well, that's where you're wrong." Harper laughed at his dubious expression. "For women, that *is* a power position. It means she's right in the center of all the gossip. Women love to chat while getting their hair done. I learned that from my mother."

"I guess I'll have to take your word for it. I would imagine being a hairdresser is stressful because you're completely dependent on the whims of others to make your livelihood. I'm guessing, when times get tough, haircuts and dye jobs are among the first things to go."

"Maybe not go, but pared down," Harper corrected. "That's the thing. I was thinking about Madeline back then and she always had the best of everything. We're talking coats, purses, and shoes. Her mother made sure she never went without. That couldn't have been easy."

"Or wise," Jared noted. "Madeline's mother basically taught her that things were important. Maybe not more important than people, but still important. It's probably no wonder that she opted for an unhappy life in the lap of luxury rather than a comfortable one without the money."

"Yeah." Harper rolled her neck. Something about the situation continued to niggle at the back of her brain, although she couldn't put her finger on exactly why. "Just because you decide to go for the money, that doesn't mean that you completely turn off the emotions."

Jared arched an eyebrow, confused. "I don't know what you're getting at."

"I'm saying that I think I would've always fallen in love with you. Imagine somehow our lives were different and there were different circumstances when you arrived in town. What if I was married to Quinn or something?"

Jared scowled at mention of her ex-boyfriend, who was currently in jail awaiting trial for threatening her life. "Let's not imagine that, huh?"

"I'm not saying I want that life. I'm just saying that if something absolutely ridiculous had happened and I was already with someone else when you came to town, I'd like to think that our pull is too great and we still would've found our way to one another."

Things finally clicked into place for Jared. "Oh. You're wondering if someone crossed paths with Madeline over the years and she tried to figure out a way to hold onto the money and somehow embrace the love, too."

"Basically," she agreed. "There's nothing that could keep me from you. I'm not the sort of person who needs obscene wealth. Not at all. I do need love. Maybe Madeline needs love, too."

"You think she might be holed up with a man somewhere."

"It makes sense. She's living a very lonely existence. Maybe it's not as lonely as we think and that's how she survives."

"I like where your head is at. That makes sense. She still had to get off this island somehow without anybody noticing."

"Yeah, well, I've been thinking about that, too. How difficult would it be for someone to bring their own boat out here and dock at the far side of the island? I'm guessing not as difficult as we're making it out to be. Heck, if someone was really dedicated, they could've rowed out here. It probably wouldn't take more than twenty minutes or so. This is barely an island."

Jared looked dubious. "Rowing is a lot of work."

"It is ... but if I was out here and you wanted to see me, would that work keep you from seeing me?"

She had a point. "No. Nothing would keep me from you. Still, I don't know many guys who would put up with being the side piece. That's an ego thing."

"Unless she found someone willing to compromise his ego for money. If the female version of that individual exists, I guarantee the male version does, too."

"Fair enough. What does that have to do with Jennifer's disappearance?"

"Maybe nothing. Probably nothing," she corrected hurriedly thanks to his expression. "The timing still bothers me, though. Jennifer knew about Madeline's relationship with her father before she disappeared. That's already been established. That means Byron dated Madeline when she was still in high school. Sure, she might've been eighteen, but that's still frowned upon."

Jared was thoughtful as he sipped his juice and thought about the scenario

Harper was setting up. "Do you think Madeline had something to do with Jennifer going missing?"

Harper shrugged. "I'm not ruling it out. If she did, I think it's far more likely a fight broke out and whatever happened was an accident. Madeline may be a money-hungry viper, but she doesn't strike me as a murderer ... mostly because she wouldn't want to do the work associated with being a murderer."

"I think, if you really want to pursue this angle, we need someone who is part of the family but not exactly close to Madeline. Someone who would have skin in the game and want to protect Byron. Most of the people here probably don't care about Byron ... other than the fact that he signs their paychecks."

"I was thinking the same thing." Harper's eyes shifted over the room until they found the person she was looking for. Evangeline. "Byron is her son. Jennifer is her granddaughter. I think she pays attention to what's going on under this roof more than people give her credit for."

Jared followed her gaze. "I have no issue if you want to hit her up for information. I am concerned that you seem fixated on the fact that Madeline's disappearance is most likely tied to Jennifer's disappearance. Odds are they have nothing to do with one another."

"I get that. It makes sense."

Jared sighed. "But you're going to stick with your theory."

"I am." Harper nodded without hesitation. "I just have a feeling. I can't explain it."

"Then I have faith in your theory."

EVANGELINE WAS READING THE NEWSPAPER and drinking coffee when Harper and Jared approached. She seemed surprised by the intrusion, but she didn't act out of sorts. George, on the other hand, was already drinking bourbon in a coffee mug and seemed to be in a foul mood.

"Oh, good," he muttered. "More ghost hunters. I can't tell you how happy I am this is the last day I have to spend with you folks."

Harper slid him a narrow-eyed look but didn't respond. Instead she focused on Evangeline. "Anything good in the newspaper today?"

Evangeline was a smart woman. She clearly sensed that Harper had an agenda for approaching. "Lots of little tidbits," she replied, handing over the A section. "You're welcome to it if you're interested."

"I'm fine." Harper forced a smile. Now that she was in the thick of things, she felt out of place. "So, I was with Bates yesterday and he told me about the attic room that can't be entered. That room belonged to your mother, right?"

Evangeline arched an eyebrow, clearly surprised by the conversational shift.

"That was my mother's room," she confirmed after a beat. "Nobody has been up there in years."

"I know." Harper exhaled heavily. "The thing is ... I'm curious how it worked. Was this house left to you following the passing of your parents?"

Evangeline darted a quick look toward George, who was looking unbelievably surly, and then nodded. "Technically, yes, but George and I were married when I inherited so everything was split between us. That's how it should be between a husband and wife."

"Unless you have a wife like Madeline," George muttered.

"Of course." Evangeline folded her hands in her lap, discomfort practically rolling off her in waves. "That goes without saying."

Harper was genuinely uncomfortable with the way the couple interacted. "But Evangeline's family is the one that had the money, right?" she prodded. For some reason, she enjoyed poking George. He was one of the most disagreeable people she'd ever met and there was joy to be found in messing with him. "She was the one who passed the house on to Byron ... although I'm wondering why you did that before your death." Harper's gaze was heavy when it landed on the uncomfortable woman.

"I never liked this house," Evangeline admitted, letting loose a nervous laugh. "I always thought it was haunted when I was a kid. My mother told me I was being ridiculous, but I always felt it."

"How old were you when your mother died?"

"Eight." Sadness washed over Evangeline's features. "I always loved my mother more than anything. My father was a good man, mind you, but he traveled on business a lot. They were the ones who built this house."

"And we were the ones who perfected it," George offered, sipping from his glass of bourbon. "We're the ones who made it great and then you just gave it away to Byron as if it was nothing. You didn't even ask me what I thought about it."

Harper sensed a very interesting story. To get it out of Evangeline, though, she was going to need to get rid of George. She sent Jared a pleading look, one that he clearly wanted to argue with. After a few moments of staring at one another, he let loose a sigh and got to his feet.

"I hear you have an antique gun collection here, George," he offered through gritted teeth. "People say it's the best collection in the entire state. I happen to love antique weapons. I don't suppose you want to show it to me, do you?"

Jared might not have been keen on being the sacrificial lamb but he understood his part in this set-up and he recognized the one thing that would propel George to perk up.

"We do." George's eyes lit with interest. "Do you have knowledge of antique weapons?"

"Some. I'm sure you can teach me a lot, though."

"I'm sure I can, too. Come on."

Harper shot Jared a profoundly grateful look as he disappeared with George and waited until she was sure the two men were gone to start speaking again.

"George is very lucky to have found a woman like you," she offered. "I mean ... most men can't say they married into riches like this."

Evangeline's expression was hard to read. Finally, she heaved out a world-weary sigh. "You're not very good at this, are you?" She almost looked amused. Now that her husband wasn't breathing down her neck, she was much more relaxed. "You can just ask me whatever it is you're curious about. We promised Byron we would cooperate with you — yes, even George — and I'm willing to open myself up to the process simply because my son asked."

Harper nodded, pursing her lips. "That's good. The thing is, I want to see your mother's sewing room. My understanding is that it's locked and no one can find the key. Everyone has given up even trying to find it. I think that's kind of odd."

Evangeline's eyes sharpened. "Why do you care about my mother's sewing room? Why would that possibly be of any interest to you?"

"Because I've seen your mother." Harper decided to lay it out there. "You said before that you always thought this house was haunted. That's why you didn't like it. I'm betting your husband didn't like the fact that you gave the house to Byron before it was necessary. I'm not going to pretend I'm not curious about that, but it's really none of my business.

"What I'm more interested in is the ghosts," she continued, opting for honesty. "Your mother is most definitely here. I've seen her twice now. The first time was down by the cemetery. The second was in the library last night. She had two other women with her, both in dated dresses. None of them spoke."

Evangeline worked her jaw. "Why are you telling me this?" she asked finally, her voice raspy. There was a hint of anger that couldn't be ignored. "What's your angle?"

"I don't have an angle. My only angle is wanting to find Jennifer. I went to school with her. You know that, right?"

"So? It's not as if you were friends. She always liked you, but you were all about your friend Zander. When you actually could've helped, you were too busy to be bothered."

Harper found the statement odd. "She talked about me back then?"

An emotion Harper couldn't identify flitted across Evangeline's features and then it was quickly shut down into polite disinterest.

"I don't believe in ghosts," Evangeline volunteered. "I know what I said, but I was a child then. I only believed in ghosts because of the constant fog and the fact that the house looked like a castle. I remembered reading stories about haunted castles when I was a kid and my mother fed my imagination."

"It's good to have a parent who feeds your imagination," Harper offered, earnest. "My mother never fed my imagination. In fact, she was often embarrassed by what I could do. My father was better. He didn't give me as much grief as she did. He wasn't easy either, though.

"My grandfather was the one who fueled my imagination," she continued. "He was the first ghost I ever saw. After he died, he came to visit me."

Despite herself, Evangeline was intrigued. "What did he say?"

"Just that he loved me, that I was going to be okay, and he didn't want me to be afraid. He said he was leaving much sooner than he envisioned and there were things he wanted to tell me. It wasn't until I was much older that I realized what those things were."

"Was he like you?"

Harper nodded. "Yeah. Maybe you are, too. Have you ever considered that you thought this house was haunted because you're sensitive to certain things?"

"Ghosts aren't real."

"I think you're just saying that because George says it. He's a real jerk, by the way. You could do much better."

"He's ... the father of my son."

Harper understood what Evangeline wasn't saying. "Your son is grown and he's saddled himself with a loveless marriage, too. It must have been difficult for you. His first marriage was probably more than you could've hoped for. He loved her and it sounds like she was a wonderful person. His second wife, however, was the exact opposite."

Evangeline's expression turned dark. "Madeline was a mistake."

"I have no doubt. She's still missing, though, and I'm bothered about the fact that no one seems to care about her. You might not like her as a person, but she's still a human being. What if something happened to her?"

"Nothing happened to her. She's just looking for attention."

That seemed to be the Jessup family mantra. "You've kept an eye on her since she married Byron. I know it. Is she involved with someone else?"

Whatever question she was expecting, that wasn't it. Evangeline immediately started shaking her head. She was too fast, though. Harper realized she was on to something within a split second.

"She is seeing someone, isn't she?"

"I don't know what you're talking about," Evangeline lied. "I ... ." Whatever she was going to say died on her lips when Bates appeared at the door to announce breakfast was ready.

"Wait." Harper tried to grab the woman's arm, but she was too fast. She was out of the parlor before Harper could drag the answers she was looking for from her clenched lips.

"What was that?" Zander asked, appearing at his friend's side. "That looked intense."

"It's not finished, is what it is." Harper's annoyance was on full display. "We're nowhere near done. I think I'm going to need a ghost to help me with this one, though."

"That sounds intriguing."

Harper could only hope it would turn out fruitful as well.

SIXTEEN

Harper couldn't shake the feeling that Evangeline was the key to figuring things out ... at least as far as Madeline was concerned. The woman was clearly hiding something. But what?

"You look agitated," Jared noted as he wiped the corners of his mouth after breakfast. "I'm the one who should be agitated. I mean ... I had to spend thirty minutes with George and his gun collection. No one has suffered like me."

Despite the deep thoughts threatening to bury her, Harper couldn't stop herself from smiling. "I'll make it up to you later in a very fun and inventive way. I promise. I might need you to do it again, though."

Jared frowned. "Why would you need me to do it again? I figured you got what you needed."

"Not even close."

"And what are you looking for again?"

"Information," Harper replied simply.

"And you think Evangeline has it?"

"On Madeline? Absolutely. She said she never liked this house because she thought it was haunted. She's right. It is haunted. There are three ghosts running around, maybe more. None of them are Jennifer as far as I can tell, though."

"I don't understand what you're getting at," Jared pressed. "We're here because of Jennifer."

"But Madeline is missing, too. Have you heard from Mel?"

Jared scowled as he shook his head. "As a matter of fact, I haven't. He said he would be in touch as soon as he had information. That was last night, though."

Harper nodded absently. "I doubt she's with her parents. If she's with anyone, it's someone else."

"You mean like a boyfriend. Listen, we had this talk already. I'm right there with you. I think it's likely she has a boyfriend. We need to figure out where she met this guy ... and how they manage to interact."

"And what their overall plan is," Harper added. "Byron isn't going to rip up that pre-nup. Madeline cannot inherit unless he does. Byron's money will be split between Jennifer's estate and Richard. Madeline is fresh out."

"Which brings up an interesting theory," Jared noted, his eyes traveling across the room, to where Richard chatted with Bertie and laughed gregariously, as if he didn't have a care in the world. "I wonder how Richard feels about half his father's money being left to a ghost."

Harper followed his gaze, surprised. "I never really thought about that. Still ... half Byron's money is more than enough to live on comfortably for the rest of his life."

"Greed is a funny thing. What would be more than enough for some people isn't even close to enough for others."

He had a point, Harper mused. "Maybe he's the one having the affair with Madeline." It was an off-the-cuff remark but it caught Jared's full attention. "Maybe they joined forces to get all the money."

"You know ... ." Jared rubbed his chin.

"You're going to say that's a good idea, aren't you?" Harper scowled before he answered. "That's a gross idea."

"It's a gross idea, but it's not out of the realm of possibility. I think it's feasible that you're right. Richard would be the more appropriate age. Maybe they joined together back when they were kids and launched a plan to get all of Byron's money, including Jennifer's half. Maybe they killed her, but something went wrong and nobody found the body. Maybe seducing Byron was always part of it and they really did think they could get him to back down on the pre-nup."

Harper was chilled by the notion. "I don't know. That's really out there."

"It is," Jared agreed. "It makes as much sense as anything else we've come up with, though."

"Yeah, well ... ." She shook her head. She couldn't dwell on it. "I need your help on something before you start digging on that theory."

He adopted an innocent expression. "What makes you think I'm going to start digging on that theory?"

"Because your eyes light up when you have a new angle to work. I know because the same thing happens to me. We're very similar that way."

"We are," he agreed, squeezing her hand. "You said you had a favor you wanted me to do for you before I chase my angle, though. You need me to do something so you can chase your angle."

"I definitely do. You might not like it, though."

"Try me."

"Okay ... but it's going to involve breaking the law."

His smile widened. "That sounds intriguing. What do you have in mind?"

JARED WAS SURPRISINGLY FINE helping Harper break into the attic room. He didn't put up more than a token fight. He even had the proper tools on him for the job, which made Harper wonder if he knew she would ask before she did.

"You're awfully prepared," she noted as she kept a lookout in the hallway.

He laughed at her impish expression. "I'm a Boy Scout. That's the motto, right?"

"You're ... something." The sound of the lock clicking caused her heart to skip a beat. "Are we in?"

He nodded without hesitation. "We're in. Hold up." He grabbed her arm before she could push past him. "Just ... let me go first, huh?"

She furrowed her brow. "What do you think is in there?"

"Probably nothing but old sewing stuff ... like needles and ... yarn ... or stuff. What do people sew with?"

She grinned. "You're such a man."

"Luckily that works out well because you're such a woman." He gave her a quick kiss and then turned back to the door. "Stay behind me, okay?"

"Nothing is going to jump out at you," Harper promised. "No one has been in there for fifty years."

"So they say."

She stilled. She hadn't really considered that they'd been lying, not even deep down. "You don't think there's a body or two in there, do you?" She swallowed hard at the notion.

He hated the way her excitement diminished. "I think that's unlikely. Still, you are the love of my life. I want to make sure the room is safe for you to be in."

"Fair enough."

There were stairs on the other side of the door. There was no light in the stairwell, though, which Jared found frustrating. He used his cell phone for a bit of light and started up the stairs. He could hear Harper behind him but remained focused on the path ahead. When they reached the top, he was relieved to find a light fixture. He wasn't certain a lightbulb had survived in the attic for fifty years and would remain usable, but he was happy to find that some things were made to last ... including, apparently, lightbulbs.

The room was cozy, which he found surprising. It was dusty, signifying it had been empty for a very long time. Before being closed up, though, it was obvious someone had loved the space ... and spent a lot of time hanging out in the room.

"What is this?" He moved closer to an antique table that had an odd piece of machinery perched on it.

"Oh, look at that." Harper wasn't the domestic sort but she recognized an antique sewing machine. "It doesn't even run on electricity. It's one of the old pump pedal kinds. This is probably worth some money."

Jared arched an eyebrow. "You still haven't told me what it is."

"It's a sewing machine."

He cocked his head sideways. "Get out."

"No, it's true." Harper ran her hands over a faded settee. "Obviously Beatrice loved it up here. This must've been her favorite place in the house."

"It was," a new voice called out, catching both Jared and Harper by surprise.

Jared, protective as always, swung out a hand to keep Harper behind him in case some sort of attack was imminent. Since Evangeline was the only one standing at the top of the steps, though, he allowed himself to relax ... although only marginally.

"How did you get in here?" she asked, her eyes on the shelf resting against the wall. There were framed photographs all over it.

"Jared is very good with locks," Harper replied automatically.

"I picked the lock," he corrected, shooting her a quelling look when it appeared she might argue. "Harper was determined to get up here. She's convinced she'll be able to find your mother in this room."

"I see." Evangeline looked lost as she glanced around the dusty setting. "When I was a little girl, I was only allowed in here if I knocked and promised to be quiet. My mother insisted on those two rules ... but she let me play up here as much as I wanted because she knew the rest of the house bothered me."

"You see ghosts, don't you?" Harper was convinced it was true. There was something about Evangeline that felt familiar to her ... like she was looking at herself.

"It would probably be easier for you if I said yes, huh?" Evangeline's gaze was sympathetic. "I don't, though. I do, occasionally, hear things. That's what happened when I was a child. I heard Belle and Dorothy after they died and my father was convinced I should be locked up."

Harper stilled. "Who are Belle and Dorothy?"

Jared felt as if he was intruding on what should be a private conversation but he didn't make a move to leave. He wasn't comfortable abandoning Harper in the long-forgotten room with a woman who seemed to be struggling. For now, he was content sitting back and allowing Harper to run the show.

"Belle and Dorothy were my mother's servants, for lack of a better word." Evangeline was rueful. "They were more than that, though. They did things for her, cleaned and cooked. They were her confidants, too. My father wasn't the easiest man to get along with."

Harper was alarmed at the way she said it. "Abusive?"

"Verbally, yes. He wasn't physically abusive unless he took to drinking. Thankfully, out on an island like this, it's not as if you can just run to the corner store for a bottle. My mother became clever about making sure there was no alcohol in the house. My father would bring some home with him occasionally – and some of the male staff members supplied him with bottles – but that usually meant only one night of him being ... horrible ... and then he was back on the wagon for a few weeks. It wasn't perfect, but it was tolerable."

"I'm sorry you had to live like that." Harper opted for sincerity. "What happened to Belle and Dorothy?"

"There was a fire in the storage shed around back. I still don't know how it happened. It wasn't a very big shed. They were somehow trapped when they went back to get something ... and they never got out. My mother was devastated and she never got over it. I loved them, too. They were always kind to me, and after they passed, I kept thinking I heard them talking. My father thought I was crazy and my mother admonished me about what I said in front of him. The house frightened me after that, though."

Harper thought back to the spirits she saw with Beatrice. "Can I describe two women to you?"

Evangeline nodded.

"One looks to be in her fifties, hair that was probably blond but could've been the early signs of gray, too. Very friendly green eyes. She wore a fitted brown dress that probably required a corset."

Evangeline made a strangled choking sound. "That sounds just like Dorothy. My mother always made fun of her for the corsets, but she was determined a proper lady always wore a corset. Thankfully my mother disagreed. How did you know?"

"I saw her with your mother in the library. The other woman, she was smaller. She had very long, very black hair and blue eyes. She was striking, but tiny. She also had two fingers on her right hand that jutted out at an odd angle."

Evangeline took a purposeful step toward Harper. "That's Belle. Are you saying you've seen them?"

Harper nodded. "They're still here. They're with your mother. I tried talking to your mother when I saw her down at the cemetery, but she was afraid. She didn't say much."

"You actually talked to her?" Evangeline's expression turned to marvel. "I can't believe you really saw her."

"I did. The thing is, most souls don't stay behind unless they had a traumatic death. I can see why Belle and Dorothy stayed behind. They died in a fire ... that kind of sounds suspicious."

Evangeline jerked up her head. "What do you mean?"

"It was a storage building," Jared interjected. "How could they die in a small building like that and not be able to escape? It doesn't make a lot of sense."

"You think someone killed them?"

He shrugged. "I don't know. That would be my guess. It was a long time ago. Even if someone did kill them, there's probably no one left to punish. Did anyone dislike them?"

"Just my father." Evangeline clenched her jaw. "I'm sure he arranged it. He didn't like that my mother was so close with them."

"What about your mother?" Harper prodded. "Are you sure she died peacefully in her bed?"

"I ... ." Evangeline tilted her head to the side. "I'm not certain about anything right now. This is all so much."

"I'm sure it is." Harper slid her eyes to the left when she caught a hint of movement out of the corner of her eye. Sure enough, Beatrice and her ghostly friends had joined the party and were listening intently. "Your mother is here now. So are Dorothy and Belle. Maybe ... maybe you should try talking to them."

Evangeline was clearly taken aback by the suggestion. "Talk to them? But ... how?"

"They can hear you. They're listening right now. Maybe you can hear them again, like you could when you were a kid, if you spend some time with them. I'm not telling you what to do with your gift, but it seems a shame not to at least try to communicate."

Evangeline remained uncertain. "But ... what if I'm crazy and they're not really there?"

"Then we'll be crazy together." Harper made up her mind on the spot and sat in the middle of the floor. She motioned for the ghosts to move closer, which they did. Jared looked at the spot she indicated but could see nothing. He had faith that she was the most gifted person he'd ever met, though, so he sat on the floor next to her and grabbed her hand.

"Come on, Evangeline," he prodded. "I think we should do this as a group."

Evangeline, quite simply, looked amazed. "Why do you want to help me?"

"Because Harper does," he replied simply. "She doesn't do anything without having a good reason. She's giving of her time and heart and if she feels this is important, I'm right there with her."

Evangeline still wasn't convinced. "Why do you think this is important? I really want to know."

"Because I think this is a family with a lot of secrets," Harper replied simply. "I think something happened to your mother ... and I think something happened to Jennifer. Quite frankly, I'm not sure something didn't happen to Madeline either, despite what everyone keeps saying. One of those mysteries is important to me because I can't help feeling I failed Jennifer in school. I think all those mysteries are important to you."

"Not all," Evangeline countered, lowering herself to the ground. "I honestly don't care what happened to Madeline. I mean ... I don't want her dead or anything, but if she were to take off and never return it would be better for this family."

Harper was intrigued by the statement, but she knew better than pushing Evangeline. The woman had information to share. She simply needed a push from beyond the grave to get her to the place she needed to be to share it.

Harper had decided on patience. She could only hope things would work out how she envisioned, because otherwise, they were right back where they started.

SEVENTEEN

Jared had never participated in something quite as extraordinary as the reunion of a mother and daughter decades after they were separated. He marveled at Harper's poise as she helped Evangeline open herself up and communicate.

And then, out of nowhere, he silently acquiesced when Harper grabbed his hand and dragged him from the center of the room. He opened his mouth to argue, but Harper very firmly shook her head, not speaking until she was at the top of the stairs and then addressing the room in an airy fashion.

"I'm going to leave you to it for a bit, Evangeline. I'm sure you and your mother want some privacy."

Evangeline seemed surprised when she realized Harper and Jared were no longer sitting next to her. "Oh, um ... thank you." Tears were rolling down her cheeks and she seemed so happy that Jared felt a tug on his exposed heartstrings.

"I'll talk to you at dinner," Harper offered, keeping a firm hold on Jared's hand. "Have a good reunion with your mother." She tugged him until they were halfway down the stairs and then slowed. "I know you're confused," she started.

"I am confused," he confirmed. "I thought you wanted to talk to her about Jennifer ... although I'm not convinced she can help on that front."

"She *can* help." Harper was certain of that. "I think she's always been the answer to that question."

Jared cocked a dubious eyebrow. "You think she killed Jennifer."

Harper shook her head. "No. I think she knows what happened to her granddaughter, though."

"Why do you think that?"

That was a good question and Harper didn't know how to answer. "I don't know. It's just ... I saw something in her that's hard to explain. It's honestly not important right now. The most important thing right now is that Evangeline feels comfortable giving me the answers."

"Because you're absolutely certain she has them."

"I feel quite confident she has them," Harper clarified. "I don't *know* anything. I feel many things. This house ... when Evangeline said this house was haunted, she was right. It's more than just ghosts, though. It's haunted by a family that lost its way. Evangeline is the only one who sees that. She's the one who gave up the house. The rest of them consider it a status symbol."

Jared furrowed his brow. "I don't understand."

"That's because you've been watching from a different perspective than me. I've been watching the family. You've been looking for clues."

"And you think that was wrong?"

"I think that clarification comes best when watching the players," she countered. "The people in this house aren't even playing the same game."

Jared held her gaze for a long time. "You're not going to tell me what you suspect, are you?"

Harper shook her head. "Not yet. I'm not ready. We need to check some things when we get back to the guesthouse."

"What things?"

"I'll tell you when we get there. As for Evangeline, she's going to be more open to helping in a few hours. I guarantee it."

"How can you be sure?"

"How would you feel if we were separated for fifty years and then suddenly we got to spend a few hours talking?"

She was smiling, but he couldn't match her expression. "Heart, it would be best if you didn't say things like that. The idea of living without you for fifty years ... ."

"Okay. Maybe that was the wrong comparison." She held her hands up in capitulation. "We're planning a life together. I'm not supposed to die a significant amount of time before you."

"You're not," he agreed. "In fact, I demand that I either go first or we go together."

"Like *The Notebook?*"

He grinned. "Maybe. I don't care if you think it's schmaltzy."

"I'm fine with the schmaltz. The thing is, you need to stop thinking of death as an ending. Just because we die, that doesn't mean we don't go on. I've told you about what I see when I use the dreamcatcher, right?"

"Yeah." His fingers were a gentle kiss against her cheek. He felt the need to touch her. Talk of separation gave him anxiety he didn't even know he was capable of before they met. "You said it's a beautiful place, warm and inviting. That doesn't change the fact that I don't want to go there for a long time ... and I want us to be together when it happens."

"I want that, too." Harper wrapped her fingers around his wrist to reassure him. "There are no guarantees in life, though. At least ... not the sort you want. I can guarantee that I want to spend the rest of my life with you. I can guarantee I see wonderful things for our future.

"I can also guarantee that, if something terrible happens and we're separated, I'll be waiting for you on the other side," she continued. "I'll want you to be happy, even if it's without me. When we reunite, it will be like no time has passed ... just like with Evangeline and her mother."

He frowned. "No. I don't want that."

"Jared ... ." She was starting to feel exasperated. "You can't control everything. It's important to me that you know I love you. Don't sleepwalk through life if something happens. Don't be Byron. Life is meant to be lived."

"I know you mean well by saying stuff like this but ... I don't like it and I don't happen to agree. If something happens to you, I'm going to turn into a bitter man who wallows. I'm going to sit in a chair and pout for the rest of my life. No joke. That's what's going to happen."

Harper let loose a sigh, the sound long and drawn out. "You mean you're going to punish me."

He balked. "Not punish you. Why would I punish you for something you can't control?"

"I don't know. That's what you would be doing, though. You wouldn't be helping anything."

"See, I think you're the one with the control problem," he countered. "You want me to feel something I'm incapable of feeling. Once my sunshine is gone, I won't be happy. You can't change that."

She rolled her eyes. "Okay, that was taking it a step too far."

He laughed despite the serious conversation. "You know, I realized that the minute I said it. I couldn't take it back, though, so I decided to roll with it."

"I don't want you being afraid of death. We're going to be together on the other side. Have faith."

"I have faith we're going to be together." He honestly didn't doubt that. "I can't be happy without you, though. It's not going to happen so I want you to stop trying to convince me otherwise. I know what I'm capable of and I'm not capable of that."

Her heart ached at his earnest expression. "Fine." She threw up her hands in defeat. "I guess I'll just have to live forever so I'm assured you're okay, huh?"

He broke out in a wide grin and grabbed her around the waist. "Now you're talking. That's exactly what I want." He smacked a loud kiss on her lips before she could complain and then pulled back suddenly when he heard an odd noise at the bottom of the stairs.

"Don't stop now," Harper groused, reaching for him so they could continue kissing. "We're not done making up."

Jared kept a firm grip on her waist, but his eyes were on the bottom of the stairs. "We weren't fighting — just for the record — but I'm fine with making up when we get back to the guesthouse."

"Then let's do that." Harper started for the bottom of the stairs, but Jared held out his hand to still her. "What?" Her forehead wrinkled. "Is something wrong?"

"I heard something." He looked at her long enough to convey a message — *don't go racing into trouble* — and then descended the stairs on soft feet. He barely made any noise. When he reached the door, which felt as if he'd opened it hours before rather than minutes, he took a moment to scan the corridor. He couldn't shake the feeling that someone had been watching them ... or at the very least, listening.

"Anything?" Harper asked, appearing behind him.

He cast her a quelling look as he glanced over his shoulder. "I told you to stay where you were."

"You did not."

"I did so."

"Um, no. I'm pretty sure I would've heard that if you said it."

"I said it with my eyes."

"Then your eyes need to be more direct because that's not what I heard."

He held her gaze for a long beat and then sighed. There really was no sense in arguing with her. She was too cute to stay angry with. "I guess we'll have to practice our non-verbal communication."

"I thought that's what we were going to do at the guesthouse."

"Good point." He gave her a quick kiss before linking his fingers with hers and pulling her out the door. He was anxious to head back to the guesthouse, but he couldn't dislodge the earlier feeling that someone had been watching. "Evangeline will be safe here, right?"

Harper bobbed her head. "Why wouldn't she be? That's her mother."

"That's not really what I meant."

Harper finally caught on to the change in his demeanor. "You think someone was listening to us."

He nodded without hesitation. "I do."

Harper ran the conversation they'd been having through her mind. "Then they're going to think we're the schmaltz twins. We weren't talking about anything serious."

That was the way Jared remembered it, too. He was still worried. "Let's just get out of here, huh? I could use a few hours of downtime. This is our last night here. I'm guessing that means the Jessups are going to pull out all the theatrics."

That was exactly what Harper was hoping for. "If we're lucky."

He graced her with a soft smile. "I thought we were going to make our own luck."

"Good point. Let's do that."

They were still laughing when they hit the end of the hallway, in their own little world. That's why neither of them noticed the shadow hiding in the corner of an alcove, an unhappy face making an entirely different plan.

It was definitely going to be an interesting night.

JARED AND HARPER SPENT WHAT they jokingly referred to as "quality time" together before climbing into comfortable clothes and hitting the research in bed.

"Don't fall asleep," Harper warned as she propped her laptop on a pillow and situated herself in the crook of his arm. "We really do have research."

"You're such a taskmaster," he teased, brushing his lips against her cheek. Honestly, he could've fallen asleep. He was feeling satiated, warm, and happy. That was the perfect combination for an extended nap. He recognized Harper wasn't going to allow that to happen, though, so he was resigned to his fate. "What are we researching?"

"For starters, I want more information on our purported psychics. I know that Molly, Eric, and Zander recognized them, but I would like some background information."

"Because you think they're involved with Jennifer's disappearance?"

"There are two separate cases here," Harper argued. "You keep forgetting that."

"I haven't forgotten. And, technically, if you include the deaths of Beatrice, Dorothy, and Belle, we're dealing with a lot more deaths."

"Yeah, I've been thinking about that, too." Harper thoughtfully tapped her chin as she took on a far-off expression. "I think it's obvious that

Dorothy and Belle didn't die by accident. That's why they're still hanging around."

"I would agree. I don't think there's any retribution to get for them, though. That happened a really long time ago."

"I don't think they want revenge. I think they stayed for Beatrice."

"Why?"

"Because ... well ... sometimes there are different sorts of soul mates. I think Dorothy and Belle were her soul mates ... just not in a romantic way."

"Kind of like how you have two soul mates, Zander and me."

Harper cocked an eyebrow. This was the sort of conversation that shriveled her innards and made her queasy. "I don't know that we should talk about this," she hedged.

Jared chuckled. "Oh, look how uncomfortable you are," he teased, tickling her ribs. He seemed to be enjoying himself, which was a great relief to Harper. There were times Zander's and Jared's insistence on poking one another gave her indigestion.

"Harper, I'm well aware that you're tied to Zander in ways that I won't ever be able to touch," he noted. "It's okay. I don't expect you to suddenly stop loving him. Besides, he makes you happy. If something ever happens to me, I'm thrilled you'll have him. I honestly love him, too. There are simply times I also want to strangle him."

Harper laughed, as he'd intended ... and then turned serious. "How come you can talk about things like that and I can't?"

"Because you're stronger than I am and can take it."

"That's complete and total nonsense."

"Maybe," he conceded. "I'm a police officer, though."

"And I hunt the dead for a living."

"Yeah, but ... going down in the line of duty is always going to be a risk for me. You need to live forever."

Harper barked out a laugh. "That doesn't seem very balanced."

"Hey, I didn't ever claim to be a balanced guy. I want what I want when I want it ... and I want you safe forever. That's simply the way it is."

The sigh she let loose was exasperated. "I think we need to stop talking about this for the time being. We're doing nothing but circling and it's keeping us from our goal."

"True story." He poked her stomach. "Let's talk about your psychics. Why are you worried about them?"

"Because they're going to be a part of whatever goes down tonight."

"And what do you think that is?" Jared was genuinely curious. "You're acting strange, as if you're lining up something important. I don't understand."

"I don't expect you to. In fact, I'm not sure if I understand it either. It's a feeling." She tapped the spot above her heart. "Something is going to happen."

"Regarding Jennifer or Madeline?"

"I don't know. Maybe both."

"Let me ask you something." Jared searched for the right words to phrase his question. "Do you think that Madeline's disappearance has anything to do with what happened to Jennifer?"

"Yes."

His eyebrows flew up at her easy answer. "You do? Should I have Mel get the state police out here?"

"I don't know." Harper was taken aback by the question. "I haven't really thought about it. Do you think you need to do that?"

It was a simple question, but it frustrated Jared to no end. "Heart, I'm asking you. You're the one who seems to think you've got this all figured out."

"Oh, you misunderstand. I don't think I've got it all figured out. I simply think the answers are coming tonight."

"Why?"

"Because it's time."

He kind of wanted to shake her over the vague answer. "Harper ... ."

"I don't have the answers you're looking for," she insisted, cutting him off. "Something is going to happen tonight, though. I have no doubt about that."

"Is Evangeline going to be part of this something?"

"Most definitely."

"What about the others?"

Harper tilted her head to the side, considering. "Like I said, I think the Jessup family has a lot of secrets. It's only a matter of time until those secrets come spilling out."

"You're being purposely mysterious."

"I am." She grinned. "That's half the fun."

"I think I have to be done talking to you for a little bit," he admitted on a sigh. "I still love you — that will never change — but you really are on my last nerve with the way you're acting. I can't pretend I condone it or understand it."

"Fair enough. We can conduct research in silence."

"Fine." He threw up his hands. "I expect you to answer every single question I have when this is over with, though. I'm not kidding."

"I would expect nothing less."

EIGHTEEN

W hen the invitation for dinner came it insisted on formal dinner wear. Harper wasn't really surprised. When the initial instruction sheet was delivered — by Byron himself — one formal outfit was listed. She knew a big dinner would eventually be part of the festivities. It made sense that Byron would want to embrace the pomp and circumstance of the occasion on their last night together.

"I hate dressing up," Jared complained as he fumbled with his tie in the bathroom mirror.

He might hate it, but Harper happened to adore the way he looked in a suit. "Oh, come on." She slid between him and the bathroom counter so she could help. "You look ridiculously handsome."

He met her sea-blue eyes and smiled. "I look like a guy in a suit. You look like every dream I've ever had about you." He admired her long legs in the skirt as she attacked his tie with determination. "You know when I said you were the prettiest woman I ever met in real life?"

She nodded.

"I meant it."

She fumbled the tie slightly and then smiled. "You really are charming when you want to be."

"I know."

She laughed. "I thought you were angry at me. Isn't that why we had a really awkward research session this afternoon?"

"I happen to think that was the best research session ever. It was warm ... quiet ... and we were naked in bed. How could I not enjoy that?"

Harper snickered. "Good point. It was the best research session ever. We also got important information."

On that, Jared wasn't sure they could agree. "Harper, I don't think the information you found is nearly as interesting as you do."

"That's because you're looking at it the wrong way."

"No, I'm looking at it the same way you are. You simply have no proof of what you've convinced yourself is true."

"That's what's going to happen tonight. We're going to find proof."

"If you say so. I ... ." Jared trailed off and stared at his tie, which now looked perfect. "How did you manage that while I was so distracted?"

"I'm a great multitasker."

"You're ... something." He gave his tie another look and then focused his full attention on Harper. "I know you expect big things from this dinner. What are you going to do if they don't happen? You're basing a lot of your assumptions on faith — which I'm fine with — but I want to make sure you aren't disappointed if none of these things actually occur."

"They're going to happen."

She sounded so sure of herself there was nothing Jared could do but sigh. "Fine. They're going to happen." He held up his hands and shook his head. "Frankly, I just want this to be over with. I'm ready to go home and resume our normally scheduled lives."

"Me, too." Harper planted a soft kiss at the corner of his mouth, using a tissue to remove the lipstick she left behind when she was done. "I know you think I'm acting weird. I'm not trying to be difficult. I can't explain why I feel the way I do. It's simply something I can't hide from."

He was careful as he stroked his hand down the back of her head. He didn't want to mess up her hair. She spent twenty minutes fiddling with it, something she rarely did. "Harper, you're the most amazing person I know. You're special in ways I didn't even know existed until I met you.

"I have every faith that you know what you're doing," he continued, realizing as he progressed that he really meant it. He thought he had doubts, but he realized now that he had total faith in her. "I know you're going to get your answers tonight."

"Yeah." She threw her arms around his neck and hugged him. "I think we're going to get a lot of answers tonight."

He didn't know what to make of that proclamation but, ultimately, he knew it didn't matter. "It's going to be an interesting night."

"You can say that again. I just wonder how many people actually realize how interesting it really is going to be."

Another riddle, Jared internally mused. She really was all over the place. The thing he hoped most is that she found the relief she needed to progress. That really was the most important thing to him.

She pulled back and offered him a pretty smile. "Are you ready?"

He nodded. "Yup. I hope we at least get some good eats at this thing ... since it will probably be our last meal here."

Harper's grin widened. "Only a man would think with his stomach at a time like this."

"I'm practical."

"Well ... I don't think you have to worry about the food. I'm betting they pull out all the stops."

"Because ... ?"

"Because this dinner was always the ultimate plan. Byron knew when he was setting things up that tonight would be the most important night."

Jared was flustered. "How do you know that?"

"Just trust me. I finally understand what he was doing. It's going to be an adventure. I promise you that."

Jared believed that with every fiber of his being, and it wasn't just the night he was convinced would be an adventure. Their entire lives would be an adventure, and he was looking forward to sharing every moment with her.

"Then let's do this. I'm ready."

"Me, too. I can't wait to see this all play out."

HARPER STROLLED THROUGH THE FRONT door of the Jessup mansion as if she owned the house. Jared trailed behind her, dumbfounded, and pulled up short so he could ask Zander the question that had been bothering him all day.

"Has she ever done something like this before?"

Zander didn't look nearly as worked up as Jared felt. Instead, the smile he shot in Harper's direction was indulgent. "Once or twice."

Jared waited for him to expand. When he didn't, he cleared his throat to prod him. "When was that? Oh, and it didn't come back to bite her, did it?"

Zander chuckled. "You know, there are times you really bug me."

Jared's expression was dry. "Thank you for telling me that ... and right now, when it's so important."

"Now is not one of those times," Zander offered. "Right now, I love you like a brother, man."

Jared rolled his eyes until they landed on Shawn. "Is he drunk already?"

Shawn looked legitimately amused. "Not last time I checked."

"I'm not drunk." Zander flicked Jared's ear, causing the detective to shoot him a dark glare. "I love you like a brother. Do you want to know why?"

"Probably not."

"I'm going to tell you anyway. You're wound tighter than a spring coil on a trampoline right now. It's not because you're anxious for answers or anything, though. It's because you want to make sure that Harper's ego doesn't get bruised. You want the best for her no matter what."

Jared found the leading edge of his agitation with Zander had not only dissipated but completely dissolved. "I love you like a brother, too."

Zander beamed.

"Not all the time, though," Jared stressed. "Only some of the time ... when you're not being a complete and total turd sandwich."

Shawn barked out a laugh as Zander rolled his eyes.

"As for Harper, I've seen her like this a few times." Zander voluntarily changed the subject. "People always said I had the bigger ego between us – which I'm sure is true – but there are times when she has an ego so big you could take a nap under it on a sunny day."

Jared's lips curved. "She's certain that everything is going to be magically fixed by the end of the night. I don't want her upset."

"Are you sure she expects things to be fixed?" Zander challenged. "From where I'm standing, I think it's far more likely that she thinks there are answers to be found. I very much doubt she thinks Jennifer's life is going to be fixed after the fact."

Jared rubbed his chin as he regarded his girlfriend, who was standing next to Harris and Delphine and seemed to be deep in conversation. It was the first time she'd willingly tried to talk to either of them. "I guess," he said finally. "She's certainly worked up, though."

Zander offered him a saucy wink. "I bet that will benefit you later."

"It already benefitted me this afternoon," Jared shot back, causing Zander to frown.

"Don't talk dirty about my best friend. Be respectful."

"You started it."

"I'm allowed because I've known her longer. You can't get away with stuff like that."

"Good to know."

BY THE TIME DINNER ROLLED around, Harper had managed to take a tour of each small group so she could converse with everyone ... whether she found them of interest or not. She was no longer smiling when she circled back to Jared and Zander.

"What's wrong?" Jared asked, instantly alert. "Did something happen?"

She slid her eyes to him, confused. "Why would you assume something bad happened?"

"Because you're no longer happy."

"Oh, that." She waved off his concern. "I was never really happy. I was excited. I'm still excited, don't get me wrong, but I'm a little nervous, too. I didn't think I would be."

"Nervous for what?" Jared felt like a broken record. He kept asking her the same question in a myriad of different ways and she kept putting him off. His temper was starting to fray.

"Soon." Harper squeezed his hand and nodded when Bates appeared in the doorway to announce dinner was served. "Showtime."

Jared dragged a restless hand through his hair as he followed her, shaking his head. He was relieved when he reached the table and found Harper had been seated next to him. Byron was on her right – a position he'd been claiming on a regular basis – and Harris and Bertie were across the table.

Jared and Byron both pulled out Harper's chair before she could sit, causing her to smile.

"Thank you. Such gallant gentlemen."

Jared managed to refrain from rolling his eyes, but just barely. "Sit down, Heart."

Byron chuckled as he took his seat, his eyes appreciative as he took in Harper's pretty dress and warm smile. "I'm glad you're here, my dear." He patted her hand. "I think the fact that you knew Jennifer makes this somehow ... easier."

Jared narrowed his eyes, suspicious. "Makes what easier?" he asked after a beat.

"What?" Byron recovered from whatever melancholy had momentarily overtook him and shook his head. "I was just talking to hear myself talk. I do that sometimes."

"I know a lot of people who do that," Harper offered. "My mother does it all the time."

"As does Zander," Jared added. Thankfully, Zander and Shawn were positioned at the other end of the table and couldn't hear the dig.

"How well did you know Jennifer?" Harris asked, grabbing a roll from the basket at the center of the table. Harper kept count over the appetizer hour in the parlor. He downed three drinks. Most people would be tipsy. Harris seemed relatively normal. "Were you close friends?"

"I wouldn't say we were close," Harper replied, unfolding her napkin and placing it gently in her lap. "We were certainly friendly. Zander was my best friend in high school – still is today – and we were kind of in our own little world. I wish I would've taken the time to talk to Jennifer. I think I might've been able to help her."

"Help her with what?" Harris was fixated on buttering his roll and didn't bother looking at Harper. If he'd taken the time, he would've seen the sly way the corners of her mouth turned up and been suspicious. "There was an accident in the woods. I already told you how she died. It's tragic, but she didn't suffer."

"I don't believe she suffered either," Harper offered, her gaze moving to the center of the table, to where Evangeline sat. The woman looked lighter, as if the weight of the world had been lifted from her shoulders. Her husband sat next to her, chattering away, and she paid him zero attention. Instead, she stared at nothing and smiled at everything.

"You believe she died in the woods, too?" Byron asked, his voice raspy. "I thought ... ."

"I don't believe she died in the woods," Harper countered quickly. "I don't think she's been here since the last time you saw her."

"What do you mean?"

"Of course she died in the woods," Harris snapped. "I told you I talked to her spirit."

"And I don't believe you." Harper was firm, pointed, before turning back to Byron. "I need to ask you something."

Byron nodded. "Of course. Whatever you wish to know, I will try to answer."

"Okay. Did you know your grandfather killed your grandmother's best friends in the storage shed?"

Whatever question he was expecting, that wasn't it. Byron let out a huge gasp, and there was nothing theatrical or fake about it. He was legitimately stunned. "What?"

"Their names were Dorothy and Belle." Harper barreled forward, barely taking a breath. "They somehow got locked in some storage shed behind the house and burned alive."

"What does that have to do with anything?" Harris challenged.

"I know the story," Byron interrupted. "They weren't murdered. There was some sort of tragic accident."

"I honestly don't think so." Harper saw no reason to lie. It was time to put her cards on the table. "Your grandmother was extremely close with them and your grandfather didn't like it."

"How do you know that?" Byron seemed legitimately curious.

"Because I spent some time with them this afternoon," Harper replied. "Not a lot, mind you, but a fair bit. They're hanging around with your grandmother."

Byron shifted in his chair. "Excuse me?"

"What is she saying?" George asked.

"She says Grandmother's ghost is still hanging around. I didn't realize that."

"Why would you realize that?" George challenged. "Ghosts aren't real. You set up this entire thing to prove something that can't be proven. You invited a bunch of crackpots here, Byron. You need to kick them out."

Byron ignored his father and held Harper's clear gaze. "Are you saying you talked with my grandmother?"

Harper nodded. "I did. What's more important is that your mother talked to her."

Byron snapped his eyes in Evangeline's direction. "Is that true?"

"Of course it's not true," George scoffed. "Ghosts aren't real."

Harper opened her mouth to yell at the man to shut up – she respected her elders, but she'd had her fill of George Jessup – but Evangeline handled the heavy lifting this go-around for her.

"George, if you can't say anything nice, then don't say anything at all," Evangeline snapped. "I'm in the middle of a conversation with my son. It has nothing to do with you and everything to do with me, so ... shut up."

George's eyes flashed with fury. He was in his seventies, but it was obvious he was ready to throw down. "Now you listen here ... ." He reached for his wife, but Jared was on his feet.

"If you put your hands on her, I will arrest you," Jared warned, his eyes flashing with ominous intent. "Keep your hands to yourself."

George appeared surprised to be addressed in such a manner. "I want you out of my house," he hissed.

"It's not your house, Dad," Byron shot back, rolling his neck as he glanced between faces. Finally, he focused on Harper. "I don't understand what you're trying to do here."

"I'm sure you don't," Harper replied, her hand automatically going to Jared's suit sleeve so he didn't crawl over the table to give George a piece of his mind. "I'm going to explain, though. Before that, I need to ask you one more time about Madeline. Are you sure you don't know where she is?"

Byron's face twisted. "Why do you keep asking me that? She's not here.

She takes off like this all the time. She's a complete idiot. She thinks that this is going to get me to change my mind and leave her everything in my will."

"I've told her I get everything, but she just won't let it go," Richard offered with a wink.

"Except you don't get everything," Harper countered, watching the younger man closely for a reaction. Instead of being upset, though, he seemed more amused.

"I will be inheriting more than I can ever spend," Richard replied. "I've tried to talk my father into donating a building in downtown Detroit – maybe an art studio for inner-city kids or something – but apparently he's going to let me decide what to do with my half of the money. I'm leaning toward that, in case you're interested."

He hadn't missed a beat, Harper realized. That answered one of her questions. "I think that sounds like a great idea. Leaving your mark on a community like that ... well ... it's great."

"It's a waste of money is what it is," George barked. "That's all the people in this family do is waste money."

"Since it's our money to waste, perhaps you should stuff it, George," Evangeline shot back. She was clearly at her limit with her husband. "In fact ... you should definitely stuff it." She took the roll that George was buttering and shoved it in his mouth. "I think we've all had more than enough of your mouth."

"Hear, hear." Zander lifted his hands in the air and applauded.

"Yes, Father. Now would be a good time for you to be quiet," Byron agreed. "Harper, you're upending dinner a bit. I would really like to know what's going on."

"And I would like to tell you. It's just ... ." She trailed off when Bates appeared in the open doorway and cleared his throat. The butler looked shockingly pale, which told Harper she'd been right on the money.

"What is it, Bates?" Byron feigned patience as he focused on his butler.

"Sir, there is a fresh vehicle in the driveway," Bates offered, his voice shaky.

"A fresh vehicle?" Byron's forehead wrinkled. "I don't understand. I didn't clear the ferry for anyone. How did someone get over in a vehicle?"

"I cleared the vehicle," Evangeline replied, her gaze landing on Harper. "I really am sorry for all of this, Byron. You'll never know how sorry. I did what I had to do, though."

"I don't understand." Frustration practically oozed out of Byron's pores. "What's going on? Who is outside?"

Harper rested her hand on his wrist to get his attention. "I think you're supposed to see this one for yourself. Don't worry. We'll all go with you – stopping us at this point would be a wasted effort – and we'll help you understand."

Byron was still beyond puzzled. "But ... who is it?"

Harper's smile was warm enough that it lit up her entire face. "It's Jennifer. I think you're going to want to answer the door yourself. Trust me on this one." With those words, she got to her feet and headed out of the room. "Come on, everybody. The main event is finally here."

Jared shook his head but hurried to catch up with her. "You and I are going to have a really long talk about secrets later."

She smiled benignly at him. "I'm looking forward to it."

NINETEEN

Jared had to scramble to catch up with Harper. She was tall, boasted long legs, and that meant she could stride with the best of them. She made a striking figure in the dress. He took a moment to admire her ... and then turned to business.

"I hope you know what you're doing," he muttered in a low voice.

"It's going to be okay," she reassured him. She didn't have to look over her shoulder to know everyone else was following. By the time she reached the foyer, she was almost shaking she was so excited. She still wasn't one-hundred-percent sure she was right. She was mostly sure ... but not totally certain. She was rewarded for her faith when she hit the parlor and found a striking woman standing beneath the chandelier.

"Jennifer."

The woman turned slowly and smiled when she caught a glimpse of the blonde. "Harper. You haven't changed a bit."

Harper couldn't say the same. "You're different. Only your eyes are the same."

Jennifer chuckled. "That's what happens when you're in hiding."

"Yeah, well ... welcome home." Harper smoothly stepped out of the way when she heard a gasp behind her.

Richard was the first to break through the milling crowd and he immediately stalked toward his sister. "What are you doing here?"

Jared narrowed his eyes as the siblings embraced. There was no weirdness between them, which made him suspicious. "You knew she was alive."

Richard took a moment to run his hand down the back of his sister's hair, probably to collect himself if Jared had to guess, and then nodded as he turned back. "I knew."

"You knew!" Byron's face was so red when he finally stepped to the fore-front of the group that Harper worried he was about to have a heart attack.

"You should sit down," she insisted, taking a step toward him.

Byron easily sidestepped her, pretended he didn't see her, and remained focused on his daughter. "I knew it." The statement was barely a whisper and then he recovered. "I knew it," he said more forcefully this time. "I knew you weren't dead."

"Which is why you set up this shindig, right?" Harper pressed. She was determined to find answers ... for everybody. "You hired those who communi-cate with the dead to prove she was alive. You wanted to force the issue by bringing together everyone – including your family – and then shoving us inside a pressure cooker."

Jennifer held her father's gaze a long time. They still hadn't embraced. Finally, she turned back to Harper. "I think the better question is, how did you know?"

"I didn't. Not fully. I had a feeling. This house has a lot of secrets ... and three souls that know all of them."

Jennifer furrowed her brow. "You're talking about the ghosts."

"Belle, Dorothy, and your great-grandmother," Harper confirmed. "They whisper if you listen ... constantly really ... and you listened. You're like your grandmother. You can hear them. That's why you tried to hang out with us in high school.

"I apologize for that, by the way," she continued, her mouth flapping away without any true direction. "I thought you glommed on to us because you felt like an outsider, too. I was too involved with my own stuff back then. I didn't realize ... any of it. I wish you would've told me, though."

"I was afraid to tell you," she admitted, rueful. "You were starting to make a name for yourself even back then. People said you could see ghosts, talk to them. I'd been hearing voices for a long time. I didn't tell anyone because I was afraid they would lock me up."

"Which is why your grandmother didn't tell anyone either," Harper surmised. "Her mother told people and it didn't end well for her ... or the people she told."

Jennifer's reaction was muted. "How did you figure that out?"

"I wasn't sure I had it completely right," Harper admitted. "I had a feeling ... and a few dreams. Then I started really thinking about things. I was angry at myself for never looking for you. That should've been one of the first things I did ... and yet it never even occurred to me.

"I know Zander and I were all about each other and shut out the rest of the world a bit when we were younger, but I like to think we weren't so self-absorbed that we would completely forget about you," she continued. "That's when I realized I didn't look because I never believed you were dead. Sure, that could've been wishful thinking, but I thought it was more."

"You were smart even then," Jennifer said on a laugh. It was obvious she was uncomfortable with the conversation. "When I heard from Richard that my father called you in, I figured it was probably time to come home. I didn't want you spending all your time looking for a person who wasn't really dead.

"I read about what happened with Quinn Jackson," she explained. "You spent years looking for him, right? That's what Richard said. You spent years looking for a man you thought was dead and sacrificed yourself in the process. Then he came back from the dead and almost killed you. It must be weird for you to know two people who came back from the dead, huh?"

"You were never dead. You disappeared."

"Most people believed I was dead."

"Only because they couldn't see beyond the money," Harper pointed out. "They thought you had no reason to run. I remember how sad you were ... and afraid. I wish I would've known why. Maybe then you wouldn't have gone into hiding."

"This is all lovely," George interjected, his tone rough. "I'm sure you can catch up later and pat each other on the backs for being so smart and great with your ghost stuff. That doesn't answer the question: Where have you been, young lady?"

Jennifer's lip curled as she regarded her grandfather. "It doesn't matter. You don't need to know."

To Harper, that was another confirmation. "Your grandfather is one of the reasons you left, isn't he?"

Jennifer nodded, visibly swallowing before turning to her father. "*One* of the reasons. The other was fear. I was afraid to tell my family what was going on. I thought they would judge me ... and then lock me up."

"Did your mother know?" Harper asked. "Did she know you heard things?"

Jennifer nodded. "She was trying to get me in to see someone when it happened. She told me not to say anything, that Dad ... and especially Grandpa ... wouldn't understand. She told me, if I was ever in trouble, to confide in Grandma.

"So, after Mom died and the voices got worse — they were always yelling at me, warning me to run away there at the end — I told Grandma what was happening and she decided the best thing to do was get me out of the house," she continued. "We came up with a plan. She arranged for a boat to pick me up on the south side of the island the night I left. I wasn't to tell anyone what was happening ... or take anything I held dear. My disappearance had to be a mystery because she was afraid that if it became public knowledge that I ran away that ... well ... they'd win."

"Who is they?" Zander asked automatically.

Harper shot him a quelling look and shook her head. "Let Jennifer tell her story in her own time."

Zander frowned at her. "That's easy for you to say. You've figured the bulk of this out. Some of us are still struggling to keep up."

Jennifer shot him a cheeky grin. "You're exactly like I remember you, the both of you. That makes me happy. I always thought you guys had the best relationship ... although I guess you guys never got married like I imagined you would in middle school."

"We don't roll that way," Zander replied. "We're life mates of a different sort."

"As well you should be," Jennifer enthused, her eyes briefly landing on Jared. "Besides, I think Harper has done well for herself. I've read about you in the newspaper, too, Detective Monroe. I'm glad you found each other. It's hard for people who are different. You seem to embrace those differences. That is the greatest gift you can ever give anyone."

"Thank you," Jared replied softly. "Harper is my gift, though."

"This is all lovely," George drawled, his eyes flashing. "I want answers!"

"Shut up, George," Evangeline snapped, moving around her husband and offering her granddaughter a warm hug. "Not everything happens on your schedule. In fact, this is happening because I'm no longer interested in your schedule ... or plans ... or the plots you've hatched over the past ten years. I'm done."

George's eyes flashed with malice. "What is that supposed to mean?"

"I think you're about to be in trouble," Harper replied for the older woman. "That's just a guess, though." She held Evangeline's gaze for a long beat. "You helped Jennifer escape because you understood about the voices. Even though you didn't want to admit what you were capable of, you understood ... and you wanted to help your granddaughter.

"You got her off the island that night and you funded her lifestyle to keep her hidden," she continued. "I don't know where you stashed her — and it's honestly not important to the story — but you hid her and then eventually brought Richard in on the plan. You knew, in case something happened to you, that Jennifer would need a touchstone. That's when he was involved."

"How did you figure all this out?" Richard asked, legitimately awed. "We thought we were being so careful."

"I don't understand any of this," Byron muttered, rubbing his forehead. "How could you keep this from me?"

Richard ignored his father's outburst. "I've known for about five years. Grandmother approached me, told me what happened, and I wanted to help. I insisted on seeing Jennifer with my own eyes, though. I visited her on the ranch where she lives and spent an entire month learning about her new life and hearing about the old one we shared ... and realizing that she was in very real peril. When I came back, I started working the angles. I knew what had to be done, but it wasn't as easy as you might think."

"What peril?" George snapped, earning a dark glare from his grandson.

"You're going to want to be quiet," Richard warned. "No, I'm being serious. You have done enough to this family and I'm not going to put up with you for another second. I don't have to. We're taking back this family, and you're not going to be part of it."

Byron was even more bewildered than before. "I don't understand!" He practically bellowed the words. "Someone needs to tell me what's going on right now!"

Jennifer took an uncertain step toward him. "I didn't want to hurt you. Believe it or not, that was the last thing I wanted to do. I had to make a choice, though, and I wasn't sure you were in on it after Mom."

Byron furrowed his brow. "I don't understand."

"Her accident wasn't really an accident," Richard volunteered. "The brakes on her car were tampered with. She was killed."

Byron made a protesting sound. "But ... no. I would know if that were the case."

"It's the truth." Richard was firm. "Mom knew about Jennifer's ability. She was trying to protect her, was making moves to make sure nothing could happen to her, and *Grandfather* found out."

Richard's demeanor had Jared moving closer to the older man. He didn't insert himself in the conversation, but he was obviously ready to step in should something terrible go down.

"Who found out about what?" George adopted an innocent expression that was so saccharine it threatened to rot Harper's teeth. "Are you talking about me?"

"You've been involved in all of it from the start," Harper supplied, opting to get to the heart of matters. "You were a stable worker on the grounds when you were a teenager. I found an article about you online today, a piece you did for a local magazine where you talked about how your life changed. You were trapped outside looking in. Evangeline's mother was special ... and her father was a drunk.

"Evangeline said that her mother tried to outsmart him with the alcohol and keep it off the island," she continued. "A stable boy helped him get alcohol from time to time. The husband was an angry man and thought Belle and Dorothy were filling Beatrice's head with nonsense. To combat that, he killed them in the shed ... and you helped."

George's eyes flew up his forehead. "You can't prove that."

"Actually, we can," Richard countered. "We've been working on this for ten years. We tracked down people who worked on the island back then. They made specific statements. Sure, you helped with the fire on orders from Great-Grandfather, but you were still part of it. Then, later, when it came time for Great-Grandmother to die, you were involved in that, too."

Evangeline looked impressed. "My mother just told me about that thanks to you. I finally gave up the fear and embraced what I can do — what Jennifer can do — and I spent a wonderful afternoon with my mother and two women who were near and dear to me. I can't thank you enough."

"You don't owe me anything." Harper felt distinctly uncomfortable with the woman's gratitude. "Seriously. I was happy to help."

"I'm still in the dark," Jared prodded. "George obviously had a hand in multiple deaths. I have no doubt about that. What did he have to do with Jennifer's disappearance?"

"May I?" Harper asked.

Evangeline's lips quirked. "I think you've earned it."

"George managed to weasel his way into the family despite being an hourly worker," Harper explained. "He had ambitions ... and they revolved around this house. He had to work the grounds and dreamed of being master of this domain ... and he was, but only for a short time.

"Evangeline's father was a jerk, but he maintained an iron grip on the property," she continued. "George married Evangeline and they all lived here together. George couldn't have the control he wanted with Evangeline's father around, though, and when he died the property passed to Evangeline through a special trust."

Realization dawned on Jared. "George couldn't take ownership of the house."

"Right." Harper bobbed her head. "Evangeline realized at a certain point that George was a bad man. That didn't mean she could divorce him. Women of her station weren't allowed to divorce ... and by then she was afraid what he would do to her. That didn't mean she had to follow the rules George wanted to set.

"She had one child with him, an heir, and then she made sure that the house trust her father set up worked to her advantage and passed the house off to Byron long before she had to," she continued. "George was furious, but there was nothing he could do. Evangeline had a family lawyer who set it up for her — something Jared and I found out while researching today — and it was an ironclad trust.

"George brought his old buddy Bertie in to work on family documents after that, but he couldn't break the trust on the house no matter how hard he tried. He's considered a shyster in law circles and there are endless stories about him screwing over clients for money on the web. He worked hard to break the trust for George, who has always wanted this house above all else. He came up empty."

"You're very good," Jennifer noted, her lips quirking. "I can't believe you figured all this out."

"It was the ghosts who made me realize what was really going on," Harper admitted. "The fact that Evangeline could hear them was another clue. I inherited my ability to see and talk to ghosts from my grandfather. It made sense that your family ability would pass from generation to generation."

Byron's expression was dark as it landed on his father. "Did you kill Celeste?" Of course the first question he asked would be about his beloved wife.

George worked his jaw. "That is the most preposterous thing I've ever heard. Everything they've said so far is complete and total nonsense. You can't believe them."

"It's not nonsense," Richard argued. "We've done painstaking research on this. We have enough evidence to turn over to the police ... and that's exactly what we plan to do. You're going to prison, old man. Don't think for a second it's not going to happen because after what you've done to this family, you've earned it."

Harper slid George a sidelong look. He was elderly but the way he eyed the door told her he was considering running. Jared was close enough to stop him, though, so she wasn't particularly worried.

"Tell me the rest," Byron ordered. "I want to know all of it."

"You were going to leave the house to Mom in your will," Jennifer replied, weariness practically wafting off her in waves. "Richard and I would inherit from her after the fact. Grandpa didn't want that. He wanted the house. Like Harper said, he always wanted the house and Grandmother pulled the rug out from under him just when he was getting comfortable.

"He killed Mom to eliminate the problem and then he started working on you," she continued. "I heard the conversations. I know it's true. He tried to convince you the house was cursed and to sign it over to him."

Byron's eyebrows hopped. "I can't believe you heard that. I told him there was no way it was going to happen."

"Which is why he spent a few years trying to come up with a new plan," Harper volunteered. "This plan involved a local girl he somehow managed to convince to do his bidding — I'm guessing money was involved — and she infiltrated your house."

Byron lifted his chin. "Madeline. You're talking about Madeline."

"They were in on it from the start," Jennifer explained. "I heard them talking not long before I left. I saw them together. They were ... doing things."

Byron was horrified. "They were together?" The accusatory look he shot his father promised mayhem. "I can't believe you did this."

"They knew I overheard them and I was afraid. I was already suspicious about what they were capable of. Grandpa threatened he was going to lock me up in a hospital and everyone would assume I was crazy. He said he had proof I was crazy and had already started the process.

"I was frozen in fear," she said, her voice cracking. "I was terrified ... and he said he already had you on his side. I wasn't sure if that was true, but I was scared enough that I didn't want to risk it. That's why I went to Grandma."

"The plan was to gather enough information on George to lock him away and then Jennifer could return home," Evangeline said. "It took a lot longer than we thought it would. During that time, Jennifer found a home she loves ... and a man she loves. She found a life she could enjoy. That didn't stop us from working, though.

"When we heard what you were doing, Byron, we knew we couldn't leave you in the dark any longer," she continued. "It was obvious that Jennifer's disappearance was weighing on you more than I realized. I thought you'd shut off access to your heart. I was wrong about that, and I'm sorry, but I'm not sorry about hiding her."

"You planned to bring her here and spring her on Byron in private, right?" Harper queried. "You only changed your mind after talking to your mother this afternoon."

"Pretty much," Evangeline agreed. "Mother told me that George and Madeline have been plotting for years. They're stuck, though. They thought they could get Byron to void the pre-nup if they just worked at it long enough. George always acted disdainful of Madeline in public so no one would suspect their affair. Once the pre-nup was gone, they planned for Richard and Byron to be involved in an accident together and Madeline would inherit ... at which point George and her would marry following my elimination."

Zander made a face. "Gross. I can't believe she was sleeping with that old dude. That is just ... sick."

"You shut your mouth," George hissed. "I'm as virile as I ever was."

"I think you should tell the other prisoners that when you get locked up for the rest of your life," Jared suggested. "I think it's going to go over well."

"I'm not going to prison." George was defiant. "You can't prove any of this."

Jared shifted his eyes to Richard, something unsaid passing between them. "Maybe not," Jared replied after a beat. "That's going to be up to the prosecutor to decide, though. For now, you're going into custody. That's the only way I can guarantee that Jennifer has a happy reunion with her family. Although ... what about Madeline?"

Harper had been expecting the question. "She never left the house. She was the one listening to us in the stairwell today. She's been hiding in George's room ... a place we never checked because we assumed that George and Evangeline were sharing a room. Turns out, that wasn't true."

"Really?" Jared was officially intrigued. "Well, I think that means we're going to need to secure George and Madeline and then call Mel. We should probably have help transporting them."

"What about dinner?" Zander whined. "I thought we were going to get prime rib."

"Dinner is still on the table," Byron offered. "Everyone can eat." He looked as if he'd aged twenty years in the past twenty minutes. "After that, though, I'm going to ask everyone to retire early. I would like to spend some private time with my daughter."

Harper smiled. "I think that's a fine idea."

Harris, who had been quiet for the entire exchange, cocked his head in Delphine's direction. "We're still getting paid, right?"

Harper scowled at him. "I bet you're not getting paid until you find Jennifer's body in the woods, you big fraud."

Harris glared. "It could've happened to anybody."

"Not me."

"Well ... aren't you special."

"She is," Jared agreed, pressing a quick kiss to her temple before moving toward George, who looked panicked. "You have no idea just how special."

❧ 20 ❧

TWENTY

Madeline was taken into custody without incident. She seemed stunned when Mel and Jared arrived at George's suite to arrest her. Immediately, barely taking a breath, she announced it was all George's idea. She claimed he threatened to kill her if she didn't participate in the plan. Byron, of course, didn't believe her. He sent her off in the back of Mel's squad car with a wave and a reminder that she had no access to his money, which meant she couldn't pay for her own defense. He seemed pleased.

George was another story. He was spitting mad and vowed revenge. Evangeline, no longer fearful of the stigma of divorce or adamant about doing her wifely duty, informed him that she'd cut off his funds as well. Apparently George and Madeline had public defenders in their future, which Byron found amusing.

As for the family patriarch, he was in remarkable spirits considering everything that happened. He sat next to his daughter — demoting Harris to the far end of the table — and asked her every question he could think of about her life.

She lived in Idaho — a state Harper knew absolutely nothing about — and raised horses with her husband, who was wealthy (although not quite on the Jessup level). She invited her father out for a visit, something he readily agreed to, and then said her husband would be arriving the next day. He wanted to meet his father-in-law, something that flustered Byron at the same time pleasure washed over his features.

After dinner, Harper and her group excused themselves to the guesthouse to pack. Jared had to stop in at the police station when he arrived back in town but, after that, he planned to drag Harper to bed for snacks and alone time. He'd already planned it out.

They were almost out the door when Jennifer showed up. She appeared shy but determined as she asked to see Harper.

"I don't want to delay you," she explained to Jared as he showed her inside. "I know that you probably want to get away from here as soon as possible. This island has always been crazy."

Jared smiled at her. "I live with Harper. Zander lives across the street with his boyfriend. I don't think you know the true meaning of the word 'crazy.'"

Jennifer laughed, delighted. "Harper did a good job picking you."

"No, I got lucky when I found her."

"I think maybe you're both lucky."

"I happen to agree," Harper announced, appearing in the doorway. She didn't seem surprised to see Jennifer. "I figured I would see you before we left."

"I'll be around for a while," Jennifer replied, stepping past Jared and focusing on the blonde. "I plan on staying at least a month. That's already been decided. My father is ... profoundly grateful for what you've done for us. He wanted me to tell you that. He was going to come down himself, but I insisted that it should be me."

"You don't have to thank me," Harper insisted. "I'm just sorry it took me so long to realize what was going on. Maybe ... maybe if I understood what was happening before you wouldn't have had to leave."

"I'm not sorry I left." Jennifer was earnest. "I have a husband I love, a life I adore. I have plans for a future that are massively bigger now than they were twenty-four hours ago. As for owing you, I do. You helped my grandmother find the strength to bring this to a close. She was the one we were waiting on."

Harper had already figured that out herself. "I'm still sorry. Your family has experienced so much loss. To have your grandfather be a part of it, too ... well, I think that's too much for anyone to absorb."

"I absorbed it a long time ago. I never liked him, even when I was a small child. I sensed he was evil. My father couldn't see it. He believed that you're supposed to respect your father no matter what. I think he's over that now, though."

"I should say so." Harper rolled her neck. "As for Madeline—"

Jennifer held up her hand to still Harper. "Honestly, the less said about her the better. I think she was used in some respects. I think she was fine with being used, though. That being said, she wasn't involved in any of the murders. She won't be facing nearly the punishment my grandfather will."

"Also, they'll probably offer her a deal," Jared supplied. "She'll get off with a minimum sentence, community service, and fines. Your grandfather is the big catch."

"I'm fine with that." Jennifer looked sincere. "I think her life has been a prison of her own making for the past ten years. I honestly think she had no idea what she was getting herself into."

Harper nodded and smiled. "I know you just got back and you probably have a million things you want to do in a limited amount of time, but I would like to have lunch once you're settled. I think we have a lot to talk about."

Jennifer's lips curved. "Like ghosts?"

"Like ghosts ... and high school ... and how I kind of took over your homecoming because I was feeling good about myself for figuring everything out. Sorry about that, by the way. Zander is usually the dramatic one and I totally stole his thunder tonight."

"You definitely did," Zander bellowed from the second bedroom, causing Jennifer to laugh.

"I would love to have lunch with you," she enthused. "That's honestly why I came down here. I want to talk to you, too. My father doesn't want to be away from me right now, though. He's a little ... clingy."

"Do you blame him?"

"No. I want to spend time with him. I feel bad for all of it, but I honestly wasn't sure if he would believe me and I was terrified about ending up in a hospital. You have no idea the fear I was operating under."

Since Harper operated under the same fear for many years, she was the only person who could truly understand. "You might be surprised."

"Yes, well ... ." Jennifer shifted from one foot to the other, antsy energy coming out to play. "Thank you for everything. I really should get back to my family, though. We have years to make up for."

"You don't have to do it all in one night," Harper pointed out. "You should take your time."

"That's the plan."

The two women embraced, warmth and knowledge passing between them, and when they separated, Harper was a little misty.

"I didn't know I would be so emotionally affected," she admitted, swiping at her tears.

"Me either." Jennifer dabbed at her eyes. "I'm glad we reconnected, though."

"Me, too."

"I'm looking forward to our lunch."

"Me, too."

Jared slipped his arm around Harper's waist and offered Jennifer a staid handshake. "I'm glad to have met you," he supplied. "I'm very glad you're alive. I have a feeling we'll be talking a bit in the next few days, too. Until then, though, you should take it easy."

"Oh, I plan to. Nothing but family and food for a week. After that, I'll be able to include friends."

"Now that's something to look forward to." Jared kept Harper in his arms until Jennifer departed, holding her tighter as soon as it was just the two of them. "What you pulled off this evening was ... amazing."

"Things just sort of fit together in my head. It wasn't that amazing."

"Don't sell yourself short," he chided. "I don't like that. You were a regular little genius this evening. It was beyond impressive."

"It just fit together like a puzzle in my head. I wasn't even sure I was right."

"There's one thing I don't get," he said. "The psychics. Why were they so important to what went down?"

"Byron picked two of the psychics and Madeline the other two. She knew Harris and Delphine were frauds. You heard Byron. He knew in his heart Jennifer was alive. That's why he wanted real psychics ... and having someone who knew Jennifer was important."

"Yeah, but ... everything had to come together perfectly. How did that happen?"

"Sometimes things simply happen exactly as they're supposed to happen. This was one of those times."

"I guess I'll have to take your word for it." He pulled back so he could stare at her face and then gave her a soft kiss. "Do you know what else happened exactly how it was supposed to happen?"

She nodded without hesitation. She knew exactly what he was going to say. "Us."

"That's right." He gave her another kiss. "What do you say we pack up and head home? If we time it right, we can spend all day tomorrow in bed. It will be just you and me for thirty-six hours. How does that sound?"

"It sounds perfect."

"Don't forget about me," Zander called from the bedroom. "Sunday is my morning with Harper."

"You've already had three mornings this week," Jared groused.

"Yes, but I'm a creature of habit. I need my Harper time." Zander poked his head through the door and winked. "I promise to only take an hour of her time, though. That seems fair given the fact that I'm in love with both of you right now."

Jared eyed him for a long beat and then nodded. "One hour. It's a compromise I can live with."

"That makes two of us ... I'll bring doughnuts, too."

Jared brightened considerably. "Now you're talking."

"I knew you would see the benefit of having me in your life eventually."

"I see the light," Jared teased.

Harper wrapped her arms around Jared's neck and sighed. "Thank you." She was sincere. "You have no idea how much it means to me that you're making things work with him."

Jared ran his hands over her back. It was worth it, he realized. There were all different kinds of families. The one he was in — for the rest of his life — was the sort that lived on emotion, not material possessions. It was what he always wanted, and he wouldn't give it up for anything.

"We're a family," he said simply. "That's what families do."

"Still ... thank you."

He tipped up her chin. "No, thank you." He kissed her, long and deep. She was breathless when they separated. "Now, let's get out of here. I have plans and they don't revolve around this island. I want to go home."

That was one thing they could always agree on.

*To Billie Kay, the best mama-in-law
a girl could ever ask for.
I know you're in heaven right now telling
all the other angels about your
daughter-in-law's "sexy books."*

CHAPTER ONE

SWEETHEART MAE HOLIDAY, or Sweetie as everyone called her, was running on empty.

Literally and figuratively.

The fuel gage on the Mustang GT her daddy had bought her for her sixteenth birthday was sitting below the empty mark and had been for the last fifty miles. She'd tried to get gas in the last town, but her credit card had been declined. She wasn't surprised. A busted car radiator, a trip to the dentist for an aching tooth, and a moment of madness while browsing the Lucchese boot website had pushed her already high credit card debt to the limit. She was tanked out on money, tanked out on gas . . . and tanked out on hope. Her mama's phone call had been the straw that broke the stubborn mule's back.

A heart attack?

Sweetie still couldn't believe it. She had always thought of her daddy as being invincible. Hank Holiday could lift fifty-pound hay bales and toss them off the bed of a trailer using just one hand, walk twenty miles back to the house after his horse went lame and still put in a full day of ranching, get gored by a longhorn bull and stitch himself up without anesthesia . . . or saying a word to anyone.

But what he couldn't do was give his six daughters any say in their lives when they'd been living under his roof. Which was why they had all moved out as soon as they'd turned eighteen. Daddy was just too darn stubborn for his own good.

Of course, Sweetie was stubborn too. Which was why she hadn't been home in twelve years. She'd been waiting for her daddy to see the error of his ways. He'd been waiting for her to do the same. Now, egos didn't matter. All that mattered was her daddy getting better.

Tears welled into her eyes at just the thought of her larger-than-life daddy falling from his horse, then lying there for who knew how long before one of the sons of the neighboring rancher had found him. He was lucky he wasn't dead. His daddy had died of a heart attack around the same age. The image of her daddy being buried beneath the old oak, alongside her grandfather, made her push harder on the accelerator.

Through the blur of her tears, she saw a road sign up ahead.

Wilder 9

The name of her hometown caused a flood of memories to wash over her. Memories of Friday night football games, Fourth of July parades, harvest festivals, Christmas hayrides, and all the usual celebrations of a small town. But her daddy's stubbornness wasn't the only reason she hadn't been home in twelve long years. Pissing off every man, woman, and child in Wilder was the other one. She didn't doubt for a second that they were still pissed off.

Texans were a friendly lot, but there was a reason *Don't Mess with Texas* was the state motto. If you stomped on one of their sacred traditions, they didn't forget and forgive easily. And she had done some major stomping. Which was why she had no intention of setting foot in town while she was there. In fact, nothing short of divine intervention would get her to face the townsfolk.

A sharp blast of a siren had her glancing at the rearview mirror. A sheriff's SUV was gaining on her with lights flashing. She quickly let up on the gas and hoped the patrol car would drive right on by. Instead, it hugged her bumper and blasted its siren again.

"Dagnabbit!" She used her Grandma Mimi's favorite swear word as she pulled over to the shoulder of the two-lane highway. She turned off the engine so as not to use any more gas and waited for the officer to get out. He took his good sweet time. In the side mirror, she could see him sitting behind the wheel with his tan cowboy hat pulled low and his aviator sunglasses reflecting the midmorning sun.

There was something about the way he was just sitting there that made her wonder if he recognized her car. She wouldn't be surprised. Even though Mustang Sally was fourteen years old and looked a little worse for wear, everyone in town had known Sweetheart Holiday's candy

apple-red muscle car. Especially the law enforcement officers. Sweetie had gotten more tickets
in high school than she could count. Not that
she'd ever had to pay one. Her daddy's friend,
Judge Hanover, had taken care of that. The law
enforcement in the county had finally just given
up pulling her over.

But that had been Sheriff Dauber. The man
who climbed out of the vehicle wasn't short with
a potbelly and man boobs. One brown, high-pol-
ished cowboy boot hit the ground first and
another followed before a tall man unfolded like
a 3D image any red-blooded woman would love
to have as a screensaver.

Sweetie sucked in her breath. Lord have mercy.
She had forgotten just how well Texas made men.

His well-worn, soft-as-butter jeans fit him just
right—snug in the lean hips and muscled thighs
and loose around his boot shanks. The long sleeves
of his khaki sheriff's shirt were cuffed, revealing
strong forearms dusted with dark hair. Sweetie
had always had a thing for masculine forearms.
There was something about the tight collection
of muscles and thick veins that made her stomach
feel like her mama's famous Jell-O Surprise.

With the hat and sunglasses, she couldn't see
much of his face. Just a prominent jaw and serious mouth—a prominent jaw and serious mouth
that, thankfully, she didn't recognize. Which
meant she had a chance of talking her way out
of a ticket. All she needed to decrease her bank
account even further was a ticket and higher
insurance premiums.

As he headed toward her, she quickly took her hair out of the bun and fluffed it before rolling down the window and pinning on a smile. She had to look wa-a-ay up. Past a sexy leather holster riding nice hips. Past a flat stomach and a well-defined chest. Past the open collar of his shirt that displayed just a hint of dark chest hair. Past a prominent chin with a covering of dark stubble and serious lips. To the dark lenses that she saw her reflection in.

"Good mornin'!" she said brightly. "You want to tell me why a good-lookin' lawman like yourself has stopped me on this beautiful Texas day, Officer—" She glanced at the gold nameplate attached to the left side of his chest, but before she could read it, he flipped up the flap of his pocket and covered it. He pulled out a citation pad and a pen, then spoke in the kind of low, husky voice that was perfect for talking dirty in the dark.

"I need to see your driver's license and registration."

With that sexy voice, he could have asked for just about anything and she would have given it to him. She reached for her purse in the seat next to her and pulled out her driver's license. The car registration was a little harder to locate. When she finally found it beneath the pile of unpaid bills she'd stuffed in her glove box, she realized it was expired by seven months. Something she hoped he wouldn't notice.

He noticed.

As soon as he looked at it, he started filling out the citation.

Her smile faded. "You aren't gonna give me a ticket, are you? I promise I'll get my car registered first thing. And I was only goin' a little over the speed limit."

"Eighty-two in a seventy-mile-an-hour zone isn't a little over." He continued to write.

Pinning on another smile, she reached out the window and placed a hand on his forearm right above his wrist. The warmth of his bare skin and the flex of his muscles had her stomach taking a dip. He slowly lifted his head. She couldn't see his eyes behind the dark lenses, but she could feel his anger in the fisting of his hand. Not one man had ever gotten angry with her for touching him. In fact, her ex-boyfriend had broken up with her because she hadn't touched him enough. But this angry man, she wanted to touch . . . A LOT.

Her strong physical attraction to him set off a warning in her brain. *Get a grip, Sweetie.* She was not there to start something up with a complete stranger. She was there to see her daddy and help out her mama. Her life was in Nashville. Not in Wilder, Texas.

She removed her hand and tried to ignore her tingling fingers.

"Look, I'm sorry. You're right. I was going well over the speed limit. But I had a good reason. You see my daddy had a heart attack. You might know him. Hank Holiday. He runs the Holiday Ranch. Anyway, as you can imagine, I'm pretty upset and I was in such a hurry to get home that I wasn't even paying attention to how fast I was going. As for the registration, I'm sure other folks have forgotten to get their car registered and you let them off with just a warning. So if you could just give me a break this time, I would really appreciate it."

Men didn't always give her what she wanted. Her failure in the country music business was a perfect example. But they had never refused her with as much hostility as this man did. The snort that came out of his mouth was filled with pure contempt. He finished filling out the citation and tore it from the pad in one rip. Instead of handing it to her, he dropped it and her license and registration onto her lap as if he couldn't stand the thought of accidentally touching her. Then he turned and strode back to his SUV while Sweetie sat there in stunned shock.

She glanced in her rearview mirror and watched as Mr. Badass Lawman got back in his car. She raised her hand and gave him the one-finger salute in the mirror.

"Asshole," she grumbled as she started her car.

Or tried to. Mustang Sally immediately sputtered and then died. Sweetie tried again and again, but the car had finally run out of gas. She wanted to bang her fists on the steering wheel and let out a frustrated squeal, but she refused to give the arrogant lawman the satisfaction. Nor would she give him the satisfaction of asking for help.

After rolling up the window and stuffing the ticket and registration into the glove box, she grabbed her purse and got out. Her parents' house was a good six miles away, but if she cut across a few fields, it would be closer to four. Hooking her purse over her shoulder, she started walking. She wasn't surprised when the patrol car pulled up next to her and the side window rolled down.

"Get in. I'll take you home and call you a tow truck."

She kept walking, refusing to even spare him a glance. "No thanks."

He swerved in front of her so fast, she had to stop or run right into the bumper of the sheriff's car. Badass Lawman jumped out. He didn't look stern now. He looked pissed. Which was fine with her. She was feeling a little pissed herself.

"What?" She held up her hands. "Are you going to give me a ticket for running out of gas, Officer . . .?" She glanced down. His pocket flap was buttoned back in place and she had no trouble reading the name engraved on the shiny gold plate.

Sheriff Decker Carson.

She might not recognize the face behind the dark sunglasses, but she knew the name. Her gaze lifted as she tried to find any sign of the boy she remembered. But nothing about this stern, well-built lawman reminded her of the eleven-year-old boy who had shown up in Wilder to live with his grandparents after his parents had died in a car accident.

Back then, he'd been a shy city boy who was scared of horses and cows and bees . . . and Sweetie. She'd been fourteen at the time and he'd stammered and blushed every time she looked in his direction.

He wasn't blushing now as he held open the passenger-side door of his patrol car and waited for her to get in. As much as she wanted to ignore his silent order, her curiosity got the better of her. Once they were both in the car, she studied his profile as he pulled out onto the highway. From this angle, she could see a glimpse of the boy he'd once been. How old had he been when she'd left? Fifteen? He'd been almost as tall as he was now, but not nearly as muscular. How old was he now? She did some mental calculation.

"Twenty-seven is pretty young to be a sheriff, isn't it?"

"Thirty is pretty old to still be driving your high school car."

"What can I say? When I love something, I love it for life."

His jaw flexed. "I think Jace would disagree."

At the mention of his cousin, Sweetie looked away and stared out the side window. The last person she wanted to talk about was Jace. She now knew why Decker had refused to let her off with just a warning. He had idolized his cousin and with good reason. Jace had taken Decker under his wing after Decker's parents had died. They were as close as brothers.

She changed the subject. "So why law enforcement? And why here in Wilder? I thought you were a big city boy."

"Just because you come from a big city doesn't mean you want to go back." He glanced over at her. "And just because you come from a small town doesn't mean you want to stay."

Sweetie hadn't wanted to stay. She'd wanted to shake the dust of Wilder off her boots as soon as she'd graduated and never look back. She had. Or, at least, she'd tried. But small-town dust is hard to get rid of.

"So how goes your quest to become the next Dolly Parton?" he asked.

A lot of replies popped into her head: exhausting, frustrating . . . a true nightmare of disappointment. But she'd lie naked in a bed of hot coals before she'd admit that to anyone in Wilder, Texas.

"Exciting."

He glanced over. Even though she couldn't see his eyes, she knew he didn't believe her.

Thankfully, before he questioned her more, they came to the turnoff for her family's ranch. The sight of the entrance to the Holiday Ranch had a swell of emotion rising up in her that completely took her by surprise.

As Sweetie took in the Austin stone arched entryway with *Holiday Ranch* spelled out in weathered steel letters, the American and Texas flags that waved proudly in the stiff January wind, and the plaque with the date her great-great-grandfather had first purchased the land, one word popped into her head. A word that had been missing from her vocabulary since she'd moved to Nashville.

Home.

CHAPTER TWO

SWEETIE FELT LIKE Dorothy when she woke up in her bed at Auntie Em and Uncle Henry's after the journey to Oz. She felt like everything that had happened in the last twelve years had been nothing but a strange dream. Or possibly a nightmare. But unlike Dorothy, she hadn't fought to get back home. Instead, she had stubbornly stayed away until she could return a famous country music superstar and prove to her daddy and the townsfolk that she had chosen the right path.

She still wanted to prove herself. Not just to her family and the townsfolk, but also to herself. But now she realized she had let her stubborn pride keep her from her touchstone, from the one place that filled her up rather than drained her dry.

She was so overcome with emotions she didn't realize that Decker had stopped the car, or that she was bawling like a little baby, until a hand-kerchief landed on her lap. Not a bandana like most country boys carried around in their back pockets, but a white linen hankie with a border of bluebonnets embroidered along the scalloped edge.

She glanced at him, but he kept his gaze on the road as he drove under the entryway.

On the way to the house, Sweetie expected to see herds of longhorn cattle grazing along the white slat fences and lazing in the shade of scrub oak and mesquite trees. She didn't see a one. Or one horse. Or one goat, sheep, or herding dog. Or ranch hand. The only animal she saw was a prairie dog peeking its head out of a hole, then ducking back down as the tires spit out gravel.

Sweetie was more than a little confused.

Thankfully, the house looked the same. The two-story farmhouse was still painted her mama's favorite color of pale green with white shutters and a wide porch to beat all porches. Big enough to hold a table and eight chairs on one side and a cushioned wicker sofa and chairs on the other. It even had room for a porch swing on the very end. A porch swing her great-grandfather had made himself out of old barn wood.

Even though it was well past Christmas, the red-and-green ornament wreath, Sweetie remembered from her childhood, hung on the front door and colored lights lined the windows and eaves. Obviously her mama had been too busy taking care of Hank to take down the Christmas decorations and put up the Valentine hearts and wreath.

Darla Holiday had married into the right last name. She loved celebrating any and every holi

day and had filled the attic with plastic bin after plastic bin of decorations for Christmas, Valentine's, St. Patrick's Day, Easter, Fourth of July, Halloween, and Thanksgiving. When Sweetie had popped out on February 14th, she'd taken it as a sign from God to name all her children after something related to the holiday closest to their births.

Sweetheart. Clover. Liberty and Belle. Halloween. Noelle.

Halloween, or Hallie as she demanded to be called, had never forgiven her mother for her obsession with holidays.

"How long are you staying?" Decker's question pulled Sweetie from her thoughts and she turned to find him studying her. His mouth was stern again. Not that he had ever been a smiler. Even as a kid, she'd had to work hard to get the solemn look from his face. The rare times he had caved and flashed his teeth, she'd always felt like she had achieved something special.

"Trying to get rid of me so soon, Deckster?" She'd given him the nickname after she'd found out he was a straight-A student. It used to make him smile. Now it made his jaw tighten.

"You might be welcomed home, but you won't be welcomed in town. It would be best for everyone if you stay out here."

She knew he had good reason to be upset with her. She had hurt his cousin. She had hurt him badly. But that didn't mean she was going to be bullied.

"Well, I guess we'll have to see about that. I've

had a hankering for good Texas barbecue and no one makes it better than Bobby Jay."

Decker studied her. "If you cause problems for me, I won't hesitate to toss you in jail."

"Ooo, did the big bad lawman just threaten me?"

"Not a threat. Just a promise. And unlike you, I keep my promises."

Before she could tell him that what happened between her and Jace was none of his damn business, the screen door swung open and her mama came charging out. Darla Holiday was a petite ball of energy and always had been. She started her day at five in the morning and didn't stop until everyone else was in bed.

She loved as hard as she worked.

As soon as Sweetie stepped out of the car, her mama had her in her arms. Nothing had changed about her mama's hugs. They were warm, tight, and scented with the honeysuckle lotion she applied every morning.

"Why didn't you tell me you were getting here so early, Sweetheart Mae? I haven't even had time to get the Christmas decorations down and your decorations up or change the sheets on your bed or finish baking your favorite gooseberry pie." Her mama drew back and gave Sweetie the once-over. "And it looks like you could use a few pies. You've lost weight since the last time I saw you. You're nothing but skin and bones. Isn't she, Mimi?"

Sweetie glanced back at the porch and saw her grandmother standing there with a soft smile on

her wrinkled face. Most of Sweetie's memories of Mitzy Holiday were of her kneeling in her gardens with a wide-brimmed hat perched on her head and bees dancing around her like flies to honey.

Sweetie hadn't gotten her grandma's way with bees or her patience for gardening. Or her sweet disposition. Like Sweetie's mama, Mimi was a soft-spoken woman who had never raised her voice or interfered with running the ranch. Or the raising of her granddaughters. But she had always been there with a wise word or a shoulder to cry on when her son's stubbornness had upset the Holiday sisters. Unlike Sweetie's mama, who had visited Sweetie in Nashville often over the years, Mimi didn't care for long road trips or flying. She did call Sweetie weekly and text her questions about Sweetie's love life, followed by a row of wedding emojis. But phone calls and texts didn't compare to seeing her grandmother in person.

"Mimi!" Sweetie hurried up the porch steps to hug her grandmother.

Mimi's hugs were just as good as Mama's. But instead of smelling like honeysuckle lotion, she smelled like the earth she loved to dig in and the Icy Hot she rubbed into her sore joints.

"There's my girl. I was worried I'd never see your sweet face on this ranch again." She drew back and patted Sweetie's cheek. "But here you are. And your mama is right. You have lost weight. You've even lost your boobs."

"Mimi!" Sweetie glanced over her shoulder to

see if Decker had left. He hadn't. In fact, he had gotten out and now stood at the bottom of the porch steps. Her face heated as Mimi continued.

"Well, it's the truth. And how are you gonna catch a man with no boobs?" Mimi was sweet as sugar snap peas, but also had no filter when it came to what popped into her head. "Isn't that right, Deck?"

"I think I'm gonna leave that question alone, Ms. Mimi."

"Smart boy." Mimi grinned. She had always had a soft spot for Decker. And so had Mama.

Mama hooked an arm through his and beamed up at him. "Why are you bringing my baby home, Deck? Don't tell me she's already gotten in trouble with the law?" Sweetie waited for Decker to tattle about the ticket, but, surprisingly, he didn't.

"No trouble, Ms. Darla. She ran out of gas and I gave her a lift."

"Out of gas?" Her mama shook her head. "Good grief, Sweetie. You'd forget your head if it wasn't attached. Well, I appreciate it, Deck, and would be happy to repay you with dinner anytime."

"Thank you, ma'am, but no payment is necessary. How's Mr. Holiday doing?"

"He's much better." Mama sighed. "Although keeping him calm and rested has been a full-time job."

Mimi nodded. "My boy never could sit still. Thankfully, all our girls are coming home to help keep him entertained." She shot a pointed look at

Sweetie. "Although they should have been home a lot sooner. Then maybe this ranch wouldn't be in the mess it's in."

Sweetie wanted to ask Mimi for details about that mess, but she refused to air their dirty laundry in front of Decker. It looked like he wanted no part of that either.

"Well, ladies. I'd best be going." He pulled on his hat and tipped it. "Ms. Mimi. Ms. Darla." Sweetie got no hat tip. "Sweetie." When he turned and headed back to his sheriff's car, it was hard not to notice the way his jeans fit his fine butt.

"That's one fine-looking man," Mimi voiced her thoughts as all three women watched the sheriff's car pull away. "It's too bad he's not a wealthy rancher. It would be nice to have a third option."

Confused by the comment, Sweetie started to ask what she meant when her mama climbed the steps of the porch and joined the conversation.

"I thought we were going to lose Decker like we've lost so many of our young folks—especially when his grandparents passed away and his aunt remarried and moved. But he turned out to be the type of man who knows where he belongs. He's the best sheriff Wilder has ever had."

Sweetie snorted. "From what I've seen, he's got a bad attitude."

"Can you blame him for being a little standoffish with you? You broke his cousin's heart."

"From what Hallie told me, Jace got over it pretty quickly," Sweetie said. "He's been thoroughly enjoying life as a Canadian football

player—including dating plenty of beautiful models."

Mimi shook her head. "No country boy wants a big-city model when they can have a sweet hometown girl."

Sweetie rolled her eyes. "Don't start, Mimi. I'm not getting back with Jace."

"Did I say I wanted you to? I'm just saying that he's not going to fall for some city girl. You mark my words." Mimi lifted her eyebrows. "Just like you aren't going to fall for some city boy. Your heart is country and only a country boy will know how to claim it. Now, I'm gonna let you two catch up while I check on the pies."

When she was gone, Sweetie sighed. "I see she's still holding out hope that I'll settle down in Wilder."

"You can't blame her. She misses you girls something fierce."

"I've missed her too." She glanced around. "And the ranch. I didn't realize how much until I got here. What's going on, Mama? Where are all the cattle?"

"Your daddy has been trimming down the herd for a while."

"It looks like he's done more than trimming. I didn't see one cow. What's a cattle ranch without cattle?"

Mama hesitated. "Your father and I have decided to sell the ranch."

If her mother had told her she was going to the moon, Sweetie wouldn't have been any more surprised. "Sell the ranch? Are you kidding?"

Her mother sighed and sat down in a chair. For the first time, Sweetie noticed how tired she looked. Darla Holiday had never looked tired. No matter how much she did around the ranch, she had always looked vibrant and full of life. Now she looked drained.

"I know it's hard to let go of this ranch, but selling only makes sense. Running a ranch this large is a lot of work, Sweetie. More than three aging people can deal with. I realized it before your father's heart attack. It took a near brush with death for Hank to realize it too. Mimi is the only one holding out. Which is another reason I wanted you girls to come home. I'm hoping you can convince her that it's time to sell."

Sweetie sat down on the couch next to her mother. "But this land has been in the Holiday family for over a hundred years. It's not just a ranch. It's our heritage. Holidays are ranchers. They've always been ranchers."

"That's just the problem, Sweetie. The next generation of Holidays don't want to be ranchers."

She wanted to argue, but she couldn't. Her mama was right. The six Holiday sisters had left the ranch the first chance they got and had no intentions of returning. Cloe was a speech therapist in College Station. The twins, Liberty and Belle, were event planners in Houston. Hallie worked for a brewery in Austin. And Noelle was going to pastry school in Dallas and working at a bakery. The chances of any of them coming home to live under their father's ironclad rule were slim to none.

Her mama patted her arm. "I know you think of the ranch as home. But home is where the heart is. Your and your sisters' hearts aren't here anymore."

Sweetie had thought the same thing. But if that was true, then why did her chest feel so full when she stepped inside the house onto the colorful rag rug her grandmother had made out of her and her sisters' baby blankets? Her heart continued to swell as she looked around.

Pictures of all the family holidays they'd spent together cluttered the top of the standup piano her daddy had bought her mama when they first got married. The same piano Sweetie had learned to play on. The Duncan Fife china cabinet Mimi had inherited from her mama not only held china, but also handprints of all the sisters, along with misshapen bowls and Crayola drawings they'd made over the years.

There were other memories as well. Memories that weren't as obvious. Like the dark stain on the wood floor that had been put there when Sweetie had tried to sneak a glass of Mimi's homemade elderberry wine up to her room and spilled it. The burn spot on the end table when Liberty had been in her scented candle-selling stage. The chipped lamp Noelle and Hallie had knocked over when they'd been wrestling over a box of Milk Duds.

All these memories assailed Sweetie as she breathed in the scent of lemon oil furniture polish, baking piecrust, and the dried-out Christmas tree sitting in the corner.

When she saw her daddy napping in his favorite recliner, her heart filled to almost bursting. He looked like the man she remembered, but also different. He was still a big man who would have no trouble wrangling a steer to the ground, but there was much more gray in his wheat-colored hair and more wrinkles around his eyes.

"Daddy," she whispered in an aching voice.

His eyes fluttered open. In them she saw surprise and love . . . quickly followed by anger. "What are you doing here?" When she didn't answer right away, he flipped up the recliner. "Well, answer the question, Sweetheart Mae. What are you doing here when I told you to never set foot in this house again?"

Sweetie glanced at her mama. "I thought you said he wanted me to come home."

The guilty look on her mama's face said it all. "Well, he didn't say it in so many words."

"I didn't say it in any words!" her daddy bellowed as he got up from his chair. "I won't have Sweetie staying under this roof after the way she spoke to me before she left."

"What about the way you spoke to me?" Sweetie said.

"I only told the truth. What you did was wrong, Sweetie. You broke your mama's and grandma's heart, not to mention Jace's"—Sweetie noticed that he didn't mention his heart—"and all over a silly pipe dream of becoming a country singer."

"You're just mad because I didn't give you your

silly pipe dream of me marrying Jace and him taking over the ranch. Jace never wanted to run this ranch, Daddy. He wanted to play football."

Hank snorted. "You could have changed his mind."

Sweetie had sworn to hold her temper with her father, but she had forgotten how annoying he could be. "I didn't want to marry Jace!"

Hank's eyes narrowed. "Because you never have known what's good for you. Neither have your sisters. I should have had sons like Sam Remington. But instead I had six daughters who don't know the difference between bullshit and a horse's ass."

"Oh, believe me, I know the difference. Right now I'm looking at a horse's—"

"That's enough!" Mimi appeared in the doorway of the kitchen. Since Mimi rarely raised her voice, both Sweetie and her daddy shut up and turned to her. "Now I've put up with both of y'all's stubbornness for twelve long years and I'm through putting up with it." She pointed a finger at Sweetie. "You won't disrespect your daddy." She pointed at Hank. "And you won't make my granddaughters feel unwelcome when they arrive."

Her daddy's eyes widened. "Your granddaughters? You mean more are coming?"

"That's right. And I'd say it's about darn time." Mimi's eyes filled with tears. "You know what scared me the most when you were lying in that hospital bed, Hank? It was the thought of you leaving this world with you and your daughters

estranged like you were with your daddy when he passed. And I won't sit back and watch it happen again. Now you stop letting your stubbornness put stress on your heart." She turned to Sweetie. "And you help your mama by putting clean sheets on the beds."

When neither one of them moved, she clapped her hands. "I mean now!"

CHAPTER THREE

DECKER CARSON WAS having a bad day and it looked like it wasn't over yet.

"I mean it, Sheriff. If you don't nip this in the bud right now, we're going to become like those big cities where homeless people set up tents on the sidewalks and pee in the streets."

Decker sighed. "Dan Wheeler isn't a homeless person, Mrs. Nichols. He lives three doors down from you. He probably just had a few too many at the Hellhole last night and made a bad choice."

"He peed in my petunias. It's all right here." Mrs. Nichols held up her cellphone. Once again, Decker had to watch the Ring video of Dan spraying down Mrs. Nichols's petunias before he zipped his fly and stumbled down the street. Mrs. Nichols lowered her phone and pointed to the flowers in question. "Just look at how wilted my beautiful babies are. They'll be dead by morning. I'm sure of it. Petunias don't do well with overly moist soil. Now are you going to arrest him for being drunk and disorderly or not?"

"How about if he buys you some new petunias and personally apologizes? I'm sure he's real sorry."

"If he was sorry, he would have already been here to apologize. He's had all day. Speaking of which, it took you long enough to get here, Sheriff. I called and complained early this morning after seeing the Ring alert on my phone and it's now almost dinnertime."

Decker's stomach knew it. After skipping lunch, he was starving.

"I'm sorry about that, Mrs. Nichols. I've had some more important issues to deal with." He knew immediately that he'd misspoken by the pinched look on her face.

"What is more important than keeping derelicts from urinating on people's petunias?"

He could have gone into detail about the semi that had flipped over in the wee hours of the morning. Thankfully, there had been no injuries, but it had still taken him and the highway patrol two hours to clear the highway and deal with irate travelers. Then there was the town meeting where he was called out for not issuing enough traffic violations because they needed more money to fix the potholes on the main road that ran through town. Which led to him setting up a speed trap. Which led to the main reason for his bad day.

Sweetheart Mae Holiday was back in town.

And she was still as spoiled and stubborn . . . and beautiful as she'd been when she left. It took every ounce of willpower he had not to get lost in the startling spring-green eyes that had looked up at him when he'd stepped to the window of her car.

A car that looked worse for wear.

Mustang Sally had once been the envy of every teenage girl and boy in Wilder. Now, it was just an old muscle car with faded paint, chips and dings in the doors, and a back bumper that looked like it had had a run-in with a light pole and lost. Decker wasn't surprised she still had the car. Or was wearing the University of Texas hoodie she'd worn all through high school. Or had the rainbow scrunchie she'd had ever since he'd known her wrapped around her wrist.

Sweetie hung on to things she loved.

Things she didn't love she easily let go of.

Like his cousin, Jace.

And Decker.

It galled him to no end that Sweetie's leaving still upset him. He thought he was over it—he'd worked so hard to get over it. And all it had taken was a flash of red Mustang for that wound to open and start aching all over again.

The ache had grown almost unbearable when she'd cried. He had seen a lot of Sweetie's emotions over the years. When she was happy, her smile could light up an entire high school gymnasium. When she was excited, her whoops could be heard in three counties. When she was amused, her laughter could ring out louder than the First Baptist Church bell.

The only emotion she didn't show was sadness. There wasn't a time that Decker could remember when Sweetie had shed real tears. Not when her horse had gotten spooked in the Fourth of July parade and tossed her off, breaking her arm. Not when her dog, Cricket, had gotten run over and killed. And certainly not when she had broken his cousin's heart.

Sweetie Holiday didn't cry.

Until today.

Tears had shimmered on the lower lids of her eyes like heartbreaking diamonds. If one hadn't escaped, he might have been able to look away. But the sight of that single tear trembling at the corner of her eye had unraveled the badass persona Decker had been hiding behind like a missed stitch in a knitted sweater.

When she'd turned those eyes to him, he'd felt like he had as a kid every time Sweetie Holiday had glanced his way—flushed, breathless, and flooded with hormones.

The abrupt ringing of a cellphone snapped him out of his thoughts. Mrs. Nichols quickly lowered the phone she had shoved in his face and answered it. "Hey, Rita. I'm with the sheriff right now so I'll have to call you back . . . What? . . . You're kiddin'? . . . You say he saw her red Mustang just outside of town?"

Decker mentally groaned. He had hoped he could keep Sweetie's visit a secret. He should have known better.

"Well, I tell you what," Mrs. Nichols continued. "If she thinks she can just waltz back into town and let bygones be bygones, she can think again. That little gal didn't just burn bridges when she left town. She incinerated them into ash. I, for one, have no intention of forgiving and forgetting. I'm sure everyone else will feel the same way. Of course, they need to be warned . . . yes, exactly . . . we need to get the word out. You call the garden club and I'll call the book club. Talk to you soon." She hung up and looked at Decker. "Sorry, Sheriff Carson, but something much more important than Dan Wheeler being a disorderly drunk has come up. Sweetheart Holiday is back. Can you believe that?"

Before Decker was forced to comment, Mrs. Nichols tapped the screen of her phone and turned to head back into her house, telling whoever she was talking to about Sweetie being back. Decker was happy he didn't have to hear any more about her wilting petunias, but he was not happy that he now had to worry about the citizens of Wilder forming a lynch mob.

Of course, the townsfolk wouldn't actually lynch Sweetie. But when they were pissed at someone, they could raise a ruckus that would make Decker's job of keeping the peace much more difficult.

And they were pissed at Sweetie.

She and Decker's cousin, Jace, had been hometown sweethearts—the kind of beautiful, talented teenagers people loved to live through vicariously. The men of Wilder loved to talk about every pass Jace made in a game and how he was destined to play in the NFL. The women loved to talk about what a great singer Sweetie was and what super Texas babies she and Jace would make.

But then Sweetie had done the unthinkable.

She'd broken up with Jace. And not just any time of year. She had broken up with him right smack dab in the middle of the most sacred time of year there was for Texans.

Football season.

And no one was more shocked than Jace.

After his father had run off and left him and his mama when Jace was only eight, Jace had never liked surprises and worked hard to avoid them. He'd planned out his entire life from going to a top-ten football college and playing in the NFL to marrying the most dependable girl in town.

Sweetie never let anyone down. If she said she was going to do something, she did it. If she told her daddy she would clean out the barn, she cleaned out the barn from top to bottom. If she told her sisters she'd be at their dance recital or softball game, she'd be there. If she promised her mama she'd help her bake cakes for the church bake sale, she'd bake cakes. If she told Jace she'd marry him one day, she'd marry him.

Instead she'd broken up with him. Publically. In the parking lot of the high school football stadium after a game, with everyone in town watching, she'd completely lost it and started yelling and hollering about how she wanted out—not only of her relationship with Jace, but also the town of Wilder.

Jace had been completely blindsided. His grades cratered and so did his quarterbacking ability. He led the Wilder Wildcats to six straight losses and ended their chances of winning a third state championship under his leadership. The townsfolk couldn't forgive Sweetie for that. Or for denouncing their beloved town.

Of course, Decker couldn't forgive her either. He wished it only had to do with her hurting his cousin.

After leaving Mrs. Nichols, Decker headed down the street to Dan Wheeler's house. Dan was real embarrassed about getting caught peeing on Mrs. Nichols's flowers and promised to deliver petunias and an apology to his neighbor right away. Once that was taken care of, Decker decided to call it a day and head home.

A few months back, he'd purchased his grandparents' house from Aunt Lou, Jace's mama, who had inherited it when Gramps and Nana had passed. The three-bedroom brick home sat on the south edge of Holiday Ranch. Gramps and Nana had lived in it for close to sixty-five years before they passed away within two weeks of each other. They'd raised two sons . . . and a grandson after their youngest son and his wife were killed in a car accident.

Decker had been eleven years old when his perfect childhood had come crashing down around him like a Jenga game when someone removed the wrong piece.

His parents were that piece.

As an only child, Decker had been doted on. He'd gone to a private school in Denver, Colorado, where his father worked as an executive for a big tech company. His mother had been a stay-at-home mom who took Decker to baseball practice and swimming lessons and play dates.

When his father got off work, he would take Decker to the park to play catch or just to sit on a park bench and talk about their day.

They were the best parents . . . and then they were gone and Decker went to live with his grandparents.

Decker had spent holidays and short summer vacations with his grandma and grandpa. But visiting a small town and actually living there were two different things. Decker had felt like he'd lost his entire world. His parents. His friends. His house. His school. His city.

His grandparents did everything possible to make him feel loved and welcomed—to help him fit in and heal. But it was Jace who helped Decker the most. Jace had been fourteen at the time and a budding football star with plenty of friends. Decker was sure the last thing he'd wanted was his eleven-year-old cousin tagging along behind him. But Jace had never complained or made Decker feel like a third wheel. The first day after he'd arrived, Jace had taken him to the Holiday Ranch where Jace had gotten a summer job.

That's when Decker had first met Sweetie. She had come bouncing out the front door like a petite, perfect doll, her ponytail swinging back and forth like a golden pendulum of a clock.

"Good mornin', y'all!" Her green-eyed gaze had pinned Decker and he'd lost his ability to think. Or speak. "So you're the new ranch hand who's going to help Jace." A smile lit her face as she'd held out her hand. "Hey, Deck. I'm Sweetie Holiday."

In his brain fog, he hadn't heard her correctly. "I-I-It's nice to m-m-meet you, Sweets," he'd stammered.

She'd laughed. "Sweets." She tipped her head in thought. "I think I like that. Now come on and I'll teach you how to shovel horse poop. Believe me, I'm an expert."

He'd believed her. He'd believed everything that came out of Sweetie Holiday's perfectly shaped lips. She had been like a bright ray of sunshine busting through the darkness that had surrounded his soul. It didn't matter that she looked at him as just a kid. It didn't matter that a year later she became Jace's official girlfriend. All that mattered was being near her.

And then just like his parents, she was gone.

Decker's house looked the same as when his grandparents had lived there. It needed to be renovated on the inside and painted on the out, but Decker didn't have the money or the time. Besides, he liked the familiarity of things remaining the same.

He parked behind Jace's old truck and got out. When he got to the porch, he had to step over his hound dog to get to the front door.

"Hey, George. Don't get up. It's only the man who feeds you, removes your ticks, and picks up your dog poop."

George didn't even open a droopy eyelid.

Decker laughed. "Lazy dog."

Once inside, he changed into some comfortable sweats, filled George's water and food bowls, and grabbed a beer from the fridge. While most men might watch sports on television or read a book after a stressful day, Decker didn't turn on the television or pick up the mystery novel sitting on the end table next to grandpa's old recliner. Instead, he sat down in Nana's needlepoint rocker and reached into the knitting basket.

The navy-and-white afghan was almost finished. All he had to do was a few more rows and then finish it off before it went in the box in the back of his sheriff's SUV. It was surprising how comforting a hand-knitted blanket was to folks who had gone through a tragedy. The truck driver had certainly seemed to appreciate it when Decker had placed a knitted blanket around his shoulders that very morning.

Decker had come up with the idea when he'd answered a call where a man had suffered a stroke and died. His poor, distraught wife had been in shock. When Decker had placed the scratchy wool blanket, he'd been issued by the sheriff's department, around her shoulders as they sat outside on the porch waiting for the funeral home, he'd thought how much nicer it would be to have one of his grandma's afghans to comfort her. He'd asked Nana if she would make him some and she'd started that day. Once she was gone, it seemed only right to continue making them. Whenever he sat down to knit, he imaged her watching from heaven and smiling.

As he worked with the soft yarn, the tension he'd felt since running in to Sweetie started to dissipate. So what if she was back in town? She'd been gone soon enough. Until then, he just needed to pretend she wasn't there.

His cellphone rang and he quickly set down his knitting and answered it.

It was Melba Wadley.

Melba was his office manager, dispatcher, and mother hen. She was efficient, dedicated, and a force to be reckoned with. She had worked for the sheriff's department for the last forty-four years and knew Texas law better than anyone in the state. She was divorced and had raised three kids mostly by herself, was a grandma to eight grandkids and foster mama to a zoo of dogs and cats that she kept trying to pawn off on Decker—which was how he had gotten a lazy hound dog. She could shoot a row of tin cans off a fence from twenty yards away, had won more than her share of ax-throwing contests, and went dirt bike riding with her kids and grandkids. She sang in the choir at church every Sunday, but never refused an offer to get a cold beer on a Saturday night.

Decker pretty much adored her. Even if she did get after him a lot.

"I'm not making you chicken salad for lunch anymore if you're not going to come back to the office to eat it."

His stomach growled at just the thought of Melba's chicken salad. "I'm sorry. It's been one helluva day."

"So what was Donna Nichols so up in arms about?"

"Dan Wheeler got drunk last night and peed on her petunias."

Melba chuckled. "Serves her right. I swear that woman needs someone to pull that self-righteous corncob out of her butt. Too bad her milquetoast husband doesn't have enough balls to do it. Oh, and speaking of balls, Viola Stanley came by to see you with a plate of brownies. The girl still can't cook worth beans—yes, I tried one—nor is she very bright. Anyone with eyes can see you're not interested."

"What makes you say that?"

Melba snorted. "You are one of the most intense men I have ever met in my life. When you focus on something, you give it one hundred percent of your attention. Whether it's ironing your clothes, eating one of Sheryl Ann's muffins, or filling out a report. And you're about as interested in Viola Stanley as you are in learning to two-step—which I've repeatedly told you is one of the prerequisites of being a true Texan. So just let the woman know so she can poison some other poor fool with her cooking. And speaking of poor fools, I just got a call about a beat-up Mustang being broken down on the side of Highway 333. I called Dave to tow it back to town."

Decker should thank her and let Dave handle it. It wasn't like word about Sweetie's return wasn't already spreading like a lit fuse through Wilder. He should make dinner, have another beer, and then see if he could teach George to fetch a ball.

But, for some reason, that wasn't what he did.

"Don't bother Dave. I'll handle it."

CHAPTER FOUR

SWEETIE DIDN'T EVEN remember falling asleep. One second, she'd been struggling to tuck a fitted sheet over the edge of her mattress, and the next, she woke up tangled in that sheet with her cheek pressed to the drool-dampened mattress.

Rolling to her back, she blinked at the late afternoon sun streaming in the window. When her eyes had adjusted, she glanced around the room.

Everything looked exactly like it had when Sweetie had packed up and headed for Nashville after she'd graduated from high school. Cloe's side of the room was neat as a pin with a book-case filled with perfectly lined-up books and her collection of childhood toy horses. Sweetie's side was stuffed to the gills with life mementos: the giant-sized stuffed animals Jace had won her at the county fair were crammed on top of each other in one corner, the shelf above her dresser held a jumble of childhood trophies, beloved dolls, and a Miss Soybean rhinestone tiara. The full-length mirror frame on her closet door was lined with pictures and concert and school dance ticket stubs. And her bookcase was stuffed full of notebooks filled with all the song lyrics she'd written over the years.

As long as she could remember, she'd had melodies and words swimming around in her head. When she learned to write, she'd started jotting them down in notebooks.

Getting up from the bed, she sat cross-legged on the floor in front of the bookcase and pulled out the first one. She couldn't help but smile as she read the first song she'd ever written. "I Love Mi Hors" had only three verses. *I love mi hors, I love mi hors, I love mi hors.* The next song was more complex. *I hat gren beens, I hat gren beens, I hat gren beens . . . but I love mi hors.*

As time went on, Sweetie's handwriting and spelling had gotten better and so had her lyrics. Most of the songs were still about her horse, but she'd started adding verses of why she loved her horse so much. *He always takes me for a ride, even wen it's cold outside.*

Sweetie didn't know how long she sat there going through notebook after notebook. It was like reliving her life through lyrics. Like a journal written in songs. There were songs about her life on the ranch: "Cattle Drive" "Muckin' Life" "Sunday Supper" "Skinny Dip." There were songs about her family. "Mama's Hugs" "Stupid Sisters" "Grandma's Garden" "Daddy's Girl." There were songs about growing up. "Little Boobs" "One Big Pimple" "Eve's Curse." Then there were songs about Jace. Love songs from a teenage girl completely besotted. "Football Hero" "When He Smiles" "One Lucky Girl." But in the next notebook the songs became sadder and darker. "Look Right Through Me" "Who Am I" "Fighting to Breathe."

She remembered writing those songs. Remembered feeling like she was trapped underwater struggling to get to the surface and no one seemed to know she was drowning. Not her parents. Not her grandmother. Not her sisters. And especially not Jace.

"Leaving to Live" was the last song she had written before she'd left town. She hadn't taken any of the notebooks with her. These songs were her past life. They had no place in her new one. When she got to Nashville, she planned to write better songs. Hit songs.

And she had tried. She had filled numerous notebooks with all kinds of words. But that's all they were. Words. They hadn't come close to conveying feelings and telling a story like these songs did. It was like she had left the real Sweetie right here on these shelves—in this room, on this ranch—while the fake Sweetie had gone to Nashville to become a star.

But people didn't want a star with no substance. They wanted the real thing.

Somewhere along the lines, she had lost the real Sweetie.

"Sweetie! Come down here!"

Her mother's voice startled her out of her thoughts and she carefully placed the notebooks back on the bookshelf. She dreaded going downstairs to supper and having to deal with her daddy. As much as she hated to admit it, his rejection had hurt. There had been a time when she had been the apple of his eye—his Sweetie Pie. But only because she'd done everything he'd ever asked of her. She couldn't be that daddy's girl again. She wouldn't be. She was a grown woman with her own dream.

She looked at the notebooks on the shelf.

But what if Daddy was right and her dream had been the wrong dream all along?

When she reached the bottom of the stairs, she expected to see her mama waiting to give her a list of things that needed to be done before her sisters got there.

She did not expect to see Decker Carson.

He no longer wore a pressed sheriff's shirt. Now he had on a faded western shirt that molded to his body as well as his jeans did. Without the hat and sunglasses, she had a clear view of his face in the evening light spilling in through the windows.

Jace had always been the better-looking Carson. The golden boy.

But things had changed.

Decker might not have hair that reflected the sunlight like a gold coin, but his thick dark brown hair caught the light like the rippling surface of a moonlit lake. While Jace's eyes were a dark midnight blue, Decker's were the same color of the pictures her roommate had shown her of the ocean around the Caribbean islands—translucent turquoise with a splash of sandy shores around his dark pupils. They held her gaze as if she was his sole focus, making her feel like she did when she was sitting on stage in a single spotlight—vulnerable and completely exposed.

"Good Lord, Sweetie." Her mama hurried over to Sweetie who was still standing frozen on the last stair. "You look like you just stepped out of the eye of a tornado." She finger-smoothed Sweetie's hair, then licked her thumb and wiped at the corner of Sweetie's mouth.

Sweetie felt her face heat. "Mama!" She stepped off the stair and self-consciously swiped at her mouth before glancing at Decker.

"What are you doing here?"

"Sweetheart Mae!" Her mama swatted her on the butt. "Mind your manners. Decker was nice enough to stop by to take you to get your car."

"I don't need his help."

Her mama rolled her eyes at Decker. "Forgive her, Deck. She's always grumpy when she first wakes up. I'm sure she appreciates your kindness. And if you'll wait here just a second I've got something for you." She hurried into the kitchen.

When she was gone, Sweetie turned to Decker. "Thanks for coming, but my mama can take me to get my car."

"It sounds like your mama has enough to worry about getting ready for your sisters and taking care of your daddy." He hesitated. "How's your daddy taking y'all coming home?"

"Just peachy."

Again, he hesitated. "He might not act like it, but I know he's happy to have y'all here."

"Thanks, but I don't need you to tell me how my daddy feels."

He pinned her with those piercing turquoise eyes as Mama hustled back into the room.

"Here we are." She held out an aluminum foil-covered pie tin. "If I remember correctly, you always loved my gooseberry pie, Deck."

Gooseberry?

Sweetie's eyes widened. That was her pie Decker was accepting with a smile that would have stunned her if she hadn't already been stunned about her mama giving away her pie. Was it her imagination or was there a knowing twinkle in his eyes when he said, "Thank you. Gooseberry *is* my favorite." He pushed open the screen door and held it for Sweetie. "After you."

She was about to decline when her mama shoved her purse at her and pushed her out the door. "I'll keep your supper warm!" She closed the door in Sweetie's stunned face.

Sweetie stood there for only a brief second before she turned to Decker and glanced down at the pie plate he was palming in his oversized hand. "That's my pie."

He followed her gaze. "It sure doesn't look that way."

"Well, looks can be deceivin'." She swept past him and down the steps of the porch. She froze when she reached the bottom. She'd expected to see his squeaky-clean sheriff's SUV. Instead, a mud-splattered old Ford truck sat at the end of the path.

A truck she remembered well.

It was the same truck Jace had driven in high school. The same truck they'd first kissed in. The same truck she'd thrown up in after drinking too many sloe gin fizzes at the junior prom. The same truck she had refused to get into the night she had broken his heart. Instead, she had remained in the parking lot and caused a scene in front of the entire town. All because she felt like if she got in that truck, she would be trapped in Wilder forever.

"Is there a problem?"

Decker's words brought her out of her thoughts. She took a deep breath and reminded herself that she wasn't a scared teenager anymore. She was an adult. An adult who could leave Wilder anytime she wanted.

"No problem." She pulled open the door and climbed in. Once inside, there was a moment of déjà vu. But it quickly passed when Decker slid into the driver's side.

He was as different from Jace as night and day. He had always been quiet whereas Jace was talkative. He had always been hesitant whereas Jace had charged forward. He had always been intense whereas Jace had always been nonchalant.

About everything but football.

Decker had never played football. He'd never played any sport. And yet, he looked like he had. As he placed the pie on the torn bench seat between them, then put the idling truck into drive and pulled away, she couldn't help taking in the hard muscles that filled out his western shirt. The solid curves of his chest. The bulge of bicep beneath his sleeve. The strong cords of his forearm hooked over the steering wheel.

A feeling settled in her belly. A feeling she had no business feeling for Jace's cousin. Trying to distract herself from the sexy, muscled man next to her, she turned on the radio. The stations had been programmed differently than when Jace drove the truck. There was not one country station. Just classic rock stations, one news station, and talk radio.

"Do you have something against country music?"

"No. It's just not something I enjoy listening to."

She snorted. "You never said a word when I used to serenade you with the songs I wrote while we were cleaning the barn."

"Would you have stopped if I had?"

She laughed. "Probably not."

The smell of warm gooseberry pie had started to fill the cab of the truck and Sweetie's stomach protested loudly. She hadn't eaten since the Sausage McMuffin she'd gotten that morning at the McDonald's in Dallas and she was starving. Since it *was* her pie, she lifted the tin foil and broke off a piece of flaky crust. Decker shot her an annoyed look and she sent him a smug smile in return before she popped the piece in her mouth.

He looked back at the road. "I don't like the crust anyway."

"Liar." She broke off another piece and ate it slowly, savoring the buttery flakiness. "You used to beg me to bring you my mama's cinnamon piecrust cookies." This time the growl came from his stomach. She laughed as she broke off a piece and held it out. "I can't let an officer of the law go hungry. So I'm willing to share . . . my pie."

His ocean gaze shifted to her and he hesitated for only a second before he leaned over, opened his mouth, and took the crust from her fingers. The feel of his lips and tongue brushing her fingertips caused her stomach to drop like she was on the downward slide of a roller coaster. All the air whooshed out of her lungs, but thankfully, he didn't seem to notice. His eyes were closed as he licked a wayward flake of crust from his bottom lip.

Her stomach took another dive and she turned away. What the hell was wrong with her? It had to be the truck. Her hormones were just taking a walk down memory lane without her brain.

And with the wrong Carson.

Except Jace's touch had never made her feel like she was riding a roller coaster.

"Okay, I lied," Decker said. "I love your mama's piecrust." He reached over and snapped off another edge of the pie.

"Hey!" She grabbed the pie plate and set it on her lap. "I will share when I—" She cut off when she saw her car up ahead.

Mustang Sally had been defiled.

Or maybe not defiled. It wasn't the first time the Mustang had had its windows shoe polished. But usually the words were something uplifting. *Go Wildcats! Juniors Rule! Happy 17th Birthday,*

Sweetie! Now the words shoe polished across her windshield were just plain mean.

Get Gone, Sweetie! You Ain't Welcome!!!

She tried to make light of it, but it was hard when a huge lump had formed in her throat. "Well, I guess that answers that question. The townsfolk *are* still carrying a grudge."

Decker muttered something under his breath that sounded like *immature imbeciles* before he made a quick U-turn and pulled in behind Mustang Sally. There was no message on the back window . . . just a splatter of raw eggs and broken eggshells.

With a muttered curse, he shoved open the door and got out. She followed behind him and watched as he took two red plastic gas containers from the bed of the truck. While he filled her gas tank, she opened her trunk and got an old car wash towel to clean off the windows. The eggs had dried so she had no luck getting them off, but the shoe polish came off with a little elbow grease.

"It was probably just some punky teenagers. This isn't the first broken-down car that's been tagged."

She glanced up to see Decker standing on the other side of the hood. "And all of them were tagged with *Get Gone, Sweetie?*" She laughed. "Don't try to make me feel better, Deckster. I know you feel the same way."

The sun had set and the soft purple of twilight surrounded his tall frame making it hard to read his expression.

"Why'd you do it?"

She could have acted like she didn't know what he was talking about, but she didn't. "Jace and I never would have worked. We both had different dreams."

"And you couldn't have figured that out sooner?"

It was a good question and one of the reasons she still blamed herself for how she'd ended things with Jace. She had known long before that night at the football game that she didn't love Jace. She just hadn't had the guts to tell him. So she had held it in and held it in until she had exploded like a shaken can of Coke. But she didn't need to explain anything to Decker.

She went back to cleaning the window. "I don't owe you an explanation."

He shook his head. "No, but you owed Jace one. He didn't have a clue what he'd done to make you stop loving him."

"He hadn't done anything. It was me. All me. I told him that."

He made air quotes. "'It's not you, it's me.' Yeah, we've all heard that one before. Jesus, Sweetie. Couldn't you have come up with something a little less clichéd?"

She straightened. "Like what? What could I possibly have said that would have made him feel better?"

"How about something other than 'I don't love you. I've never loved you. I just dated you to please my daddy' in front of the entire town?"

She hated that Decker remembered word for

word what she had yelled at Jace. Of course, the shallow, insensitive words were hard to forget.

"You're right," she said. "I shouldn't have said that. It was insensitive and cruel. The only excuse I have is that I was young and stupid and feeling like I didn't have a choice in my life."

Decker moved around the car and stood in front of her. "And you think Jace didn't feel that way? He had all the coaches expecting him to take the Wildcats to another state championship. He had college scouts showing up at every game scrutinizing his every play. And he had the entire town's hopes that he'd not only give them another state trophy, but also become an NFL superstar. And you were feeling like you didn't have a choice?" He turned away. "You are so damned selfish."

She felt her anger rise. "Selfish? I was selfish? I supported your cousin all through high school. I was at every damn game and town pep rally, cheering louder than anyone else—including you. If I remember correctly, you don't even like football and rarely showed up at the games. But here you are, acting all holier than thou." She stepped closer and jabbed a finger at him. "Well, let me tell you something, mister. I was a good girlfriend to Jace. A damn good girlfriend. Especially when it wasn't exactly an easy job. I had more dates than I can possibly count interrupted by people wanting to know how his arm was and how he thought the Wildcats were going to do this year and what college he was planning to play for. I just sat there and smiled through it all until I couldn't sit there and smile anymore."

"Like I said. Selfish. You couldn't stand that he was getting all the attention from the townsfolk and you weren't."

She had always had a temper, but over the years she'd learned how to control it. But there was something about her daddy and Decker that unraveled the tight hold she'd kept on her anger and it spilled out before she could stop it.

The ringing sound of her open hand connecting with his face snapped her out of her rage haze, but it was too late. There was no way to take back the vivid red handprint on Decker's clenched jaw.

In a nanosecond, he had her pushed up against the car with a hard body that gave no quarter. Once again, her stomach took a roller-coaster ride and her breath hung suspended in her lungs as he spoke in that low, sexy, bedroom voice.

"Just because Jace put up with your spoiled tantrums, doesn't mean I will. You mess with me again and I'll toss your ass in jail and throw away the key. You got that, Sweets?"

Before she could do more than blink, he was gone and she was left staring at the red taillights of Jace's truck.

CHAPTER FIVE

"SO WHAT'S GOING on with you?"

Decker glanced up from the cup of coffee he'd been staring into. Melba stood in the doorway of his office wearing her usual outfit of tie-dyed Crocs, black yoga pants, and a floral shirt that hurt his eyes. Today, she had added a cartoon-dog-print purse strapped across her body.

"You going somewhere?" he asked.

"Do I ever go anywhere during work hours? Now what's up with you? You've been acting like a bear with a thorn in its paw ever since you walked through the door. Are you constipated?" No subject was taboo for Melba.

"I'd rather not discuss my bowels, thank you very much. And nothing's wrong with me. I just didn't sleep well last night."

"Because you're probably constipated. Blockage can do that."

His sleepless night had nothing to do with blockage and everything to do with him making a big mistake. He should have stayed away from Sweetie Holiday. He'd had no business going to her house. No business taking her to get her car. And no business bringing up the past.

He deserved to be slapped. He should have taken it like a man and walked away. Instead, he'd hadn't just left with an imprint of her hand on his cheek. He'd left with the imprint of her body.

He could still feel the fullness of her breasts against his ribs, the low strum of her heart echoing the rapid thump of his. He could feel the soft press of her stomach and the hard jab of the button on her jeans. He could feel the curves and hollows of her hips and the long lines of her thighs.

All those feels had kept him up for most of the night. When he *had* finally fallen asleep, his dreams had taken over. In those, he hadn't just pressed her against the car. He stripped her naked and took her right there on the candy apple-red hood of Mustang Sally. He'd woken up with a hard-on that could pound nails and a boatload of guilt he didn't know if he could ever get rid of.

What the hell was the matter with him? It was bad enough when he was eleven and lusting after his cousin's girlfriend. Now he was an adult man who knew the hell that woman put men through. He had no business remembering how she felt. He had no business feeling her at all. He needed to stay away from Sweetie Holiday.

"Does this have to do with Sweetie Holiday coming back to town?

Decker choked on the sip of cold coffee he'd just taken. It took a good amount of coughing to clear his throat. When he finally did, he glanced over to see Melba giving him a knowing look.

"That's what I figured. Sweetie coming home has caused quite a stir."

As always, Melba had hit the nail right on the head. Sweetie had stirred Decker up all right. She'd stirred him up real good. Thankfully, there would be an end to the stirring.

"She'll be leaving soon enough," he said.

"And that's a shame. One of those Holiday girls needs to stick around and take care of family. I realize Hank is hardheaded, but so are most Texas daddies—or Texas men, for that matter. That's why Texas women need to be tough-skinned. You don't run when your men get stubborn. You just take the tiger by the tail and let them know who's really running the show. But enough about Sweetie Holiday. There's another sweetie I'd like to tell you about. Dixie Chick is the cutest little gal you'd ever want to meet and I think she'd make a great friend for George Strait."

People who didn't know Melba would think she was talking about country singers. But Melba had taken to naming all her foster animals after country singers. She had fostered Gene Autry, Kitty Wells, Morgan Wallen, and Kelsea Ballerini. Just to name a few. It was like she knew that giving them a beloved country singer's name would make them hard to say no to. But Decker didn't need another dog. He hadn't even needed the first one.

"No, thank you, Mel. George Strait doesn't need a friend. All that animal wants to do is sleep.

When you said he was a gentle soul, I thought you meant he had a sweet disposition. I didn't think you meant he had narcolepsy."

"George doesn't have narcolepsy. He just enjoys naps. And who doesn't like a good nap?"

"All day long? You put a leash on the dog and he drops to the floor like he's been shot between the eyes. You toss a ball or a stick and it sits where it is until I run over it with the lawn mower. He doesn't enjoying hunting or fishing or riding in the truck. He will meander over to his bowl when you fill it with food. And not just any food. It has to be the refrigerated kind that costs an arm and a leg."

Melba smiled. "Admit it. You love that lazy, finicky dog."

"Yes. I love him. Besides his eating habits, he's not demanding. And with my job, demanding animals won't work. So no on another dog."

"Dixie Chick isn't demanding. How can you say no before you meet her?" She opened the purse she had strapped on and pulled out a . . . hairy rat. No, make that a hairy mouse with ears too big for its golf ball–sized head. But it had teeth. Tiny sharp teeth that it bared as soon as it saw Decker.

Melba stroked its head and spoke soothingly. "Now calm down, little mighty mite. Decker isn't gonna hurt you." As soon as she got the dog quieted down, she held it out to Decker, but he shook his head.

"Nope. You aren't going to get me this time, Mel. Once was enough."

She shrugged. "Well, it was worth a try." She set the dog down on Decker's desk. "But at least watch her while I run to the bathroom." Without waiting for a reply, she turned and headed out of the office.

Decker studied the miniature cross between a Chihuahua and a rat. She was the littlest dog he'd ever seen in his life. But she was kind of cute. Besides big ears, she had huge brown eyes that covered more than half her face. They studied him with suspicion and fear.

"Melba is right. I'm not gonna hurt you." He reached out to pet her, but she bared her teeth again. He held up his hands. "Fine, but don't get too close to the edge. And don't even think about pee—" He cut off when a flash of red drew his attention to the window. He swore when he saw the tail end of Mustang Sally passing by.

Without giving the bared teeth a second thought, he scooped Dixie Chick up and headed to the window. He arrived just in time to see Sweetie pulling into a parking space in front of Nothin' But Muffins. If someone wanted to draw attention to themselves, all they had to do was show up at the café in the mornings. Everyone in town stopped by for coffee and Sheryl Ann's famous muffins.

Decker should have turned away from the window and gone right back to his desk. Whatever the townsfolk dished out, Sweetie was obviously asking for. But when she got out of her car, he couldn't seem to look away.

Yesterday, she'd looked all nap-tousled and sexy as hell when she came down the stairs.

Today, she looked refreshed . . . and sexy as hell. Her long hair had been curled and those curls waved in the stiff breeze like a field of overripe wheat. She wore the UT hoodie and black leggings that clung to the sweet curves of her butt like a second skin. Flaming-red cowboy boots came up to her knees and begged to be wrapped around a man's waist.

Desire settled low and heavy inside Decker.

He tried to remember the last time he'd felt such a strong sexual pull. It was scary he couldn't pull up one woman who had made him feel so . . . hungry. Well, there was one and he was looking at her. But that was when he was a randy teenage boy. He wasn't that boy anymore.

"Get a grip, Decker," he muttered under his breath. He started to turn away, but then the door of the café opened and Cob Ritter and his gang of troublemakers stepped out. He hoped they wouldn't notice Sweetie. It was a fruitless hope. There was no way any man could not notice Sweetheart Holiday. And when Cob smiled in a lecherous way, Decker knew he couldn't hide in his office any longer.

By the time he got out the door of the sheriff's station, Cob and his buddies had surrounded Sweetie and Cob was being his usual asshole self.

"Well, if it ain't Miss High and Mighty Sweetie Mae Holiday. Of course, it doesn't look like you're all that high and mighty anymore." He placed a hand on the Mustang's hood. "What? Couldn't you afford a new car with all that country star money you're making?"

Sweetie didn't back down. "Touch my car again, douchebag, and I'll break your nose like I did in second grade. Or did you forget how I made you cry like a baby for his mama?"

Cob's eyes darkened and he reached out and grabbed Sweetie's arm. Decker had always been a calm and collected sort of lawman who never lost his cool and rarely chose to use physical force over levelheaded logic. But there was something about the sight of Cob's hand on Sweetie's arm that made him feel . . . feral.

"Get your fuckin' hands off her," he growled as he shoved his way into the group. Both Sweetie and Cob turned to him with surprise. Cob released her and held up his hands.

"Don't go postal, Deck. I was just welcoming Sweetie back to town."

"I'm sure you were. And it's Sheriff Carson to you."

"Oh, come on now. We played dodgeball together when we were kids."

"I don't ever remember you playing, Cob. I do remember you viciously throwing the ball at kids' heads."

Cob grinned. "Potato potahto. We grew up together."

"That doesn't make us friends."

Cob's smile faded. "No, I guess it don't." He glanced at Sweetie. "But I'd think that you wouldn't be so quick to serve and protect after what she did to your cousin."

"That's between her and Jace. Not you. Or me. Or anyone in this town." As soon as he said the words, he realized how hypocritical they were. He had been taking his anger out on Sweetie. Just not for what she'd done to Jace as much as what she'd done to him.

Cob smirked as if he could read Decker's mind. "Or maybe you don't care what she did to Jace because you have plans of your own for Miss Sweetie Holiday."

Decker felt his face heat with anger. "What I have is the responsibility of keeping everyone in this town safe. Everyone. Now are you going to move along or do I need to help you?"

Cob laughed. "You and who else?" He looked down. "Your big, mean police dog?" Decker had been so focused on getting to Sweetie that he hadn't even realized he still had Dixie Chick tucked in the crook of his arm. Her buggy brown eyes were focused on Cob and when he reached out to pet her, she bit him. "What the—?" Cob drew back to examine the puncture marks in his finger that were welling with blood.

Decker grinned. "You might want to get that looked at, Cob. I'm not sure my police dog has her rabies shots."

Cob sent him a mean glare before he motioned to his friends and they left. When they were gone, Decker patted Dixie Chick's head. "Good girl."

"Females don't like being talked to in such a patronizing way."

Decker glanced at Sweetie. He hadn't expected a smile or a thank you—especially with how they had left things the night before—and he wasn't disappointed.

"I could have handled Cob Ritter," she said. "I don't need you to play hero."

"I wasn't playing hero. I was saving myself the hassle and paperwork of having to arrest someone. Now what are you doing in town?"

"That's none of your damn business." She went to move past him, but he took her arm. She gazed down at it, then up at him with eyes that held a warning. "The men in this town seem to have forgotten I don't like to be manhandled. I never broke your nose, but there's a first time for everything."

He dropped his hand. "Go home, Sweetie."

"I intend to, Sheriff Carson. But until I do, I'm not going to hide out like some scared rabbit. If the townsfolk want to take their anger out on me . . ." She held out her arms. "Here I am. Now if you'll excuse me, I need a cup of coffee in a bad way. Mama can cook like nobody's business, but her coffee has always tasted like weak tea." She reached out and gave Dixie Chick a scratch on the ears. "You aren't a good girl because you did something a man happened to like. You're strong because you stood up for yourself. Don't you ever forget it, girlfriend."

Then she turned and headed into the café.

CHAPTER SIX

SWEETIE WAS SHAKING in her boots. Not because of her run-in with Cob Ritter. Or because of the hostile looks she was getting from every patron at Nothin' But Muffins. She was shaking in her boots because Decker Carson rattled her and made her feel things she didn't want to feel.

Like a needy woman.

She had told him she didn't need him playing the hero. And she didn't. But she had liked it. She had liked it a lot. When he had gone all alpha male on Cob, her insides had turned warm and gooey. His blue eyes had been snapping fire and his clenched fist had caused his forearm to flex in a way that took all the air right out of her lungs.

What topped off the big scoop of angry, virile man was the tiny little dog he had protectively cradled in his muscled arm the entire time. Sweetie had always been a sucker for animal lovers. And Decker had always had a way with animals. When he first came to the ranch, he'd been scared of horseflies. But within a few weeks, he'd relaxed around animals and his calm demeanor had drawn them to him.

Just like he was drawing her.

She shook her head to clear it. *No, Sweetie. Just, no.* She had made a big mistake with one Carson boy. She didn't need to make another. Especially when she was still paying for that mistake.

"Is there something you needed?"

The words had her glancing at the woman standing behind the counter.

Sheryl Ann had run the café for as long as Sweetie could remember. Her parents had started it when they were a young, newlywed couple and Sheryl Ann had taken over managing it as soon as she was out of high school. She was a stout woman with thick black hair she had inherited from her Cherokee relatives and a friendly face that always wore a toothy smile.

She wasn't smiling today.

Sweetie held up her hand in an awkward wave. "Hey, Sheryl Ann." She glanced around the café at the people sitting at the tables. Most of whom she knew. "Hey, y'all. Long time no see."

No one said a word. They all just stared at her. Or more like glared.

She cleared her throat and returned her attention to Sheryl Ann. "There sure is something I need. I need a cup of strong black coffee with plenty of sugar and one of your famous muffins. Sour Lemon Poppy, please."

Sheryl Ann sprayed some cleaner on the counter and started wiping it down. "Out of coffee. Muffins too."

Sweetie looked down at the display case where tray after tray of different-flavored muffins sat. It was difficult to keep the bright smile on her face. "Well, that's too bad. Nobody makes coffee or muffins like you do, Sheryl Ann. I guess I'll just have a Diet Coke."

"Coke machine is broke." Sheryl Ann stopped wiping the counter and glanced up. "You should probably go somewhere else."

There was nowhere else to get breakfast in town. Bobby Jay's Hellhole didn't open until four and Tito's Taco truck opened at eleven. Not that Sweetie was hungry. Her mama had already made her a huge breakfast of waffles and bacon that morning, before giving her a list of errands she needed to run in town. Sweetie couldn't say no. Especially when she was there to help her mama. So since she had to come to town, she figured she'd start with Nothin' But Muffins and let most of the townsfolk get all their anger out at once.

She hadn't realized how hurtful it would be.

"Okay," she said. "I'll go. But before I do, I have a few things I'd like to say. I'm sorry for what I said that night at the football game. Not just to Jace, but also about this town."

Sheryl Ann scowled. "You mean the part about you hating this stupid Podunk town and not being able to wait until you could shake our dust from your boots."

It looked like the town had as long a memory as Decker did.

Sweetie swallowed hard. "I didn't mean it."

"Which is why you didn't come back once in the last twelve years," Sheryl Ann said snidely.

"That had nothing to do with y'all. It had more to do with the fight I had with my daddy over me not marrying Jace."

Coach Denny Wilson jumped up from his chair, the whistle he always wore around his neck swinging against his barrel belly. "You should have married Jace! Instead, you broke that kid's heart and were responsible for him losing his chances of getting a scholarship to a top-ten football college!"

As always when Coach Denny yelled, spit flew from his mouth. "The boy was the best quarterback I've ever had the privilege to coach, and if you hadn't publically humiliated him and made him lose his focus, he would've gone on to play for the Longhorns or the Aggies." Half the people in the café lifted their pointer fingers and pinkies in the Texas University Longhorns' "hook 'em, horns" sign and the other half lifted a thumb in the Texas A&M Aggies' "gig 'em" sign as Coach Denny continued. "And there's no doubt he would have gone on to be a top pick in the draft and been one of the best damn quarterbacks in the NFL." He placed a hand over his heart. "Maybe even better than Roger Staubach."

Everyone covered their hearts with their hands.

Sweetie knew that, where football was concerned, there was no arguing with the town's beliefs. It would be best if she made a quick exit with her tail between her legs. But before she could, a loud snort came from the corner of the café. Sweetie turned to see Fiona Stokes sitting at her usual table by the window.

Sweetie was happy to see the old gal looking so well. She still dyed her stiffly sprayed bouffant hair a dark red. She still wore full makeup and enough jewelry to sink the Titanic. And she still dressed in matching skirts and jackets, hose, heels, and a mink stole she wore in all seasons.

Although the mink was starting to show its age. Not so Mrs. Stokes.

"That is just plain horse hockey," she snapped before she fell into a smoker's coughing fit. Something she did a lot. Mrs. Stokes had smoked Winston cigarettes all her life . . . and had still outlived three husbands and six boyfriends. According to Sweetie's mama, she was now seeing a retired podiatrist nineteen years her junior. Sweetie didn't doubt it. Mrs. Stokes might be old, but old could be overlooked when a person had a boatload of oil leases their daddy left them.

Not wanting to catch hell, everyone waited quietly for the coughing fit to end. Mrs. Stokes was meaner than a rattlesnake and the one person in town everyone feared. Mostly because it was her money that kept the town going. Without it, Wilder would have become just another small town of vacant buildings and lost dreams. Instead, it was one of the prettiest, well-maintained small towns in Texas.

After one last phlegmy cough, Mrs. Stokes continued talking as if she'd never stopped. "Jace didn't have the arm to make it in the NFL. Y'all were just too caught up on the idea of having the next Staubach come from this town to realize it." Her eyes narrowed on Sweetie and Sweetie swallowed hard. Like the rest of the town, Mrs. Stokes scared the crap out of her. "But that doesn't excuse what you did, missy."

"Yes, ma'am. I know I handled things all wrong with Jace."

"I'm not talking about what you did to Jace. Relationships are never easy to navigate. Especially when you're young." Mrs. Stokes shot a mean glance over at Coach Denny. "Some ignorant people might think you should've stayed and continued to kiss Jace's ass, but I don't agree." She looked back at Sweetie. "While the Carson boys have always had nice asses, no woman should feel like she's only there to support her man's dreams."

Sweetie released her breath, relieved that someone in this town understood her side of things.

Her relief was short lived.

"But that doesn't excuse what you did to us," Mrs. Stokes snapped. "This is your hometown. You were born just down the road at the county hospital. You got your first doll from Crawley's General Store. You chipped a tooth when you fell off the statue of David Bowie at Remember the Alamo Park and broke your arm right out there on that street in the Fourth of July parade. Joe Baca sitting right there bonded that chipped tooth you broke and Decker Carson carried you all the way to Doc Weaver's when you broke your arm. Everyone here cheered when you hit a home run on your softball team, when you were crowned Miss Soybean, and every time you played the piano or your guitar and sang."

She had another coughing fit, then started right back up. "I get that you wanted to leave and stretch your wings in a big city. But no matter how high or far away you fly, you should never forget where you came from. And you, missy, forgot us."

There was more nodding before Sheryl Ann spoke. "You didn't even write to give us your address so I could send you a birthday card or your favorite lemon poppy seed muffins for Christmas."

"You didn't text either and we used to text all the time." Tammy Sue joined the conversation.

Tammy Sue had gone to high school with Sweetie. She was one of those overachievers who excelled at everything. Sweetie took note of her large stomach and the double stroller she rolled back and forth with two sleeping toddlers. Obviously, she overachieved at baby making too.

"I'm sorry, Tammy Sue," she said. "I thought everyone in high school hated me for breaking up with Jace and causing us to lose the state championship and wouldn't want to hear from me."

"At first, we did. But not because of the championship. You and Jace were the perfect high school sweethearts. When you broke up, I guess we felt a little blindsided. We thought for sure if anyone got married and lived happily ever after, it would be you two. But we would have gotten over it, if you hadn't shunned us. After you broke up with Jace, you became this angry person who treated all of us as if we were suffocating you."

Sweetie wanted to deny it, but she couldn't. She *had* been angry. Back then, she had wanted to blame Jace, her daddy, and the entire town for making her feel like she couldn't breathe. Now, she realized there was only one person to blame.

Herself.

She was the one who had let her father dictate her life. The one who so wanted to please him that she hadn't stood up for what she wanted until her senior year in high school. Until then, she had acted like she wanted to run the ranch, marry Jace, and live in Wilder. If she had stood up for what she wanted sooner, maybe she wouldn't have hurt her daddy. Or Jace. Or every person in town.

Maybe she wouldn't have felt like she had to leave and couldn't come back until she was famous and had proven she was worthy of their love. But it looked like she had been worthy. She was the only one who hadn't realized it. Now it was too late. There was no way to make up for the years she'd ignored them. It was obvious by the way they were looking at her now.

Not with love, but with hurt and distrust.

She was standing there with tears brimming in her eyes and her heart in her throat when the door opened and Decker stepped in. The cute little dog was gone and his hat was pulled low. It didn't take long for his blue-eyed gaze to zero in on her. His jaw tightened. She wasn't surprised by his show of anger. He seemed to be perpetually angry with her. She waited for him to get after her for being there . . . or maybe just for breathing. Instead, he turned that angry look on the townsfolk.

"Is there a problem?"

"There's no problem, Deck," Sheryl Ann said. "I'll get your usual Cinnamon Monkey Swirl and a cup of coffee heavy on the vanilla creamer." When she started filling his order, everyone went back to their coffee and conversation.

Sweetie should be relieved she was no longer the center of their attention. She wasn't. The townsfolk's attention had always made her feel special—like she could do anything. She'd give about anything to have it back. But she knew it was too late. They could forgive her for breaking up with Jace, but they wouldn't forgive her for breaking up with them.

Accepting her fate, she turned for the door. Decker stopped her.

"Did you forget your coffee?"

She shrugged. "I guess the coffee machine is broken."

He sighed. "I tried to warn you."

"I don't need your warnings, Sheriff. And why are you following me around?"

He snorted. "I have better things to do than to follow you around. I just needed some coffee."

"Bull. I know for a fact that the sheriff's office has a coffee maker. You came to watch the townsfolk take me down a peg or two."

"If I had wanted to see that, I wouldn't have intervened earlier."

"So why did you?"

"Like I said. I'm responsible for the people in this town." He hesitated. "Even the ones who no longer belong here."

After what she had already gone through, that hurt.

"Order up, Deck!" Sheryl called and Decker walked over to get his cinnamon muffin and coffee. Sweetie should have let it go. But she was having a hard time letting anything go with Decker. She waited outside for him and ambushed him as soon as he stepped out of the café.

"I belong here just as much as you do, Deckster. More so, since I was born here and you weren't. So if you think you can bully me into leaving sooner, you got another think coming. Got it?"

Decker's Caribbean-blue gaze held her captive for a long moment before it lowered to her mouth. The sexual awareness hadn't gone anywhere. It was right there singeing her nerve endings and making her knees feel like overcooked pasta.

"Got it," he said in his low, bedroom voice before he turned and walked away.

It wasn't until Decker had disappeared into the sheriff's office that she noticed the white bakery bag sticking out of her purse. When she opened it, she discovered a muffin.

Not a cinnamon muffin, but a lemon poppy seed.

CHAPTER SEVEN

DECKER SPENT THE rest of the morning trying to stay away from the window . . . and failing miserably. Like some kind of pathetic stalker, he kept going back to peek between the slats of the mini blinds and watch as Sweetie made her way around town. After stopping at Nothin' But Muffins, she had headed next door to Hammer and Nail Hardware. She came out only a few minutes later carrying a big bag of gardening mulch. No doubt for her grandma. After she put it in the trunk of her car, she went to the bank, then the post office, and finally Crawley's General Store.

She didn't stay long at any place. It was obvious no one in town was welcoming her back with open arms. But that didn't keep her from running her errands. Sweetie Holiday had never been the type of woman who let anyone stop her from doing what she wanted to do. Whether it was winning a softball tournament or the title of Miss Soybean. If she set her mind on something, she did it come hell or high water.

It looked like she had set her mind on proving to the town that she wasn't going to let their grudge send her packing before she was ready to leave.

Around lunchtime, she stopped by Tito's Taco truck. If anyone forgave her, it would be Tito. He had always had a soft spot for Sweetie. But he wouldn't even come to the window to take her order, and Sweetie loved soft chicken tacos with extra hot sauce and guacamole as much as she loved lemon poppy seed muffins.

Once again, Decker had the strong urge to come to her rescue and damned if he knew why. The sooner Sweetie got it through her head she wasn't welcome here, the sooner she would be on her way back to Nashville. Then things could get back to normal.

And Decker could stop being a damn stalker.

But even after Sweetie left town, Decker couldn't seem to focus on work. It was a relief when the day was over and Melba came in to tell him she was heading home.

"Have a good weekend, Mel," he said as he shut down his laptop.

"I will. It's two-for-one baby backs and beer at the Hellhole tonight." She glanced down. "So are you going to give my dog back?"

Decker looked down at Dixie Chick sleeping in the crook of his arm. The dog seemed to sleep as much as George. Decker got to his feet and carefully handed the dog off to Melba. Dixie woke up as soon as Melba slipped her into the doggie carrier. There was something about those furry ears and big brown eyes peeking over the edge of the carrier that tore Decker's heart in two.

"Fine," he grumbled as he scooped the dog back out. "I'll take her. But only on a trial basis."

Melba fought back a grin. "Sure. You bring her back whenever you're ready. If you come out to my car, I'll give you her bed, food, leash, toys, and favorite treats."

"You have all that in your car?" He scowled as the truth hit him. "You knew I was going to take her, didn't you?"

Melba shrugged. "Of course I did. I also know that you won't bring her back. She's just what two bachelors need."

Decker wasn't so sure.

As soon as he got home, he realized what a mistake he'd made. His yard didn't have a fence. Which was fine for a hound dog that didn't want to move off the front porch, but not so fine for a tiny dog who could wander away and get run over or hurt.

He was sitting in his car thinking about taking Dixie Chick back to Melba when a black Ram truck pulled in behind him.

Rome Remington was Decker's best friend. They were two years apart in age so they hadn't been close in high school, but grew close after Decker came home from college. Rome was a straight shooter and an all-around good man . . . unlike his father, Sam, who was one of the biggest hard-asses Decker had ever met. Sam expected a lot from both his sons. The younger, Casey, let his father's expectations roll right off his back. Rome had taken them to heart. Although after Rome's wife had left him, Decker had noticed he wasn't as dedicated a son as he'd once been.

"Hey, Deck!" Rome said as they both climbed out of their trucks. "I stopped by to see if you wanted to go to the Hellhole for ribs and—" He cut off when he saw Dixie Chick wiggling around in Decker's arms. "What the hell is that?"

Decker used his elbow to close his car door as he tried to control Dixie Chick. "A huge mistake."

Rome shook his head. "Let me guess. Melba talked you into taking another one of her foster dogs. Believe me, I understand. If she pawns any more of her dogs and cats on Casey and me, we'll need to get a bigger ranch. Although I don't know that this one qualifies as a dog or a cat. It looks more like a hamster with big ears." He reached out to scratch Dixie Chick's head, then quickly jumped back when the dog snapped at him. "Jesus!"

Decker laughed. "You scared of a little hamster, Rome?"

"Hell, yeah. That hamster has some sharp teeth. It also looks like it needs to pee."

Decker had already figured that out, but he was nervous about setting the little dog down. "You see George?"

Rome glanced around. "No, but that dog is too lethargic to care one way or the other about a new dog being added to the pack." He squinted at Dixie Chick. "You sure you want something that small? He looks like he could get blown away in a strong wind."

"She. Dixie Chick. And I haven't decided yet if I'm going to keep her. I guess that will depend on how she and George get along."

Dixie Chick continued to squirm and, after one more glance around, Decker set her down. She looked even smaller standing in the middle of the big yard. She shook, the tags on her collar jingling, then proceeded to lower her nose to the ground and sniff out her new surroundings. Decker followed behind her, looking for anything that might cause her harm. Since the sun was setting, he unhooked his flashlight and turned it on, keeping a circle of light around her as she wandered the yard.

Rome laughed. "You'll keep her. You've always had a hero complex, Deck."

He sent Rome an annoyed look. "I don't have a hero complex."

"I don't know what you'd call it. Even as a kid, you were always rescuing or helping out someone. You rake Ms. Davidson's leaves every fall after her husband passed away. You took Janet Levitt to senior prom when no one else would ask her. You declined a great paying job with Microsoft to stay here and become the town sheriff."

"Seattle didn't sound appealing. I like the sun too much."

"You love the people of this town too much."

Decker shrugged. "And you don't?"

Rome's smile faded. "Yeah. Even though sometimes I wish that wasn't true." He crouched and held out his hand to Dixie Chick. "Come here, darlin'. Come say hello." Dixie Chick moved closer to Rome's hand and took a sniff, then lifted her nose in the air and trotted away. Both Decker and Rome laughed. "Looks like you got yourself a finicky female." Rome stood. "And speaking of finicky females. I heard Sweetie Holiday is back in town."

It was Decker's turn to lose his smile. "Yeah. She came back to spend time with her daddy after his heart attack."

"Makes sense." Rome hesitated. "I heard she didn't get the welcome carpet rolled out."

The image of Sweetie standing in the middle of the café with her eyes brimming with tears popped into Decker's head and his fists clenched. "The damn fools just can't let anything go."

Rome's eyebrow lifted beneath the brim of his cowboy hat. "I didn't think you had let it go either. I mean we've spent quite a few nights together where we've ranted and raved about things that piss us off. Sweetie always seems to be top of your list." He hesitated. "It always made me wonder if maybe you had a thing for her."

Decker forced a laugh. "Me and Sweetie? No way. She was Jace's girl. I never even considered dating her."

It was an out-and-out lie. Decker couldn't count the times he'd thought about that exact scenario. If he were the one dating Sweetie, he wouldn't cancel a date because his football buddies wanted to eat pizza and go over game film. If he were dating Sweetie, he wouldn't take her to another school's football game on a date so he could scope out his rivals. If he were dating Sweetie, he'd buy her tulips—her favorite flowers—and give her notebooks to write more of her songs in and do everything he could possibly do to let her know how lucky he was to be dating her.

While he was lost in his thoughts, George came barreling across the yard like his tail was on fire. The sight of the normally lethargic dog running at top speed was so surprising it took Decker a moment to react. By that time, George had reached Dixie Chick.

The large hound dog could have easily swallowed the miniature dog in one bite. But he didn't look like he wanted her for dinner. He looked completely lovestruck. He danced around the little dog with his tail wagging a mile a minute while Dixie Chick completely ignored him and continued to sniff and mark her territory. The one time George got too close, he got snapped at and immediately dropped to his belly and started whining an apology.

"Well, I'll be damned," Rome said. "It looks like all he needed was a female to get his motor running."

Decker laughed as he watched George's antics. "I guess so. Maybe I should start calling him Smitten."

They watched George continue to vie for Dixie Chick's attention until it got dark. Then Decker scooped her up and turned to Rome. "I can't compete with Bobby Jay's ribs, but you're welcome to come in for beer and gooseberry pie."

"I never refuse pie," Rome said.

Once inside, Dixie Chick proceeded to do what she did in the yard and sniff around while George followed behind her with his tail wagging and his tongue lolling. Leaving the dogs to get acquainted, Decker and Rome headed for the kitchen. Decker pulled out a couple beers and handed them to Rome to open while he filled the feeding bowls Melba had given him with food and water. Once he finished, he filled George's bowl.

Only a few seconds later, Dixie Chick came prancing in, her nails clicking on the hardwood floor, and started eating . . . out of George's bowl. George just sat there and watched with a goofy look on his face.

Rome laughed. "Looks like he knows the 'ladies first' rule."

Decker only shook his head as he grabbed two forks out of the drawer. A few minutes later, the gooseberry pie was completely gone.

"Damn," Rome said as he sat back in the chair. "Darla Holiday makes a good pie. Of course, her blackberry is my favorite."

Decker glanced at him. "When did you taste Darla Holiday's blackberry pie? With the feud going on between your daddy and Hank Holiday, I didn't think you'd ever been to the Holidays' for supper."

"She made me one after I helped Hank." Rome had been the one who had found Hank after his heart attack and called 911. "How is he doing, anyway?"

"I saw him in town the other day. He looks like he's lost a little weight, but other than that he seems to be as headstrong and opinionated as always. I got to hear his thoughts about cattle prices being too low and politicians being too lazy and his daughters being too uninterested in running 'their own damn ranch.'"

Rome took a sip of beer. "If he wasn't so hard-headed like my daddy, maybe one of his daughters would have stayed . . . and maybe he wouldn't be in danger of losing the ranch."

Everyone in town knew the Holiday Ranch wasn't doing well. Hank had sold most of his livestock off well before his heart attack, which wasn't a good sign for a cattle ranch.

"Do you think the sisters know?" Rome asked.

"If they didn't before, they will when they all get there."

"So all the sisters are coming home?"

Decker nodded. "That's what I hear. And I don't think it's a good thing. Those girls can get into a lot of trouble when they're together."

Rome grinned. "Worried you'll have to haul them in, Deck?"

He was a little worried. They were all as obstinate as Sweetie and he was going to have his hands full.

"Speaking of the Holiday sisters." Rome tapped his bottle of beer on the table. "I got a weird prank text the other day."

"From one of the sisters?"

"No. From Ms. Mimi. At least that's what it claimed. Since I don't have Ms. Mimi's cell-phone number, I can't be sure. Although it seems unlikely given the proposition."

Decker laughed. "Ms. Mimi propositioned you? And here I thought she was such a sweet little ol' gardening grandma."

"Which is why I think it's a prank."

Decker watched with surprise as George picked up the ball he'd ignored for the last month and dropped it at Dixie Chick's feet. The ball was much too big for the little dog's small mouth. Which could explain why she ignored it. Or it could have been George's dog slobbers covering it.

"So what did the text say?" Decker asked as he reached down and picked up the ball to see if George would fetch it now that he had a female to impress. But the ball dropped right back out of his hand when Rome answered his question.

"It said if I could convince one of her grand-daughters to marry me, Mimi would give me the ranch. Every last acre."

CHAPTER EIGHT

SWEETIE ARRIVED BACK from the errands her mother had sent her on to discover the Christmas lights and wreath had been taken down and a string of heart lights and a red-ribbon-and-glittery-heart-festooned wreath had replaced them. But it wasn't the Valentine's decorations that held her attention. It was the two cars sitting in front of the farmhouse. One was a beat-up Chevy. pickup with a bumper sticker that read: *Beer, the official champagne of Texas* and the other was a plain white Honda Civic.

Just the sight of the vehicles made Sweetie squeal with joy.

She parked behind the truck and got out. Before she could make it to the porch, the screen door opened and her two sisters came charging down the porch steps.

Or Hallie charged. Cloe moved at a more sedate pace and waited for Hallie and Sweetie to stop hugging, squealing, and jumping up and down before she took her turn at greeting Sweetie. Which was so like Clover Fields Holiday. She had always been the one who waited patiently for her turn. She didn't jump or squeal. She just gently pulled Sweetie into her arms. While Sweetie was short like their mama, Cloe was tall like their daddy and always smelled like clean country air. Even when she no longer lived in the country.

Hallie, on the other hand, always smelled like homemade bread, probably due to the yeast she used to brew her beer.

Sweetie hooked an arm around Hallie, pulling her into the hug with Cloe. "I've missed you both. I wish y'all could've come out to Nashville in August like Liberty and Noelle. A year is too long to go without seeing y'all."

"I was too busy getting ready for the school year," Cloe said. "You should have come to College Station for Thanksgiving."

"I should have. That gig singing in the mall for Black Friday turned out to be a waste of time. Everyone was too busy shopping to stop and listen to me sing Christmas carols."

"Maybe they would've listened if you sang your own songs," Hallie said. Cloe shot her a warning look, but Hallie had never paid any attention to warnings. "What? I know the Holiday Secret Sisterhood voted that we weren't going to mention Sweetie's phobia of singing songs she writes in front of people, but how is she going to make it big if she only sings songs someone else writes?"

Sweetie didn't know what surprised her more—the fact that her sisters knew about her phobia or the fact they had called a Holiday Secret Sisterhood meeting to discuss it.

The Holiday Secret Sisterhood had been Belle's

idea after she had read *Divine Secrets of the Ya-Ya Sisterhood* in sixth grade. Sweetie had been in ninth grade at the time and thought herself above a silly club. But since Belle rarely asked for anything, Sweetie had gone along with it. Besides, as the oldest sister, it was up to her to make sure her younger siblings weren't going to do something stupid. Over the years, she'd had to veto Hallie's idea of blood oaths using a sharp kitchen knife. And Belle's idea of summoning their deceased ancestors by having a séance in the hayloft using real candles.

But she'd gone along with most of the other sister bonding ideas: Swimming buck naked in Cooper Springs every full moon—Liberty's idea. Stealing a bottle of Mimi's homemade elderberry wine from the cellar every New Year's Eve—Noelle's idea. Swearing on the family Bible to never ever poach another sister's boyfriend—Cloe's idea.

The sisters still met to discuss life issues and family problems. Sweetie just didn't think they would meet to discuss her.

"You had a Holiday Secret Sisterhood meeting without me?"

Cloe narrowed her eyes at Hallie before returning her attention to Sweetie. "We were just worried about you. Every time we talk on the phone, you seem depressed."

"I'm not depressed. And I don't have a phobia of singing my songs in front of people. If I wrote good songs, I'd gladly sing them. But no one wants to hear the garbage I've written while in Nashville."

Cloe looked at her with sympathetic eyes. "What about the songs you've written here? You have dozens of notebooks filled with them, Sweetie, and none of us have heard a one."

"I'm not hiding them. You can look at the notebooks anytime."

"I tried once," Hallie said. "I could decipher your early songs about Major, but once you learned cursive and started writing in your chicken scratch, I couldn't read a word. Besides, this isn't about us reading your lyrics. It's about you being unable to sing them—at least in front of people. The only person I ever heard you sing them around was Decker and we all know he's really a robot so that doesn't count."

Decker had been a pretty robotic teenager who didn't show his emotions. Maybe that was why Sweetie had been able to sing her songs to him. He didn't give her any kind of feedback whatsoever. He just listened quietly and kept working. She hadn't realized until now that her barn concerts were probably the reason he hated country music.

She sighed. "Okay, maybe I am depressed. But anyone would be depressed if they'd spent the last twelve years at a career that has gone absolutely nowhere. But y'all don't need to worry about me. You know I always figure things out. What we *do* need to worry about is what's going on at this ranch. Have you noticed that there are no cattle grazing in the pastures?"

"It was the first thing I noticed on the drive in," Hallie said. "I tried to talk to Mama about it when I got here, but then Daddy walked in and she clammed up. I tell you what, I will never marry an arrogant man I have to walk on eggshells around."

"She's just worried about upsetting him after his heart attack," Cloe said.

Hallie snorted. "As long as I can remember, Mama has worried about upsetting Daddy."

"I don't think she was worried about upsetting him when she brought up selling the ranch," Sweetie said.

Hallie stared at her. "Selling the ranch? You're kidding, right?"

"I wish I was, but Mama and Daddy have decided to sell the ranch. After talking to Mama, I understand why. Running a ranch isn't easy, and Mama, Daddy, and Mimi aren't getting any younger."

"I don't think that's the only reason." Cloe glanced back at the screen door before she continued. "I think the ranch is in trouble, which is why Daddy's been selling off the cattle. I tried to talk to him about it, but he's still mad at all of us for moving away and refused to tell me anything. He said if I cared about the ranch so much, I should've stayed and helped take care of it. And we all know that Mama and Mimi have never cared about the business side of things. So neither one of them could give me any details about what was going on, except that money has been tight." She paused. "So I did a little snooping."

Cloe might be quiet and introverted, but she could also be devious when the situation called for it.

"Why, you little sneak, Clo," Hallie said with glee. "What did you do?"

"I called Gilbert McWilliams at the bank and said I was doing Daddy and Mama's taxes and needed their account information."

"So what did you find out?" Sweetie asked.

Cloe leaned in closer and lowered her voice. "There's only a few thousand in the ranch checking account—no doubt due to the large monthly payments he made last year to Oleander Investments. I googled the name and discovered it's an investment company that gives loans to businesses. If Daddy took a loan out, he must have finished paying it off. There were no payments to Oleander for the last six months."

"Well, that's a relief," Hallie said. "At least they don't have a huge loan hanging over their heads."

"But they still don't have enough money to keep the ranch going," Sweetie said.

All three of the sisters stood there for a long time without saying a word. Sweetie knew they were all thinking the same thing. How could they let the ranch go when it held so many memories?

Behind the house was the big red barn where she and her sisters had groomed horses, helped deliver foals, milked cows, and played in the hayloft. Next to the barn was the chicken coop where they'd collected eggs and been chased by a mean rooster they'd named Mister Hastings, after their strict grade school principal who had a head of red hair that looked like a rooster comb.

Beyond the barn and the henhouse were acres of land that had been their own personal playground. Riding, roping, and herding cattle hadn't been work to them. It had been a daily adventure.

When they weren't helping on the ranch, they'd had campouts in pup tents, built campfires, and then told ghost stories as they gorged themselves on burnt marshmallow s'mores. They'd spent the sizzling Texas summers at Cooper Springs, playing Marco Polo, doing cannonballs, and picnicking beneath the huge cypress trees. In the fall, they'd carve pumpkins Mimi had grown in her garden and enter them in the Fall Carnival Pumpkin Carving Competition. Hallie had won almost every year for most terrifying pumpkin while Noelle had won for most creative.

In the winter, Daddy had hitched up the hay wagon to a couple horses and driven them around the ranch with them singing "Jingle Bells" at the top of their lungs.

In spring, they would pick wildflowers and make flower crowns and pretend they were all fairy princesses who had accidentally slipped through a portal and were stuck in a human's world and the only way to get back was to swing as high as they could on the rope swing on the old oak tree.

That was how Hallie had broken her nose.

Mama and Mimi had been in town at the time. Daddy and the ranch hands, including Jace, had been branding cattle. It had been Sweetie's responsibility to watch her younger siblings. Instead, she'd been in her room scribbling down a song called "Shirtless Jace" when she heard her sisters' screams. She'd raced outside to see her other sisters in a panic and Hallie holding her nose . . . along with a handful of blood.

Sweetie had frozen.

Thankfully, Decker had been working in the barn. He hadn't been more than thirteen, but as soon as he came out, he'd taken charge, sending Sweetie for a bag of ice and calming down the rest of her sisters. Now that Sweetie thought about it, Decker had always been calm and collected in a panic situation. He'd grabbed the hose the time Liberty had set off a firecracker and the sparks caught some dead grass on fire. He'd scooped Noelle out of the way when a stallion had broken out of his stall. He'd been the first one to reach Sweetie when Major got spooked by a firecracker in the Fourth of July parade and tossed her off. She had been in a lot of pain and he had told her some silly story about the pet hamster he had as a kid to keep her mind off her arm as he carried her three blocks to Doc's house.

"Are you listening, Sweetie?"

She returned to the present and looked at Hallie. "Sorry. What?"

"We can't let Mama and Daddy sell the ranch to complete strangers. This land is Holiday land. It should remain in our family."

"I agree, but are you coming back to help run it? Because I'm not. Daddy and I are like a lit match and gasoline. There's no way we could work this ranch together. Not to mention that I have no desire to be a rancher."

"I wouldn't mind being a rancher as long as I could brew beer too. Although I can't get along with Daddy either." Hallie looked at Cloe. "You, Belle, and Noelle are the only ones who can."

Cloe shook her head. "I can't leave my job. Or Brandon." Cloe was the only one of the six sisters who had a steady boyfriend. "And Belle has a successful business in Houston and I'm sure she won't want to leave it—not that Liberty would let her."

Liberty and Belle were killing it as event planners. While Sweetie was thrilled for her sisters, she was also a little jealous. They had succeeded at their dreams while she had failed.

"What about Noelle?" Hallie asked.

"You know she's never loved ranching as much as she loves baking," Cloe said.

"So we're just going to let the ranch go?" Hallie asked. Both she and Cloe looked at Sweetie for the answer to the question like they had always looked to her for answers. But this time, she didn't have an answer.

Or maybe she just wasn't ready to accept that it was time to let the ranch go.

CHAPTER NINE

USUALLY, MEALTIME AT the Holiday table was a chaotic affair with plenty of laughter and people talking over each other as they passed around the plates and bowls of Mama's home cooking. But tonight, no one seemed to be in a jovial or talkative mood.

Except for Mimi.

She didn't seem depressed at all about selling the ranch. Which made Sweetie worry that maybe she was getting a little senile and had forgotten. Especially when all she wanted to talk about was Rome and Casey Remington.

"Those two boys are fine catches, I'm telling you. Besides being good-looking as sin, they know how to run a ranch. Any woman would be lucky to have one of them as a husband."

"If that's the case, why did Rome's wife leave him?" Hallie asked around a big bite of biscuit.

"Rumor has it, she just wasn't cut out for ranch life. Rome and Casey need a strong woman who understands the hardships that go along with running a ranch." Mimi swatted Hallie's arm. "And don't talk with your mouth full. Regardless of the time you spent in ours, you weren't raised in a barn, Halloween Jean."

Hallie's eyes darkened and Sweetie knew she was upset over Mimi using her full name. She hated her name as much as she hated high heels, makeup, and arrogant men. But instead of saying something, she stuffed the rest of the biscuit in her mouth as Mimi continued.

"I hear that Sam Remington is wanting grand-kids. I figure it will only be a matter of time before Rome chooses another wife."

Daddy sent his mother a sharp look. "I'd prefer you not use that man's name at my table, Mama."

Mimi didn't cower. "It's time for you to get over your feud with Sam. His boys might just be our salvation."

"What are you talking about? I won't be taking any help from a Remington."

"You already did. If Rome hadn't found you and called 911, you might not be sitting here at this table."

"I didn't ask for his help."

Mimi sighed. "No. You never ask for help. Which is one of your major flaws. If you knew how to ask for help, maybe this ranch wouldn't be in the trouble it's in."

Sweetie might have taken the opportunity to ask exactly what kind of trouble the ranch was in if Mama hadn't quickly put an end to the conver-sation. "Let's not talk about the ranch's problems tonight. Let's just enjoy our girls being home. Now who wants pie?"

After they finished dessert, Sweetie volunteered

to do the dishes. Hallie and Cloe started clearing the table while Daddy and Mimi headed to bed and Mama headed to the laundry room to fold the load of towels she'd washed earlier.

"What should we do tonight?" Hallie asked as she set a stack of dirty plates on the counter next to the sink. "And I'm not watching those old song and dance movies you love to watch, Cloe. What's with that anyway when you don't like to sing or dance?"

Cloe set some glasses on the counter. "You don't have to know how to do something to enjoy watching other people do it."

"Then I think we should go to the Hellhole and watch some dancing in person."

Sweetie shook her head as she washed a plate. "Not me. Half the town already shunned me today. I don't need to be shunned by the other half."

Cloe wasn't a person to lose her temper . . . unless it involved one of her family members. Her voice shook with disbelief and anger. "The townsfolk shunned you?"

Hallie snorted. "Idiots! Don't tell me people still haven't gotten over what happened with Jace."

"Actually, they're not mad about that as much as they are about me leaving Wilder and not returning until now," Sweetie said.

Cloe's voice softened. "Because they love you, Sweetie."

She nodded. "I know. And they're right. I should have come back sooner. Not just for the townsfolk, but for Daddy, Mama, and Mimi. I let my own pride and anger keep me from the people I love."

"Well, hiding away in this house isn't going to get the townsfolk to forgive you," Hallie said. "I say we walk right into the Hellhole as if we have every right to be there and raise some Holiday Sister hell of our own."

The Hellhole was one of the county's most popular restaurants and bars. Partly because of Bobby Jay's signature barbecue and partly because of the huge dance floor Bobby kept sanded as slick as ice over asphalt. Texans loved to dance as much as they loved the baby back ribs Bobby cooked in a big ol' smoker and then braised on an open-faced grill. Bobby's barbecue kitchen had a huge pass-through window. As Sweetie walked by, she could see Bobby in his tall ten-gallon hat and barbecue sauce-stained apron cutting thick slices off a slab of brisket.

It looked like very little had changed at the Hellhole in the last twelve years. At least that's what she thought until they were seated at a table in the bar and she saw the stage where the old jukebox had once been.

"Since when did Bobby Jay start hiring live bands?" Sweetie yelled over the Miranda Lambert song the lead singer was belting out . . . and quite well. Damn her.

"I don't have a clue," Hallie yelled back. "But I love it!" She glanced around. "What I don't love is how everyone is staring."

It was the truth. Everyone had stopped their own conversations and was now staring at Sweetie and her sisters.

"I knew this was a bad idea," Sweetie said. "I'll be lucky if Bobby doesn't toss me out on my butt."

"Over my dead body." Hallie glared back at the staring townsfolk as if daring someone to say something. "I'll grab us some beers at the bar."

"Margarita for me," Sweetie said.

"Dr Pepper for me," Cloe added. She always appointed herself the designated driver and she took her job seriously.

A few moments later, Hallie returned with their drinks. "Well, it looks like the men in this town don't hold grudges. Every cowboy at the bar wanted to buy all of us drinks. Sweetheart Holiday included."

"You're kidding." Sweetie took her margarita.

"Nope. I didn't have to spend a dime. Which is good because I don't have many dimes to spend." She handed Cloe her soda before holding up her beer. "To the Holiday Sisters and the generosity of Texas men!"

The margarita was strong, sweet, and salty . . . and so were the next two sent over to their table. After the second one, Sweetie started to feel buzzed. By the third, the buzz had turned into a happy drone. It had been a long time since she had cut loose and forgotten about everything but having fun. In Nashville, when she was at a bar, she was always working. When she didn't have gigs, she waitressed to help pay the bills. There was no time for enjoying life.

She jumped to her feet. "Come on, you two. I want to dance!" Hallie immediately stood, while Cloe stayed seated.

"You two go on," she said. "I'll hold our table."

Since the bar had gotten a lot more crowded in the last two hours, it seemed like a good idea. Of course, everything seemed like a good idea. Including two-stepping with her little sister who had always wanted to lead.

"Let me lead, Hal!"

"I am!" Hallie stepped on Sweetie's toe for the third time and they both burst out laughing. While they were having a giggling fit, someone tapped Sweetie on the shoulder. When she turned, she found herself looking at a big ol' wall of a cowboy.

Sweetie looked way up at the cowboy's face. "You is one big boy,"

The cowboy pulled off his hat. "I'm Bud Wilkes. We went to school together. Remember?" Sweetie remembered. Bud had been a defensive tackle on the football team. The same football team Jace had quarterbacked for. She figured she was about to be yelled at, but she was too drunk to care.

"Well, hey, Bud. How you doin'? I guess you're pretty pissed at me for breaking Jace's heart and ruining your chances to win state." She waved a hand. "So go ahead and let me have it."

Bud shifted uncomfortably. "Actually, I was going to ask you to dance."

Sweetie blinked. "You want to dance with me? But don't you hate me for breaking your star quarterback's heart in front of the entire town?"

"Well, I was pretty upset when we lost state. But I figured it's time to let bygones be bygones."

Hallie poked Big Bud in the barrel chest. "Or maybe you just figured out that you guys sucked and didn't deserve to win state and my sister breaking up with Jace was none of your damn business."

Sweetie shouldn't laugh. But she did. So did Hallie. They laughed until tears rolled down their cheeks. She thought Bud would be insulted and leave.

He didn't.

"I guess you're right. It was our fault we lost state more than Sweetie's. So about that dance?"

"Thanks, Bud," Sweetie said. "But I haven't seen my little sis here for a long time and I want to—"

Before she could finish refusing, another cowboy stepped up. This man Sweetie recognized immediately. So did Hallie.

"Hey, Billy Lee!" Hallie said. "You still have that old truck that farts every time you start it up?"

Billy Lee Riley laughed. "Nope. I sold The Bean a couple years back. Now I have a brand-new GMC with Bose speakers and heated seats. You want to go check it out?"

Hallie shook her head and weaved on her feet. "Nope. I'm not a new-truck, heated-seats kind of gal. I like my trucks old and cranky . . . and gassy."

"I have an old truck," Freddy Dupree stepped

up next to Hallie. "I'd be happy to take you for a ride in it, Hal."

"Me too." Dave Creswell joined the fast-growing group of men. "I'd love to take either one of you pretty ladies for a ride."

"Now wait one damn minute, Dave," Bud said. "I already called first dibs on Sweetie."

If Sweetie hadn't been feeling so damn happy, she might have taken exception to that. But she *was* feeling happy. Not just because tequila was humming through her veins, but also because it looked like people had started to forgive her. At least the younger men had. The older men and all the women were still shooting her daggers. But she figured you had to start somewhere.

She thumped Bud on his massive chest. "No need to worry, Bud. I'm not riding in anyone's truck." An image of Decker's strong forearm hooked over the steering wheel of Jace's truck popped into her head and her lips moved without her brain. "Except maybe Jace's."

Bud's face fell. "I should've known you'd pick Jace."

Billy Lee slapped him on the back. "That still leaves five other sisters in the running, Bud."

Since Liberty and Noelle weren't there, Sweetie struggled to figure out what he was talking about. Before she could, Cloe came hurrying up.

"You are not going to believe what Henry Jenner just did. We need to go. And we need to go now."

Hallie frowned at her sister. "But I don't want to go. I want to dance."

All the men spoke at once. "I'll dance with you!"

Cloe grabbed Hallie's and Sweetie's arms. "No one is dancing with anyone. Do y'all understand me? We're leaving. And we're leaving now." Cloe might not be as aggressive as her sisters, but when she made up her mind about something, there was no stopping her. With a strength that surprised Sweetie, she dragged them off the dance floor and toward the door.

They were halfway there when Cob and his buddies stepped in front of them.

"Hey, now, what's your hurry, ladies?" Cob said. "The fun is only starting." His gaze wandered over each sister before landing on Hallie. "My, my, you've grown into a hot-lookin' woman, squirt. I remember when you were just a skinny, flat-chested kid with pimples."

Sweetie bristled. Drunk or not drunk. No one talked to her sisters like that. But before she could let Cob have it, Hallie did.

"Unfortunately, it looks like you haven't grown out of being an uglier-than-a-mud-fence jackass."

Sweetie laughed as she hooked an arm around Hallie. "Damn straight, little sis. Now get out of our way, Ugly Jackass."

Cob smiled snidely. "Looks like the Holiday sisters still think they're better than everyone else. Which is why your daddy has decided he has to pay men to marry y'all off."

Sweetie snorted. "You been smokin' loco weed

again, Cob? My daddy has no say in who we marry."

"Sweetie," Cloe said. "Let it go." She looked at Cob. "Please move, Cob. We need to get home."

Cob's gaze ran over Cloe. "I always thought you were the plain Jane of the sisters, but there's something to be said for a woman who knows how to talk to a man." He tugged Cloe into his arms. "You want this man to show you a good time, Plain Jane?"

Sweetie let out an enraged growl and went to attack Cob, but Cloe kneed him in the balls before she could get there and Cob dropped like a sack of rocks. One of his buddies took exception to that and grabbed Cloe's arm, but he didn't hold it for long. Rome Remington appeared out of nowhere and punched him so hard he flew into a table and fell to the floor in a crash of wood and broken beer bottles.

Then someone yelled, "Fight!"

And all hell broke loose.

CHAPTER TEN

DECKER HAD JUST gotten to sleep when he got the call from Bobby Jay. Since it wasn't the first time alcohol and rowdy cowboys hadn't mixed, he wasn't surprised.

He *was* surprised when he got to the Hellhole and found it completely closed down. Bobby Jay's bouncers usually had the troublemakers in the parking lot waiting for Decker to deal with while everyone else continued to party inside. Tonight, there was no one waiting in the parking lot. When Decker got inside, the lights were on and the band was gone and broken glass and busted chairs littered the floor.

It looked like it had been one humdinger of a bar fight. Since Cob and his cronies sat in a group of chairs surrounded by bouncers, Decker figured he knew who had started it. He couldn't say he wasn't thrilled about slapping a pair of handcuffs on Cob.

Just not on the two men sitting in chairs a few feet away.

Rome and Casey didn't look any worse for wear. In fact, Casey looked as happy as a pig in mud. He was always up for a good fight. Rome, not so much. Decker couldn't help wondering what had caused his friend to lose his cool.

"Glad you're here, Deck," Bobby Jay said. "It's been one helluva night."

Bobby was a small man. No more than five and a half feet tall. Although the white ten-gallon hat he always wore added another five inches. He was a good-natured man who took everything in stride. Which helped when you ran a rowdy bar.

"Hey, Bobby." Decker moved over to the bar Bobby stood behind. "You want to tell me what happened?"

Bobby shrugged. "I didn't witness it myself so I can only tell you what people told me." He glanced over to the corner. "But from what I heard, they started it."

Decker turned expecting to see some rough-looking cowboys. Instead, he saw three Holiday sisters . . . who looked like they had been in a bar fight. Their hair was wild and their shirts and jeans were splattered with bar beverages. But their hair and clothes didn't hold his attention as much as Sweetie's bleeding lip.

Once again, a feral, protective feeling swelled up inside him. "Who hit her?" he growled.

"I did!" Hallie raised her hand over her head like she had been sitting there waiting to answer the question. "But I was aiming for Cob when Sweetie jumped in the way."

Anger faded and he turned back to Bobby. "Get me some ice, Bobby." When Bobby brought him ice wrapped in a towel, he walked it over to

Sweetie and handed it to her. Their gazes locked. He expected to see annoyance. She had made it clear she didn't like him coming to her rescue, but there was no annoyance in her clear green eyes. Just a warm, sultry look that had him swallowing hard and turning back to Bobby.

"Start from the beginning."

While Bobby relayed the story, Decker tried to stay focused on him and not on the woman who sat there swinging a red cowboy boot. When Bobby was finished, Decker looked at Rome.

"You threw the first punch, Rome?"

Before Rome could answer, Cloe Holiday spoke. "I started the fight. I kneed Cob in the . . . privates when he grabbed me."

Decker was surprised. Growing up, Cloe had been a quiet introvert like Decker who seemed to enjoy watching more than partaking. Things would have been so much easier if Decker had had a crush on Cloe.

"Cob grabbed you?" he asked.

"He sure as hell did!" Hallie jumped to her feet. Decker couldn't help grinning. He had always had a soft spot for Hallie's feistiness. "Cob wouldn't let us leave and started being insulting."

Cob finally spoke up. "I wasn't being insulting. I was just stating the truth. Cloe is plain and your daddy did—"

Casey got to his feet. "Shut your mouth, Cob, or I'll shut it for you!"

Decker held up a hand. "Sit down, Casey. I got this. And exactly what part did you have in the fight?"

Casey sat back down. "This time, I wasn't in the fight." He flashed a grin at Rome. "I'm just here for moral support . . . and to watch my perfect brother, who never does anything wrong, being hauled off in handcuffs."

"I hope it won't come to that." Decker turned to Bobby. "How much damage do you think we got here, Bobby?"

Bobby glanced around. "Probably no more than a thousand, but that doesn't include the sales I would have made if I'd kept the bar open for the rest of the night."

"Give me the total and I'll make sure you're reimbursed."

Cob started to argue, but Decker cut him off. "You really want to push it, Cob?" Decker would love nothing more than for Cob to push it so he could haul him in. But if he hauled him in, he would have to haul in Rome. And the Holidays. Cob would have his day. Decker didn't doubt it for a second.

"Fine," Cob grumbled. "But I'm not paying for it all."

"I'm the one who threw the first punch, I'll pay for it," Rome said. "I should have handled it differently."

Decker agreed. But if today in town was any indication, he wasn't good at keeping his cool around the Holiday sisters either. "You good with that, Bobby, or do you want to press charges?"

"I'm good with it." He glanced at the Holiday sisters. "But I'd appreciate it if they didn't come back in while they're in town."

Hallie's eyes narrowed. "I'll go where I want to in this town and nobody can tell me—"

Cloe grabbed Hallie by the arm and cut her off. "We'll steer clear, Bobby. Thank you. Come on, y'all. Let's get home."

Not wanting Cob to start something again, Decker followed the Holidays out to the parking lot. Rome and Casey walked with him.

"Sorry, Deck," Rome said. "I'm not sure what happened."

Casey slung an arm over his brother's shoulders. "I know what happened. It's called three years without sex."

"Shut up, Casey," Rome growled.

"See what I mean, Deck. He's a corked bottle of sour wine just waiting to explode." Casey dropped his arm and called to the Holiday sisters. "Excuse me, lovely ladies, but would anyone like to continue this party at a little bar just a few miles from here?"

All three sisters stopped and turned to him. Hallie looked amused. Cloe looked like she was struggling to come up with an excuse. And Sweetie looked . . . straight at Decker. Her gaze slowly perused him while he tried to ignore the wave of heat that followed in its wake. When she lifted her eyes, a smile played with the corners of her mouth. A mouth that still looked slightly swollen.

"Where's the ice pack?" he asked.

"I didn't want to steal Bobby's towel. Especially after busting up his bar."

Hallie laughed. "We did bust it up, didn't we? That was my first bar fight."

"And, hopefully, your last," Cloe said.

"Now come on, Clo," Sweetie said. "Don't act like you didn't enjoy busting that cowboy over the head with the beer bottle."

Rome studied Cloe with a smirk on his face. "That took me completely by surprise. As did sending Cob to his knees. Are you drunk, Clover Holiday?"

"Of course not. I'm the designated driver. And since you and Casey have been drinking too, I'll be happy to drive y'all home."

Rome grinned. "Even though we're the enemy?"

"That's your daddy," Hallie said. "You two are just the sons of Satan."

Both Casey and Rome laughed as Cloe got after her sister. "Hallie!"

"That's okay," Casey said. "I've been called worse by a Holiday sister." He looked at Rome. "Come on, big brother. If I can't convince these lovely women to join us, I guess it's time to head back to hell." He tipped his hat. "See you around, ladies." He thumped Decker on the arm. "See ya, Deck."

Rome shook his head as he followed his little brother.

After they were gone, Hallie released a low whistle. "I don't think I care if they are the sons of Daddy's sworn enemy. Those two sizzling-hot cowboys might be worth Daddy's wrath."

"Don't even think about it, Hal." Cloe took her

sister's arm. "Now let's go before Decker changes his mind and tosses us all in jail."

"Y'all go on," Sweetie said. "I need to talk to Deck."

The last thing Decker wanted was to be alone with Sweetie, but there wasn't anything he could do about it when Hallie and Cloe were already heading across the parking lot.

"What did you need, Sweetheart?" he asked, hoping to get whatever she wanted to talk about over quickly.

But she didn't seem to be in any rush.

She tipped her head and studied him. "Did you know I've never liked my name? Sweetheart sounds like something your granddaddy calls your grandma."

"You need to go on home with your sisters, Sweetie."

She shook her head. "I don't like that name either. Sweetie sounds like something you'd call a tiny pet dog. Now Sweets. Sweets sounds like something special . . . something that's hard to resist." She leaned closer. "Did you struggle to resist me, Deck?"

He had.

He still was.

"You're drunk."

She nodded. "Yep. And I'm sure tomorrow I'll regret everything I say . . . and do . . . tonight."

"Then go home so you don't regret too much." So they both didn't.

"You're probably right." But she didn't leave. And neither did he. They just stood there staring at each other until Decker noticed the drop of blood on her bottom lip.

"Your lip is bleeding again." He pulled the handkerchief from his back pocket and held it out.

She took it and studied the poppies embroidered along the edge before she pressed it to her lip. "What's with you and flowered hankies? Is there something you haven't shared with the townsfolk, Sheriff Carson?"

"There are a lot of things I haven't shared with the townsfolk."

"Like secret crushes?"

He didn't lie. "Yes."

She stared back at him. "Who?"

"If I told you, it wouldn't be a secret."

"I guess not." She lowered the handkerchief and ran her tongue over her plump bottom lip. He had to close his eyes and count to ten. When he opened them, she was staring at him. "So why flowered handkerchiefs? Do you just have a thing for Texas spring flowers? Or were they a gift from a woman?"

"I guess you could say they were a gift from a woman."

"Viola Stanley? Mimi told me you were dating her."

He didn't deny it. Maybe if she thought he was dating Viola, it would end this conversation. "Viola doesn't embroider. She bakes." And not well.

"So she prefers baking for her man."

Since it looked like nothing was going to end

this conversation, he told her the truth. "The handkerchiefs were my mother's. After Nana and Gramps passed, I found them in Nana's dresser drawer when my aunt and I were boxing up her things. Carrying them around in my pocket makes me feel like my mama's still with me." The pain of losing his parents and grandparents was there again, nestled right beneath his ribs like a sore ache that wouldn't ever completely go away.

Sweetie's eyes softened. "I remember your mama. She was beautiful. I remember trying to fix my hair like hers after y'all had come to visit your grandparents."

Decker took in Sweetie's long, golden locks. They had always reminded him of his mama's.

"I was sorry to hear about your grandparents passing," Sweetie continued. "They were good folks. Every time I came over to visit Jace, your grandpa would tell me about how he met your grandma while your grandma tried to teach me how to knit."

"You were horrible at it."

A smile lit her face. A real smile that he hadn't seen in a while. "I was, wasn't I? I couldn't stand the repetition. Knit one, purl two. Knit one, purl two."

"That's exactly what I love about it." As soon as the words were out, he wanted them back. Especially when those moss-green eyes pinned him like a butterfly to a display board.

"You knit?"

His face heated and her real smile returned.

"There's the blushing Deck I remember. You blushed every time I looked at you."

"I did not."

"You did too." She hesitated. "Was I your secret crush, Decker Carson?"

There was a part of him that wanted to get the truth out in the open and be done with it. The other part knew it would only make things more difficult. And things were already difficult enough.

"Not likely," he said. "I knew you were Jace's."

The words hung heavy between them. A barrier he needed to place there.

It was too bad she was drunk and didn't know what was good for her.

Her smile vanished. "I was never Jace's."

"The entire town would disagree."

Her eyes flared as she stepped closer. "Then the entire town can go to hell. I belong to myself. Not Jace. Not Daddy." She grabbed the front of his shirt in her fist. "Myself. I'm the one who decides what I do, where I go . . . and who I kiss."

She kissed him.

If he hadn't spent half his life dreaming about this moment, he might've been able to resist her. But he had. And he couldn't. She *was* Sweets to him. A decadent dessert he couldn't help indulging in. He couldn't stop his hands from gripping her arms and tugging her closer. He couldn't stop his lips from parting at the first touch of hers. Or the groan of pleasure that escaped his throat when the heat of their mouths collided.

She tasted like tequila, lime . . . and blood. Her blood. He couldn't get enough of the heady flavor. He didn't think about Jace. All he thought about was his need for this one woman. A need he couldn't seem to control.

But she could.

One second, she was fisting his shirt and hungrily kissing him, and the next, she shoved him away and stared at him like she didn't know who he was.

"I . . ." She started, but didn't finish before she turned and ran off.

Decker stood there like a stone statue and watched as she jumped into the back seat of a white Honda Civic. It wasn't until the taillights had faded into the darkness that he ran a hand over his face.

He felt guilty as hell. He also felt . . . happy. Which made him feel even guiltier. And stupid. Sweetie had just been drunk and mad about him calling her Jace's girl. The only reason she had kissed him was to prove a point.

She belonged to no man.

She would kiss whomever she wanted to kiss.

Even Jace's cousin.

She *had* kissed him. She had kissed him like no woman had ever kissed him before. She might belong to no man, but she had made him feel like he belonged to her.

Or maybe he had always felt that way.

He took long, deep breaths until he felt like he was balanced enough to walk, then he turned to his car. That's when he noticed Bobby Jay standing by the dumpster holding two large bags of trash.

He tried to act nonchalant. "Hey, Bobby. Closing up for the night?"

Bobby looked back at the spot where the Honda had been parked. "Family can forgive a lot of things, Deck. But stealin' their women isn't one of them."

CHAPTER ELEVEN

OVER THE YEARS, Sweetie had come up with a lot of different methods to sober up after a night of too much drinking: Drink tons of water. Fill up on Taco Bell. Throw up. Or sleep it off. But she had never tried kissing. It worked better than all other methods combined. As she slipped into the back seat of her sister's car, Sweetie wasn't drunk anymore. She was stone-cold sober . . . and stunned. Completely stunned. And it had nothing to do with her kissing Decker and everything to do with him kissing her back.

Although kissing was too mild a word for what Decker had done to her. He had used his mouth and lips and tongue to scorch her to the core of her very being and made her feel completely lost . . . and at the same time, found.

It scared the crap out of her.

"What the hell, Sweetie! Did you just kiss Deck?"

Damn. Sweetie had hoped the parking lot was too dark for her sisters to see what had happened. Obviously not.

Hallie had completely turned in the passenger

seat and was holding her open hand between the seats for a high five. "Way to go, Sweetie!"

Sweetie ignored her sister's hand and glanced out the window. Decker was still standing there. She knew he couldn't see her in the dark car, but that didn't stop her from feeling like he could.

"Just drive, Cloe. Please."

"Why are you so upset?" Hallie asked as Cloe pulled out of the parking lot. "Any woman in their right mind would jump at the chance to swap spit with Decker Carson. The geeky calf has become a studly bull. And did you get a look at Rome and Casey? Whatever hot manly vitamins they've started putting in the water here in Wilder, I want to take some back with me to Austin. The last two guys I went out with asked permission to kiss me. Permission! While some women might find that sweet, I don't. I want a man who is smart enough to tell if a woman is interested and takes the bull by the horns. Or the Hallie by the lips. Believe me, if I don't like it, I'll let him know. And if I want to kiss him, I'll go for it. So spill. Did Decker kiss good? Or is he still a cold robot?"

Cold robot?

That didn't come close to describing the way Decker kissed. Sweetie's body still felt like a pressure cooker ready to release steam. She couldn't help comparing Decker's kiss to his cousin's. While Jace had been a good kisser, he had always kissed her as if it was a chore he needed to finish before he could take off for football practice. Decker had kissed her like he never wanted to stop. Like nothing, including a major catastrophe, would pull him away from her lips.

"Well?" Hallie prodded.

Sweetie mentally shook herself out of her thoughts. "It doesn't matter because it shouldn't have happened. I've done enough to Jace without drunk kissing his cousin."

"So you kissed him?" Cloe's eyes studied her from the rearview mirror.

"Yes, but only because that bartender makes strong margaritas."

It was so easy to blame her actions on the margaritas. But deep down, she knew it was a lie. She had still been buzzed after the bar fight, but she hadn't been so drunk she didn't know what she was doing.

She had wanted to kiss Decker. She'd wanted to ever since he had walked into the bar with his messed hair, sleepy eyes, and wrinkled sheriff's shirt, looking nothing like the pressed, rigid lawman he normally did. All she could think about as he interrogated Bobby Jay was if that was what he would look like in the morning after a hot night of sex. When he had turned that Caribbean-blue gaze on her, she had melted like a light dusting of Texas snow.

No. Alcohol hadn't played a role in her need to feel his lips against hers. But she wasn't about to tell her sisters that. Although the look in Cloe's eyes said she already knew.

"You're leaving, Sweetie. It would be best if you didn't start something with Decker."

"I'm not starting anything with Decker." She

wasn't. The kiss had been a mistake. One she wasn't going to repeat. Not only because he was Jace's cousin, but also because they lived in two different places. Nothing could come of starting something with Decker . . . nothing, but some more unbelievable kisses.

"Good," Cloe said. "And after what just happened, I think it's best if we stay away from town completely."

"I'm not staying away from town," Hallie grumbled. "Men get in fights all the time and nobody says anything to them. Look at Cob. That guy is a real asshole and Bobby didn't tell him to stay out of his bar."

"I don't care about what Bobby said," Cloe said. "I'm the one who doesn't think it's a good idea to go back to town."

"Because of the fight?"

"Not only that, but also because of the weird thing that happened before the fight. The way all the men were flocking around us like bees to honey. I've never been the type to get a lot of male attention, and tonight, I was surrounded by cowboys wanting to take me to dinner, or horseback riding, or fishing. Henry Jenner started talking crazy about how he'd always admired my brains and thought we'd made a good couple. He'd run the ranch and I could homeschool our kids."

"Your kids?" Sweetie stared at the back of her sister's head. "And what ranch? Henry doesn't own a ranch."

"Exactly. I think he was talking about our ranch."

There was only one explanation. "Mama must have told other people that they're selling the ranch. Or more likely Mimi. You know she's never been good at keeping a secret."

Hallie shook her head. "But that doesn't make any sense. Mimi doesn't want to sell the ranch. Why would she tell people that we are?"

"I don't know," Cloe said. "All I know is that Henry was talking weird. And after what Cob mentioned about Daddy having to pay people to date us, I think there might be something to it."

Hallie turned to her. "And here I thought you and Belle were the logical sisters. But there is no logic in that, Clo. Daddy wouldn't ever give away the ranch for free."

Cloe sighed. "You're right. I just can't explain what happened tonight."

Now that tequila wasn't fogging her brain, Sweetie realized it *was* weird how all the men had flocked around them. Especially when the townsfolk were still angry with her. Any man who decided to marry her would have to have a good incentive. Like a ranch. But like Hallie had pointed out, Daddy wouldn't give away the ranch.

"Maybe the single female population has shrunk so much men are just getting desperate," she said. "Mama did say a lot of young people have left."

"Well, the poor fools are looking in the wrong spot for wives," Hallie said. "Not one of us is ready to tie the knot."

"I'm ready."

Cloe's declaration had Sweetie sitting up in her seat. "Brandon asked you to marry him?"

"Not yet, but I think he's going to. He said he wants to have a serious talk about where our relationship is headed when I get back."

Cloe had been dating Brandon for close to six years. It made sense that they would finally get married. Which didn't explain the green-eyed monster that was suddenly sitting on Sweetie's shoulder and whispering in her ear. *She has a great career and now she's going to have love and a family, while you have nothing to show for the last twelve years of your life. Nada.*

Ignoring the monster, Sweetie reached up and squeezed Cloe's shoulder. "That's awesome, Clo. Really awesome."

Hallie wasn't as supportive. "Are you sure you want to marry a man who spent all of Thanksgiving talking about how many miles he'd ridden on his Peloton?"

"There's nothing wrong with a man being fit," Cloe said.

"No, but there is something wrong with him being an arrogant butt wipe."

"Hallie!" Sweetie chastised.

"I'm sorry, but he is. I mean, he didn't even compliment the dinner we'd slaved away on."

Cloe glanced over at her. "You slaved away on?"

"Okay, you, Liberty, Belle, and Noelle slaved away on. But I did bring the beer. And he had the gall to drink most of it and then say it was a little too yeasty for his tastes. I'll have you know I make some of the best beer in Texas. If I could get a backer, I would open my own brewery and prove it."

"Brandon was just nervous at Thanksgiving. The Holiday sisters aren't easy to take all at once. But he's a nice man who is a great teacher and he'll be a good husband and father."

Hallie snorted. "Wow. Those sound like the perfect reasons to marry a man."

Sweetie had to agree. "But you love him, right, Cloe?"

There was a long hesitation before Cloe answered. "Of course I love him. I mean it's not a wild, crazy kind of overwhelming love, but I'm not a wild, crazy kind of girl. I don't need a lot of excitement or passion. I just want a partnership where my opinions are valued. Brandon values my opinions."

Sweetie knew where Cloe's desires came from. Their parents' relationship hadn't been a partnership where her mother's opinions were valued. Daddy ran the ranch the way he saw fit without asking what Mama, or even Mimi, thought. Maybe if he had, they wouldn't have to sell the ranch.

"We're happy for you, Cloe." Sweetie reached between the seat and the door and pinched Hallie on the arm.

"Ow—yes! We're happy for you. I'll even brew you some beer for your wedding reception. Where do you think you'll get married?"

"I always dreamed about having my wedding and reception in the barn. But now . . . "

"Why do Mama and Daddy have to sell the

house and barn?" Hallie asked. "Couldn't they just sell the land and have enough to live on for the rest of their lives?"

Sweetie had to agree. It would make sense to just sell the land and keep the acre the house and barn sat on. But maybe Mama was tired of taking care of the house too. There were a lot of empty rooms now that Sweetie and all her sisters were gone.

Cloe pulled up in front of the house. As always, Mama had left the light on for them. It looked like she had added more Valentine decorations. Pots of fake flowers filled the porch. There were red roses and yellow roses and pink roses. Daisies and lilies and carnations. Some were in elaborate arrangements and others were just lying on their sides in floral cellophane.

It was the cellophane that made Sweetie realize they weren't fake. And there was no way her mother would put real flowers out on the porch in January.

"What the hell?" Hallie voiced Sweetie's thoughts. "It looks like one of Mrs. Stokes's husbands' funerals."

"Do you think they're for Daddy?" Cloe asked as she turned off the engine.

"Red roses aren't usually a flower people give to a man when he has a heart attack," Sweetie said. "Besides, Mama said most folks sent or brought plants and flowers to the hospital."

"Well, we're not going to figure it out sitting here." Hallie jumped out of the car and hurried up the steps. By the time Cloe and Sweetie had joined her, she was already pulling cards from the flowers. "They're for us."

"Us?" Sweetie said. "You mean the family?"

Hallie shook her head as she continued to take out cards and read the envelopes. "No. I mean us girls. You, me, Cloe, Liberty, Belle, and Noelle."

"But why?" Cloe asked as she looked around at all the flowers filling the porch.

Sweetie shrugged. "It looks like the single men of Wilder really are hard up for women."

"Oh, they don't just want a woman," Hallie said as she turned the card she'd just pulled out of one of the envelopes.

Across the white cardstock two words were scrawled.

Marry Me!

CHAPTER TWELVE

SOMETHING WEIRD WAS going on. For the second time in twenty-four hours, Decker was on his way to deal with a fistfight. This time, it was at Nothin' But Muffins. There had never been a fight at the café that Decker could remember. Not even when Sheryl Ann had gone to visit her mama in Big Springs and left her husband in charge and he'd burned all the muffins. It was probably just an argument over why the Texas Longhorns football team hadn't won the conference title.

When Decker stepped into the café, he wasn't sure what he'd find, but it wasn't Jarod Tate and Matt Milford face down on the floor with Mrs. Stokes standing over them pointing her derringer.

Not wanting to startle her, Decker spoke in a calm voice. "You can lower your gun now, Ms. Stokes. I'll handle things from here."

Mrs. Stokes shot him an annoyed look. "It's about time you got here, Deck. My coffee's getting cold." She opened her beaded purse and dropped the small gun inside before she adjusted her mink stole and took a seat at her regular table.

Since there was no damage done to the café besides a turned-over chair, Decker had the men take a seat so he could find out what had started the fight.

It turned out to be a woman.

"I knew her in high school," Jarod said. "It's only fair that I get her."

Matt glared at him. "So what? I knew her too. I sacked her groceries when she and her mama came in the general store. She always smiled at me and winked."

"Because she thought you were just a kid with a crush on her. She would never take you seriously."

Jarod's words struck a little too close to home and Decker lost track of their argument as his mind wandered back to the night before. The kiss hadn't been serious. Sweetie had only been toying with a man who had once had a crush on her. It hadn't meant anything.

At least, not to her.

To Decker, it had meant way too much.

He had spent all night going over every single detail of their kiss. The hot slide of her lips and the seductive licks of her tongue. The way she'd held tightly to his shirt as if she didn't ever want to let him go.

But he hadn't thought she'd let Jace go either. And she had. Sweetie toyed with men. She'd proven it. He had no business letting her toy with him.

". . . Sweetie probably won't even remember you. But she'll remember me. I had chemistry with her for an entire year."

Both Decker and Matt stared at Jarod and spoke at the same time. "Sweetie?"

While Decker tried to process what he'd just heard, Matt spoke. "I don't want Sweetie. I'm still mad at her for losing us that state championship and my mama is still mad at her for leaving town without a word. I want Liberty. She's the prettiest of the bunch."

"She might be the prettiest," Jarod said. "But Sweetie is a determined country gal. Look how long she's been trying to break into the music business. And you'll need a determined country gal to run a ranch."

"Wait a second," Decker said as he held up his hands. "What are you two talking about?"

Sheryl Ann spoke from her spot behind the counter. "You haven't heard?"

"Heard what?"

Coach Denny butted in like he always did. "Hank Holiday is going to give his ranch to the first man to convince one of his daughters to marry him. I'd give it a go, but I'm a coach not a rancher."

"You're also too old and hard of hearing," Sheryl Ann said. "Hank's not giving away the ranch to the first man to marry one of his daughters. He's giving it away to the first man who can get the ranch out of debt. A daughter is just an added bonus. Like when I throw in an extra muffin when you buy a dozen."

Mrs. Stokes snorted. "Neither one of you got it right. It's not Hank giving away the ranch. It's his mama, Mitzy Holiday. She told me at our last book meeting that she was hoping to marry off one of her granddaughters to one of the Remington boys. Which leaves you two yahoos out completely."

"Well, damn." Jared looked at Matt. "You want to go fishing, Mattie?"

"Hell yeah. If that's okay with you, Deck."

Decker was so stunned by what he'd just heard all he could do was nod.

Both he and Rome had laughed off Mimi's text. But now it looked like it hadn't been a prank after all. Of everyone in town, Mrs. Stokes was one of the few people who didn't gossip unless she had all the facts.

Decker couldn't wrap his head around the fact that Mimi had come up with the plan. Or that she thought it would actually work. Grandmother wishes carried a lot of weight. But he couldn't see Sweetie or her sisters marrying a Remington just because their grandmother asked them to. And how could Mimi give away the ranch when Hank was the one who owned it?

Decker needed to stop the crazy gossip before it caused him more headaches.

"Look," he said. "I don't know what Ms. Mimi said, but the Holiday sisters are not up for grabs like some prize at the county fair. Nor is the Holiday Ranch."

"Of course it's up for grabs," Mrs. Stokes said. "Everyone knows the ranch is in trouble. I won't be surprised if it goes up for sale within the month. That could be why all those girls came home. They came to say goodbye to the place where they grew up."

Decker didn't know why the thought of the Holidays selling the ranch bothered him so much. Maybe because it had been the place where he'd grown up too. It seemed wrong for it to belong to someone besides the Holidays.

"I'm sure the Holidays aren't selling the ranch," Decker said. "They're not giving it away either. Now everyone needs to get back to their business and stay out of other people's."

But that was easier said than done for the townsfolk. Everywhere Decker went that day, he overheard people talking about the Holiday sisters being on the marriage mart. Decker figured there was only one way to clear things up. If he wanted to stop the gossip, he needed to talk to Mimi.

After the kiss, he hoped he could avoid Sweetie, but she was the first person he saw when he pulled up to the ranch.

The second was Rome's little brother, Casey.

Decker had always liked Casey. It was hard not to like someone so rascally and charming. While Rome was the responsible, dedicated, hardworking older brother, Casey was the irresponsible, carefree, devilish younger brother. He was also the biggest flirt in Wilder, Texas.

Right now, he seemed to be flirting with Sweetie.

They were sitting on the porch swing and

Casey's arm rested on the back as he leaned in and whispered something into Sweetie's ear that had her doing the snorty laugh that had never failed to make Decker smile.

He wasn't smiling now. The feral feeling he'd been struggling with since Sweetie came back to town reared its ugly head and he slammed the door a little harder than necessary when he got out.

"Hey, Deck!" Casey greeted him with a big smile.

Decker tried to get ahold of his temper as he climbed the porch steps. "I thought you were going to Abilene to buy horses."

"I am, but I got an interesting text this mornin' and thought I'd come check it out." Casey tipped his head. "You okay, Deck? You look a little flushed. This hot January getting to you?"

What was getting to him was Casey's arm on the back of the swing . . . way too close to Sweetie.

"What are you doing here?" he asked, even though he knew damn good and well why Casey was there. He'd gotten the same offer as his brother had. "I thought Hank chased you off with a shotgun last time you showed up here."

Casey winked at Sweetie. "Some things are worth risking your life for."

Sweetie rolled her eyes. "Which is why you made sure my daddy wasn't home before you got out of your truck."

"My mama didn't raise no fool."

Sweetie laughed. "Just the biggest flirt this side of the Pecos."

Casey held a hand over his heart. "A man comes courtin' with sincere intentions and you mock him?"

"You didn't come courtin'. You want to get married about as much as I do."

Casey laughed. "True. But just because I don't want to get married, doesn't mean I don't enjoy courtin' a beautiful woman. And you, Miss Sweetheart Holiday, are one beautiful woman."

"Well, thank you kindly, Mr. Remington. But if I got with you, my daddy would have another heart attack. In fact, you need to leave before he gets home."

Casey leaned closer to Sweetie and Decker's hands tightened into fists. "We could sneak around. I've always been good at sneakin'."

"I bet you have, but I'm not staying long enough to start anything up with a charming cowboy." She glanced at Decker. "Or anyone for that matter."

She was letting him know in no uncertain terms that the kiss had been a drunken mistake. He couldn't help feeling annoyed that she felt like she had to tell him so he wouldn't get the wrong idea.

"Don't worry, I'm not here to see you. I'm here to talk to your grandmother."

"Mimi? Why do you want to talk to her?"

While Decker tried to decide how much he wanted to tell Sweetie, Casey cut in. "I think I know why Deck is here. He's here the same reason I am. To find out if the Holiday girls know about their grandmother's proposition."

Sweetie turned to Casey. "Proposition? What proposition?"

Casey grabbed his hat from the arm of the swing and got to his feet. "I think I'll let Deck explain that." He smiled at Decker. "You are the sheriff, after all." He tipped his hat at Sweetie. "If you ever change your mind about sneaking around, you let me know." He playfully punched Decker on the arm on the way past. "See you later, Deck."

Once Casey was gone, Decker returned his attention to Sweetie. She had her hair piled up in a messy bun on top of her head. Blond tendrils surrounded her face like spun gold. Her green eyes were no longer twinkling and her full lips were turned down in a frown.

"What exactly was Casey talking about?" she asked. As he tried to figure out how to break the news, his gaze got stuck on Sweetie's bare feet peeking out from the edge of her jeans. He couldn't remember ever seeing her without boots. Her feet were petite and her red-painted toes were lined up in a perfect row. Like five glossy cherries he suddenly had the strong desire to take a nibble of.

"Well?"

Sweetie's question pulled his gaze from her toes and he cleared his throat. "There's a rumor going around town that your daddy will give the ranch to the first man to marry you or one of your sisters."

"I figured as much when I got home last night and found this porch flooded with flowers and marriage proposals. I just can't figure out where the gossip started. I thought it might be Daddy, but he didn't know anything—" She cut off and her eyes widened. "Mimi. That's why you want to talk to her? You think she's the one who started the rumor?"

Decker hated to throw Mimi under the bus, but he figured Sweetie would find out soon enough. "I know she is. She texted Rome Remington and told him she'd give him the land his daddy wants if he could convince one of her grand-daughters to marry him. I'm guessing she sent Casey the same text."

The stunned look on Sweetie's face lasted for only a second before she jumped to her feet and pushed past him. "Mimi!"

He followed her down the porch steps. "Now don't go yelling at your grandmother."

"Oh, I'm going to yell at her. She sat there at breakfast this morning and didn't say a word the entire time my sisters and I were being asphyx-iated by the pungent scent of roses and talking about what happened at the Hellhole last night. Not one word." She headed around the side of the house to the garden. "Mimi!" When Mimi wasn't in the garden, Sweetie turned to the barn.

The barn had always been Decker's favor-ite place on the Holiday Ranch. The first time he'd seen the huge bright red building with its high-pitched roof and massive hayloft, a nostal-gic feeling had washed over him. His daddy had loved barns—probably because he'd grown up surrounded by them—and every time he'd colored with Decker, he'd always put a barn in his picture. One that looked just like the Holidays'.

As Decker stepped inside, he was assailed with memories of being there with Sweetie. Of listening to her sing while they cleaned stalls or groomed horses. He had loved listening to the songs she'd written. She had made him a fan of country music. When she'd left, he'd never wanted to listen to it again.

"Mimi!" Sweetie yelled. The word echoed off the rafters. If Mimi was there, she was hiding. And with good reason. Having witnessed Sweetie's temper before, Decker knew she could blow up like an explosive grenade and then regret her words later. So he stepped in front of her when she turned to leave the barn.

"Calm down. I don't think your grandmother meant any harm."

Sweetie stared at him. "She's put me and my sisters on the auction block like brood mares and you don't think she meant any harm?"

"She only wants to keep one of you here with her."

"At the expense of our happiness?"

"Maybe she doesn't view marriage as something that makes people unhappy."

Her shoulders relaxed and she released her breath in a long sigh. "You're right. She thinks marriage is the only thing that's going to make us happy. But I never thought she'd go to such extremes." She glanced at him. "So how do we fix this?"

"I'm not sure. Even if Mimi takes it back, the

rumor has already spread . . . and turned into something else entirely."

"Well, that explains what happened last night at the Hellhole and all the flowers that arrived on our doorstep." She shook her head. "The men of this town are stupid if they think all they have to do to get one of us to marry them is send a few flowers or ask us to dance."

"Most men are stupid when it comes to court-ing women." He hesitated. "Although it might help if you didn't flirt with them."

Sweetie's eyes narrowed. "Excuse me?"

"Men think you're interested when you get drunk at a bar and dance with them . . . or cuddle with them on a porch swing." He knew he was overstepping his bounds, but the image of Casey's arm perched on the back of the porch swing so close to Sweetie was still front and center in his brain.

"Cuddle?" Sweetie stared at him. "I was not cuddling with Casey Remington. And even if I was, that's none of your damn business. I thought I'd made it clear that I'll kiss whoever I want to kiss."

"Even if they don't want to be kissed?"

Her eyes widened. "Are you saying you didn't want to kiss me, Decker Carson?"

He should let it go and leave. But he wasn't good at doing what he should where Sweetie was concerned. "You were the one who kissed me."

She took a step closer and leaned in. "And you were the one who didn't want to stop. So don't you dare play the victim with me."

Since she knew the truth, he should apologize and get the hell out of there. He certainly didn't need to rile her more. But he couldn't seem to stop himself from asking the question that still plagued him.

"Why *did* you kiss me?"

She stood there for a long, tension-filled moment before she finally spoke. "Because I've never been good at resisting things that are all wrong for me."

He wished like hell that his heart hadn't done a cartwheel at just the thought of Sweetie being unable to resist him. But it did and he couldn't ignore it. Or her.

"You're right," he said as he took a step closer. "We are all wrong for each other."

She tipped her head up and her tongue swept over her bottom lip, leaving it wet and too tempting to look away from. "Just plain wrong."

He leaned in. "One hundred percent wrong."

If possible, the first brush of their lips was even more electric than the night before. But this time, he wasn't surprised. He now knew kissing Sweetie was like stepping into the eye of a tornado: deep inside him, everything was calm and still like he was right where he was supposed to be, while the rest of his body was a whirling, trembling cyclone of need.

With a groan, he surrendered to the storm and tugged her into his arms, kissing her like he'd wanted to kiss her since stepping out of his car.

Her arms came around his neck and her fingers threaded through his hair, knocking off his hat.

Like last night, she held on like she never wanted to let go. He prayed she wouldn't. He wanted to be absorbed into her soft skin and remain there forever. The sexy sound that came from deep in her throat had him backing her up against the wall of the barn so he could press closer.

She drew away from the kiss and her head fell back as she spoke in an aching whisper that made him feel reckless and wild. "Say it, Deck. Please say it."

He trailed kisses along her neck to her ear where he sucked in the soft skin behind her lobe. "Sweets." He nipped her with his teeth. "My Sweets." He came back to her lips and hungrily kissed her again.

The sound of slamming car doors penetrated his sexual haze, but not enough to make him pull away from the hot woman in his arms.

Nor did the high-pitched squeals of females greeting each other.

It wasn't until five giggling Holiday sisters stepped into the barn that he was finally able to pull away.

CHAPTER THIRTEEN

WHEN DECKER TRIED to pull away, Sweetie tugged him right back. She had let him go last night, but she wasn't going to let him go again. It wasn't until she heard a collective gasp of surprise that she realized they weren't alone.

"Well, it looks like Sweetie hasn't wasted any time making herself right at home," Liberty said.

Sweetie drew away from Decker and saw all five of her sisters standing just inside the open barn door. The sight of Liberty, Belle, and Noelle had her desire fading beneath the joy of seeing her sisters. She pushed past Decker and hurried over to hug them.

"It took y'all long enough to get here."

Noelle drew back from the hug and cocked an eyebrow. "And I see that you were just twiddling your thumbs waiting for us." She glanced over Sweetie's shoulder and her eyes widened. "Deck?"

Sweetie turned to see Decker standing there looking thoroughly kissed. His hair was messed from her fingers and his lips were puffy from her kisses . . . and the fly of his jeans had an obvious bulge.

He followed her gaze and he quickly picked up his hat from the ground and held it in front of him with his cheeks flaming. "Hey, Noelle. Liberty. Belle. How are y'all doing?"

Liberty fielded the question. She loved to field questions. In school, she was constantly being sent to the principal's office for not raising her hand before she blurted out an answer. "Not as good as you, obviously."

Decker cleared his throat and glanced at Sweetie. "Could I speak with you outside for a second?"

Sweetie nodded and followed him out of the barn. She figured he would want to talk about the kiss. Instead, he acted like it had never happened.

Which annoyed her.

"I'll see what I can do about stifling the gossip, but there will still be some randy cowboys showing up here wanting to win a Holiday sister and the ranch. I'm afraid things won't settle down until you and your sisters leave town."

Her annoyance grew. He wasn't just acting like they hadn't kissed. He was also trying to get her to leave. "So you're going to kiss me and then try to get rid of me, Deck?"

His gaze lowered to her mouth and she couldn't help the tremble that ran through her. "It would make things a lot easier if you left."

It *would* make things easier. If she went back to Nashville, she wouldn't have to deal with her matchmaking grandmother, the grudge-holding townsfolk, and the land-grubbing single men in the town. She wouldn't have to deal with her stubborn daddy or the ranch being sold. And she wouldn't have to deal with the intense physical attraction she had developed for the man standing in front of her.

It was too bad Sweetie had never taken the easy way out.

"Thanks for coming out, Sheriff. But like I told you before, I'll leave when I'm ready. You and a bunch of ranch-crazy cowboys aren't going to run me off."

Decker studied her for a long moment before he nodded. "Okay then." He pulled on his hat. "If men do show up and start causing trouble, call me."

"Not likely." She turned and headed back into the barn.

All her sisters were waiting with expectant looks on their faces. She knew they wanted answers and she wished she had them. But she didn't understand what was going on between her and Decker either. So instead of explaining the kiss, she flopped down on the nearest bale of hay and covered her face with her hands.

"Damn."

Belle sat down next to her. "Are you okay? He didn't force you, did he? Because if he did—"

"Not likely, Belly," Hallie cut in. "Considering what happened between Decker and Sweetie last night at the Hellhole, it was probably Sweetie doing the forcing."

Sweetie lowered her hands. "I did not force Decker to kiss me!"

"It looked like mutual kissing to me," Liberty said.

"Me too," Noelle agreed. "In fact, y'all looked like you were only seconds from the main event."

Cloe sent Sweetie a confused look. "I thought you weren't going to start something with Decker."

"I wasn't—I mean, I'm not."

"Oh, you've started something," Liberty said. "You've definitely started something. That man was boasting one impressive boner."

"Libby!" Sweetie glared at her sister.

Liberty shrugged. "Sorry, but it was hard not to notice."

Hallie laughed. "Real hard."

"Enough teasing," Belle said as she placed an arm around her. Belle and Liberty were identical twins. Both were dark-haired, tall, and beautiful. Liberty was assertive and driven and Belle was more soft-spoken and compassionate. "Can't y'all see Sweetie's upset?"

Sweetie rested her head on Belle's shoulder. "I don't know what happened. I don't even like him."

"Of course you like him," Noelle said. "You used to go out of your way to hang out with him."

Sweetie straightened. "What are you talking about? I didn't go out of my way to hang out with Decker."

"Now that Noelle has pointed it out," Hallie

said. "I do remember you choosing mucking out the stalls with Decker to herding cattle with Jace. Which was weird because Jace was your boyfriend and Decker was just a kid. Although he never acted like a kid. He's always acted like he was fifty."

"He had just cause," Belle said. "Losing his parents made him have to grow up fast."

"Well, he's not a kid now," Liberty said. "So I don't see why you're so upset about sharing a few kisses with a hot cowboy, Sweetie."

"Because he's not just some random cowboy," Sweetie said. "He's Jace's cousin. I struggled to forgive myself for what I did to Jace. I certainly don't want to break Decker's heart and spend the next few years feeling guilty."

Hallie rolled her eyes. "Believe me, from what I've seen on Jace's social media, his heart wasn't broken for long."

"Decker is different than Jace. He's more . . ." She struggled to find the right word and found more than one. "Sensitive. Caring. Loyal."

All her sisters stared at her as Cloe spoke. "Are you starting to develop feelings for Decker, Sweetie?"

"Of course not."

But she was developing something for him. It was like he had cast a weird spell on her. When he was around all she could think about was touching him . . . and having him touch her. And she didn't get it.

"Mama!"

The sound of their father's loud bellow had all

the sisters startling and turning to the open door. Daddy and Mama had gone into Austin to see Daddy's heart specialist and it looked like they were back. It also looked like Daddy was pissed about something. It didn't take a genius to figure out what that was. He'd found out about the gossip Mimi had spread.

Sweetie jumped up and headed outside. She might be mad at her grandmother, but she didn't like the thought of her daddy taking his anger out on her. Or of her daddy getting upset and having another heart attack. She intercepted him and Mama on their way around the side of the house. Daddy looked mad as hell and Mama was trying to calm him.

"Now, Hank, don't get upset. You could be wrong. It could be someone else who started the rumor."

"What rumor?" Mimi came around from the back of the house. Her sunbonnet hung so low it obscured her eyes and she had to tip her head back to look at her son. "Everything go okay at the doctor's?"

"Everything went fine . . . until Darla and I stopped in Wilder for some barbecue."

"I hope you didn't bring any home for supper. As much as I love it, barbecue no longer agrees with me."

"I didn't get any barbecue. And you know why? Because before I could order, men surrounded me and started asking for my daughters' hands in marriage. I thought the entire male population of Wilder had gone plumb crazy until I ran into

Decker leaving the ranch. And you know what he told me, Mama? He told me you had started that rumor."

Sweetie's sisters, who had followed her out of the barn, showed their shock in gasps and a few *"What the hell"*s before Daddy continued.

"What were you thinking, Mama?"

Mimi tipped her chin even higher. "I was thinking what everyone in this family should be thinking. How can we keep from selling the ranch?"

"Selling the ranch?" Liberty, Belle, and Noelle said in unison.

Daddy ignored them and continued to glare at Mimi. "Have you lost your mind, woman?"

Mimi pointed a dirt-covered finger at him. "There's nothing wrong with my mind and you better watch the way you speak to me, young man. I have kept my mouth shut and allowed you to run this ranch the way you saw fit and look where that has gotten us. Now I'm stepping in and doing what I think is right."

Sweetie jumped in. "You can't auction us off like mares, Mimi."

"I'm not auctioning y'all off. I would never force any of you girls to marry someone you don't love. Which is why I never said a word when you broke up with Jace. I knew you two weren't meant for each other. Just like I know you're not meant to be a country singer. I thought you'd fig- ure that out when you were in Nashville, but you seem to be as hardheaded as your daddy is about accepting the truth. It took him until now to figure out that he isn't a businessman. If we want to keep this ranch and make it successful, we need to run it like a business. Which is why we need one of the Remingtons. They know how to run a successful ranch."

Daddy's eyes bulged out of his head. "The Remingtons! You want to give this ranch to a Remington? You have lost your mind."

"I'm not giving this ranch to anyone. I'm doing just the opposite. If one of our girls marries Rome or Casey, my great-grandchildren will not only keep this ranch, but they'll also own the Remington Ranch. In my book, that's a win for everyone."

"Not for us!" Hallie entered the conversation. "No woman wants to be sold into marriage. I feel like I just stepped into one of those Regency romances Belle loves to read."

"She has a point," Liberty said. "You can't sentence one of your granddaughters to a life of married hell just because you don't want to lose the ranch, Mimi."

"Marriage isn't hell," Mama said as she smiled at Daddy. "If you get with a man you love, it's about as close to heaven as you'll ever get."

"The key word being *love*," Noelle said. "None of us are in love with Rome or Casey Remington. In fact, what I feel for Casey is as far as you can get from love."

Mimi huffed. "That's because your daddy has never let you get close enough to either one of those boys to find out what good men they are. If Rome hadn't found you after you had your heart attack, Hank, you probably wouldn't be here. You didn't even thank him properly because of the ridiculous feud you have with his daddy."

"Well, I sure as hell don't want to thank Rome by giving him one of my daughters," Daddy snapped.

Mama placed a hand on Daddy's arm. "Now keep your calm, honey." She looked at Mimi. "I know you would love one of our girls to get married and start a family right here, Mimi. I would love that too. But you can't swap ranches for love. And I'm sure the girls are now so embarrassed that they don't ever want to see Rome and Casey again."

"Not just Rome and Casey," Sweetie said. "The entire town knows about the offer." She looked at Mimi. "And I'm wondering how everyone found out."

It was easy to read the guilt on Mimi's face. "I might have mentioned it at the Wild Women's Book Club."

Sweetie rolled her eyes. "That's like yelling it through a megaphone at a football game. Those ladies are the worst gossips in town."

"Now don't be talking about my friends. Besides, it hasn't done any harm."

Cloe stared at her. "Any harm? Mimi, we won't be able to go anywhere in town without being chased around by single men."

"And exactly why is that a problem? It's high time that all of you get married. Of course, I'm only giving the ranch to a Remington."

"You're not giving the Remingtons any part of my ranch and that's final!" Daddy hollered.

Mimi swept off her hat and her green eyes snapped. "Your ranch? I believe my name is on the deed of this ranch. Something you seemed to have forgotten when you and Darla started talking about selling it. I'm not selling this ranch. Do you hear me? And that's final!"

Sweetie was stunned. She had thought her grandmother had signed over the ranch to her father long ago. She certainly had acted like it belonged entirely to him. Not once had she interfered.

Until now.

And, boy howdy, had she interfered!

For the first time, Daddy was speechless. He just stood there for a long moment staring at Mimi. Then his shoulders wilted and he released a sigh that held such pain Sweetie was instantly concerned. Before she could ask if he was okay, he spoke.

"You're right, Mama. I should have figured out that I wasn't a businessman sooner. Then maybe things would have turned out differently. But now, we don't have a choice. We have to sell the ranch. If we don't, it's going to be taken from us."

CHAPTER FOURTEEN

SWEETIE COULD COUNT on one hand the times she'd been invited into her father's study. The room located behind the stairs had always been his domain—where he went to get away from the gaggle of females in his family. It had belonged to his father and his father before that and his father before that. Its paneled walls held the scent of cigar smoke, its shelves held history books on Texas, cowboys, and ranchers, and its old leather chairs held the imprint of past Holiday men's butts.

Which probably explained why Sweetie felt so uncomfortable sitting in one. Of course, the bomb her daddy had dropped on the entire family had left everyone feeling uncomfortable and shaken.

Mostly Mimi, who sat in the chair next to Sweetie looking lost and confused.

"I don't understand, Hank," she said. "You acted like the document you had me sign was for a small loan from the Wilder bank, not a huge loan from some kind of shady, big-city loan shark. Why did you need that kind of money?"

Daddy sat behind his desk looking totally defeated. As always, Mama stood by his side, her hand resting on his shoulder as he spoke. "I thought if I had the capital, I could make this ranch twice as large and twice as successful. So I bought land. Then land prices dropped and so did cattle prices. Then we lost half the herd during that bad freeze. I kept thinking next year would be better." He swallowed hard. "But it wasn't."

Sweetie knew exactly how he felt. For the last twelve years, she'd kept telling herself that next year would be better. She'd write better songs and get better gigs. Next year, she'd be able to sing her songs in front of people without freezing on stage like a fool.

But next year had yet to come.

"How many loan payments have you missed, Daddy?" she asked.

Daddy rubbed a hand over his face. "Enough that they could start foreclosing proceedings anytime. The only way we can stop it is if we pay the loan off in full. Which is why we need to sell the ranch. At least, that way, we might end up with a little something to start over."

Mimi jumped up from her chair. "You'll sell this ranch over my dead body!" She stormed out of the room, slamming the door behind her. Daddy started to get up from his chair to follow her, but Mama stopped him.

"Let me talk to her."

When Mama was gone, Sweetie looked at her father. She had always fantasized about something or someone knocking the arrogance out of him.

But she had never wanted him to be brought this low.

"It's okay, Daddy. We'll figure it all out."

A sorrowful look passed over his face before he swiveled his chair toward the window.

It was so like her father to refuse to let anyone see his pain. Sweetie was a lot like him. She hadn't let anyone know how badly things were going for her in Nashville. She had only told them the highlights of her life—as if telling the truth would somehow make her less in the eyes of the people who loved her. She realized now how wrong she'd been.

Love never saw less. Just more.

She got up from her chair and moved behind him. Outside the window, the sun was setting. The golden rays stretched out as far as the eyes could see on land that had belonged to their family for over a hundred years.

"I love winter sunsets," she said. "They always seem to be prettier than summer ones. It's almost like the cooler air condenses the colors and makes them more vibrant." She hesitated. "The last twelve years haven't been good for either one of us, Daddy. But we're Holidays. We'll get through this . . . together." She rested her hands on his broad shoulders and gently squeezed. "I love you."

She didn't expect him to say anything, and he didn't. But he didn't pull away either. She stood there with her hands resting on his shoulders until the sun disappeared completely. Then she turned and headed for the door. Before she got there, he spoke.

"I love you too, Sweetie Pie."

For the first time in twelve years, the Holiday Secret Sisterhood met in the Holiday barn hayloft. The last time had been when Sweetie had told her sisters she was leaving home. There had been a lot of tears at that meeting. Which probably explained why Sweetie's eyes welled up as soon as all her sisters were gathered in the loft.

What if this was the last time they would ever gather in the barn? The last time they would sit cross-legged in a circle with the smell of hay and the cool night air surrounding them? The thought was heartbreaking. But she hadn't called the meeting to commiserate.

She held up her hand. "I call this meeting to discuss the trouble the ranch is in."

"I think we already figured that out, Sweetie." Liberty unzipped the backpack she had brought with her and pulled out a bottle of Mimi's homemade elderberry wine. Then another. And then a third. "I know it's not New Year's Eve, but I figured we could use a little fortification—not to mention a little warming up. It's colder than a witch's titty up here."

Belle handed her the folded quilt she had tucked under her arm.

"Good thinking, Belly." Liberty pulled the blanket around her and hooked one edge around Belle before picking up a bottle of wine. She scowled. "Damn, I forgot—" Belle pulled a corkscrew out of her hoodie pocket. Liberty grinned. "That's why we make such a great team." Once Liberty had a bottle opened, she took a long drink before she passed it to Belle who took a much more tentative sip. Sweetie waited until the wine bottle had been passed around once before she continued.

"Daddy took out a loan and he's missed enough payments that the ranch is in danger of foreclosure. Which means we need to sell quickly and pay off the loan so Mama, Daddy, and Mimi will, at least, have something to start over with. Unfortunately, Mimi is the one who owns the ranch and she's not willing to sell."

"What did Daddy do with the money from the loan?" Belle asked. "Especially when he has no cattle to show for it."

"He bought land."

Hallie snorted. "And probably paid twice as much for it just to keep Sam Remington from getting it."

It did make sense. Daddy had always been willing to do anything to best Sam.

"Well, it doesn't matter what happened. The point is that we need to figure out a way to convince Mimi to sell."

"We?" Hallie took the corkscrew from Libby and opened another bottle of wine since the first bottle was empty. "Daddy is the one who screwed up. He's the one who should figure out how to convince Mimi."

"That's not going to work," Noelle said. "Mimi

is pissed at Daddy for talking her into signing for the loan. She's not going to do anything he says now. And she's still convinced one of us marrying a Remington is going to fix everything. As if, any of us would ever consider doing that. I would marry Satan before I'd marry Casey Remington."

"Now all we have to do is convince Mimi of that," Sweetie said. "And we don't have a lot of time to do it. Daddy has already been delinquent on the payments for months."

Liberty spoke. "Maybe we can pool our money to make the back payments and give ourselves more time. Belle and I have put most of our extra money back into our business, but we could probably pull together ten thousand."

"Don't look at me," Hallie said. "I barely have enough money to pay my bills." She took a swig of wine and wrinkled her nose. "Damn, this is awful. I should have brought a case of my beer."

"I have a little savings," Cloe said. "But even together with Liberty's and Belle's, it won't be enough to cover all the payments Daddy has missed."

Noelle accepted the bottle from Hallie. "Like Hallie, I don't have any extra money. But even if I did, I feel like we're trying to use one of those wine corks to keep Old Faithful from erupting. Eventually, we're not going to be able to make the payments. And Daddy's proven he can't run the ranch successfully. As hard as it is to watch, maybe we need to just let things run their course."

Sweetie shook her head. "If the ranch is fore-closed on, everyone in town will find out about it. Y'all know how gossip spreads. That wouldn't just hurt Daddy's pride, but also Mama's and Mimi's. We need to convince Mimi to sell."

"How do we do that?" Belle asked.

Sweetie sighed. "I don't know. But I do know that one of us needs to stay here and try."

"One of us?" Liberty lowered the bottle she'd just taken a drink from. "Belle and I have a business to run. We can't just take off indefinitely while we try to convince our grandmother to stop being pigheaded." She looked at Hallie. "What about you, Hal?"

Hallie stared at her. "Me? Why me?"

"Because brewing beer at a brewery isn't a real job," Noelle said.

"And you think decorating cakes is?"

"At least I have a viable skill."

"Brewing beer is a viable skill. People drink more beer than eat pastries. Once I get a backer and start selling my beer, I'll make more than you ever will selling cupcakes."

"While you wait for a backer, you could brew your own beer right here at the ranch," Liberty said. "It does make sense."

"To you, Libby. Not to me. And just because you can tell Belle when to take a pee doesn't mean you can tell me when to."

Belle's eyes widened. "Liberty doesn't tell me when to take a pee."

"Really? Then why don't you let her run your business while you stay here and help figure out how to convince Mimi to sell?"

Belle turned to Liberty. "Maybe I should—"

"Absolutely not!" Liberty cut her off. "Valentine's Day is just around the corner and we have too many events." She glared at Hallie. "Unlike a hobby, we have a profitable, successful business."

"Brewing beer is not a hobby," Hallie snapped. "I'm sick of everyone thinking that my career dreams aren't as important as theirs. What about Sweetie? She's spent twelve years in Nashville and no one is pointing out that her chances of making it big after all this time are as good as us saving this ranch." As soon as the words left Hallie's mouth, she turned to Sweetie with wide eyes. "I'm sorry, Sweetie. I didn't mean that. As usual, my temper got ahead of my brain."

Sweetie shook her head. "It's okay, Hal. You're right. The chances of me making it big after all these years is slim to none."

Cloe rested a hand on her arm. "That's not true, Sweetie. It could still happen."

"Of course it could," Liberty said. "You just need the right break."

It was what Sweetie had been telling herself for twelve long years. As she looked around at her sisters—none of who could look her in the eye—she suddenly realized she was more like her daddy than she thought. Not only did she hide her emotions from people, she also stuck her head in the sand and refused to see things for what they were. His daughters had all left him, his stress was killing him, and he was losing the thing he'd strived all his life to keep. All because he refused to accept the truth that he was never going to have a ranch as large as the Remington' . If he had only scaled down his dream, they might not be losing the ranch.

Sweetie needed to accept the truth too. She wasn't good enough to make it as a country singer. If she'd been good enough, she would have made it by now. But she couldn't even sing the songs she wrote in front of people. Every time she'd tried, she'd felt like she was standing on the stage naked as the day she was born. The songs were all her emotions in music and lyrics. If she couldn't tell people how she felt with words, what had made her think she could tell them how she felt in song?

"I'll stay," she said.

All her sisters stared at her.

"No, Sweetie," Cloe said. "We aren't going to ask you to give up your dream."

"I'm not even sure what my dream is anymore, Cloe. It makes sense that I'm the one who stays to help untangle this mess."

Cloe got the determined look on her face she always got when she had made up her mind about something. "Then we'll all take turns coming back and helping." She glanced around at her sisters. "This is a family crisis. And as a family we need to put aside our other responsibilities and face this crisis as a team. As sisters."

There was a long stretch of silence before Belle spoke. "I move that we all take turns coming back and helping. Not only do we need to convince Mimi to sell, but Mama and Daddy will need help putting the house on the market and packing up everything and finding a new place to live. They'll need us all to pitch in."

"I second that," Noelle said.

Her sisters looked at Sweetie expectantly and she said, "All those in favor?"

Four hands went up quickly. Liberty's took a little longer, but she finally raised it.

Sweetie smiled. "The motion passes unanimously."

Once the meeting was over, they stayed in the hayloft and continued to drink wine and reminisce. It was obvious that they would all be sad to see the ranch go. Once the wine was gone, Noelle glanced out the door of the hayloft.

"Hey, y'all. It's a full moon."

Sweetie turned and saw the moon hanging like a beautiful golden disk in a sky filled with glittering stars. When she moved to Tennessee, she discovered the stars didn't shine nearly as brightly. Obviously, it was much harder to be a star in Nashville.

The thought made her laugh. Or maybe it was Mimi's elderberry wine. Whatever the reason, she couldn't seem to stop. Her sisters joined in. Soon all the Holiday girls were leaning against each other in a fit of giggles.

Even though it was January and the temperature couldn't have been more than sixty degrees, Sweetie got to her feet and yelled,

"Last one to Cooper Springs is a rotten egg!"

CHAPTER FIFTEEN

"OKAY . . . this . . . was definitely . . . a bad idea." Decker stopped running and rested his hands on his knees as he gasped for air.

Rome, who was a good ten yards ahead, ran back to him. It was annoying that he wasn't even out of breath. "You okay?"

"I'm fine." He wasn't. The five beers he'd drank were threatening to come back up.

"Deep breaths, buddy." Rome patted him on the back. "I won the bet, by the way."

"Only because I'm wearing cowboy boots."

"I'm wearing cowboy boots."

"Yeah, but you came out of the womb wearing boots. You do everything in them."

"Not everything."

Decker straightened to find Rome grinning. Normally, Decker would have smiled or laughed at the sexual innuendo. But tonight, he didn't find it funny. Something Rome noticed.

"So are you ready to tell me what's going on with you?"

"What do you mean?"

"I mean the entire competitive thing that happened tonight. I've been to your house hundreds of times before and not once have you even pulled out a deck of playing cards. Tonight, you wanted to play checkers, washers, and Jenga, and then you forced me into racing you. So what's going on?"

What was going on was that Rome was one of two men Ms. Mimi thought worthy of her granddaughters. That stuck in Decker's craw. It was like Rome and Casey had been offered a free pass to court Sweetie. A pass Decker desperately wanted. He knew his jealousy was ridiculous and childish, but damned if he could help it.

Nor would he admit it.

"Can't a man just want a game night with his best buddy?"

Rome squinted at him. "Not a guy who has never shown any signs of being competitive. Which is one of the reasons you and I get along so well. Competition is everything to my father and I've spent my entire life having to compete for everything I got. I thought I didn't have to compete with you, Deck."

Talk about feeling like a real jerk. "You don't." He shook his head. "I'm sorry. I've just felt a little out of sorts lately."

Rome studied him. "It's Sweetie, isn't it?" When Decker started to argue, he held up a hand. "I know you have a huge sense of honor, Deck. It's another reason I like you. But you can't help how you feel. And any fool can see that you feel something for Sweetie."

"It's just leftover feelings from my teenage crush."

"Okay. So it's just leftover feelings. It's still feelings. Believe me, I get it. I don't want to still have feelings for Emily, but I do. And sometimes the best way to get over them is just to accept them. Does Sweetie have feelings for you too?"

If their kiss was any indication, she did. There was only one problem. "She was Jace's girlfriend, Rome. And not just a girlfriend, but the girl he planned to marry."

Rome hesitated before he spoke. "Look, Deck, Jace is a great guy and he was a damn good cousin to you and one helluva quarterback. But I went to school with Jace and played football with him and I never got the feeling he was madly in love with Sweetie. He cared about her. But he didn't care about her as much as he cared about football. If he had a choice between weight training and watching game film or being with Sweetie, he always chose training and game film. To be honest, I didn't blame Sweetie for breaking up with him."

Rome wasn't telling Decker anything he hadn't witnessed with his own two eyes. But a part of him had always believed his perception of Sweetie and Jace's relationship was skewed by his feelings for Sweetie. He had wanted Jace to be a bad boyfriend because he so desperately wanted to be the good boyfriend. And maybe it wasn't that Jace was a bad boyfriend. Maybe it had more to do with him being a teenage kid who wasn't ready to make a lifelong commitment. Just like

Sweetie hadn't been ready. If that was the case, then the only person making Jace and Sweetie's relationship into something more than what it was . . . was Decker.

As he stood there and allowed that thought to sink in, a female scream rent the night air, causing both him and Rome to startle.

"What the hell was that?" Rome asked as he glanced around.

Another high-pitched scream had Decker taking off at a dead run in the direction it had come from. He'd thought it was hard running on the dirt road in boots. It was even harder running across a pasture of wild grass and gopher holes. He stumbled more than a few times, but picked up his speed when there was another scream.

"Cooper Springs," he yelled back at Rome.

When he came to the copse of thick mesquite and oaks that surrounded the springs, he had to slow his pace to push the low-hanging branches out of the way. Another scream had him barreling through the trees so quickly he lost his footing in the soft soil that surrounded the springs and ended up stumbling down the incline and head-first into the water.

Damn, it was cold. He surfaced with a gasp, then scraped his hair out of his eyes so he could spot the woman who needed help.

It turned out it wasn't just one woman.

It was six.

You would think picking Sweetie out of a group of women at night would be difficult, but he had never had a problem finding Sweetie in a crowd. His gaze zeroed in on her not more than a few feet away from where he stood chest-deep in water. Her hair was wet and slicked back and her bare shoulders were speckled with water droplets that sparkled in the moonlight like diamonds. Unless she was wearing a strapless bathing suit—that had inched low enough to show the tops of two soft breasts every time her treading brought her farther out of the water—she wasn't just swimming with her sisters. She was skinny-dipping.

"Just what in the heck do you think you're doing, Decker Carson?" she asked.

He swallowed hard and tried to keep his gaze above her neck. "I heard screams and assumed someone was in trouble."

She tipped her head. "And you thought you needed to come to the rescue?"

"You can rescue me, Deck."

He wasn't sure which sister had spoken and he was too damned embarrassed to try to figure it out. "I'll just let y'all get back to your . . . swim." He started to turn to shore when Rome came crashing through the trees and did the same thing Decker had done. He slid down the incline and fell into the creek. Decker reached out and pulled Sweetie out of the way. He only intended to move her so she wouldn't get hurt, but the waves Rome made when he entered the water pushed her flush against Decker.

And yep, she was naked.

He didn't think he could get an erection in ice-cold water. He proved that theory wrong. If he felt all her soft curves, she had to feel all his hard ones. He couldn't help the heat that flooded his cheeks any more than he could help his reaction to having a naked Sweetie in his arms. Probably because he'd spent many a night as a teenager jacking off to this exact scenario. And if he were honest, not just as a teenager.

Her eyebrows hiked up before a soft smile spread over her mouth. "Shouldn't I be the one blushing, Deckster? I mean I'm the one naked while you're fully clothed."

He didn't need the reminder.

Rome's "Oh, shit" pulled him from Sweetie's twinkling green eyes and he released her and turned to see his friend surrounded by bobbing Holiday sisters.

"God must be on Mimi's side," one sister said. The sassy tone had him guessing it was Hallie. "She wished we'd get to know the Remingtons better and one just fell right into our skinny-dipping party."

"Skinny-dipping?" Rome sounded as stunned as Decker had been, but he recovered much quicker. "Beg pardon, ladies. Decker and I just heard screams and got concerned."

Hallie spoke again. "That was just Liberty and Noelle being wussies about jumping into cold water."

"We're not wussies." Decker was pretty sure it was Liberty who spoke. She'd never had a problem voicing her thoughts. Even if they were inappropriate. "This water is too damn cold. I move that the Holiday Secret Sisterhood's full-moon swims be done only when temps are above seventy. I'm so cold, my nipples could cut glass."

"Libby!"

"It's the truth, Cloe. And I don't care if Rome and Decker get an eyeful, I'm getting out." Liberty started swimming toward the shore.

Decker kept his gaze on Sweetie. "The Holiday Secret Sisterhood?"

She laughed. "I guess we can drop the secret part now. But Liberty is right." She turned to the remaining sisters. "I second the motion! All in favor?" Ayes filled the air and all the sisters— except for Sweetie—started swimming toward the bank.

Rome cleared his throat. "Since I'm already wet, I think I'll do some laps." After he tossed his boots up on the bank, he ducked under and started swimming.

Decker should have followed his lead and left the Holiday sisters to get dressed in private. But something held him right there. More than likely, the gorgeous moonlit woman treading water in front of him.

"So you want to explain what you were doing lurking around in the shadows?" she asked.

"I wasn't lurking. Rome and I were having a race."

"In the middle of the night and in cowboy boots?"

"I didn't say it was a smart idea. But neither is skinny-dipping in January."

She laughed. "Fair enough."

Her good mood had him asking, "Are you drunk?"

"I was a little tipsy earlier, but ice-cold water has a way of sobering you. So you don't have to worry about me forcing myself on you again."

He should have let it go. He didn't. "There was no forcing involved."

She studied him for a long, breathless moment before one of her sisters yelled.

"Sweetie! Come on!"

Decker glanced over his shoulder and saw that her sisters were dressed and waiting. He knew he should let her go. It was damned cold in the springs and the chivalrous thing to do would be to turn his back and let her leave. But that's not what he wanted. What he wanted was treading water right in front of him with moonlit green eyes that held a look that made him forget about everything but the heat that radiated between them.

"I want to kiss you again so bad it hurts," he said.

Before she could say anything, her sisters called her name louder and more insistent. She could have easily used the excuse to leave. She didn't. She didn't even glance at the shore as she spoke. "I want to kiss you again too." He curved a hand around her waist and drew her closer, but before their lips met, she stopped him. "This is just casual fun, right?"

At that moment, he would have agreed to just about anything. "Just casual fun."

Her lips were cold, but they warmed quickly

beneath his. Her sisters stopped yelling and all
Decker could hear was the lap of water and the
beating of his heart as Sweetie answered every
soft pull of his lips. Every gentle brush of his
tongue.

Her arms were locked around his neck, her soft
body flush against his. Through his wet clothes,
he could feel the hard points of her nipples and
press of her hips. Desire settled deep inside him,
but so did something else. Something stronger
than passion. Something that consumed his mind,
body, and soul. By the time he finally drew back
from the kiss, he realized there would never be
anything casual about his feelings for Sweetie.

It scared him. Just not enough to let her go.

He kissed her again, this time, softer and gen-
tler before he sipped the trail of water droplets
from her cheek and then along her neck. When
he reached the spot behind her ear, he sucked the
soft skin into his mouth until she released a sexy
moan and hooked a leg around his hips.

"We're leaving, Sweetie!" one of her sisters
yelled.

It was followed by another sister's laughter. "I
don't think she cares."

Sweetie drew back. She looked dazed and he
couldn't help feeling happy that his kisses were
responsible. "I need to go."

He nodded. But instead of releasing her, he
tightened his hold and walked her out of the
creek. Which wasn't easy when his boots were
being sucked down into the mud with every step.
When they were close to shore, he set her on her

feet and tried not to look at all the moonlit skin on display as he peeled off his soaked western shirt and wrapped it around her.

She smiled. "Always the hero."

He struggled to find something to say. Something witty and charming, but he had never been witty and charming.

"I want to see you again. What's your phone number?"

She hesitated for only a second before she gave it to him. "You'll remember it?"

"Yes." He would remember every single thing that had taken place that night. Every word. Every touch. Every kiss.

She smiled as if she could read his thoughts. "Well, if you forget it, you know where I live."

He did. He just didn't know for how long. He wanted to ask the question so he could mark it on his calendar—so he would at least know when to expect the pain. But then he realized it was better if he didn't know. All he would do was count down every second, instead of enjoying the time he had.

"See you later, Deckster." She leaned in and gave him one more heated kiss before she turned and presented him with the view of twin butt cheeks peeking out from beneath the edge of his wet shirt as she splashed her way onto the bank. As soon as she reached it, she was surrounded by her sisters like bees to their queen.

Sweetie *was* a queen. Somehow Decker had gotten his hands on her. If only for a brief time.

Decker continued to stand there until the Holiday sisters disappeared into the trees and their laughter and voices faded away. Then he turned to the full moon and let out a whoop that could be heard in the next county.

CHAPTER SIXTEEN

DECKER DIDN'T FORGET Sweetie's number. Her cellphone rang the following morning bright and early, waking her out of a sound sleep. She reached for it and pulled it under the covers to look at the screen. She didn't recognize the number, but she knew it was Decker. Decker was reliable. If he said he would call, he would call.

So why wasn't she answering?

She wanted to. Her heart thumped madly at just the thought of Decker saying good morning in his husky, bedroom voice. But now that her head wasn't filled with elderberry wine and a starry sky and a handsome lawman with the prettiest blue eyes and sweetest lips, she could think clearly. Starting something up with Decker was just wrong.

"So you're not going to answer it?"

Sweetie pulled the covers off her head and saw Cloe sitting up in the bed next to hers. While all her other sisters had been thoroughly excited about her kissing Decker, Cloe hadn't said a word.

Probably because Sweetie already knew how she felt.

"I know," she said. "Starting something with Decker is a bad idea." Her phone stopped ringing and disappointment settled in the pit of her stomach like a heavy brick. She fell back on her pillow and sighed. "Why am I such a hot mess?"

"You aren't a hot mess."

Sweetie rolled to her side to face Cloe. "Oh, yes, I am. I'm almost thirty years old and I don't have a clue where my life is heading. For twelve years, I've been in Nashville and I'm not any closer to my dream than when I started. I'm starting to wonder if it was really my dream or just an excuse to leave home."

"What do you mean?"

Sweetie hugged a pillow to her chest. "I thought I was going to take Nashville by storm. But once I got there, I realized there were hundreds of other people who thought the same thing. People who are prettier and more talented than I am, and have no problems singing the songs they write on stage without having a major panic attack. And the thing is, I don't even enjoy singing other people's songs on stage."

Cloe stared at her with disbelief. "But you used to love singing in school programs, at church, and here at home with the family."

"That was different. That was with people I know. With strangers, I'm just a bundle of nerves every time I step on stage."

"Why didn't you say anything?"

"Because I kept thinking it would go away and

all I needed was a little more experience. But no matter how many gigs I do, I still don't get that high other singers talk about when they're performing in front of a crowd. All I feel is scared and . . . suffocated. Like I did when I lived here. See what I mean about being a hot mess?"

Cloe got out of bed and climbed in with Sweetie. Once she was settled under the covers, she took Sweetie's face in her hands and got the stern look she always got when she meant business. "You are not a hot mess. You are smart and talented and beautiful. So what if you don't like singing in front of people? You can still be a country music star."

Sweetie laughed. "And just how is that going to work? Am I going to become the next masked singer and hide behind a giant dragon's head?"

"You can write songs for other people to sing. Songwriters are music stars. They just don't get all the attention and notoriety."

"Thanks, Cloe, but I don't think my songs are that good."

"How do you know unless you let people hear them? Or at least, see them. Have you even shown them to anyone in the music business?" When Sweetie shook her head, Cloe continued. "Then you need to. You have close to a hundred notebooks on that shelf over there that say you're a songwriter. Now all you need to do is believe it."

Sweetie hugged her sister close. "I love you, Cloe."

"I love you too. And just so you know, you're

not the only one who questions whether or not their life is on the right track."

Sweetie drew back. "You don't like being a speech therapist?"

"No, I've always loved working with children and helping them overcome their impediments. But I just thought my life would be further along by now. I thought I'd be married and have a couple kids and maybe a dog and some cats. Instead, I'm living with Brandon in a small apartment that doesn't allow pets."

"But I'm sure that will change when you and Brandon get married. I'm sure you'll start a family and get a house of your own."

Cloe smiled weakly. "Of course it will." Sweetie's phone pinged with an incoming text and Cloe nudged her. "Answer it."

Sweetie shook her head. "It would be a mistake."

"I thought so at first, but then I saw the way he was with you at Cooper Springs. He couldn't look away from you."

"I was naked."

Cloe laughed. "True, but so were five other women that were surrounding him. He didn't pay attention to any of us. And you couldn't look away from him either."

Sweetie sighed. "When he's around, it's like I can't think straight. All I can think about is being in his arms. When I'm not around him, my brain kicks in and pulls up all the reasons why getting into a relationship with him is a really bad idea. And not just because of Jace. Decker and I are complete opposites. I'm loud. He's quiet. My life is a hot mess. His is stable and secure. He's the beloved town sheriff. I'm the town outcast. Us starting something makes absolutely no sense."

Her phone pinged again and she pulled it out from under the covers and quickly turned it off.

"No. Decker is not for me. I need to accept that and move on."

For the rest of the day, Sweetie silently repeated that mantra and refused to turn on her phone. In the morning, she helped her mama organize all the holiday decorations in the attic. In the afternoon, she and her sisters met in their daddy's study to go over all the things that needed to get done before they left town.

"We need to talk to the investment company that gave Daddy the loan and see what the payoff is going to be," Cloe said.

Liberty raised her hand. "I'll do that."

"Great." Cloe checked it off her list. "I'll talk with the real estate agent in town and see what we can get if we have to put the ranch on the market?"

Noelle shook her head. "That's a waste of time. Mimi is not going to sell. If the house gets fore-closed on, they'll have to take her out kicking and screaming."

"Maybe we won't have to sell the house," Sweetie said. "For now, find out what the land is worth without the house and barn, Cloe."

"I don't know why we don't just go to the Remingtons and ask what they'd pay for it," Hallie said. "I bet Sam with want to buy it."

"Sam will lowball us," Liberty said. "Not to mention, Daddy will only let Sam buy this ranch over his dead body."

Cloe made a check on her list. "No on trying to sell it to the Remingtons."

"Good," Noelle said. "I'd hate for Casey, the devil incarnate, to get this ranch after the way he's treated me."

"You haven't exactly been nice to him either, Elle," Hallie pointed out. "In school, you two were like two feral cats put in a cage."

"Let's stay on subject," Sweetie said. "What's the next thing on your list, Cloe?"

Cloe's look answered the question before she even spoke. "Someone has to start trying to convince Mimi to sell the ranch."

Not one sister raised her hand. Sweetie sighed. "Fine. I'll do it."

Later that day, she found Mimi working in the large vegetable garden next to the chicken coop. All Sweetie could see was the top of her wide-brimmed hat as Mimi hacked at the cold ground with a small garden spade.

"Isn't it a little early for planting vegetables, Mimi?"

Mimi continued spading. "That's what most people think. But gardening isn't just about planting. It's also about preparing the soil so that when you do plant, your seeds will have the perfect home to grow in. There's nothing like a perfect home to make a flower grow. You girls are a perfect example. You had a good start in perfect soil and you grew up to be good, strong flowers."

She glanced up at Sweetie. "Even if you and your sisters refuse to consider a perfect plan."

Sweetie knelt beside her grandmother and picked up another spade. "What about if we sell the land, but keep the house?"

Mimi stopped spading and squinted at her. "I'm not worried about keeping my house. I don't care anything about a pile of wood. I care about this land. Land that has belonged to Holidays for over a hundred years. Yes, I know I'm not a Holiday by blood. But I loved your granddaddy and know in my heart that he wouldn't want us to sell this land. He'd want it for our grandchildren and great-grandchildren to enjoy just like we did. So, no, I won't sell."

"But, Mimi, you don't have a choice. The investment company Daddy got the loan from will foreclose if we don't pay them."

"Then we need to figure out how to pay them." Mimi went back to spading.

With no other arguments, Sweetie sighed and started helping her grandmother turn the soil.

As a kid, she had never been much of a gardener. In fact, she'd thought up any excuse not to help in the garden. But once in Nashville, she had missed Mimi's flowers so much she couldn't go by a nursery without stopping in to buy a new plant. Her bedroom and the small balcony off it were filled with all kinds of potted flowers.

Maybe she should get a job at a greenhouse when she got back to Nashville. She didn't know if it was the thought of working at a greenhouse or the thought of returning to Nashville, but suddenly she felt extremely depressed. The depression turned to panic when she glanced up and saw the sheriff car heading up the road that led to the house.

She jumped up with every intention of hiding in the barn, but she was only halfway there when Decker pulled in front of the house and got out. He didn't look happy. He looked determined as he strode toward her.

"Something wrong with your phone?"

She turned and tried to act like she hadn't been running away. "Hi, Deck. And no, there's nothing wrong with my phone."

Her answer said it all and she hoped he would get the hint and not make her explain. She wasn't that lucky. He stared at her for a long, unnerving moment before he walked over and hefted her up on his shoulder.

She would have yelled at him to put her down if all the air hadn't left her body when her stomach met hard muscle. Luckily, her grandmother came running.

"Just what in tarnation do you think you're doing, Decker Carson!"

Decker turned to face Mimi, swinging Sweetie like a rag doll. "Beg pardon, Ms. Mimi, but your granddaughter and I have some unfinished business we need to attend to and she's refusing to attend to it."

Mimi chuckled. "Well, in that case, I'll leave you to it."

"Mimi!" Sweetie yelled as Decker turned and headed to his car. But her grandmother didn't answer as she disappeared around the corner of the house.

Decker deposited her in the back seat of his sheriff's car. Once he slammed the door, she tried to jump back out, but she couldn't get the door open.

"You let me out of this car right now," she said as soon as he slid into the driver's seat.

He put the car into drive and took off down the road. "Sorry, but like I told your grandmother. We have unfinished business and I'm not conducting it where we can be interrupted by your family."

"Fine." She sat back and crossed her arms. "Go ahead and conduct your business."

His blue eyes looked at her from the rearview mirror. "What happened between last night and today?"

"I figured out we aren't going to work."

His shoulders tensed beneath the cotton of his western shirt. "Why? And don't give me the same crap you threw at Jace—it's you, not me."

Her temper flared. "You want to know what happened? I'll tell you what happened. I woke up and realized that starting something with you is a really bad idea. I'm leaving. Maybe not this week or next week, but once I get the ranch mess untangled, I'm out of here. And I don't want anyone to get hurt."

"You mean you don't want me to get hurt."

"Okay. I don't want you to get hurt."

"Well, thanks for worrying about me, but I'm not a little kid you have to watch out for anymore, Sweetie. I'm a big boy who can take care of himself. I get that this isn't forever. I get that nothing is going to stop you from going back to Nashville and following your dream."

"Then you should also get that it makes no sense for us to start something we can't finish."

He pulled up in front of his grandparents' house. It had been a while since Sweetie had been there. It looked exactly the same. A time capsule of her youth and the times she had spent there with Jace and his grandparents . . . and Decker. Decker who always stood on the sidelines silently watching.

He wasn't standing on the sidelines now.

As soon as he parked, he hopped out of the car and opened her door. A second later, she was in his arms.

He kissed her like he always kissed her. Like she was his sun and his moon and his stars and his entire universe. When he had completely claimed every one of her brain cells with the hot slide of his lips, he drew back just enough to whisper.

"We already started something, Sweets. All we can do is finish it."

CHAPTER SEVENTEEN

SWEETIE EXPECTED DECKER to keep right on kissing her and take the decision out of her hands. But after he had turned her into a puddle of need with his expert lips, he released her and stepped back.

"What do you want, Sweets?"

At one time, she thought she knew the answer. She wanted to be a country superstar and travel the world singing her songs. She wanted to come back to Wilder as the hometown celebrity everyone had forgiven. She wanted her daddy to accept he'd been wrong all along and be proud of her. She wanted to build a mansion on the ranch and come home whenever she wasn't touring and garden with her grandma and bake with her mama and hang with her sisters who would all move back to Wilder to be close to her.

It had taken twelve years to realize how unrealistic her dream had been.

Even if she became part of the one percent of singers who make it big in the music business, that didn't mean the townsfolk would forgive her. Or her daddy would be proud of her. Or her sisters would come back to Wilder to live.

She couldn't control people's feelings and actions. She couldn't even control her own.

But standing in front of her was something she wanted—something she wanted badly. And she could have it. All she had to do was be willing to take a chance.

With her insides trembling with emotions, she stepped back into his arms.

"You. I want you."

"Sweets." He breathed the name against her lips as he scooped her up into his arms and carried her toward the house. As soon as they stepped in the door, two excited dogs greeted them. A floppy hound dog with sleepy eyes and the cute little dog Sweetie had met before.

"Get down, Dixie Chick and George." Decker tried to maneuver around the jumping dogs.

Sweetie laughed and reached out to scratch the hound dog's ears. "Hey, George. You're a handsome boy." She glanced at the little dog that danced backward as Decker moved into a bedroom. "Hey, Dixie Chick. Where did you get that cute pink sweater, girlfriend?" She glanced at Decker. His blush answered her question. The thought of him knitting his little dog a sweater made Sweetie's heart twist. When he placed her on the bed, she couldn't help pulling him in for a kiss.

It was interrupted by wet doggie kisses as both George and Dixie Chick joined them on the bed.

Sweetie couldn't help giggling as Decker

scooped up Dixie Chick and grabbed George's collar.

Once both dogs were on the other side of the closed door, he turned to Sweetie with a sheepish look. "So much for me romantically carrying you to my bed."

She smiled. "I like the sweater you made Dixie Chick, Deck."

His cheeks grew redder. "I'm trying for sexy here."

She laughed. "You knitting your dog a sweater is damn sexy, believe me."

"Yeah?"

She nodded. "Yeah. So why are you still standing over there?"

His gaze was intense as it swept over her. "I need a minute to realize that this isn't a dream. You're here. You're actually here."

Her heart twisted even tighter. "I'm here."

He released his breath as if he'd been holding it. "Do you know how many times I pictured this?" When she shook her head, he told her. "A thousand . . . no, make that a million. This moment is fulfilling a lot of my fantasies." A sexy smile tipped the corners of his mouth. "You want to fulfill a few more?"

When he smiled at her like that, she was willing to give him just about anything.

But it turned out she wasn't the one who did the giving.

After removing his boots, he started unbuttoning his shirt and the chest revealed when the cotton slipped from his shoulders made Sweetie's breath catch. He didn't have an athlete's body with muscle on top of muscle, but the muscles he had were strategically placed in all the right spots. Which somehow made them even more impressive.

She had never thought that pectoral muscles could be pretty. Decker's were. They started just below his collarbone and spread out like two hard slabs of granite that were lightly sprinkled with dark hair and topped with light brown nipples almost the same color as his tanned skin. Book-casing those pecs were defined biceps that flexed as he unbuttoned and unzipped his jeans.

Sweetie's attention was pulled away from his perfect chest and heat pooled in her body as Decker slipped out of his jeans and she took in the thick, hard length that strained against his boxer briefs. By the time he removed his socks and joined her on the bed, she was nothing but a puddle of need.

He kissed her. Not like he had kissed her earlier—rushed and desperate. This kiss was slow and thorough, as if he wanted to savor every taste and texture of her mouth. He didn't close his eyes and neither did she. Their gazes remained locked as he took slow sips.

No one had ever kissed Sweetie like this. Every gentle pull of his lips and brush of his tongue made her feel things no man had ever made her feel. Not carnal, physical things—although he could certainly make her feel those. But the way he was kissing now didn't make her feel sexual as much as . . . cherished . . . worshipped . . . special.

Growing up with five sisters, it was hard to feel special. Maybe that was why she'd wanted so desperately to become a superstar. She'd wanted to stand out in the crowd. But she'd come to realize that standing out in a crowd didn't make her feel special. It made her feel terrified. She suddenly realized that people who didn't know you couldn't make you feel like you were unique. Only the people who really saw you for who you were could.

Decker saw her for who she was.

"Sweets," he whispered against her lips as his fingers found the buttons on her shirt. He slowly unbuttoned them one by one as he continued to make slow love to her mouth. Once her shirt was off, he traced the strap of her bra in a gentle back and forth motion before sliding it down one shoulder and releasing her breast from the cup.

A shiver of anticipation ran through her as she waited for his touch. He took his time cradling her breast in his large, warm palm. He didn't squeeze. He just gently held it as if he was counting each one of her heartbeats. Feather soft, he slowly stroked his thumb over her nipple, sending wave upon wave of heat rippling through her body. She closed her eyes and let her head loll back as he masterfully played her nipple with light rolls and pinches while brushing hot kisses along her throat.

Sweetie literally saw stars—or at least light spots—when his mouth finally reached her nipple and he tugged the stiff nub into his hot, wet mouth. He suckled her like he kissed with deep pulls of his lips and lush sweeps of his tongue. When he had turned her into nothing but whimpering need, he lowered her other bra strap and pushed her back against the pillows where he cupped both breasts and feasted on them as if he wanted to eat her whole.

She was so completely caught up with what he was doing with his mouth that she didn't realize he had unbuttoned and unzipped her jeans until his hand slid into her panties. Her breath rushed out in a gasp as his fingers slipped between her wet folds and circled and teased until her body jerked with need.

"Decker, please."

"Please what?" He spoke against her nipple.

"You know what."

He sucked her nipple deeply into his mouth as he drove his fingers into her wet heat and flicked his thumb over her clit, sending her spiraling into an amazing orgasm. She moaned out her release as he sucked, thrust, and flicked—drawing out the sensations that assailed her body until there was nothing left but a drained, twitching shell.

When she finally became coherent, she could hear the dogs whining outside the door. No doubt they were confused about the moaning woman shut in the room with their dad. She was just as confused. She had always struggled to reach orgasm with other men. Sometimes she never reached it. But she had reached it with Decker. And quicker and higher than she had ever reached it before.

When she opened her eyes, she couldn't help

blushing when she discovered him rested on his elbow studying her. She was at a loss for words. Fortunately, he didn't seem to expect any. He smoothed back her hair from her forehead, then leaned down to give her a soft kiss.

"I knew you would look beautiful when you came. I didn't realize you'd look even more beautiful after."

Now she was really at a loss for words. How could a man be so perfect? She wanted to give him what he had given her. She wanted to make him feel as special and beautiful.

Pushing him over, she straddled him. Beneath her butt, she could feel his erection. His obvious desire caused her own to resurface and she shifted her hips, sliding his hard length along the damp center seam of her jeans.

"Sweets," he gritted out between his teeth. "Stop. I'm too close."

She rolled her hips again as she reached back and unhooked her bra, allowing it to slip down her arms. He stared at her breasts that were abraded from his stubble—her nipples hard and rosy from his mouth's attention—and grew even harder beneath her. He leaned up as if to kiss them again, but she drew away and shook her head.

"No. My turn."

She scooted down his thighs so she could release the straining muscle beneath his briefs. It sprang out impressively. She watched his face as she took him in hand. His eyes rolled back as she stroked him from base to moist tip and back down again. She had never wanted to taste any other man, but she wanted to taste Decker. She lowered her head and took him into her mouth. She only got to take a few deep pulls before she was flipped over to her back.

He made quick work of removing the rest of her clothes. When she was completely naked, his gaze swept her from head to toe. "Damn," he breathed. "Are you sure this isn't a dream?"

"No dream." She held out her arms. "Come here and I'll show you."

It turned out she was wrong. Making love with Decker was a dream. There was no other way to describe it. Once he had his boxer briefs off and a condom on, he took his time getting her ready with heated strokes of his fingers and gentle sips of his lips. When she was wet and trembling, he eased into her carefully.

"This okay?" he asked.

"I'm not my grandma's china, Deck."

"Are you saying you like it a little rough?"

"I'm saying do what feels good."

"Everything with you feels good, Sweets." He withdrew and thrust deep, his eyes closing as he groaned. "Every damn thing."

Everything did feel good. Decker seemed to know exactly how to angle each thrust to set Sweetie on fire.

"Faster," she coaxed as she dug her nails into his butt.

With a low growl, he pumped into her with hard, deep strokes that banged the headboard against the wall. "Dammit! I can't hold back."

Sweetie didn't want him to hold back. Seeing the normally controlled man so turned on and out of control was hot as hell. She hooked her legs around his waist and met each of his thrusts. He swore a blue streak as he gripped her thighs and pounded out his passion. When his entire body tensed, she came right along with him.

He collapsed on her for a brief second before he pulled out and rolled to his side to dispose of the condom. When he rolled back, his voice held concern. "Are you okay? I didn't mean to be so rough."

She was so relaxed that it took a real effort to turn her head and look at him. His hair was boyishly mussed and his eyes held concern. She had seen that look in his eyes before. Like when she'd had too much of Mimi's elderberry wine one New Year's Eve and showed up at his grandparents' house acting a fool and looking for Jace. Decker had taken her keys and walked her home. Then she had just thought he was a weird kid who acted too much like an adult. Now she saw him for what he was.

A hero.

Her hero.

She smoothed back the lock of hair that had fallen over his forehead and smiled. "Thank you."

"You don't have to thank me, Sweets. I should be thanking you. That was . . . unbelievable."

She smiled. "It was pretty awesome, but I wasn't thanking you for the sex. I was thanking you for not letting me jump out of the hayloft when we were kids. And for taking my keys when I was drunk. And for coming to my rescue when Major bucked me off in the Fourth of July parade. And for always watching out for me even when I never paid you any attention at all."

He leaned in and brushed a kiss over her forehead. "That's not true. You paid me the best kind of attention. You accepted me without pitying me. To you, I wasn't the orphan who'd lost his parents and had to come live with his grandparents. I was just Jace's weird cousin."

"Well, you were kind of weird. I mean, when you first got here, you dressed in polo shirts, khakis, and pristine white sneakers. You were scared of bees, spiders, and even butterflies. It took months before I could get you to say 'y'all' and even longer to get you on a horse."

He smiled. "See, you did pay attention to me. You made sure I spoke and rode like a true Texan."

"I just didn't want you getting beat up after Jace left for college."

"Then I guess I should be thanking you too." He rolled on top of her, framing her head with his perfect forearms. "So how should we go about thanking each other, Sweets?"

She looped her arms on his shoulders and slid her fingers through his hair. "I think we can figure it out."

CHAPTER EIGHTEEN

L IFE WAS SWEET.
     Or maybe life was Sweets.

Decker felt like he hadn't really started living until Sweetie had come home. For the last week, he'd woken up every morning feeling like he'd won the lottery and gone to bed every night feeling the same. He would have loved to hold her hostage in his house and never venture out into the real world. But he had to work and she had to help her sisters untangle the financial mess the ranch was in.

He had known things weren't good at the Holiday Ranch. But he hadn't known how bad they were until Sweetie had told him. He wished he could help her and her family out, but he'd spent most of his savings on buying his grandparents' house. Still, he had offered what he had. In the last week, he had come to realize that he would give Sweetie anything to keep her here . . . including his heart.

She had refused both.

His money she had refused with words. His

heart she had refused with actions. No matter how passionate her lovemaking or how tenderly she held him afterwards, she never stayed the night. He hated the moment when he had to walk her to her car and say goodbye. He never complained or begged her to stay. He refused to smother her and make her leave sooner. But it was becoming harder and harder not to think about her leaving and to just enjoy the time they had together.

A piece of hay brushed over the bridge of his nose, pulling his attention to the woman who lay next to him in the hayloft. Her hair was mussed and littered with hay and her eyes were sated from their lovemaking.

"Whatcha thinkin' about?" She ran the piece of hay over his bottom lip.

"I'm thinking about how itchy my bare behind is."

She laughed a soft laugh that made his stomach feel all light and airy. "And here I thought the prissy city boy was completely gone."

He rolled on his side to face her and lifted his eyebrows. "Prissy?"

"That's what I said. Hardy country folk don't mind dealing with a little itch. But if you're too soft, I guess we just won't tumble in the hay again."

He growled and pulled her to him, giving her a long, deep kiss before drawing back. "I can deal with a little itch."

She looked up at him with twinkling eyes. "Well, I can't." She reached down and scratched her butt cheek. "Next time, I'm bringing a blanket."

"Here, let me scratch that itch for you." He pushed her hand away and filled his palm with her soft flesh.

"That's not scratching. That's squeezing."

"But it feels better, doesn't it?"

She hooked her arms around his shoulders and her smile faded. "Every time you touch me, I feel better."

Her words made hope flare, but he was still too scared to say what he wanted to say: *Then don't leave. Please don't leave. I love you, Sweets. I've always loved you.* Instead, he kissed her, slowly and deeply, trying to communicate everything he couldn't say.

When he drew back, he changed the subject. "So how is everything going? Have you had any luck convincing Mimi to sell?"

She shook her head. "No. She stubbornly refuses to even talk about it."

"I'm sorry," he said. "Is there anything I can do?"

"I don't think there's anything that anyone can do ... unless one of my sisters or I want to marry Rome or Casey Remington." He knew she was kidding, but just the thought of Sweetie marrying Rome or Casey made Decker feel a little crazed. Something he tried to hide as she continued. "There's something we need to talk about."

His heart picked up its pace. He knew this time would come. He just hadn't thought it would come this quickly. Or hurt this much. He tried to brave his way through it.

"I guess since you can't talk Mimi into selling, you're leaving."

Her eyebrows popped up. "Trying to get rid of me so soon, Deckster?"

He didn't laugh. "I don't want you to leave, Sweets."

She cupped his jaw in her hand. "Then you'll be happy to hear that I've decided to stay here in Wilder a little longer."

Every muscle in his body relaxed and he wanted nothing more than to jerk her into his arms and kiss her silly. "What about your singing career?"

"I don't really have a singing career. Something I've been lying to everyone about—including myself."

He should have kept his mouth shut. He was getting exactly what he wanted. Sweetie staying longer. But damned if he could let her feel badly about herself. "It's not a lie. You're the best singer I've ever heard, Sweets. Your songs are better than anything on the radio."

She laughed. "Which is why they soured you on country music forever. They were so damn good."

A blush heated his cheeks. "Actually, after you left, listening to country music—any country music—made me sad."

Her smile faded. "You're the only one I've ever been able to sing my songs to. I think it was because I knew you wouldn't judge them harshly."

He smoothed back her hair. "Sing me one now."

She hesitated for only a brief second before she started singing in a soft voice that had always made his heart swell with pride. She sang a song about a small-town girl leaving home to make it in the big world and how much that girl had missed her family and her friends and the people of her town. Decker knew she was that girl. When she finished, he hugged her close.

"I love it. What's it called?"

"'Small Town Regrets.'" She drew back. "Do you really like it? I just finished it last night when I was waiting for you to get home from work and I know it needs some work."

"I think it's perfect just the way it is. The towns-folk need to hear it." He could read the hurt in her eyes. "They love you, Sweets. They just need to know that you love them too."

She gazed into his eyes with a look he couldn't describe. "How did you get so calm and level-headed, Decker Carson? From your daddy? Your mama?"

Talking about his parents had always been painful. But strangely now, in Sweetie's arms, he could smile when thinking of his mom and dad. "Definitely not my mama. She was stubborn and feisty and had no patience whatsoever." He hesitated. "A little like someone else I know."

Her eyes widened. "I don't have a clue who you're talking about." She plucked a piece of straw from his hair. "So I guess it was your daddy who was calm and collected like you."

"I haven't been all that calm and collected since you came back to town."

"I rile you, do I?"

"Just a little bit." He kissed the tip of her nose. "And maybe that's a good thing. My mama used to rile my daddy all the time. She loved teasing him until he chased after her and flipped her over his shoulder." He smiled at the memory. "When I was younger, I'd wrap my arms around my daddy's legs until he picked me up too."

Tears glistened in Sweetie's eyes. "I bet they were awesome. Only awesome parents could make an awesome son like you."

Words pushed at his throat, but he swallowed them back down and changed the subject. "Want to go to dinner with an awesome guy? I was thinking about taking you to Houston tonight on a real date."

"I would love to go on a real date with an awesome guy, but my sisters are leaving in the morning and it might be the last family dinner we have all together in the house."

He hated that he wouldn't get to be with her tonight, but he was thrilled she wasn't leaving like her sisters.

At least not for a while.

To show his gratitude, he kissed her. When he finally drew back, her eyes were dazed and passion filled.

"Does that kiss mean you aren't too prissy for another tumble in the hay?"

He tumbled her. Not even the itch of the hay stopped him from giving her a tumble she'd never forget. And one he'd never forget. He'd never forget the liquid green of her eyes when he brushed his lips over her wet heat. Never forget the tight hug of her thighs or her soft breathy hiccups as he used his tongue to delve deeper. Never forget the way she gasped his name when he pushed her over the edge.

"Decker," she whispered like a prayer.

After he had pleasured her, she used her mouth to pleasure him. When they finally climbed down from the hayloft, they looked like they had been tumbling around in the hay.

"If you walk in the house like this, your family is going to know what we've been doing," he said as he plucked hay out of her hair.

She brushed at his shoulders. "My family already knows what we've been doing. Or least my sisters do."

He stared at her. "You told them we're having sex?"

"Of course. I tell them everything. And it's not like they couldn't have figured it out on their own. Mimi loves retelling the story about how you tossed me over your shoulder and carried me off."

"Shit. Your parents and grandma must think I'm a caveman."

Sweetie laughed. "My daddy was pretty angry until I assured him you were just horsing around. I don't think Mama believed it. Neither did Mimi. She thinks you have gumption. She said if you had money and were a rancher, you'd be top on her bridegrooms' list."

He pulled her closer. "Then I guess I need to go buy some lottery tickets and brush up on my ropin'." As soon as the words were out, he wished he had them back. Marriage talk was sure to send Sweetie bolting. But she didn't look upset or uncomfortable. In fact, her smile got even bigger.

"I guess you should."

On the way home, he took a detour to a truck stop where he bought twenty lottery tickets. He knew it was foolish. The chances of him winning were slim. And even if he did win, the chances of Sweetie agreeing to marry him were even slimmer. But he hadn't thought she would stay for longer than a couple weeks and she was. So maybe, just maybe, his luck was changing.

"Jolene" came on the radio station he'd recently programed in and he sang along loudly and obnoxiously. He stopped singing when he got home and saw the rental car parked in his driveway right behind his sheriff's SUV. Since few people in town ever rented a car, he was wary. As a law enforcement officer, he had been trained to be cautious, so he took his gun out of the glove box and tucked it in the waistband of his jeans before he got out. He had only taken two steps toward the house when the door opened and George and Dixie Chick raced out.

Followed by a man.

Decker didn't need to see the face beneath the shadow of the cowboy hat to know who it was. The athletic body and swagger gave him away.

"Jace!" Decker hurried over to greet his cousin with a tight hug.

Jace thumped him on the back. "Hey, cuz." He drew back and grinned. He still looked like a golden boy. His hair was as blond. His eyes as blue. But there was a harder edge to his features that hadn't been there the last time Decker had seen him. "You haven't changed at all," Jace said. "What's it been, five years?"

"Six. My college graduation was the last time we saw each other." Decker gave George a pat on the head before he scooped Dixie Chick into the crook of his arm. "When did you get here?"

"A couple hours ago. I was gonna wait on the porch, but then figured I'd see if the key Nana gave me still worked." Jace squinted at Dixie Chick. "That's some watchdog you got there, Deck. She tried to chew my leg off when I stepped in the door."

"She's a feisty one. You still have a key to the house?"

Jace shrugged. "You know me. I never could get rid of anything." He glanced at the old truck sitting in the driveway. "Looks like you can't get rid of anything either. You didn't mention you still had my old truck when we talked last. I'd thought for sure you'd sell it."

Decker shook his head. "I knew you'd come home eventually."

"Yeah. It's been too long." Jace's eyes turned sad. "I wanted to come home for Gramps and Nana's funeral, but it was right in the middle of the season and I—"

Decker cut him off. "I know. It's okay."

Jace nodded, then glanced at the sheriff's SUV.

"You told me you were sheriff, but it didn't sink in until you drove up. Who would have thought that my skinny cousin who was terrified of bees would be defending the townsfolk of Wilder?"

"Not me, that's for sure."

Jace socked him in the arm. "Actually, it's not that hard to believe. You've always been a hero, Deck. If you weren't helping out a widow in town, you were standing up for kids who were getting bullied, or heroically carrying Sweetie to the doctor when she broke her arm."

Decker had been so happy to see Jace he hadn't even thought about Sweetie until that moment. Now guilt settled around him like a wet wool blanket. He needed to tell Jace about her coming home and their relationship.

First, he needed a beer.

"You want a beer?"

"Hell yeah." Jace crouched to give George some attention. "I didn't have a problem walking into your house uninvited and taking a nap on your couch, but I drew the line at helping myself to your beer."

"Hey, this is as much your house as it is mine. They were your grandparents too."

"Yeah, but you were the one who stayed and helped Mama take care of them at the end."

"Because you were busy with football."

His eyes dimmed and he stared off. "Yeah. Football always came first." He snapped out of whatever funk he'd gone into and smiled. "So about that beer?"

When they got inside, Jace mentioned he was

hungry so Decker made them both ham-and-cheese sandwiches to go along with their beers. They took them out to the porch and sat in the same rockers their grandparents had sat in while they ate and went through a six-pack of beer.

Decker figured he'd work up to telling Jace about Sweetie. So for the first hour, the conversation was about Jace's flight out, Decker's job, how Jace's mama and new stepdaddy liked living in Galveston, and how Decker had come to own a miniature Chihuahua mix. By the time the six-pack was gone, Decker knew it was time to tell his cousin. But before he could, Jace spoke.

"I have to quit football."

"What? Why?"

"You remember that shoulder injury I got last season?"

"Yeah, you said it was no big deal."

Jace finished off his beer and crushed the can between his hands. "Maybe I was just trying to convince myself." He stared out at the night. "The docs don't think I'll get full range of motion back. Too much scar tissue from the surgery."

Decker didn't know what to say. Football had always been Jace's life. After struggling for words, he finally just reached over and squeezed Jace's arm. "I'm sorry."

Jace nodded. "Me too."

They sat there for a long time not saying anything before Jace spoke. "So who's the woman you're dating?"

Now was the time to confess all, but damned if Decker could do it when Jace had just told him he might not ever play football again. "A woman? I'm not dating anyone." Technically, it was true. He and Sweetie had yet to go out on a date.

Jace laughed. "You never could lie worth shit, Deck. Gramps always told me to make sure you weren't around if I wanted to get away with something."

"So that's why you never told me about what you did at all the high school parties you went to."

"I didn't tell you because you weren't interested in high school parties." He cocked his head. "Come to think of it, you weren't interested in much. You didn't care about sports. You got good grades, but didn't study a lot. You didn't even date in high school." He reached over and plucked a piece of hay out of Decker's hair. "But it looks like you're making up for it. So who were you rolling in the hay with? Is it the same girl who owns the lacy panties I saw in the laundry room?"

When Decker struggled to tell him, Jace smiled. "It's okay, dude. I respect that you're not the kind of guy who kisses and tells. I figure I'll get to meet her soon enough. That's if it's okay with you if I stick around for a few days."

"Of course it is. You can sleep in Gramps and Nana's room."

"Thanks. In fact, I think I'll call it a night. That's one helluva long flight from Ontario." He got to his feet, and Decker knew he needed to say something. If Jace was staying, he'd find out soon enough.

"There something you need to know, Jace." He

forged on before he lost his courage. "Sweetie Holiday is back in town."

Jace smiled as he headed for the door. "I know. Why do you think I'm here?"

CHAPTER NINETEEN

SWEETIE COULDN'T SLEEP. Liberty had found out the payoff total for the loan Daddy had gotten and it was much higher than anyone had expected. After comparing it to the amount the Realtor had told Cloe they could get for the ranch, it was doubtful her parents and Mimi would be able to keep the house. Or even afford to buy a new one.

And worrying about where her parents would live wasn't the only reason Sweetie couldn't sleep. The other reason was a six-foot-three-inch lawman with eyes the color of a Caribbean sea and lips Sweetie couldn't get enough of. This was the first night in the last week Sweetie hadn't snuggled in his arms after they'd made love and listened to the strong thump of his heart. The first night he hadn't kissed her good night as if he never wanted to let her go.

She hadn't wanted to let him go either. But every night she had forced herself to return home. Sleeping with him was the one barrier she had placed between them in the hopes it would remind them both that this was just some casual fun.

Except it no longer felt like casual fun.

Being with Decker felt as right as her decision to stay in Wilder. It felt comfortable. More comfortable than any relationship she'd ever had in her life. When she was with Decker, she didn't feel invisible like she had when she was with Jace. Or unheard like she did with her daddy. Or pressured to be a success like she did in Nashville. When she was with Decker, she felt seen and heard and content. It didn't matter if she was the hometown sweetheart, or an obedient daughter, or a country superstar.

He loved her for her.

And he did love her. He hadn't said the words out loud, but he'd said them with every kiss, caress, and tender look he gave her.

He loved her.

As she lay there in the dark, missing Decker with an ache that physically hurt, she wondered if she might love him too.

It should have been a scary epiphany. A few weeks ago, falling in love had been the furthest thing from her mind. Her life had been too chaotic. It was still chaotic. Just not so chaotic that the thought of Decker on bended knee and holding a ring didn't seep into all her pores and warm her heart from the inside out. The feeling took her completely by surprise. She wasn't ready for marriage.

Was she?

A tap on the window startled her out of her

thoughts. She assumed it was a tree branch moving in the wind until it came again. Quietly, so as not to wake Cloe, she got out of bed and tiptoed to the window. When she drew back the curtains, her heart swelled at the sight of the cowboy standing beneath. She didn't hesitate to turn and head for the stairs.

Decker was coming around the side of the house as she was coming down the porch steps. She ran toward him and dove into his arms. He swept her completely off her feet and swung her around twice before she realized that something wasn't right. In fact, the feel of his arms and body were all wrong. When he set her on her feet, she stared in stunned surprise at the face beneath the cowboy hat.

"Jace?"

He smiled. A charming smile that had melted many a heart. Just never hers. "Hey, Sweetie."

"What are you doing here?"

"I came to see you."

"All the way from Canada and in the middle of the night?"

He flashed a grin. "I used to come and see you all the time in the middle of night."

He had. He'd tossed pebbles at her window and she'd raced out to meet him just like she had tonight. Except, tonight, she hadn't wanted it to be Jace. She'd wanted it to be Decker who had swept her in his arms.

Decker, Jace's cousin.

Good Lord, what a mess. Did Decker know his cousin was back? If so, had he told Jace about his and Sweetie's relationship? Was that why Jace was there?

"Look, I know it's late," Jace said. "But do you think we could talk?"

"Sure," she said. "Let's go sit on the porch."

Since Sweetie had run out of the house in nothing but Decker's western shirt—a shirt she had worn to bed ever since he had wrapped it around her the night at Cooper's Creek—she was shivering by the time they reached the porch.

"Here." Jace took off the jean jacket he was wearing and hooked it over her shoulders as they sat down on the swing. They had sat in that exact spot at least a hundred times before. Jace talking about football while Sweetie made up songs in her head.

"Feels like old times," he said as he took off his hat and hooked it over the arm of the swing. The porch light was on, giving Sweetie a better view of his face than she'd had in the dark yard.

He had changed very little over the years. His hair was a tad bit longer. The smile crinkles at the corner of his eyes a little deeper. And he could grow a beard now—golden scruff covered his jaw and above his top lip. If possible, he was even more handsome than he'd been in high school.

He seemed to be assessing her too. His blue-eyed gaze ran over her features before a smile broke over his face. "You can still stop a man's heart, Sweetie Holiday."

"And you're still a shameless flirt."

He laughed. "Hey, it's worked for me."

"I bet it has. I bet you have lots of Canadian football groupies at your beck and call."

His smile died, his eyes serious. "None that feel like home."

She felt it too. The comfortable feeling of knowing someone since childhood. All the shared memories. All the shared growing pains. But that was all there was. There was no rapid heartbeat. No breathless longing. No feeling like he saw her for who she really was.

Only Decker gave her those feelings.

But that didn't stop her from caring about Jace. They had shared a lot together.

"So when did you get back?" she asked.

"I got in late this afternoon."

"You've seen Deck?"

"Yeah. I'm staying with him."

She couldn't help feeling a little ticked. A warning text from Decker would have been nice. "So I guess he told you I was back in town."

"Actually, one of my mama's friends called her and said you were here." He frowned. "She also said the townsfolk are still holding a grudge about what happened. Which is why I'm here. I wanted to apologize in person."

"Apologize? It's not your fault that the townsfolk hold grudges."

He sighed and ran a hand through his hair as he looked out at the night. "Yeah, it is. I blamed you for what happened as much as the townsfolk did and that was wrong." He looked back at her. "You breaking up with me didn't cause me to lose those games, Sweetie. I jumped on that excuse because I couldn't admit the real truth . . . I had crumbled under the pressure. When the college football scouts started calling and showing up to the games, my nerves got the best of me. That's what caused me to lose those games. Not a broken heart. And I should have said that when the town started shunning you. Instead, I said nothing because I didn't want folks to think I was just a scared kid."

"We were both scared kids. I wasn't blameless either. I picked the worst possible time to break it off with you and embarrassed you in front of the entire town."

"You should have broken it off with me sooner. I was a shitty boyfriend who couldn't think of anything but football. You deserved better."

It was nice to have the confirmation, but he needed to know the truth. "You were pretty wrapped up in football, but that's not the reason I broke up with you. The summer before our senior year, I had started to feel invisible. Like I didn't have an identity. I was Hank Holiday's oldest daughter. One of six sisters. Jace Carson's girl. But I was never just me. In order to just be me I needed space from my family. From you. From the town." She hesitated as she looked out at the ranch. "I guess sometimes you have to leave everything you know to figure out who you really are."

As soon as the words were out of her mouth, she realized how true they were. She'd had to leave Wilder. She'd had to leave a daddy who saw her as the daughter who would take over the family ranch to discover that she loved her family's ranch. It was her home. She'd had to leave five sisters who she'd tried so hard to be the perfect role model for to discover that her sisters didn't need a perfect role model. They just needed a sister who would always be there for them. She'd had to leave a boyfriend who the entire town had expected her to marry to discover the type of man she did want to marry.

Because if she hadn't left, she never would have discovered all those things when she finally came home. She knew who she was now. She was a woman who loved writing country songs—just not singing those songs on stage. She was the oldest Holiday sister who loved her family and intended to make sure her career goals never got in the way of spending time with them again. She was a woman who had fallen head over heels in love with her ex-boyfriend's cousin.

She didn't realize she was sitting there grinning like a Cheshire cat until Jace pointed it out.

"By the look on your face, I'd say you've figured out who you are. I guess being a country singer agrees with you."

"Actually, I couldn't make it as a country singer and it took me twelve years to discover that I didn't really want to. It turns out that all along I was chasing the wrong dream. How stupid is that?"

"Not stupid at all. Dreams have a way of tricking you."

"Yours didn't. You've always known what you wanted."

Jace's eyes turned sad. "Yeah. I've always known." He lifted a hand and smoothed her hair away from her face. "I know I didn't say it enough, but I really did love you, Sweetie Holiday."

Her heart ached for the two innocent kids they'd once been. "I loved you too, Jace. I still do."

He sighed. "Just not enough."

"I don't think either one us ever loved each other enough. If we had, I wouldn't have left." She smiled. "And you wouldn't have let me. But that doesn't mean we can't love each other as friends." She leaned in and kissed his cheek. The sound of an approaching car had her pulling back and looking at the road.

Just the sight of Jace's old truck had Sweetie's heart leaping. When Decker got out with sleep-tousled hair and wearing nothing but a pair of faded jeans, it leaped even more. All she wanted to do was run to him and confess her love. But then he stepped into the spill of porch light and she read the anger written all over his face.

"Well, this looks cozy."

Sweetie realized that it did look pretty cozy. She stood and tried to explain. "Jace just came over—"

Decker cut her off and glared at his cousin. "Oh, I know what Jace just came over for." He looked back at her. "The question is, did he get it?"

Her eyes widened. "Excuse me?"

Sweetie figured most men would be jealous

if they caught their girlfriend sitting on a porch swing with another man in the middle of the night—especially when that girlfriend was wearing nothing but a shirt and another man's jacket. But she had thought Decker was different than most men. She had thought he knew her. Really knew her. But if he thought she could swap out cousins like she swapped out hair products then he didn't know her at all.

That hurt. It hurt badly.

Jace stood up. "What the hell are you talking about, Deck?"

Decker turned on him. "Don't play dumb jock with me, Jace. You know exactly what I'm talking about. You couldn't wait to fly back home when you found out Sweetie was back in town. Couldn't wait to take up where you two left off twelve years ago."

Sweetie's hurt quickly turned to anger. "Take up where we left off? You don't know what you're talking about, Decker Carson. And I suggest you leave now before you say something stupider than what you've already said."

"Would someone tell me what's going on here?" Jace asked. "Why are you so mad, Deck?"

Decker and Sweetie ignored him as they continued to glare at each other. Not more than a few seconds ago, she'd been ready to confess her love. Now she just wanted to beat him over the head. "I mean it, Deck. I want you to leave."

"Well, that's too bad. I'm not leaving until Jace leaves."

"What? Are you afraid we'll have sex on the porch swing once you're gone?"

Decker growled low in his throat. "Don't push me, Sweets."

That sent her over the edge. She had grown up with an overbearing man who loved giving orders. She wasn't about to put up with Decker thinking he could.

She marched down the porch steps. "I'll push you." She shoved him with both hands. "I'll push you as much as I want to push you." She shoved him again. "Especially when you show up at my house and act like a jealous, possessive asshole!"

His eyes flared. "I have every right to act like a jealous asshole when I find you cuddled up on the porch swing with my cousin."

"Jealous?" Jace came down the steps. "Wait a second. Sweetie is the woman you've been fooling around with? You moved in on my girl, Deck?"

Sweetie was about to point out that she wasn't his girl when Decker turned on Jace and growled, "She's not your fuckin' girl! You never gave a shit about her. All you cared about was football. I used to have to remind you to get her something for her birthday. And it lands on Valentine's Day, for God's sake!"

Jace yelled back, "The only reason you knew that was because you followed her around like a lovesick puppy."

"Better than treating her like she didn't exist whenever a football was around."

"So you think you'll make a better boyfriend?"

"I *am* a better boyfriend!"

Sweetie was about to jump in and tell them both off when Decker hauled off and punched Jace right in the face. She released a startled squeal as Jace stumbled back into the flowerbed and held his jaw.

"Is that all you got, baby cousin?" Jace charged Decker and punched him. Decker's head flew back, but he held his ground.

"I would think that a quarterback would throw a better punch than that. Of course, you can't even throw a football now, can you?"

"You sonofabitch!" Jace tackled Decker to the ground.

"Stop it!" Sweetie yelled.

But they didn't stop.

They wrestled around at Sweetie's feet like two adolescent teenagers. For a second, she stood there not knowing what to do. Then she remembered what her daddy had done whenever the herding dogs had gotten into a fight. She ran to where the garden hose was coiled up and turned on the spigot. When the first spray of cold water hit them, Jace and Decker released yelps and jumped to their feet. But she was too mad to stop spraying them. She continued to soak them from head to boots until they both raced for their cars.

The screen door squeaked and her entire family came charging out. Her daddy was in his underwear holding his shotgun. Mama was in her bathrobe holding a kitchen knife. Her sisters wore various sleepwear and were armed with baseball bats, a tennis racket, and a riding crop.

And Mimi was in her foam curlers and housecoat with no weapon at all. Just a big smile on her face.

"And everyone thought my plan wouldn't work. Just how much does a Canadian football player make, anyway?"

CHAPTER TWENTY

THE DRIVE BACK to the house was miserable. Not only because the heater didn't work well in the old truck and Decker was sopping wet, but also because the jealous haze that had fogged his thinking when he had seen Jace and Sweetie all cozied up on the porch swing had lifted and he felt like a complete and utter idiot.

He knew what had sent him over the edge. He had spent way too many years standing on the sidelines while Jace took what Decker had wanted. All those feelings had reared their ugly heads when he'd gotten up to let Dixie Chick out and discovered Jace's rental car was gone.

It hadn't been hard to figure out where Jace went. Especially when he had flat out confessed to coming back because Sweetie was there and he wanted another chance with her. Not that he'd said those exact words, but he didn't have to say them for Decker to know what he wanted.

Only a fool wouldn't want a second chance with Sweetie.

Decker wanted a second chance. He wanted a second chance to redo the night and not show up at Sweetie's house acting like an arrogant, jealous fool. She had been furious and he couldn't blame her. His behavior had been immature and irrational. But the sight of Sweetie leaning in to kiss Jace's cheek had unraveled all the emotions he'd been trying to keep tucked deep inside.

He hadn't just felt rage. He'd felt terrified. Terrified at the thought of Sweetie giving Jace what she refused to give him—her love. Probably because Decker still saw himself as being unworthy of it. It had always been Jace and Sweetie. The football star and the hometown sweetheart. They had a history that she and Decker would never have.

Which explained why when he arrived home and saw Jace standing in the front yard waiting for him, he couldn't help being pissed all over again.

He jumped out and slammed the door so hard the old truck swayed. "If you think you can just waltz back into town and start things up with her, you got another think coming."

Jace glared back at him. "She was mine first, cuz."

"She isn't yours anymore."

Jace snorted. "It doesn't look like she's yours either."

Decker wished he could argue the point, but he couldn't. He'd done exactly what he'd promised himself he wouldn't do. He had forced Sweetie into a corner by charging over to the Holiday Ranch and claiming her as if she was some kind of possession. Which was exactly why she had left the first time. She had felt smothered and like she belonged to everyone but herself. And there he had stood in her family's front yard and acted like some kind of arrogant, possessive Neanderthal.

What had he been thinking?

She was probably packing right now.

Just the thought of her leaving had his heart throbbing as much as his jaw where Jace had hit him. He wanted to jump back in his truck, head to the ranch, and beg her to stay so badly his hands shook. But he knew that would only make her feel more cornered. Only push her further away from him when all he wanted was to pull her close.

He fisted his hands and yelled up at the sky. "I love her. I fuckin' love her!"

"And you think I don't?"

He glared at his cousin. "Shut up, Jace, or I'll finish what I started."

"I believe I was the one winning when Sweetie hosed us down." Winning had always been so important to Jace. It had never meant that much to Decker . . . until now.

"Sweetie isn't a prize to win."

"Funny, but that's not how you acted tonight. And be honest, you don't love Sweetie. You're just infatuated with her because she reminds you of your mama."

Decker moved closer. "Watch it, Jace."

"The truth hurts, doesn't it?"

"It's not the truth."

"Of course it is. And I get it. You were grieving hard when you first came here to live. Being around Sweetie made you miss your mama less. But before you go around claiming to love her, you better make sure the feelings you have for her aren't just feelings of gratitude because she helped you get through a rough time."

"And I suppose your love for Sweetie is more authentic." Decker snorted. "You don't even know her. You don't know that her favorite muffin is lemon poppy seed and her favorite flowers are tulips. You don't know she has at least two hundred songs she wrote in notebooks in her room. Songs that speak about how hurt she was because no one seemed to care about who she was or what she wanted. It would have been so easy for her to stay here and take over the ranch. Or for her to marry you and become a football star's wife. But she wanted her own life. She wanted to be her own person.

"So she left here at eighteen and went to Nashville all by herself. I can't even image how hard that must have been—all alone in a big city where she knew no one. But she hung in there. She never gave up. For twelve years, she's been working her tail off to try and make it in the music business. That's not just feistiness. That's determination, dedication, and the refusal to let anything or anyone hold her back. Not you. Not her daddy. Not the town she loves." He swallowed the lump that had risen to his throat. "Not even me. That's the woman I fell in love with. Not when I was eleven, but when I was twenty-seven years old and thought I was over crushing on her. But I'll never get over Sweetie. Never."

When he was finished, he stood there with his heart hurting and his breath pumping in and out of his lungs. Jace stared at him for a long time before he released his breath.

"Well, shit. Why the hell didn't you tell me all this when I got here and asked who you were seeing?"

"Because I didn't want to hurt you any more than you were already hurt over losing your dream. I planned on telling you this morning, but you ran off to Sweetie's before I could." He couldn't help feeling angry all over again as the image of Sweetie and Jace sitting on the porch swing popped into his head.

Jace must have read his expression because he held up his hands. "Now don't start swinging again, Deck. Nothing happened. I didn't come back here to start something up with Sweetie. I do love her. I'll always love her. Which is why I came back to apologize to her for being a shitty boyfriend and for not defending her to the townsfolk." He sighed. "But you're right, it's not the kind of love that will last a lifetime. Sweetie and I both know it. I just got a little hurt when I found out that you not only have a good life here in Wilder, you also got a great girl. While I'm nothing but a washed-up football player with nothing to show for his life."

"You're so much more than football, Jace. It's just a game."

Jace smiled sadly. "Unfortunately, it's never just been a game to me." He sighed. "You always did have a better head on your shoulders than I did.

You always made the right choices. So make the right choice now. Don't let her go, Deck. Don't make the same mistake I made."

Decker didn't want to let Sweetie go, but deep down he knew he'd already lost her. He couldn't forget the way she'd looked at him when he'd started spouting his jealous nonsense. He had worked so hard to make her feel like he respected her enough to listen to her and he hadn't even given her a chance to explain. And why should she have to? She had never made him any promises. At least not with words. With her body, she had said things that had made him think maybe they had a chance of making it work.

But it had just been wishful thinking.

"You couldn't hold her, Jace." He tried to ignore the fist squeezing his heart. "And neither can I. Now I'm going to go get out of these wet clothes."

Once inside, he was greeted by George and Dixie Chick, but not even their slobbery love made him feel better. Nor did a long hot shower. After getting out, he planned to go back to bed and try to sleep for a few hours before he had to get up and go to work, but then he stepped out of the bathroom and saw Jace sitting in Nana's chair reading something in a spiral notebook.

"What are you doing?"

Jace glanced up. "Have you seen this?"

Decker moved into the living room. "What is it?"

"I think it's one of those songbooks you were telling me about."

"Sweetie's? But how did it get here?"

"I don't know. I found it in Nana's knitting basket."

Decker took it from him. "You shouldn't be looking through it. Sweetie doesn't like sharing her songs."

"If I remember correctly, she didn't seem to have a problem singing her songs to you. When I asked her to sing them to me, she always had some excuse for why she couldn't." He pointed at the notebook Decker had clutched possessively to his chest. "And she needs to share those songs. I don't know how to read music, but the lyrics about made me cry. Especially the second one. I think you need to read it, Deck."

Decker shook his head. "I'm not going to invade her privacy. I'm sure she left it here by accident."

Jace cocked his head. "You sure? Or maybe she left it here because it's always been easier for her to express her emotions to you in songs." His eyes grew as intense as they did when he was getting ready to throw a touchdown pass. "Go on, Deck. She wrote it for you."

Since leaving Sweetie, Decker hadn't felt a spark of hope. He felt it now. Without saying another word, he carried the notebook into his room.

George and Dixie Chick were sound asleep on his bed, Dixie on one pillow and George on the other. Decker sat down on the foot of the bed and set the notebook on his lap. He shouldn't open it, but he did.

There were only two songs in it, scribbled in

Sweetie's almost illegible writing. The first song was the song Sweetie had sung to him in the hayloft. "Small Town Regrets." The second song was called "The Right Boy."

Taking a deep breath, he read the lyrics:

A boy who sees me for who I am . . . and who I was, a boy who loves me just because. A boy who gives me space to breathe, a boy who offers a country dream . . . the right boy for me. He's the right boy for me.

"So are you going to offer her that country dream?"

Decker looked up to see Jace standing in the doorway.

"I don't have much of a country dream to offer her. I don't have a lot of money, or a big house . . . I can't even help her save her family's ranch like the Remingtons."

Jace came into the room and flopped down on the bed like he'd done a hundred times before when they were kids. "Mama told me about the Holiday Ranch being in trouble. But what do the Remingtons have to do with the equation?"

"Mimi cooked up a plan to marry one of her granddaughters to Casey or Rome in the hopes that their money will get the family out of debt."

"Shut the fuck up." Jace laughed. "That old gal has always been a character." He sobered and glanced at Decker. "Don't tell me that you're actually thinking Sweetie would be better off with a Remington. She doesn't love a Remington. She loves you." He glanced down at the notebook Decker still held. "If that song isn't proof, I don't know what is. So quit sitting here feeling sorry for yourself and let's come up with a plan to get her back."

"After what I did, I don't know if that's possible."

Jace scratched Dixie Chick's ears and grinned. "Anything is possible when the Carson boys put their heads together. The first thing we need to do is get the townsfolk to stop being idiots. They adore Sweetie. They're just scared of getting hurt again when she leaves. I figure all they need is to hear 'Small Town Regrets' and they'll be putty in her hands. That, and knowing she's not leaving again." He sent Decker a pointed look. "That's where you come in, cuz." A cocky smile tipped up the corners of his mouth. "Not that marrying a small-town sheriff is much of a dream. But I guess we all can't be hot quarterbacks."

CHAPTER TWENTY-ONE

SWEETIE WOKE UP to the sun blazing in through the window. She wasn't surprised she had slept late. After the Carson Cousin Brawl, her sisters had kept her up wanting all the details. Hallie had applauded her for hosing them down until they looked like drowned rats. Liberty had been impressed she had two hot cowboys fighting over her. Noelle had wanted to know which one had won—not only the fight, but also Sweetie's heart. Belle was more concerned about the two men being hurt. And Cloe had wanted to know how Sweetie felt.

Last night, she had just felt angry. This morning, she felt hurt and disappointed. She thought Decker was the kind of man who valued her opinions—the kind of man who would always listen to and trust what she had to say. But he hadn't listened to her or trusted her last night. He'd just assumed the worst.

It had broken her heart.

She had planned to stay at the ranch, but now all she wanted to do was run back to Nashville and try to forget Decker Carson.

Of course, she couldn't leave. Not when she had already told her family she was staying. She would just have to avoid Decker. She had already turned off her phone. She glanced at it sitting on her nightstand. As she did, she noticed Cloe wasn't sleeping in the other bed. In fact, the bed was military made with the pillow propped perfectly.

Worried that her sisters had left without saying goodbye, she quickly got up and hurried down the stairs. She was relieved to hear their voices coming from the kitchen. They seemed to be having an intense conversation.

A conversation about her.

"Well, I don't know about Sweetie, but I'd choose Deck," Hallie said. "Jace has always been an arrogant jock who thinks his poop don't stink."

"Watch your mouth at the table, young lady," Mimi scolded. "But I'm rooting for Decker too. If your sister truly cared about Jace, she never would have broken up with him. And I like the way Decker doesn't put up with any of Sweetie's shenanigans. You should have seen the way he flipped her over his shoulder and carried her off."

"I'm shocked, Mimi," Liberty said. "I thought you'd want her to pick Jace because he makes more money and can pay off the loan."

"He doesn't make that much more. I looked up Canadian football salaries on my phone last night. Truly disappointing." Mimi paused. "So it's up to one of you girls to save this ranch."

Sweetie waited for her sisters to argue and was more than a little surprised when Daddy did.

"Give it a rest, Mama. My girls aren't going to marry someone they don't love just to save this ranch. Heritage isn't about land. It's about family. I figure, even if we sell this ranch, this family will be around for a long time to come."

It was the most heartfelt, levelheaded, sweet thing her father had ever said. Sweetie couldn't believe it had come out of his mouth.

"I think your daddy is finally realizing that family is much more important than this ranch."

The softly spoken words had Sweetie turning to see her mama standing on the stairs behind her with a bundle of sheets in her arms. She'd obviously started stripping off the sheets of her sisters' beds.

"Good mornin', Sweetheart Mae. How did you sleep?"

Sweetie sighed. "As well as could be expected after witnessing two men act like kindergarteners." She nodded her head toward the kitchen. "And if my family thinks I'm going to pick a Carson cousin after that childish display, they've got another think coming."

Mama's eyebrows lifted. "So you're not in love with Decker?"

Tears came from nowhere and filled her eyes. Her mama quickly dropped the sheets and took her arm, leading her back up the stairs and into her room. When the door was closed, Mama pulled her into her arms and hugged her tightly.

Just like that, Sweetie fell apart and the tears started really flowing. Mama let her cry it out before she led her over to the bed. Once they were seated, she turned to Sweetie with tears in her own eyes.

"Jealousy is just part of love, Sweetie. It can turn the most levelheaded people into illogical fools. Your daddy and Sam Remington are perfect examples. The feud between them started because of jealousy over me."

Sweetie's eyes widened. "You dated Sam Remington?"

Her mama nodded. "I dated him before I dated your father."

Sweetie couldn't believe her ears. "But why didn't you say anything?"

"Because it's a sore subject that's better left in the past. I'd appreciated it if you didn't say anything to your sisters about it."

"I won't, but how close did you two get?"

Mama paused before she spoke. "I thought I loved him, but then I met your daddy and I realized what true love was."

"Damn," Sweetie breathed. "That explains a lot. But I still think it's a ridiculous feud. So what if you once were in love with Sam? You chose Daddy. Sam should accept that and Daddy should be happy . . . instead of acting like stubborn, jealous fools. Of course, after last night, it seems like all men are stubborn, jealous fools who assume the worst without letting you explain. While you might be able to deal with that, I can't. I won't spend my life with a jealous husband who I can't speak my own mind to."

Mama's eyes widened. "Is that what you think of me, Sweetheart Mae? You think I can't speak my own mind to my husband?"

Sweetie wanted to kick herself for not being more careful with her choice of words. But it was too late to backpedal now. "I'm sorry, Mama. But it's the truth. You have never once gotten after Daddy for being pigheaded, stubborn, and jealous."

"Of course I have. I just choose to do it behind closed doors."

Sweetie stared at her. "You yell at Daddy?"

"Yes, I yell at your father. Why do you think I made him build me a master bedroom on the back of the house when I was expecting you? Because I didn't want our children to hear us arguing. I knew the pigheaded man I'd married and I knew I was going to get mad at him. But children shouldn't have to listen to their parents fighting."

Sweetie was too stunned to speak. All she could do was stare at her mother as she continued.

"But I guess maybe I should have let you hear a few of those arguments. Especially if it made you think your mama was a weak woman who couldn't speak her mind."

Sweet took her hand and squeezed it. "You're not weak, Mama. You're the strongest woman I know. I don't come close to being as strong as you." She hesitated. "Which is why I don't think I can put up with someone as overbearing as Daddy."

"I hate to point this out, but in your and Decker's relationship, I don't think he's the one who's overbearing."

Sweetie blinked. "Mama!"

"I'm sorry, honey. I'm not trying to make you feel bad. I fell head over heels for an overbearing person so there's nothing wrong with being a little more controlling than most folks. Just like there's nothing wrong with being a little more quiet and levelheaded. Decker is the definition of quiet and levelheaded. Which is probably why you two hit it off so well."

"He didn't act so levelheaded last night."

"Because he obviously cares a lot about you, Sweetie. Your daddy wasn't the only one who made a fool of himself because of jealousy. I once caught your daddy in town talking with Jenna Leigh Jenkins. I jumped out of my car and threatened to pull out every one of her peroxided hairs if she didn't stay away from my man."

The thought of her sweet mama threatening anyone was too shocking to believe. "You didn't."

"I sure as heck did. You can ask Mimi. I couldn't go into town for a month I was so humiliated by my behavior. Especially when I found out Jenna was just asking your daddy what he thought about her throwing me a surprise baby shower." Mama hesitated. "Let me ask you something. How would you feel if you caught Decker sitting on a porch swing with Viola Stanley? A woman you know he's dated and kissed before?"

Sweetie's eyes widened. "Decker has kissed Viola? Did they have sex?" Just the thought of Decker making love to Viola like he made love to her had Sweetie feeling like she'd been punched hard in the stomach. It also made her want to pull out Viola's dyed blonde hair. Her mama must have read her thoughts because she smiled.

"See. Jealousy makes people do crazy things. So I wouldn't be too hard on Decker. You're upset with him for not letting you explain, but you aren't letting him explain either." Mama glanced at her phone sitting on the nightstand. "Is that off or on?"

Sweetie sighed. "Off."

"So you're just gonna run off like you did last time without talking things through? You didn't talk things through with Jace. You didn't talk things through with your daddy. And you didn't talk things through with the town. Look how that turned out. Running never fixed anything, Sweetie." Mama took her hands. "You mentioned that your daddy should be happy that I chose him over Sam. Does Decker know that you choose him over Jace?"

Tears welled again. "No."

Mama sighed. "I know it's hard for you to express emotions. I think that's why you love to write songs. It's a way of getting everything out without having to look people in the face when you do. But sometimes you have to face people when you're telling them how you feel."

"But what if I disappoint them?"

Mama stared at her with confusion. "Disappoint them?"

She nodded. "What if I can't love Decker

enough? I disappointed Jace and the entire town because I couldn't love him enough. What if I screw up again? Decker's their beloved town sheriff."

"Oh, Sweetie." Mama pulled her close. "I think you knew all along that Jace wasn't the right boy for you. Just like I think you know that Decker is. Trust your heart, honey."

"What about Decker's heart? He hasn't told me he loves me either."

"I think last night spoke pretty loud and clear. Maybe the reason he hasn't used words is because you're leaving. Maybe he doesn't want to throw anything in your path that will keep you from your happiness."

As soon as her mama said the words, Sweetie knew they were true. It was so like Decker to put her happiness before his. And she had made it clear she wanted to go back to Nashville . . . even when that was no longer true.

She drew back. "I don't want to go back to Nashville, Mama." It was a relief just to say the words. "I was never happy there. I love writing songs, but I'm not a singer. I want to stay right here in Wilder. Not just because I'm in love with Decker, but also because this is my home. Like Daddy said, we might not be able to hold on to this house or the ranch, but we can hold on to each other."

Mama smiled. "Damn straight, we can. And I think there's room in our family for one more person to hold on to. What do you think?"

Before she could answer, Cloe opened the door

and peeked her head in. "Someone is here to see you, Sweetie."

"If it's another cowboy wanting me to marry him, you can send him packing."

Cloe smiled and held open the door. "Actually, I think you'll want to see this one."

Decker stepped in. He was dressed in his starched sheriff's shirt and jeans. His boots were polished and his hair combed back. In his hands he held a bouquet of pink tulips. As she looked into his sea-blue eyes, her heart swelled with love and she realized how stupid she'd been to think she could leave this man.

"I'm sorry, Sweets," he said. "I had no business coming over here and acting like a jealous fool. I guess I just had a flashback to high school and all those times I wished I was in Jace's boots sitting on the front porch swing with you. But that didn't give me the right to act like I own you. I don't own you. You belong to yourself. Not me. Or Jace. Just you."

Before she could say anything, her mama got up. "I think I'll let you two talk." She patted Decker on the arm before she and Cloe left the room.

When they were gone, Decker held out the tulips.

"Thank you," she said as she took them. "They're my favorite."

"I know."

Of course he did.

"I can't stay long," he said. "I have to get to work, but I'd like to take you out tonight." He hesitated. "To the Hellhole."

"I don't think that's a good idea, Deck. Folks haven't forgiven me yet—Bobby Jay included. And they really won't forgive me if I walk in with Jace's cousin. They'll think I'm going to do to their favorite sheriff what I did to their favorite quarterback."

"Then it's time they pulled their heads out of their asses."

She studied him. "Is this why you're taking me to the Hellhole? You're going to bully the townsfolk into forgiving me?"

He didn't deny it. "If I have to."

She couldn't help smiling. He would always be her hero. "It's okay, Decker. I don't need their forgiveness."

His eyes turned sad. "Yes, you do. You might live elsewhere, but this will always be your home." He paused as if he wanted to say more. Instead, he turned for the door. "I'll pick you up at six."

When she told her sisters where Decker was taking her, they voted unanimously to stay and go with her. As much as she would love to have them as backup, she refused. Facing the town was something she needed to do on her own.

Decker was fifteen minutes early to pick her up. She was twenty minutes late getting ready. She struggled to figure out what to wear. Once she decided on a short print dress that matched her red boots, she spent a good hour doing her makeup and hair. But Decker didn't seem to be upset about the wait. When she came down the stairs, his eyes lit up.

"You're beautiful, Sweets."

She knew she would always feel that way with this man.

Even on a Monday night, the Hellhole was hopping. The band was loud and the conversation and laughter even louder. Although the last two toned down considerably when Decker and Sweetie walked in. As Decker led her to a table on the bar side, Sweetie could feel all eyes on them. Decker must have felt her tension because he gently squeezed her hand as he called out greetings.

"Hey, Dale! Heard your son was accepted at UT. Tell him congrats."

"Hey, Carrie! How's your mama after that bad case of the flu?"

"I saw your new truck, Joe. Nice!"

"Those ribs look delicious, Harvey. I might have to order me some." He glanced at her. "What do you think, Sweets? You up for some ribs?"

She was so nervous all she could do was nod. When they reached the table, he pulled out her chair and then helped her scoot in before he excused himself.

"I'll be right back."

She watched as he headed to the stage. The band was setting up. The same band that had been there the night of the bar fight. Decker spoke to the pretty brunette lead singer with the great voice before he handed her something. When he got back to the table, she couldn't help teasing him.

"What was that all about? You making arrangements with another woman in case I get kicked out?"

"I just requested a special song. And you're not going to get kicked out."

She glanced around. They had become the main focus of the bar. People didn't even try to look away as they leaned in and whispered behind their hands. "You sure about that, Deckster? There are an awful lot of mean looks being directed our way. They probably think I'm trying to get a little kissing cousin action."

"You don't have to try very hard." He leaned in and kissed her. Once his lips touched hers, she forgot all about people watching. When he drew back and spoke, she felt even more dazed.

"I love you." He held up a hand as if to stop her from talking, but with her heart in her throat, she couldn't say a word. "I didn't say it to make you stay. I just wanted you to know."

He didn't say it to make her stay? Didn't he want her to stay?

While she was mulling the question over, the waitress arrived to take their orders. When she left, Decker took her hand and continued.

"I'm not trying to make you feel cornered, Sweetie. Just because I love you doesn't mean I want to control you. Or force you to stay if you don't want to."

At one time, his words would have been music to her ears. She had thought she wanted a man who gave her freedom. She did, but she also wanted a man who didn't want to let her go. She knew it was stupid. How could she want to be free and held at the same time? But that's exactly what she wanted.

Their food arrived. Her emotions were in such turmoil she didn't think she could eat. But when the piles of spicy baby back ribs, tender chicken, thick brisket, baked beans, potato salad, coleslaw, and macaroni and cheese were sitting in front of her, she couldn't help but dig in.

After they were finished eating, she started to tell Decker how she felt, but then the brunette band member stepped up to the microphone.

"Hope y'all are enjoying the night so far. We've got some great songs picked out for you tonight. But before we start our set, your local sheriff has a special surprise for you."

Sweetie had a bad feeling. That bad feeling grew when Decker got up and headed to the stage. He thanked the singer as he took the microphone.

"Hey, y'all. No, I'm not going to give you a lecture on drunk driving. Y'all already know how I feel about that. Tonight, I get the pleasure of introducing a special guest. You might know her. She grew up in this town. Y'all are her people. Which is why she wrote a song about you. She'd like to sing it for you now. So let's give a warm welcome to our very own Sweetie Mae Holiday!"

CHAPTER TWENTY-TWO

DECKER FIGURED THIS could very easily make Sweetie walk out the door and never talk to him again. She had told him she had stage fright when she tried to sing her own songs. He also knew she didn't like to feel manipulated. But this was the only way he could think of to make Sweetie realize her songs were worth sharing.

So were her feelings.

He held his breath as she got to her feet. She hesitated as if she was thinking about making a run for it. Instead, she lifted her chin and walked to the stage. When she got there, he held out a hand and helped her up.

"I'm going to kill you, Decker Carson," she whispered under her breath.

"You're going to kill them," he whispered back. "Knock 'em dead, Sweets." He brushed a soft kiss over her cheek before he stepped down from the stage. He didn't go back to his seat. He stood in front of the stage like the Sweetie Mae Holiday groupie he was—and always would be.

Her hair was curled and fell in golden waves around the shoulders of the jean jacket she wore.

The same jean jacket he had loaned her when she'd forgotten to bring a coat with her to his house. Beneath it, she wore a pretty flowered dress that hugged her breasts, waist, and hips and flared out around the tops of her thighs. The sexy red boots finished off her outfit . . . and the last of the moisture in his mouth.

Even though he'd told her not to, he still felt a little hurt she hadn't reciprocated with words of love. And maybe she didn't love him. Maybe "The Right Boy" wasn't about him at all. If that were true, he'd have to accept it. Just like he had to accept she was leaving.

And he would survive.

For the last sixteen years of his life, he'd lived in fear of people he loved leaving him. The fear had started when his mother and daddy died and grown worse when Sweetie left. Not wanting to feel the same pain, he'd steered clear of serious relationships. Now, he saw how foolish that had been. Love was meant to be shared. No matter the pain and loss. While you had it in your grasp, you needed to enjoy every moment.

He intended to enjoy this one.

Although Sweetie didn't seem to be enjoying it.

As she pulled the strap of the guitar someone had handed her over her head, she looked like she was about to throw up. Decker regretted ordering barbecue. He should have ordered saltine crackers and ginger ale. As he watched her step up to the microphone, his own stomach threatened to revolt. The townsfolk were unpredictable. Anything could go wrong.

The guy on the keyboard started playing a soft tune. Decker hoped it was "Small Town Regrets." He had copied the song when he'd gotten to work that morning and brought it with him tonight to give to the band.

It must have been the right song because Sweetie glanced at the keyboardist in surprise before she sent an accusing look at Decker. He merely lifted his hands in a helpless shrug. She took a deep breath and leaned closer to the mic. Her voice was shaky at first. Decker had the strong desire to jump back on stage and take her hand. Instead, he willed her to look at him. When she did, her voice grew stronger as she sang of the love she had for Wilder and the people who lived there.

But the lyrics seemed to be going right over the townsfolk's heads. No one was reacting. Decker wanted to go around the bar and shake some sense into each and every one of them. But then, slowly, people started to get up from their barstools and chairs to join Decker. By the time Sweetie finished singing, the entire bar was crowded in front of the stage.

For one heart-stopping second, no one clapped.

Then the entire place erupted with applause and whistles and loud whooping.

Sweetie stood there looking out at the crowd in stunned surprise as tears started rolling down her cheeks. Decker hopped back up on stage and slipped the guitar from around her neck so he could pull her into his arms.

"You were amazing, Sweets. Just like I knew you would be."

She drew back and smiled at him with watery eyes and wet cheeks. "I really should kill you. You planned this entire thing?"

He nodded. "People need to hear your songs, Sweetie." He glanced out at the beaming crowd. "Look how happy it makes them."

She looked at the townsfolk before she turned to him. "I love you, Decker."

They were standing right in front of the microphone and her words came out of the speakers loud and clear, echoing through the bar . . . and through his heart. He had waited so long to hear those words that he took a moment to bask in their glow.

But the townsfolk never could take silence.

"Well, don't just stand there, Sheriff," Melba Wadley hollered. "Do you love her or don't you?"

"Maybe he doesn't love her," Donna Nichols yelled. "Maybe he just wants the Holiday Ranch."

"But I thought only a Remington was offered the ranch," a drunk-sounding guy said. "If that stip-lu-a-tion has changed . . . I love you, Sweetie, if Deck don't!"

Too happy to be annoyed by the busybody townsfolk, Decker ignored them and smiled at the woman in front of him. She loved him. Nothing else mattered.

"I love you too, Sweets. I love you so much it hurts. I know you're probably worried I'm going to pressure you to move here. But I'm not going to do that. I will always allow you to be your own person and follow your dreams. If the only way to achieve that dream is for you to live in Nashville, then you have to go back."

He thought his words would make her happy. Instead, she looked pissed off. "So you're just going to let me go? Just like that?"

He scrambled through his mind, trying to figure out why she was so mad. "Umm . . . I thought that's what you wanted. You wanted a boy who would set you free."

"Not that free!"

"So you're asking me to come with you to Nashville?"

"Now wait one damn minute!" The crowd parted and Mrs. Stokes shuffled her way to the front. She did not look happy. "You can't just up and leave us, Decker Carson. There's no one who could replace you. This town needs a sheriff who grew up in this town—a hometown hero— someone who knows and loves the people even when they hold stupid grudges and believe ridiculous gossip. You're that hometown hero, Decker Carson."

A chorus of "hell yeahs" erupted and Decker didn't think his heart could get any fuller. Sweetie loved him and wanted him to come to Nashville. And the townsfolk loved him and wanted him to stay here. Since he hadn't been born in Wilder, he'd always felt a little like an outsider. Jace had always been the hometown hero. Decker had just been his cousin from the big city who was afraid of bees. Maybe that was why he'd worked so hard at being a good sheriff. He had wanted the town's love. It was nice to know he had it.

Although, now that he knew, it would make leaving that much harder.

"I love y'all," he said. "But if Sweetie is heading back to Nashville—"

Mrs. Stokes cut in. "Sweetie can't leave either." She looked at Sweetie. "You can't write a song about how much you love this town and its people and how much you regret leaving us and then leave us all over again. If you regretted leaving us the first time, you'll regret leaving us the second."

"She's right." Sheryl Ann stepped up. "You can't go, Sweetie. We're sorry for ever doubting your love for us. To make it up to you, if you stay, I'll have your Sour Lemon Poppy muffin and coffee waiting for you every morning."

Tito moved up next to Sheryl Ann. "I'll make sure you always have extra guacamole and hot sauce on your chicken tacos."

"And extra barbecue sauce for your ribs," Bobby Jay called from the kitchen.

Tammy Sue weaved her way through the crowd, which was difficult when she was eight months pregnant. "Since you missed the first two being born, you can't miss this one. You can't leave. That just ain't right."

"Talking about what's not right," Coach Denny said. "Doesn't anyone care about Jace? Or how hurt he's gonna be when he finds out his cousin has run off with his girl?"

The cowboy who had been sitting in the dark corner by the stage finally got to his feet and pushed back his cowboy hat. Everyone gasped when they saw Jace's smiling face. Decker was a little surprised too. He thought his cousin had left for Galveston that morning.

"Now, Coach," Jace said. "What Sweetie and I had together ended a long time ago. She knew exactly what she was doing when she broke up with me. I was so wrapped up in getting a scholarship to a top ten school that I was a horrible boyfriend . . . and a lousy quarterback. I'd like to apologize to the town right now for getting so stressed out about those college scouts that I lost us a chance for another state football trophy." He sent them a puppy dog look that beat out Dixie Chick's when she was begging for a piece of bacon. "Can y'all forgive me?"

Coach Denny headed over and gave Jace a big hug, followed with a hard thump on the back. "Of course we can forgive you, son." He turned to the crowd. "Ain't that right?"

Everyone nodded and voiced their agreement as they followed Coach Denny's lead and welcomed Jace home with hugs and backslaps. When they were finished, Jace was grinning from ear to ear. "Then I guess there's nothing left to do but congratulate Decker and Sweetie." With a mischievous twinkle in his eyes, he held up a bottle of beer. "To Decker and Sweetie. May they have a long marriage . . . hopefully, right here in Wilder."

Decker wanted to throttle his cousin. All Decker had planned for tonight was to get Sweetie to forgive him and the townsfolk to forgive her. Talk of marriage would only make her feel trapped.

He quickly put a stop to the toast. "Now hold up, everyone. Sweetie and I aren't at the marrying stage yet."

"Just what stage are we at?"

He turned to find Sweetie standing there with her arms crossed looking as mad as Mrs. Stokes. "You think you can just come with me to Nashville and move into my apartment without putting a ring on my finger, Decker Carson? My daddy would have a fit. And Mimi and Mama would never forgive you. And just what do you intend to do when you get to Nashville? Do you actually think you can find a job you love as much as you love being the sheriff of this town? Of course you can't. And I'm not about to let you give up a career you love for me. Just like you aren't about to let me give up a career I love for you."

Frustration filled him. "So that's it? We're just going to love each other and say goodbye? Sometimes love takes sacrifice, Sweets. If you want me, I'm willing to sacrifice whatever I need to be with you." He patted his chest. "I'm your right boy and I want to give you your country dream."

A soft smile lit her face. "I know you're the right boy for me. So it's a good thing that my country dream is staying right here in Wilder."

He stared at her. "What? But what about being the next Dolly Parton?"

"There's only one Dolly," Mrs. Stokes said, and a chorus of "amen" broke out.

Sweetie laughed. "I wish I'd realized that twelve

years ago. I also wish I'd realized I love writing songs, but I don't enjoy singing them." She cupped Decker's face in her hands. "Except to my right boy." She looked out at the crowd. "And the folks of my hometown."

Decker couldn't believe what he was hearing. "Are you sure, Sweets?"

"I've never been more sure in my life."

Decker pulled her into his arms as the bar erupted in whistles and whoops again. Then someone yelled out from the back.

"Well, don't just stand there hugging. Ask her to marry you so you can win that ranch!"

Sweetie drew back and he figured she'd look as frustrated with the townsfolk as he was. But she didn't look frustrated. Her eyes twinkled with love and happiness. "What do you say, Deckster? You won't get a ranch. All you'll get is the girl."

His heart filled with joy as he dropped to one knee. "The girl is more than enough for me."

CHAPTER TWENTY-THREE

"I THINK YOU'VE LOST your mind marrying Decker only weeks after you two hooked up." Hallie tugged at the hem of the short dress she wore. "But if you're dead set on marrying the lawman, why did you force me to wear a dress that shows my panties every time I bend over?"

Liberty fielded the question as she continued arranging Sweetie's hair into an upsweep of curls. "Because long bridesmaid's dresses are rarely worn again. These dresses can be worn to church, on dates, and clubbing."

Belle, who was zipping Noelle's dress, turned to her twin. "And when do we ever go to church, on dates, or clubbing, Libby? All we do is work."

Liberty lifted her chin. "Well, we'll have the perfect dress if we do decide to do those things."

Hallie snorted. "Pink dresses aren't what I would call perfect. And Mama would have a heart attack if we wore a dress this short to church." She glanced at Cloe, who was fluffing Sweetie's veil. "Except for Cloe's. How did she get a longer dress?"

"I took down the hem." Cloe stopped fluffing and glanced down at her breasts that spilled over the low neckline of her red maid of honor's dress. "Although I would take a shorter hem if I could have more material on top. I told you not to order mine so low cut, Libby."

"Don't be ridiculous." Liberty took the veil from Cloe. "That dress shows off your big boobs. And I always say that if you got it, flaunt it. It's too bad Brandon won't be here to see you walk down the aisle in it." She attached the veil to Sweetie's head and jabbed in a hairpin so hard Sweetie's eyes watered. "Has he called you to let you know how his grandmother is doing?"

Cloe turned away. "Umm . . . yes, she's much better." She walked over to Mama's dresser where she opened a drawer and started looking through the scarfs.

"So why isn't he coming?" Hallie flopped down on the bed. "College Station is only a couple hours away. He might miss the wedding, but he could make the reception. You'd think he'd want to party with his soon-to-be family."

Noelle pushed Hallie's pink boots off the bed. "And he'd get to see the ranch before we sell it."

"We still might be able to keep the house and barn," Hallie said.

A silence fell over their parents' room where the sisters had gathered to get Sweetie ready for the wedding. They were all hoping they'd get to keep the acre of land with the house and barn. But after finding out the payout amount of the loan, it was doubtful. Not that Mimi would ever agree to sell the ranch. She was still pinning all her hopes on one of her granddaughters marrying a Remington.

Which meant the ranch would probably be foreclosed on.

Either way, they would lose the ranch.

The doctors had okayed Daddy to start gradually exercising again and he had taken to going for walks in the early morning by himself. Sweetie knew it was his way of saying goodbye to the land he loved so much. Mama baked when she was unhappy. Both Sweetie and Decker had gained weight from all the pies, cookies, and cakes Mama baked.

Thankfully, getting ready for the wedding had been a distraction. Mimi and Mama had shown up at Decker's house a few days earlier loaded down with some of the family heirlooms and keepsakes. There was a quilt made by Mama's great-grandma and a seasoned cast-iron skillet Mimi had gotten from her grandma. There were sepia photographs of both Daddy's and Mama's ancestors in silver frames and the rooster salt and peppershakers Sweetie remembered Grandpa Holiday using every morning when he ate his fried eggs.

The ranch might be sold, but the Holiday heritage would live on. Sweetie would make sure of it.

"Okay, people." Liberty clapped her hands. "Let's get this show on the road. We're going by backward birth order. Noelle first, then Hallie, Belle, me, and finally Cloe." She glanced at Cloe who was adjusting a scarf over her cleavage and rolled her eyes. "Now let's do this, Holiday Sisters!"

As annoying as Liberty was, there were perks to having a controlling event planner in the family. One of them being that if you decided you wanted to get married only two weeks after being proposed to, you could still have a gorgeous wedding to remember. Liberty had been ordering around her sisters for the last couple days. Everyone but Sweetie. Liberty had wanted her to be surprised.

When Sweetie stepped into the Holiday Ranch barn and saw the transformation, she was. All the gardening tools and farm equipment were gone. The cement floor was swept clean of dirt and moldy hay and it looked like a layer of sealant or wax had been applied to make it shine. Swathes of red and pink satin hung along the walls and draped from the high beams, along with more twinkle lights than Sweetie had ever seen in her life. Pink tulips sprang out of tall white vases in the center of the harvest tables that ran in four long rows from one set of open doors to the other. Surrounding the vases were heart-shaped candleholders with tea candles, their flickering flames reflecting off the crystal glasses and the gleaming white plates and silver place settings.

But as much as her sisters had transformed the barn into a Valentine's dream wedding, it wasn't what had tears flooding Sweetie's eyes.

It was the people crowded into the barn.

Sweetie's people.

Rows of white chairs had been set up on the other side of the barn and every chair was taken, leaving standing room only for the folks who had arrived late. All those folks were turned to her with beaming smiles on their faces.

"I told you they'd forgive and forget."

Sweetie looked at her daddy who was as handsome as ever in his black western tuxedo and Stetson. "You never told me that they'd forgive and forget. That was Mama. You were too mad at me yourself for leaving."

He squinted down at her. "Mad at you? Why would I ever get mad at my Sweetie Pie?"

She suddenly realized he was teasing her, something he had started doing quite a lot lately. She swatted his arm. "Daddy!"

A smile broke over his face. "Damn right, I am. And just because you're getting married that doesn't mean I'm giving up that job."

She leaned in and kissed him on the cheek. "Of course not. You'll always be my daddy."

He nodded. "Then let's get you hitched. By the look on the groom's face, I'd say he's worried we've been standing here so long talking you're having second thoughts."

Sure enough, when she headed down the rose-strewn aisle, Decker *did* look concerned.

"Everything okay?" he asked when she reached him.

"Nope," she said. Before the concern in his Caribbean-blue eyes could deepen, she took his hand in hers and smiled. "Everything is perfect."

It was a perfect ceremony. Or perfect for Wilder, Texas.

Earlier, Hallie had talked Reverend Thompson into taste-testing the different beers she'd brewed for the wedding and the poor man got so drunk he couldn't remember the vows. After several attempts, Mrs. Stokes yelled out, "Just pronounce them husband and wife and be done with it!" Then the best man, Rome Remington, dropped the rings. Since he was acting so strange, Sweetie had to wonder if Hallie had gotten him drunk too.

Once the ceremony was over, Decker was supposed to lead her outside where the photographer was waiting to take pictures. Instead, before they reached the open doors, he took a detour to the ladder that led to the hayloft.

"What in the world are you doing, Deck? Liberty will kill us if we don't show up for pictures."

"She'll get over it." He winked. "I have a surprise for you."

Since Sweetie loved surprises, she didn't hesitate to lift her dress and climb the ladder.

When she reached the top, she discovered that Decker had made a love nest. Two glowing battery-powered camp lanterns set on either side of the fluffy comforter that covered a fresh mound of hay. A bucket of ice with champagne and two fluted glasses set next to the makeshift bed, along with a wrapped package. Through the open window the sun was setting, its deep oranges and pinks casting a magical glow over the entire scene.

Tears filled Sweetie's eyes as she climbed the

rest of the way up the ladder. "Oh, Deck, it's beautiful."

He stepped up behind her and wrapped his arms around her waist, his soft lips brushing her neck. "No, you're beautiful." He turned her and the look of love in his eyes made her melt. "I know the townsfolk want to celebrate with us until the wee hours of the morning, but I wanted just a little time alone with my new bride."

She smiled. "Your bride? I like the sound of that. But I have to warn you that there are about a hundred covered buttons on Mama's wedding dress and by the time we get it off, everyone will probably be heading home."

He pulled a hankie out of the back pocket of his tuxedo pants. A white hankie with primrose flowers embroidered along the edge. He gently lifted her chin and dabbed at the tears. "As fun as getting you out of that dress sounds, I didn't bring you up here to get you naked."

"You didn't?"

He shook his head and gave her a kiss before he took her hand and led her over to the comforter. Once they were seated, he handed her the wrapped package. "Happy birthday, Sweets."

More tears welled. "You remembered."

"Of course I remembered. I would never forget your birthday. Even if it happens to fall on our wedding day. Go on. Open it."

She carefully removed the heart-printed paper to discover a box inside. When she lifted the lid, her heart swelled to bursting.

"If you don't like it," Decker said. "You don't

have to wear it. You just liked Dixie Chick's so much, I thought you might like one."

She glanced up to find him blushing and looking just like the young boy who had first come to Holiday Ranch. A young boy who had lost everything, but refused to give up. Now that boy was hers. She was one lucky girl.

She lifted the pink knitted sweater with the big red heart on the front and hugged it close as tears rolled down her cheeks. "I love it. And I love you."

"And I love you." He handed her the handkerchief. "But if you keep taking my hankies, I'm going to have to embroider more."

She stopped wiping her cheeks and stared at him. "You can embroider too?"

He cleared his throat. "Let's move on. There's something else I need to give you." He took an envelope out of the inside pocket of his tuxedo jacket and handed it to her. It was addressed to Bobby Jay.

"What's this?"

"I don't know. Bobby Jay gave it to me the other day when I ran into him. He said he's had it for a week and just kept forgetting to give it to you."

"Bobby Jay? But why is he giving me his mail?"

"He said the card inside is addressed to you. I figured it was a birthday card."

She opened the envelope to find another envelope with her name on the front. But there wasn't a card inside. Just a folded note. She read through it quickly, her eyes widening with each word.

"What is it?" Decker asked. "Don't tell me it's another marriage proposal."

She shook her head. "It's from the band that played the other night. The one that accompanied me when I sang 'Small Town Regrets.' I guess they sent it to Bobby Jay because they didn't know how else to contact me."

"Contact you for what?"

Sweetie reread the note to make sure she wasn't dreaming before she lifted her gaze to Decker's. "They just got a recording deal and they want to include 'Small Town Regrets' on their first album."

Decker took her hand and gently squeezed it. "And how do you feel about someone else singing your song?"

She took a moment to assess all the emotions swirling around inside her. There was a small amount of disappointment that she wouldn't be singing her own songs on stage, but mostly she just felt . . . "Happy. And damned relieved that I don't have to sing it in front of people and see their reactions."

Decker lifted her hand and kissed it, his mama's diamond engagement ring that he'd given her sparkling in the sunset. "They're going to love it, Sweets. I know it." He lowered her hand and grinned. "And here you thought you weren't going to make it in the music business. I never doubted it. When Sweetheart Mae Holiday sets her sights on something, she usually gets it."

Looking at the man sitting next to her, she couldn't argue the point. "I guess that's true. I set my sights on you and now you're mine."

He easily lifted her onto his lap. "Not before I set my sights on you. I've wanted you since the moment you first strutted out the door with your ponytail swinging." He kissed her a slow, leisurely kiss that held the kind of love that lasts forever. When they were both breathless, he lifted his head and his eyes twinkled mischievously. "You know what I'm thinking?"

"Is it the same thing I'm thinking?"

He smiled wickedly. "A hundred buttons isn't that big a deal."

She drew him back to her lips.

Yep, he was the right boy for her.

THE END

**Turn the page for a
SNEAK PEEK of Katie Lane's
next Holiday Ranch romance!**

SNEAK PEEK

WRANGLING A LUCKY COWBOY!
Coming February 2024!

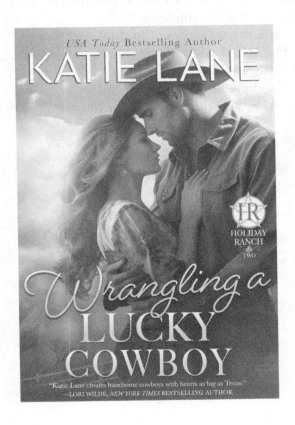

CHAPTER 1

ROME REMINGTON NEVER thought he'd find himself standing in front of the altar again. He was a man who learned from his mistakes. After his first failed attempt at marriage, he had no intentions of entering the holy bond of matrimony a second time. No matter how much his father was pushing for grandkids to carry on the Remington name.

Rome had spent his life fulfilling his father's wishes. While other kids rode bikes and played video games after school, he'd studied for hours so he could hand Sam Remington a report card filled with A's. In high school, he'd gone out for the football team regardless of the fact that he hated football. In college, he'd majored in business, even though he'd wanted to major in animal science. Once he'd graduated and returned home, he'd searched for the right woman to marry— one his father would approve of.

He still wanted to please his dad. But he wasn't willing to tie the knot again. He figured it was time for his little brother to step up to the plate and take one for the Remington team. Casey certainly had no trouble getting women to fall in love with him. Half of the female population of Wilder, Texas, was trying to win his heart.

Rome understood why. Casey had a good heart. Rome's was a little too battle scarred. Which was why he had no intentions of offering it again. Thankfully, he wasn't the one exchanging vows today.

But that didn't seem to stop him from sweating through his tuxedo. As he listened to Decker and Sweetie exchange vows, knots the size of brahma bull balls grew in his stomach as memories swirled to life in his head. Memories of the sweet timbre of Emily's voice when she promised to love, honor, and cherish him forever. The teasing sparkle of her blue eyes when he lifted the thin wisp of her veil to kiss her. The welcoming softness of her lips. The tight grip of her hand on his arm as if she never wanted to let him go.

She had let him go.

Eighteen months later, she had packed up and headed back to Georgia, teaching him that love was a fickle and untrustworthy emotion he wanted no part of.

"Rome?"

He blinked back to the present moment and found Decker holding out his hand and giving him a quizzical look. Rome quickly slipped his hand in his pants pocket and pulled out the ring. Unfortunately, when he went to hand it to Decker, it slipped from his shaky fingers and bounced down the steps of the dais. As he moved down the steps and bent to retrieve the ring, he could feel everyone's eyes on him.

He should be used to people's attention. As sons of one of the wealthiest ranchers in Texas, the townsfolk had always had high expectations of him and Casey. Casey let those expectations roll right off his back and did exactly what he pleased. Rome couldn't do that. There was something inside him that desperately wanted to meet those expectations. Everyone's expectations. The townsfolk's, his father's . . . his wife's.

He had failed.

When the ceremony ended and the preacher declared Decker and Sweetie man and wife, that failure punched Rome hard in the chest and he found himself in a full-fledged panic attack. His vision blurred, his heart started thumping like crazy, and he couldn't seem to pull a full breath into his lungs.

Decker and Sweetie started down the aisle to a loud round of applause. As the best man, Rome knew he was supposed to follow. But he was struggling just to stay standing. There was no way he could put one foot in front of the other.

Then a cool hand slid into his and gripped it firmly. He held tightly to the lifeline he'd been handed and allowed himself to be lead down the aisle and out of the barn. He barely registered the stiff February breeze as he was pulled around the side of the barn.

"Sit." Firm pressure was applied to his shoulders and his legs finally gave out. His butt had barely landed on a stack of firewood when his black Stetson was whisked off and his head pushed down to his knees. "Breathe."

It took a few wheezy tries before his lungs started to partially fill. When the spots lifted from his vision, he found himself looking at two sets of cowboy boots. His own black size thirteens and a much smaller red pair. There was only one person who had worn red boots to the wedding. Sweetie's boots were white. All four of the bridesmaids' boots were pink. Only the maid of honor wore red. And Rome would bet money that the color hadn't been her choice.

Clover Fields Holiday was not a bold red kind of person, even though she carried the surname of her mama's side of the family. Fanny Fields had run the very first house of ill repute in the county. Mrs. Fields' Boardinghouse wasn't as notorious as the infamous Chicken Ranch. But the wild things that had gone on in the house were how the town of Wilder had gotten its name. All the boys in school had often discussed which Holiday sister had taken after her mama's side of the family.

Cloe's name had never come up.

She was the reserved wallflower of the six Holiday sisters. The one who stood back and watched instead of participating. She wasn't the popular Soybean Queen like her oldest sister, Sweetheart. Or a smart bookworm like her middle sister, Belle. Nor was she an overachiever like Belle's twin, Liberty. She wasn't an athletic cowgirl like her next to the youngest sister, Halloween. Or a bouncy cheerleader like her youngest sister, Noelle.

She was just Cloe, a girl who didn't seem to waste her time trying to prove herself.

Unlike Rome.

Even now he felt like he had to prove he was fine by sitting up—even when doing so made him feel lightheaded and dizzy. When he finally focused, he discovered the familiar girl he had known most of his life staring back at him.

Cloe was only a few inches under Rome's six feet one inches and skinny as a willow branch. She always wore clothes that looked two sizes too big. Even the maid of honor's dress hung well past her knees. While her sisters either had their daddy's blond or their mama's black hair, Cloe's hair was the brownish red color of autumn leaves right before they drop to the ground. Although it was hard to tell the true color when she always kept it confined in clips or twisty buns. Today, it was fixed on top of her head in a tower of curls that tilted to one side like a lopsided fence post.

Like the rest of her sisters, she'd gotten her mama's pretty green eyes. While most people starting using contacts in high school, Cloe continued to wear glasses that always seemed to be slipping down the bridge of her button nose. Like now. Instead of pushing them up with her hand, she wrinkled her nose until they slid back into place as she continued to fan him with the hat.

"Concentrate on taking deep, even breaths," she said. "The only way to get through a panic attack is to regulate your breathing."

The fact she knew he was having a panic attack made him even more panicked. If word got out it would spread like wildfire and everyone would think he was still upset over Emily leaving. He wasn't. He damn well wasn't.

"I'm not having a panic attack. It was just hot in the barn." Considering it was the middle of February and most people in attendance were wearing jackets, it was a weak excuse. He tried to get to his feet to prove he was okay, but when everything spun again, he was forced to sit back down and put his head between his knees. Which annoyed him and made him a little snappish.

"Look, I'm fine. I just need a few minutes . . . alone."

The red boots didn't move, but the fanning stopped and she lowered his hat. There was something about the sight of her hand cradling the crown of his black Stetson that grabbed his attention. Her fingers were long and slender, the nails neatly trimmed and devoid of polish. Emily had kept her nails lengthy and painted bright colors. She couldn't open Coke cans and got upset when one chipped or broke off. While those manicured nails had been sexy as hell, he'd always worried about being impaled when she handled his man parts. That wouldn't be a problem with Cloe. Those long fingers could easily wrap around his—

Whoa, boy!

He brought a screeching halt to the thought train that had completely run off the rails. Obviously, his three-year dry spell had finally caught up with him. Cloe Holiday giving him a hand job? What was the matter with him? Shock at his wayward thoughts gave him the jolt he needed to regulate his breathing and sit up.

Her eyes behind the lenses were filled with concern and kindness. Which made him feel badly about being so snappish.

"Sorry I'm being a bear. Weddings aren't really my thing."

She smiled softly. She had a nice smile. It wasn't fake or too big. It was just . . . nice.

"Weddings are stressful, aren't they? Not only for the bride and groom, who feel like they are the hosts, but also for their parents who are watching their money leak down the drain. Then there are the bachelors who fear their girlfriends will get marriage fever and start demanding proposals. And their girlfriends who are stressed because they're worried they won't ever get that proposal." Her smile faded. "And finally there are the people who have gambled at love and lost. For those people, weddings just make them feel like . . . complete and utter failures."

Cloe had hit the nail right on the head. Rome felt like a complete and utter failure. He just wasn't able to admit it. Especially when she was giving him that pitying look. Sympathy was not something Remingtons had ever received graciously.

"A complete and utter failure? Look, just because I got a divorce doesn't mean I'm a failure. I run one of the biggest ranches in Texas and run it damn well."

Her eyes widened, and she shook her head. "Oh, no. I wasn't talking about you being a failure, Rome. I was talking about me."

Before he could ask her what she meant, Liberty came charging around the corner of the barn. While Cloe was calm, soft-spoken, and blended into the woodwork, Liberty was high-strung, controlling, and commanded attention with her stunning beauty. At one time, Rome had considered asking her out, but she scared him too much.

"Have you seen Sweetie and Decker? We're getting ready to take pictures and I can't find them anywhere. I swear trying to keep control of a bridal party after the wedding is over is like trying to corral a litter of misbehaving puppies." Liberty glanced between Cloe and Rome. "Just what are you two doing hiding over here? And why are you holding Rome's hat, Cloe?"

Rome waited for Cloe to tell her sister about his panic attack.

She didn't.

"I was feeling a little lightheaded from the heat in the barn and Rome helped me outside to get some fresh air." She fanned herself with his hat, causing the wisps of hair around her face to flutter. What *was* her hair color? Mahogany?

"Lightheaded?" Liberty said. "You've never been lightheaded in your life, Clo—" She cut off and her eyes widened. "Wait a second. Are you pregnant? Is that why Brandon has finally gotten around to asking you to marry him after six long years?"

Rome glanced at Cloe, whose face was as red

as the barn. She was getting married? Why did that surprise him? Probably because she had never dated in high school or even shown any interest in dating. Which had made him assume she would end up like his aunt Francis, who was quite happy living alone in South Padre with her three parakeets.

"I'm not pregnant," Cloe said.

Liberty's eyes narrowed. "Then why were you lightheaded? And don't give me that ridiculous excuse about the barn being hot. It's not over sixty degrees today."

Since Cloe had lied for him, Rome jumped in and helped her out. "I guess some people are just more hot natured than others. I was burning up in the barn."

Liberty studied him. "You do look sweaty. You might want to wipe some of that off before pictures." She glanced at Cloe. "And take off that ugly scarf, Clo. No wonder you're over heated with that thing wrapped around your neck." She reached for the scarf, but Cloe sent her a warning look.

"The scarf stays, Libby."

Rome was surprised. He'd always viewed Cloe as a wilting pansy next to her more aggressive sisters. But it looked like she had some steel hidden under her quiet reserve.

Liberty backed off. "Fine. Keep the scarf, but you two don't dawdle. Since I can't find Decker and Sweetie, we'll start on the groomsmen and bridesmaids photos." She whirled and hurried off as quickly as she had arrived.

"I see Liberty is still a tornado." Rome took his hat from Cloe and pulled it on. "So you're getting married. Congratulations."

Instead of replying, she studied him for a long moment before she stepped closer and reached up to adjust his hat. He didn't know what surprised him most. Her uncharacteristic actions, or the realization that he'd been wrong about her eyes. They weren't the same color as her sisters. This close, he could see that the irises were a darker shade of green. Like the color of the late summer grass that covered the south pasture.

And how did she know how he liked his hat to sit?

She adjusted it to the perfect angle on his head as she spoke. "Actually, I'm not getting married. Brandon broke up with me a few weeks ago. I just haven't gotten around to telling my family yet. I didn't want to ruin Sweetie's wedding with bad news."

Rome felt like a complete jerk. While Cloe had been trying to make him feel better about having a panic attack, she had been suffering from her own relationship ending only weeks ago. A six-year relationship.

"I'm sorry," he said.

She brushed something off the brim of his hat before she stepped back. "It's okay. Technically, we weren't even engaged. I only thought he was going to ask me to marry him . . . instead, he told me he didn't think we were well suited for each other and asked if I would consider trans ferring to another school so things wouldn't be awkward."

"Another school?"

She nodded. "We're both teachers at an elementary school in College Station."

Rome snorted. "I hope you told him go to hell."

"Why would I do that? He was right. It would be awkward seeing him at school every day."

Rome was struck speechless. Most women he knew would have set the guy's desk on fire . . . after tying him to it. Emily had had a raging screaming fit when Rome had forgotten their three-month dating anniversary. Which should have been an indication of her temper tantrums to come. Now that he thought about it, he had never seen Cloe even raise her voice. She had always been calm and rational.

"It worked out for the best," she continued. "I wanted to take an extended leave of absence anyway so I could help get the ranch ready to sell."

Rome knew the Holiday Ranch was in financial trouble. People who had owned their land as long as the Holidays didn't sell unless they had to. It was too bad. He never liked to see a ranch go under.

"So when does your ranch go on the market?" he asked.

"Probably after the wedding. You think your daddy would be interested in buying it?"

Rome laughed. "You and I both know that your daddy doesn't want my daddy owning any part of his ranch. And my daddy would never act like he was interested in Holiday land . . . even if buying it was the smart thing to do."

Cloe's green eyes were intense. "If you feel that way, then why don't you buy it?"

Before Rome could get over his surprise at the question, Liberty came charging around the corner of the barn again. "I swear I'm going to start thinking there's something going on between you two if you don't stop hiding behind his barn. Now, come on. It's picture time!"

Rome followed after the two Holiday sisters with Cloe's words ringing in his head.

Then why don't you buy it?

Order Wrangling a Lucky Cowboy today!
https://tinyurl.com/4frvsmfh
Or
www.katielanebooks.com

Also by Katie Lane

Be sure to check out all of Katie Lane's novels!
www.katielanebooks.com

Holiday Ranch Series
Wrangling a Texas Sweetheart
Wrangling a Lucky Cowboy–February 2024

Kingman Ranch Series
Charming a Texas Beast
Charming a Knight in Cowboy Boots
Charming a Big Bad Texan
Charming a Fairytale Cowboy
Charming a Texas Prince
Charming a Christmas Texan
Charming a Cowboy King

Bad Boy Ranch Series:
Taming a Texas Bad Boy
Taming a Texas Rebel
Taming a Texas Charmer
Taming a Texas Heartbreaker
Taming a Texas Devil
Taming a Texas Rascal
Taming a Texas Tease
Taming a Texas Christmas Cowboy

ABOUT THE AUTHOR

KATIE LANE IS a firm believer that love conquers all and laughter is the best medicine. Which is why you'll find plenty of humor and happily-ever-afters in her contemporary and western contemporary romance novels. A USA Today Bestselling Author, she has written numerous series, including *Deep in the Heart of Texas, Hunk for the Holidays, Overnight Billionaires, Tender Heart Texas, The Brides of Bliss Texas, Bad Boy Ranch, Kingman Ranch,* and *Holiday Ranch.* Katie lives in Albuquerque, New Mexico, and when she's not writing, she enjoys reading, eating chocolate (dark, please), and snuggling with her high school sweetheart and cairn terrier, Roo.

For more on her writing life or just to chat, check out Katie here:
FACEBOOK
www.facebook.com/katielaneauthor
INSTAGRAM
www.instagram.com/katielanebooks.

And for more information on upcoming releases and great giveaways, be sure to sign up for her mailing list at www.katielanebooks.com!